D0845155

by Carla Laureano and available from
r Point Large Print:

Saturday Night Supper Club

BRUNCH A
BITTERSWEET

Also
Cent

Th

BRUNCH AT
BITTERSWEET CAFÉ

A Supper Club Novel

CARLA LAUREANO

CENTER POINT LARGE PRINT
THORNDIKE, MAINE

This Center Point Large Print edition
is published in the year 2019 by arrangement with
Tyndale House Publishers, Inc.

Scripture quotations are taken from the Holy Bible,
New International Version,® *NIV.*®
Copyright © 1973, 1978, 1984, 2011 by Biblica, Inc.®
Used by permission. All rights reserved worldwide.

Brunch at Bittersweet Café is a work of fiction. Where real
people, events, establishments, organizations, or locales
appear, they are used fictitiously. All other elements of the
novel are drawn from the author's imagination.

The text of this Large Print edition is unabridged.
In other aspects, this book may vary
from the original edition.
Printed in the United States of America
on permanent paper.
Set in 16-point Times New Roman type.

ISBN: 978-1-68324-225-2

Library of Congress Cataloging-in-Publication Data

Names: Laureano, Carla, author.
Title: Brunch at Bittersweet Cafe / Carla Laureano.
Description: Center Point Large Print edition. | Thorndike, Maine :
  Center Point Large Print, 2019.
Identifiers: LCCN 2019014554 | ISBN 9781643582252 (hardcover :
  alk. paper)
Subjects: LCSH: Large type books.
Classification: LCC PS3612.A93257 B78 2019b | DDC 813/.6—dc23
LC record available at https://lccn.loc.gov/2019014554

For my mom, Cathy.
You've supported me in every wild dream
and change of direction.
I'll always be grateful for your love
and encouragement.

ACKNOWLEDGMENTS

Over time, my acknowledgments begin to sound like broken records, because I'm always thanking the same people for the same things. Writing a novel may be a solitary act, but publishing and the writing life itself are not. When you're fortunate enough to have an amazing team around you, you settle in and thank the lord and hope nothing ever changes.

A thousand thank-yous to the Tyndale #dreamteam: Karen Watson, Jan Stob, Sarah Rische, Kristen Magnesen, Amanda Woods, Sharon Leavitt, Mark Lane, Danika King, and our awesome Tyndale sales reps. I'm truly blessed to work with each and every one of you. The words "publishing home" are often used too lightly, but it truly does feel like home.

A big salute to Steve Laube, agent/mentor/counselor/storyteller extraordinaire. You wear a lot of hats, but you make it look easy. I want to be half the encourager you are when I grow up (even if the growing-up thing is looking less and less likely).

Chips and salsa to Audra Jennings for making my life so much easier while I was editing this book; it's the least I can do.

A thousand tiny packets of airline peanuts (and

my undying gratitude) to Vance Franks, who helped me with the aviation details, reviewed the pertinent passages, and made my sons' year by letting them climb inside his own gorgeous homebuilt plane.

Caffeine and chocolate to my writer squad: Lori Twichell, Brandy Vallance, Evangeline Denmark, Jen Turano, Elizabeth Byler Younts, and Amber Lynn Perry. You guys keep me sane, focused, and encouraged, especially on the days that our "water cooler chats" are the only thing keeping me going.

Hugs and kisses to my husband, my two wonderful boys, and my mom and dad. You take the crazy in stride and are still proud of me. I love you bunches.

And lastly, *all the books* to my wonderful readers, including Tai Sith, who came up with the fabulous fractional name AvionElite. Without all of you, I wouldn't get to live my dream. You're the reason I'm here, so *thank you*.

CHAPTER ONE

Once upon a time, Melody Johansson had believed in happily ever afters.

To be truthful, she still believed in them, but with her thirtieth birthday in the rearview mirror, the fairy-tale ending had turned away from meeting a handsome prince to owning a little *patisserie* in Paris. Even if sometimes, as she toiled away in her own version of Cinderella's attic, both fantasies seemed equally far-fetched.

Melody brushed past the ovens in the bakery's kitchen, giving the loaves inside a cursory glance, then dragged a rolling rack of rectangular tubs from the back wall. Customers no doubt had romantic ideals of what it meant to be a baker, picturing quaintly dressed European peasants kneading loaves by hand and shoving them into ovens on long-handled peels, but the American commercial bakery had far more in common with an assembly line than a charming country *boulangerie*.

Still, there were worse places to spend the dark, still hours of the night than surrounded by loaves of bread, their deep-brown, crackling exteriors fragrant with wheat and caramel and yeast. But Melody was closing on the end of a twelve-hour shift alone, and the only drifts she wanted to be enveloped in were the fluffy plumes of the down duvet on her antique bed. Not the hard, wet snow that coated the city like a sprinkling of demerara sugar on a freshly baked pastry. It looked beautiful, but the peaceful surface concealed treacherous sheets of ice, courtesy of Denver's mercurial warm-then-snowy March weather. Every time spring looked to be on the horizon, winter yanked it back for one last hurrah.

Melody muscled a forty-pound tub of dough to the benchtop and overturned it in one swift movement. She'd done this enough in her career to judge two-pound portions by eye, but she still put each piece on the scale after she cut it from the mass with her steel-bladed bench knife. Unconsciously, she matched the cadence of her movements to the music softly pouring from the speakers. Cut, weigh, set aside. Cut, weigh, set aside. Then came the more complex rhythm of shaping each loaf. A dusting of flour, push away, quarter turn. Each stroke of the scraper beneath the loaf rolled the dough inward on itself, creating the surface tension that transformed the loose, wet lump into a taut, perfectly formed round. Then the loaf went into the cloth-lined proofing basket to rise before she went on to the next one. Twenty times per tub, multiplied by the number of tubs on the rack. She was going to be here for a while.

Baking wasn't usually such solitary work. A second baker normally worked the weekend shifts to make up for the café's increased traffic on Saturday and Sunday, but he lived south of the city, just past the point where they had closed the interstate. It shouldn't have been a surprise—practically every storm closed Monument Pass. Had it been Melody, she would have driven up earlier on Friday morning to make sure she was able to make her shift on time. But then, she'd worked her entire adult life in restaurants and bakeries, where the first rule was: always show up.

That meant her usual eight-hour shift had morphed into twelve.

She muffled a yawn with the back of her arm. "Get it together, Melody. Only two more hours." Assuming the morning staff got here on time to put the proofed loaves into the oven.

Maybe it was time to cut this job loose. She'd been here for six months, which, with the exception of a single fine-dining gig, was the longest she'd been in one place in her life. She needed variety. She could churn out someone else's mediocre recipes for only so long before she felt like she'd sold out.

She'd been wanting to go back to Europe. She'd been away from Paris for eight years, and even then she'd been so busy as a baking apprentice that she'd never had the chance to explore France beyond the capital. A few months to travel sounded like heaven.

Melody sighed. That was as much a work of

fiction as any book in her extensive library. Based on the current state of her savings account, she could barely fund a trip to the airport, let alone any points beyond.

She was heading back for a fourth tub when she heard a tapping from the front of the store. She frowned, cocking her head in that direction. Probably just the snow or the wind rattling the plate-glass windows. This strip mall was old, and every storm shook something new loose.

No, there it was again. She wiped her hands on her apron and slowly poked her head out of the kitchen toward the front entrance.

A man stood at the front door, hand raised to knock on the glass.

Melody hesitated. What on earth was anyone doing out in this storm at 4 a.m.? Even worse, what was she supposed to do? It didn't bother her to be here alone, but she kept everything securely locked until the morning staff arrived to welcome customers.

"Hello?" His muffled voice sounded hopeful. Didn't sound like someone who was planning on murdering her. But what did a murderer sound like anyway?

She approached the window cautiously. "Can I help you?"

He exhaled, his breath crystallizing around him in a cloud. "My car got stuck down the street. Can I use your phone? Mine's dead, and I forgot my charger in the hotel." He pulled out a cell phone and pressed it against the wet window. Evidence, apparently.

Melody wavered. From what she could tell through the snow-crusted window, he was nicely dressed. Didn't sound crazy. And sure enough, when she peered down the street, she could see a car cockeyed against the curb with its emergency flashers on.

"Listen, I don't blame you for being cautious. I'm a pilot, see?" He opened his overcoat to show a navy-blue uniform and then pulled out a badge clip holding two unreadable cards. "These are my airport credentials. Homeland Security and my employer trust me with a thirteen-million-dollar plane. I promise, I just need a phone."

A gust of wind hit him full force, the smattering of snow crackling against the window. He turned up his collar and hugged his arms to himself, waiting for her response.

Melody sighed and pulled a key ring from her belt loop. She couldn't leave the poor guy outside to freeze, and she knew there wasn't likely to be another place open for miles. She just prayed that her compassion wasn't going to backfire on her. The lock clicked open, and she pulled the door inward.

He rushed in, rubbing his hands together. "Thank you. You have no idea how much I appreciate this."

"Sure. The phone's over there by the register." Melody pointed him in the direction of the counter.

He nodded, turned toward the phone, then hesitated and stuck out his hand. "I'm Justin Keller."

As his cold fingers closed on her warm hand, she looked up and found herself frozen by brilliant blue eyes. "Melody Johansson."

He smiled, causing her heart to give a little hiccup, and released her before moving toward the phone. She watched as he dug a roadside assistance card from his wallet and dialed.

The stranger she'd rescued was handsome. Almost unfairly so. Hair that vacillated between blond and brown, cut short and a little spiky. Those arresting blue eyes. And a crooked leading-man smile that must routinely melt women into puddles at his feet. No, not leading man . . . fairy-tale prince. Why was it that pilots seemed to dominate the good-looking end of the gene pool? Was it a prerequisite for the job?

Justin was talking in a low voice—a sexy voice, she had to admit, just deep enough to balance the boyish charm—and she realized she should probably get back to work before he caught her staring. But he turned to her and cradled the handset against his shoulder. "They said it's going to take a while. Is it okay if I wait here?"

"Sure." She might have been reluctant to

14

let him in, but her answer now was a little too enthusiastic. From the slight glimmer of a smile he threw back to her, he'd probably heard it too.

Well, a guy like that had to be aware of the effect he had on women. She had just never thought of herself as predictable.

He hung up the phone. "They say two hours, but they also said that there are people stranded all over Denver right now. I have no idea how long it will be. Are you sure it's okay? I don't want you to get in trouble for letting me in."

"It's no trouble." Especially since the opening manager was a single woman. She'd take one look at him and understand Melody's decision. "I've got to get back to work, though. Do you want some coffee?"

"I'd kill for some coffee."

"I'm not sure I like the choice of words, but I understand the sentiment." Melody smiled at the flash of embarrassment that crossed his face. "Have a seat and I'll get you a cup. One of the perks of the night shift—unlimited caffeine."

"Sounds like more of a requirement than a perk."

"Sometimes." She found a ceramic mug under the counter and then went to the vacuum carafe that held the coffee she'd made a few hours earlier. She pushed the plunger to dispense a cup and set it on the counter. "Cream and sugar are over there."

"I take mine black." He retrieved the mug and warmed his hand around it for a moment before he took a sip. "It's good. Thank you."

"Sure." She'd said she needed to get back to work, but now she found herself hovering awkwardly behind the counter. It seemed weird to leave a stranger out here by himself—even weirder that she was reluctant to walk away.

He was looking around the bakery. "So, you're the only one here?"

Now Melody took an involuntary step back, red flags waving wildly in the periphery of her mind.

He picked up on her tension and held up one hand. "Forget I said that. It sounded less creepy in my head. I just meant, are you the one responsible for all that bread? It seems like a lot of work for one person." He gestured to the metal bins behind the counter, still awaiting their bounty for the day's customers.

"Usually I have an assistant on the weekend, but yeah. It's mostly me."

"Impressive." His nod made her think he meant it.

"Not really. This isn't baking."

"What is it then?"

Melody shrugged. "Assembling, maybe? But it's a job, and working with bread all day beats sitting behind a desk in an office."

He saluted her with a coffee cup. "I hear that. Exactly why I went into aviation."

16

A little smile formed on her lips. She'd expected a guy that good-looking to be arrogant, but his relaxed, comfortable attitude suggested the opposite. "I'm not supposed to let anyone back here, but if you want to keep me company . . ."

He straightened from his perch by the counter. "If I wouldn't be bothering you. Normally I'd stream a video or put on a podcast, but . . ."

"Dead phone. Right." She moved back to the kitchen, aware of him following behind. She nodded toward a stool by the door. "You can sit there if you like."

He shrugged off his wet overcoat and hung it on the hook by the door, then perched on the stool. She couldn't resist giving him a subtle once-over from the corner of her eye. Seemed like in addition to being unfairly good-looking, he had the physique to match—tall, lean, broad-shouldered. From the way his slim-cut white uniform shirt skimmed his torso, she would not at all be surprised if it were hiding six-pack abs.

She could tell already that this guy wasn't the type to let himself go soft from too much sitting and bad airport food. He probably had a gym membership or a personal trainer or something to stay in that kind of shape.

She shook herself before she could become another pilot groupie. *Focus, Melody.*

Starting on the next tub of dough gave her

something to think about other than the man sitting a mere five feet away from her. She started cutting and weighing the dough. "So what kind of planes do you fly? 747s or something like that?"

"No. Not anymore. Light business jets."

"Like for executives?"

"Executives, politicians, athletes, celebrities. I work for a fractional, so it's different people all the time. You know, they buy a share of a particular plane so they can travel whenever they want without having to pay for the whole thing and the cost of having a crew on standby."

"Do you enjoy it?"

"Sure."

Melody cast a look his direction. "That didn't sound very convincing."

Justin chuckled and rubbed a hand through his hair. "Had you not asked me at the end of a seven-day, twenty-five-leg tour—followed by being stranded in the snow—I probably would have said yes, absolutely."

"Okay, I guess I can give you that one. You said, 'Not anymore.' You used to be an airline pilot?"

"Do you always ask so many questions?"

"By my count, that's only three."

"Five." He ticked off on his fingers. "What kind of planes? 747s? Executives? Do I enjoy it? And did I used to be an airline pilot?"

Melody rolled her eyes, but she laughed. "You

must be fun at parties. Answer the question."

"I flew for a regional 121 operator out of Texas for a while . . . one of the smaller companies that code-shares with the majors."

"And you left because . . ."

He shook his head, like he realized he wasn't going to get out of the conversation. "The pay wasn't great and the schedule sucked. I flew twenty-four days out of the month, which meant I usually stayed in hotels twenty of those. Now I work eighteen days a month for more money, and even though there's a lot of waiting around for passengers, I actually get to fly instead of babysit autopilot."

"You seem pretty young to be a pilot."

"You seem pretty young to be a baker."

"How old should a baker be?"

"I don't know. But they shouldn't be young and stunning."

Heat rose to Melody's cheeks before she could control it. "Are you hitting on me?"

"If I were trying to hit on you, you wouldn't have to ask." He caught her gaze, his expression dead serious. Just when she feared she wouldn't be able to breathe again, his mouth widened into a grin.

The flush eased when she realized he was just teasing her. "You're terrible."

"I'm honest." He hopped off the stool. "Is it okay if I get more coffee?"

"Help yourself." She let out a long exhale when he left the room. That guy was dangerous. He was gorgeous and he knew it. He had a sexy job and he knew it . . . even if he pretended to be blasé about it.

Pretty much the sort of guy she was always attracted to and lived to regret. In fact, the more attracted to a man she was, the worse off she knew she'd be at the end when the relationship imploded like a popped soufflé.

Judging from the little quivers she felt in his presence, a mere twenty minutes after their first meeting, this one was a heartbreaker.

CHAPTER TWO

Justin left the kitchen in search of another cup of coffee. He needed way more caffeine—or maybe a muzzle, considering the way his thoughts seemed to be spilling from his mouth. He hadn't lied. The woman who had saved him from a cold morning in his car was young and stunning. Everything about her was lush, from her figure to her lips to the spill of blonde waves she kept partially tucked up beneath a slouchy beanie. When he'd knocked on the door, he'd been silently pleading for someone, anyone, to answer. He wasn't quite sure what he'd done to deserve *her* being the one to open it.

That kind of thinking was the last thing he needed. She was already skittish enough being alone in the bakery with a stranger. His only job was to be as nonthreatening as possible and check the interest that had hummed to life the instant she put her warm hand in his.

Instead, he wandered to the window to peer out at the car and cursed his own idiocy once more. He should have known better than to trust the warm sunshine that saw him off on his last tour; he was a Colorado native, so he knew as well as anyone that March had an on-again, off-again relationship with spring. It had just been so long since his project vehicle had seen the outside of a garage that he'd left his much more sensible SUV behind and driven the vintage pony car to the airport.

Which was precisely why he was waiting for a tow instead of already home in his warm bed. The 1967 Mustang GT might be 271 horsepower of pure driving fun on dry roads, but it was virtually useless in conditions like these.

"You okay out there?" Melody's voice drifted from the back. "Are we out of coffee?"

He'd been out of sight for too long. He took his coffee and moved back into the kitchen, where Melody was taking golden-brown loaves from the oven, one by one, and setting them out on vertical racks to cool.

"Those smell great," he said. "Why do you say that's not really baking?"

Melody started, as if she'd forgotten he was there. Without looking at him, she batched the next set of loaves into the oven and shut the door. "The rye and the country *miche* are decent breads, even considering they come premixed. But the baguettes and *batards* aren't even close to what they should be. And of course, the clientele is used to grocery store bread, so that's what they expect bread to be like."

"What's wrong with grocery store bread?" Justin asked. "It tastes good and it fills you up."

Melody sent him a look that was halfway

between resigned and bemused. "Bread shouldn't be some sort of bland, spongy starch that you use to push down your food. When it's done right, it's as complex as wine—the pleasantly sour flavor of well-fermented dough, the nutty quality of freshly ground wheat flour, the bitter caramel notes from the crust. Haven't you ever wondered why the Bible says Jesus is the bread of life? Bread was once worthy of that metaphor. Somehow I don't think He would like to be compared to Wonder Bread."

Justin raised an eyebrow. The last thing he'd expected from the blonde bombshell was a biblical reference. He put his attention back on her words. "So why aren't you baking that sort of bread?"

Melody shrugged. "There are only a few really good traditional bakeries in Denver, and they don't tend to have much turnover. I had a pastry chef job with a lot of freedom, but that ended when the chef who hired me left."

"What happened?"

"Now who's asking a lot of questions?"

"Hey, I'm just trying to figure out how I can get my hands on some of that heavenly bread you're talking about." He couldn't help it. The sentence came out with a hint of flirtation. So much for distance.

She seemed to be struggling against a smile. "If you're really that anxious for good bread, I'll write down the names of a couple of bakeries for you."

"I get it. You don't like talking about the past."

She shot him a look, her brow furrowed. "You're really pushy; do you know that?"

He didn't mean to be, but two hours spent in silence with a beautiful and interesting woman was a wasted opportunity. "I'm just trying to pass the time. I could sit out front, but I hoped you wouldn't mind the company."

She didn't say anything, a clear answer. He could take a hint. He was about to excuse himself to the dining room when she said, "My friend was the chef, and through no fault of her own, she was pushed out of her restaurant. I left as a show of solidarity."

"Loyal. I like that."

"Impulsive, more like. Even Rachel told me I should have stayed."

"Wait. Rachel Bishop?"

"You know her?"

"I caught that feature *Altitude* did on her a few months back. She's a big deal around here. Which means that you're kind of a big deal. What are you doing at a place like this?"

"Like I said, pastry jobs are in short supply."

Justin fell silent, watching her more closely this time. He didn't know anything about baking, but there was something about the way she moved—contained, controlled, with no wasted motion—that marked her as a professional. Her hands seemed to know what to do even when she was focused on something else.

And then she stopped, her gaze locking with his. "Do you ever look at your life and wonder how you got here? I mean, I realize I made all the decisions that brought me to this point, but I haven't been working on my craft my whole life just so I could bake a corporate chef's mediocre recipes in a chain bakery. Do you know what I mean?"

The personal nature of the question took him off guard, and for a moment, he struggled for an answer.

She laughed self-consciously. "Never mind. This is why solo shifts are better. I tend to ramble at 4 a.m."

"No, it's okay." He considered how to answer her question. "I guess I've always been pretty focused. I knew I wanted to be a pilot since I was a kid, and no one was going to do the work for me. It took a lot of time and money to get here." He cocked his head and studied her curiously. "What would you do if you could snap your fingers and make it all different?"

Melody didn't even hesitate. "Open my own place. French-inspired, most likely, with all those amazing pastries I fell in love with in Paris. Maybe light lunch fare. Hearty bread, the way it's supposed to be done—heirloom wheat, baguettes baked *bien cuit*, that point just before burnt where the crust gets rich and caramelly."

"Then why don't you?" It was clearly her passion. She'd probably spent hundreds of shifts daydreaming about being her own boss. Maybe he didn't understand the love of bread or what *bien cuit* meant, but he understood that need for independence.

But Melody was shaking her head. "I don't have a hundred grand stuffed in my mattress, that's why. And it's a high-risk venture. Not easy to get a loan with no track record."

Her expression shifted toward melancholy, or maybe wistfulness, until she shook it off and plastered a smile on her face. "Tell me how you became a pilot."

"How did I become a pilot? Or when did I become a pilot? Or how did I come to do it as a job? All three of those are different questions."

Another smile twitched at her lips. "Pick one. Or better yet, answer all three. I've got about ten more of these tubs to do." She indicated the rack with a floury wave of her hand.

"The answers probably won't last you even one. My dad is an Airbus driver. He taught me how to fly in his 1966 Piper Cherokee. He sold it later when we built our own, which I know isn't strictly one of your questions—"

"You built a plane?" She paused in her shaping

26

to focus on Justin. "From scratch? How do you even do that?"

"From a kit. We assembled the pieces in our garage and then put them together in our hangar."

Melody made a face. "No big deal. You have a hangar."

He grinned as he realized how it sounded. "Yes, we have a hangar. For the Cherokee, remember? Anyway, I racked up a lot of my PIC time in the homebuilt . . . well, that and as a flight instructor, but that's not strictly one of those three questions either. So, short version, I got my private pilot's license at sixteen. Accumulated enough flight time at my dad's expense in our plane and as a flight instructor while I was in college to get my commercial license at twenty. When I graduated, I got my ATP—that's the license you need to fly passengers for anything other than skydiving or tours—and then I got a job as a first officer with a regional airline. Put in enough hours to qualify for a fractional job, and voilà. Here we are."

"Wow." Melody nodded thoughtfully. "Why a fractional? Why not one of the big airlines?"

"Seniority is a big deal, and had I gone to a major, I'd still be working my way up the first officer ranks. Maybe I'd make captain by fifty, if I was lucky and a bunch of pilots retired. Instead, I hired onto AvionElite as a captain. The advantage to being in the first wave of new hires after a fleet expansion. No waiting."

She smiled. "I'm impressed."

"You should be. It's very impressive." He shot her a grin, and as he'd hoped, she laughed.

"Somehow I don't think you need another woman stroking your ego. I'm quite certain you get enough of that already."

"You'd be surprised."

Melody rolled her eyes. "Come on. You're telling me you don't have women falling all over you the minute you say you fly jets for a living?"

Well, to be fair . . .

She took his hesitation as confirmation. "I thought so. But in case you were wondering, I'm not the type."

"Didn't say you were." She was making it pretty clear which side of the line she was on, and there was a line. Half the women he met thought dating a pilot meant spontaneous trips to Paris. The other half—the ones who instantly dismissed him—automatically assumed he had a woman in every city.

Neither was the truth, at least not completely. He had zero autonomy in where he flew, so Europe on the company dime was out. As far as women went, he'd learned a long time ago that casual flings had a way of turning out to be not so casual. He didn't need the complications or the guilt. A few dates to pass the time, no strings attached? Sure. But the minute anyone tried to attach expectations, he was out. If he'd learned anything from his parents' failed marriage, it was that this job didn't lend itself to long-term commitment.

Which was exactly why he needed to stop thinking of the best way to get Melody's phone number. Anyone who confessed her deepest dreams after thirty minutes of acquaintance surely didn't do casual.

No reason he couldn't tease her a bit, though. "I have a confession to make. I've wanted to ask you something since I got here."

She instantly went on guard. "Okay?"

"Do you think I could have one of those mini quiches over there?"

She let her breath out in a relieved laugh. "Help yourself."

"You won't get in trouble?"

"No, I'll just ring it to my account."

"Thanks. I haven't eaten since lunch yesterday." He found a plate and grabbed a savory pastry from the cooling rack. After that he limited his questions to her process of forming the endless loaves of bread until the hands on the big institutional clock edged toward six. From the front of the café he heard rattling as someone unlocked the front door.

"There's my relief. Finally." Melody pushed her last proofing baskets onto the rack and began scraping bits of dough off the wood tabletop with her steel cutter thing. She gave the whole surface

29

a wipe-down with a wet rag and then yanked her apron off over her head. Only when she took her down parka from the hook beside his overcoat did she seem to remember his presence. "Do you want me to just drop you at home on my way? I assume you live around here."

"LoHi," he said. "But I don't want to put you out. You already saved me a very cold night in a very old car."

"It's no problem."

Her expression said she meant it. He knew he should probably just go wait for the tow truck, but who knew how long it would be before it came along. At this point, he'd been awake for twenty-six hours and felt nearly dead on his feet. Too dead to resist the impulse to spend a little more time with Melody.

"Okay," he said finally. "Thanks."

Melody nodded and marched out to the front, where a short-haired woman was flipping on lights and unlocking cash registers.

"Louisa, I'm going to take off. When Patrick gets in, have him put in the baguettes and the quiches. Everything's ready to go."

"Thanks, Mel," the woman said absent-mindedly, throwing a glance over her shoulder. She did a double take when she saw Justin there . . . triple if you considered the way she looked him up and down with interest.

Melody sighed. "This is my friend Justin. He

got stuck in the neighborhood and needed a ride home. We're going to take off, all right?"

Louisa's expression changed, and she nodded. "Thanks again for covering last night. We all owe you one."

"No problem." Melody strode back into the kitchen, and Justin followed her to the back door, where she grabbed her purse and keys before breaking out into the frigid, but no longer snowing, morning. "I'm over there. That Jeep."

She gestured to a battered blue Wrangler that had seen better days, mounded with snow. He revised his impression of her once more as she retrieved a snow brush and began clearing the white coating from the windows. Then she hauled herself up into the cab and leaned across to unlock the passenger side.

As he climbed in, she pulled the knit beanie from her head and took out a pair of clips. Blonde hair spilled over her shoulders, just as long and thick as he imagined it would be. She ran her fingers through it before pulling the cap over her head again.

Just kill him now.

She shifted into reverse and twisted to see out the rear window panel, bracing her hand against his seat as she did and reigniting that earlier spark of interest. Wow. Since when did he find driving to be sexy?

She was a good driver, though, and he always

admired a woman who could handle a stick, especially in bad weather. The Jeep's big tires didn't flinch as they plowed through the snow. Neither did she, for that matter.

"You take this thing off road?"

Melody shot him a glance. "Occasionally. Why?"

"Just wondering. I'm rethinking my initial opinion of you."

"Which is?"

"Artistic and capable. Now I'm going to add 'a thwarted sense of adventure.' "

She chuckled. "That's not too far from the truth, actually."

Now he was wondering what other sorts of adventurous things she was into. She didn't strike him as a mountain climber. Skydiver? Whitewater rafter? World traveler? And why did it matter to him anyway?

They drove slowly through the downtown streets, the roads eerily silent in the dark. On a stormy Saturday morning, no one would venture out until after ten, when the sun would come out and begin to melt the snow and ice that coated the city. He was suddenly glad he'd taken her up on her offer.

"I don't suppose I could borrow your phone?"

She didn't hesitate, just rummaged one-handed in her purse and handed it to him without looking.

"Thanks." He pulled out his roadside assistance

card, dialed the number, and canceled his request for help.

"Why did you do that?"

"Doesn't make much sense to have a tow truck come when I'm already home. I'll go back and pick it up when the roads clear."

"I guess it doesn't do you any good until the plows are out anyway. How are you going to get around?"

"I have an SUV. I just got duped by the weather report before I left, figured I should run the Mustang so the gas doesn't get stale. I don't take it out much in winter for this very reason." He shrugged. "You didn't think I was dumb enough to purposely drive it in a snowstorm, did you?"

"I don't know you well enough to make that judgment." But her tone and her slight smile said that was exactly what she'd been thinking. "Project car?"

"Precisely. I'd intended on selling it when I was done, but I couldn't bring myself to let it go."

"Sentimental, then. Don't worry; I won't tell."

Justin buried his smile and only then realized he was paying more attention to her than their progress through the snowy streets. He was supposed to be giving her directions. "Turn here. And then right at the second light."

Melody followed his directions silently, but when he told her to pull up at the curb in front of an old brick building, her head whipped toward him in surprise. "This is it? When you said LoHi, I thought—"

"One of those huge new developments? No. I'm still paying off my loans. Sorry to disappoint, though." He got that a lot. One more disillusionment from the glamorous lifestyle people thought he led.

A slow smile spread across her face. "Who said I was disappointed?"

His breath caught for a moment at her expression. Call it sleep deprivation or just a loss of his senses, he found himself leaning closer to her. She didn't move away, just sat there, her eyes wide, those luscious lips parted in surprise. At the last minute, he pulled himself together and grasped the door handle. "Thanks for the ride, Melody Johansson. I owe you one."

He hopped out of the Jeep before she could reply and stepped back onto the snowy curb. She gave him a little wave through the window, then pulled back out onto the street, ice crunching beneath her tires. Justin watched her go for a minute, then turned and trudged toward the entrance of his building. He'd said he owed her one, but it was unlikely he would ever see her again to make good on the promise.

It was probably better that way.

CHAPTER THREE

Melody pulled away from the curb, blowing out her breath and shoving down unreasonable disappointment. She'd known the guy for all of four hours. Knew nothing about him but his name, his occupation, and the fact he liked to fix up old cars in his spare time. And yet she was wishing that she'd offered her number. Or asked for his. She was a modern woman, after all. There was no reason to hide her interest in him.

Scratch that. She had plenty of good reasons. Five to be exact.

Brandon. Sebastian. Luc. Leo. Micah.

Especially Micah.

All guys she'd been powerfully attracted to at first sight. All guys who had been intelligent, charming, accomplished. By all outward indicators, decent as well.

But little by little, whether it took one month or one year, she'd realized that outward appearances were deceiving and been left with nothing but a broken heart and a sense of shame over her own naiveté.

No more. She had plenty of things to worry about, first among them how to get off this dead-end path she was on. If there was one good thing about Justin's appearance tonight, it was that she'd been forced to articulate what bothered her about her life. How far from her own dreams she'd drifted. Justin had made it seem simple to make a plan and follow it. So why couldn't it be?

She found street parking outside her tiny white-brick apartment complex in Sun Valley, an area that was worlds away and not just a handful of miles from the tony Capitol Hill neighborhood in which she worked. That was another thing that would be depressing, if she allowed herself to think about it for too long. Her best friends had made something of their lives by the thirty-year mark: Rachel was an award-winning chef who owned a nice condo conversion in Cheesman Park, while Ana was a big-time publicist with a beautiful high-rise condo in Lower Downtown. It wasn't that Melody was irresponsible or profligate with her money—quite the opposite. It was just that her line of work didn't tend to pay especially well, and she didn't hang around most places long enough to get a promotion and a raise. These days she was pretty happy to afford rent, food, and health insurance. Which meant living in a not-quite-nice building in a not-quite-nice neighborhood.

She bypassed the snow-covered shopping cart that had been abandoned at the curb and trudged toward the building's front entrance. Her key stuck in the cold lock, and she had to wiggle it to get it to turn—naturally the owners wouldn't have sprung for keycard locks, not in a building of this age. She climbed the stairs through the dingy hallway to an apartment on the second floor, its door peeling and warped, where she went through the same key-jiggling routine she'd done with the front door.

The interior, fortunately, was nowhere near as depressing as the common areas. Melody had resigned herself to not getting back her security deposit and covered the plaster walls in a soothing shade of gray to contrast with the white molding. Much of the art-deco plasterwork remained, damaged and patched inexpertly, giving the apartment an air of graceful decay, like the lovely old building in which she'd lived in Paris for a short while. There wasn't much that could be done with the 1950s kitchen, but she'd decorated the rest of the living area in whimsical printed fabrics and vintage furnishings she'd thrifted or refinished. It was a beautiful cocoon, one that blotted out the loud neighbors and wailing sirens that surrounded her.

She dropped her keys on a tiny demilune table near the doorway and hung her coat on the antique doorknobs that acted as hooks. A big glass of water, a quick shower, and then she could collapse into bed beneath her pin-tucked cotton duvet cover. And if she happened to be thinking about a certain handsome pilot despite her best efforts to the contrary, there was no one here to tell on her.

An obnoxious trill penetrated Melody's dreams, peeling back the layers of unconsciousness until she could pry one eye open to squint at her cell phone. The big white numbers on the screen said 2:05. She swiped a finger across the screen, but instead of silencing the alarm, she only managed to swipe the phone off her nightstand with a cringe-inducing thud.

She fumbled back the covers with clumsy limbs and crawled under the bed, where she finally got the blasted thing to shut off. That was the drawback of shift work. She might get six or seven hours of sleep a day, but it wasn't good sleep, and she often woke in a state of confusion. She pushed the phone onto the table where it belonged, climbed into bed again, and dragged the duvet over her head.

No. It was Saturday. That meant that she couldn't go back to sleep. She had a dessert to make for the Saturday Night Supper Club.

Technically, it wasn't an official meeting; those only happened on the first and third Saturdays of the month when Rachel hosted the invitee-only dinner party at her house. For the actual supper clubs, the guests were nominated by previous attendees and selected by Rachel and her boyfriend, Alex. They pretended like the selection was random, but in reality, Rachel and Alex spent a great deal of time putting together the right mix of guests to ensure that conversation would flow and everyone would get along. Guests were expected only to contribute the cost of their meal, which could range from ten dollars to fifty depending on the extravagance of the menu, but it was a small price to pay. In the eight months since it had begun, it had quickly become the hottest and most sought-after dining invitation in the Denver metro area.

Most of that had to do with Rachel's incredible cooking, but Melody could say without arrogance that her desserts were always one of the night's highlights.

Because tonight was a girls' night—only she, Rachel, and Ana were attending—she could get away with something simple, but of course she wouldn't. She had a reputation to uphold, after all. Melody rubbed her eyes until they burned, levered herself out of bed with another yawn, and stumbled to the kitchen.

Her programmable coffeemaker was almost finished, the last drips making concentric ripples across the surface of the dark brew. She grabbed a mug from the cabinet, poured herself a cup, and added milk and sugar. She'd go through this entire pot by the time she left for Rachel's, but right now she took the opportunity to sip the first cup and let it transform her groggy state into something resembling alertness.

She was practically a Folgers commercial.

In the meantime, she could decide what to make. She selected one of her favorite cookbooks from the rack on the kitchen wall and took it to the dining room table, flipping through the pages for inspiration. She rarely baked from them—she had her own recipes for most things—but there was something about the beautifully photographed, glossy images that sparked her imagination.

She brushed a finger across a photo of a strawberry pie. The glistening strawberries and swirls of cream topping began an instant craving for summer, but fresh strawberries were months away from their peak. She could still do a napoleon, though.

With either inspiration or caffeine flowing through her veins—hard to tell which—Melody began pulling ingredients out of the cabinet. She didn't store them in the quaint little jars one would expect from the vintage style of her apartment, but rather big commercial Cambros, plastic buckets that could hold twenty pounds of flour and sugar at a time. When it came to serious baking, cute didn't quite cut it.

A proper laminated dough would take hours, folding the layers of dough and butter multiple times, interspersed with frequent rests in the refrigerator. She had neither the time nor the energy to pull off something so exacting for a casual meal. Rough puff would have to do.

This method worked on the same principle as traditional *pâte feuilletée*, cutting cold butter into the flour, rolling the dough out until it was streaked with butter, then folding it several times envelope style. As the water in the butter evaporated, it caused air pockets that rose the pastry while the fat kept it tender. The shortcut meant it wouldn't have as many layers, but it was close enough that some of the chefs she'd worked with didn't even bother with the real thing.

When the dough was folded, she wrapped it in plastic, popped it in the refrigerator to chill, and began to work on the filling. There wasn't enough time for a proper pastry cream—it had to be boiled together on the stove like a custard and then chilled before using—so she'd do a whipped cream filling with strawberry jam.

Melody lost herself in the work, her grogginess melting away as she put together a quick jam, whipped heavy cream, and baked the pastry between two sheet pans to keep it flat. When the components were finished and cooled, she cut the sheet of pastry into even rectangles and layered each with whipped cream and jam. She scooped the rest of the whipped cream into a pastry bag with a star tip and piped perfect little plumes on the upper layer. At the last minute, she pulled out a bar of bittersweet chocolate and sliced curls onto the top with a vegetable peeler. Beautiful. The girls would love it. As would her followers.

She pulled out her cell phone and brought up her Instagram account, her heart giving a little leap when she saw that she'd gained a few dozen more followers while she slept. She'd started the profile out of boredom after she left Paisley and began the first of several bad bakery jobs, needing an outlet for her creativity. In eight months, Books in the Bakery had reached over ten thousand followers—pretty impressive considering she'd done nothing but post a photo every day or two.

She glanced around for inspiration, settling on the pickled wood surface of her dining table, then pulled several colors of vintage linen napkins from a basket on top of her cabinets. The mint added a nice counterpoint to the red of the strawberry jam, two pops of color in an otherwise-monochromatic layout. She toyed with the arrangement of the napkin, then transferred the napoleon to a plate with a paper doily. No, no doily . . . just the scalloped-edge platter. A coffee cup, a tiny silver creamer, and one of her antique dessert forks later, the composition was ready for its most important element: the book.

She wandered over to the milk-painted bookshelf that acted as a TV stand and knelt before its overfilled shelves. The napoleon was an old-fashioned pastry, named after the Italian city rather than the French emperor as so many assumed, so it definitely had to be classic European literature. Melody ran her fingers across the spines of the cloth-bound volumes as if she could absorb their essences by touch. Tolstoy, Hugo, Eliot . . . Dumas.

She smiled and tipped a scarlet-bound volume of *The Count of Monte Cristo* off the shelf. Perfect. A French book about a pretend Italian count paired with an Italian dessert with pretend French roots? Her more literate followers would get a kick out of the parallels. Not to mention the fact that Napoleon himself figured prominently in the plot.

Grinning to herself, Melody crossed back to the table, placed the book carefully in the composition, and dragged over a chair to stand on. She needed height rather than depth of field for the flatlay, so her cell phone camera was more than sufficient. Half a dozen photos later, she had selected the best one, enhanced it in her photo editing app, and uploaded it to both Instagram and her Tumblr.

Almost immediately the likes started coming in.

She left her phone on the table while she went to change her clothes and twist her hair up into a messy bun, but she couldn't resist checking when she came back to pack up the dessert for transport to Rachel's house. Up to thirty. Not bad, but certainly not the record for fastest-growing post. She analyzed the photo for some clue about what wasn't resonating with her audience, but it didn't seem any different from her most popular posts. Maybe next time she'd add some greenery. Things with roses and fresh leaves always were a big hit.

She was still recomposing the photo in her head when she pulled up in front of Rachel's house and picked her way up the icy walkway to her friend's front door, balancing the dessert box carefully in front of her.

The door opened to reveal a beautiful dark-haired woman, casually dressed in a flannel button-down shirt and jeans. "Mel. You're early!"

"There's a first time for everything." Melody gave Rachel a one-armed hug and handed over the container so she could shrug off her down parka. She followed her friend into the kitchen, where Ana sat at the long, rustic kitchen table. As usual, the Filipina was impeccably put together in a stylish sweater and jeans, her makeup flawless.

Ana held up a bottle. "Wine?"

"Please." Melody lifted her face and breathed deeply. "Something smells amazing. What are we having?"

"*Moules marinières*," Rachel said. "It seemed a shame to let mussel season close without making it at least once."

"Oh la la," Melody said. "Paris must have been in the air today, because I made a napoleon."

Ana handed over a half-filled wineglass and gave Melody a quick hug. "You're killing me, Mel. I'm still recovering from last week's Death by Chocolate Mousse."

"Don't tell me you only have dessert once a week." Melody looked over Ana's trim figure, toned and sculpted in the gym, and shook her head. "Never mind. I already know the answer to that."

"Please. You and Rachel got the good genes. I have to work at it."

"Whatever." Melody rolled her eyes and plopped herself across the table from Ana, watching Rachel lift the lid on the pot. A plume of shallot and white wine–perfumed steam wafted their direction. "I see she's missing the restaurant tonight."

"You think?" Ana flashed a smile. "She was just waxing eloquent about white truffles."

"Not for this dish," Rachel interjected. "Just white truffles in general."

Melody laughed. "Hon, you've got it bad."

"That obvious?" Rachel checked the temperature of the oil in her Dutch oven and began to transfer once-fried potato strips into the oil for their final crisp. "Don't get me wrong. I've loved going to college, and I'm enjoying teaching at the culinary school far more than I ever thought

I would. I have this one student who reminds me of why I cook. She's forty years old and came to the conclusion that she'd rather die than spend one more day in an office. Normally, cooks who start any older than their twenties never make it. They realize that the life is harder than the one they left behind. But she's like a sponge. She absorbs everything I can throw at her and demands more."

"So you want a restaurant so you can hire her?"

"That's not a bad idea, actually." Rachel sent a smile over her shoulder. "You know me. This was always just a break. I just haven't found the right situation yet."

"I know what you mean," Melody said.

Ana grimaced. "Bakery job not going so well?"

"You know how it is. Low pay, long hours. Making the same boring things every day without any relief. If I've got to make one more ham and cheese quiche, I'm going to lose it."

Ana swirled her wine around in her glass, a sure sign she was thinking about how to broach a tricky subject. "You know, if you hadn't moved around so much, you could be the executive pastry chef somewhere by now."

Melody had no response to that, because it was 100 percent true. Had she stuck with the pastry chef job she'd held before she went to work for Rachel, she probably would be in charge of the entire section now. Of course, the reason she'd quit had nothing to do with the details of the job or her performance and everything to do with her bad taste in men.

"At least we can both agree that my current situation is dead-end. I'm just a cog on the wheel. You don't need a baking pedigree to do this gig."

Rachel watched her fries carefully, then began to fish them from the Dutch oven with a spider skimmer. "So what are you thinking?"

"I'm thinking that I would love nothing better than to pack up all my earthly possessions and move back to Paris, but my bank account disagrees. So maybe I should just start looking for another job."

Ana regarded her with a half-exasperated, half-doting look. Neither of Melody's friends quite knew what to do with her restlessness. She'd never been able to explain it, even to herself. It wasn't boredom exactly. It was just that for every opportunity she chose, she was all too aware of the ones she rejected. It was only a matter of time before she wondered what else was around the corner. And yet she had realized today that none of those choices were moving her *toward* anything, just away from something else.

"I saw your latest Books in the Bakery post. You've got a ton of followers, Mel! Why aren't you doing something with that?"

"Do what? Ten thousand followers does not

a business make. It's not even enough to get a publisher interested in a cookbook."

"What about a mail-order bakery?" Rachel started to transfer their dinner to serving dishes. "Surely some of those ten thousand people would love to get their hands on your work. With your design sensibility and Ana's PR skills, I'm pretty sure you could get up and running almost immediately. You know I'm willing to help however I can."

"You don't have any time, between teaching and going to college and that gorgeous boyfriend of yours." The words came out petulantly, but Melody winked so Rachel would know she was kidding. "I don't want Alex hating me for taking up all your free time."

"Alex knows how important you guys are to me. Which is why he's hanging out with Bryan tonight so we could have some girl time." Still, there was a little glimmer in Rachel's eye that made Melody think she'd rather be with her boyfriend. And who could blame her? Not only was he handsome, he was successful, kind, and he adored Rachel. You only had to see how he looked at her to know that he was head-over-heels in love. It was enough to send a single woman into twin spirals of hope and despair.

And resurrect fairy-tale fantasies faster than you could say "glass slipper."

She didn't begrudge Rachel the fairy tale, though. It was her turn, her shot. Rachel had lived for work almost her entire life, eschewing men completely in favor of climbing the ranks of the culinary world. Ironically, Alex had been the one who caused it to come crashing down, after an article he wrote in the *New Yorker* set off a chain reaction that ended in her losing her share of the restaurant she'd built with her partners. If you asked Rachel, she'd say it was the best thing that had ever happened to her, and not just because of the guy.

Maybe I need a guy to come around and ruin my career. Justin's image immediately popped into her head, and she shoved it back down.

Rachel began bringing soup plates to the table then, heaped with open mussels in a shallot-and-parsley-studded buttered broth. A basket of freshly cooked, thick-cut French fries went in the middle, along with a plate of baguette rounds for soaking up the last bits of the fragrant liquid.

Melody closed her eyes to savor the first taste of perfectly steamed mussel. Her friend really was an amazing chef. Simple dishes like this one showed off both the quality of the ingredients and the skill of the cook—no heavy sauces or elaborate preparations behind which to hide.

Ana gave a blissed-out sigh. "You need your own place again, Rachel. Not that I'm not grateful to be the recipient of your boredom, but it seems selfish to want to keep your cooking to myself."

Rachel repressed her smile, obviously pleased. Cooking was the way she loved her friends; praising the food was the way they loved her back.

They ate in virtual silence, too consumed with pleasure to be bothered to speak, until Melody jerked her head up and looked to Ana. "Oh! I forgot! You had a date last night!"

Rachel turned accusingly to Ana. "I can't believe you didn't lead with that."

"That's because it was a disaster." Ana dipped a round of bread into the broth and took a bite, chewing long and carefully. Clearly she wasn't going to elaborate.

"So we can check the setup off the list as a viable dating option," Melody said.

"Either that or I need to be set up by coworkers who have better taste."

Rachel cringed. "He was that bad?"

"He was good-looking, but all he wanted to talk about was how much money he made and how much his car cost. Plus he kept saying that he wanted to take me to his house in Vail. All in the first thirty minutes." Ana shuddered. "It creeped me out, like he thought I could be bought."

"I'm sorry," Melody said, wrinkling her nose. "Surely Rachel didn't get the last decent guy in the entire city."

"I'm beginning to think so. So you're not having any luck either, I take it?"

"When would I have time? Though, actually . . . you won't believe what happened at work this morning."

Melody hadn't planned on telling them, but the story was too good to keep to herself. She started with how Justin had shown up in the snow outside the bakery, and by the time she got to the part where she drove him home, her friends were grinning like fools.

"So you got his number, right?" Ana said. "Or gave him yours."

Melody shook her head. "No. It wasn't like that."

" 'It wasn't like that,' " Ana muttered. "She meets a hot, intelligent, employed guy who doesn't put the moves on her, and she has no interest."

"I didn't say I had no interest. Of *course* I had interest. A lot of interest. And therein lies the problem."

"Not every guy is like Micah," Rachel said. "And you've seen firsthand that sometimes the right guy comes along when you least expect it."

"For you, maybe. When I let my hormones decide, I make terrible choices."

"You're not wrong," Ana said. "But how do you plan to meet someone if you rule out anyone you're attracted to?"

"I figured he'd sit down next to me at church

51

or something and I'd hear a voice from heaven."

"When's the last time you went to church?" Rachel asked.

"You know very well. About as far back as you, before you became a lady of leisure and got all this free weekend time."

Rachel snorted, and Melody cracked a smile in return. Only a cook would consider part-time college and part-time teaching as less than a full-time job. "Seriously, though . . ."

Melody waved a hand. "No, trust me. This guy pushed all my buttons at first sight. And we all know that's bad news. Besides, even if I were interested, I have no way of contacting him."

Ana shrugged. "You know where he lives."

"I'm not going to stalk him!"

"I have no such qualms," Ana said. "I want to see the button-pusher myself. Give me your cell phone."

Reluctantly, Melody passed her the phone. Ana immediately punched the Facebook icon. "What did you say his name was?"

"Justin Keller. Wait, you're really looking him up?"

"Of course I am." Ana's fingers flew over the phone's tiny keyboard and a page of results loaded. She swiped up, murmuring to himself, "Not him . . . not him either . . ."

Then she stopped and shoved the phone in Melody's direction. "Is that him?"

Melody squinted at the photo and her breath hitched. It was her Justin all right, looking as appealing in a snapshot as he had in person. Well, he wasn't *her* Justin . . . "That's him."

Ana whistled and passed the phone to Rachel, whose eyebrows went up. "You weren't kidding."

"I never kid about ultra-hot guys. Now give it back to me."

"You should send him a friend request," Ana said.

"Absolutely not."

"Too late. I already did."

Melody snatched back her phone. "What do I do now?"

"You wait. He'll accept your friend request and then you post something cute and flirty on his wall. Ask him if he ever got his car out of the snow."

"Add a winky face," Rachel suggested.

"Do *not* add a winky face," Ana said.

Rachel's brow furrowed. "Why? Does that mean something bad?"

"Honey, I know I've been telling you to brush up on your social media skills, but maybe you should stay off of it."

"Can we get back to my problem here?" Melody asked. "I'm going to cancel it."

"If you do that," Rachel said reasonably, "he'll know you were looking him up and you pressed it by accident. Which really is stalking. Better that he just thinks you're proactive."

"I can't believe you just did that to me!"

Ana grinned. "You're welcome."

Fine. The damage was already done, so she might as well take advantage of it. Melody pressed the photos section, and several that were set to public popped up on the screen. She tapped one of Justin with a little girl, maybe two or three years old. "He has a kid?"

Rachel hopped out of her seat to look over Melody's shoulder. "Wait, what?"

"No, no. It's his niece, I think. He was tagged by Jessica Keller Costa. Must be his sister." She looked closer and read the caption. " 'Abby with her favorite uncle at church today.' "

"Jackpot," Ana said. "Christian and a good uncle."

"We don't know that," Rachel said. "Maybe his sister dragged him to her daughter's dedication or something. And she really shouldn't be posting pictures of her kids set to public."

Ana made a face. "Party pooper."

Rachel stood and began clearing the table of their dishes, practically licked clean. She piled them in the sink for later, then turned to the pastry box holding Melody's dessert. "Do you want to come cut this?"

"Gladly." Melody jumped out of her seat, taking her phone with her this time, and rushed to Rachel's side. She portioned the napoleon into slices and transferred them to small plates that Rachel provided, then helped her friend bring them to the table while the coffee brewed. Before they could return to the topic of Justin, she asked, "So who do we have invited for supper club next weekend?"

"The three of us, of course, if you can still make it. Alex invited his neighbor and the neighbor's girlfriend. That makes six. I thought each of us could invite someone new, just to mix it up a little."

Melody caught Ana's grin from the corner of her eye and held up a finger. "Don't say it."

"What?" Ana asked innocently. "I wasn't going to say anything."

"Good. Because short of Facebook, I don't intend on having any contact with Justin Keller."

And yet, on her way home from dinner, his repeated intrusion on her thoughts called her a liar. It was all she could do not to check her phone at the stoplight and see if he'd accepted her friend request. That was why looking him up had been a bad idea. Back when she thought she had no way to reach him short of showing up at his apartment, it had been easy to dismiss him as the central character of an interesting story. Now that there was the possibility of contact—real contact—she found herself making excuses, thinking up reasons why he wasn't as bad an idea as she'd initially convinced herself.

When did you go and get all conservative? she wondered as she marched up the icy sidewalk to her building's front door. *Once, you would have been the first to track him down.*

But she knew the answer to that, too. If there was one thing Micah had taught her, it was that once her heart got involved, her head took a backseat. Had she not been so stupid in love with him, she would have seen what was staring her in the face, and she wouldn't have had to walk in on her boyfriend with another woman.

In the storage room of his own restaurant.

Even worse than the eyeful she'd gotten had been his excuse: *"We were never exclusive, Melody. I thought you knew that."*

She shook off the memories with an irritated shake of her head and climbed the stairs to her apartment. She had some taste in men, all right. Chefs and pilots. Two occupations known for their groupies, and for appealing to men who were all too willing to take advantage of the fact.

Melody let herself into her apartment, her mind made up. She would cancel the friend request. Who cared if Justin thought she'd been Facebook stalking him? If she never saw him again, it hardly mattered. She pulled her phone out, her thumb selecting the app as she automatically shrugged out of her coat.

"There you are."

Melody let out a shriek and spun toward the settee near the window, her phone forgotten. Her heart pounded so hard it made her sway on her feet with every beat. When she recognized the intruder, she sagged against the wall. "Why would you do something like that to me? You just about scared me to death!"

The tall, elegant woman who unfolded herself from the seat looked enough like Melody that they could be sisters—or at least that's what she liked telling everyone. Same long wavy hair, same brown eyes. The difference of course was that this woman was whittled and toned from personal training and Pilates, her voice modulated to a sultry Southern twang that Melody knew was as fake as certain body parts. Janna Leigh had been born and raised in Denver, not the Deep South like she implied when talking about her love for Tennessee.

"I don't know how else I would have announced myself," Janna said petulantly, crossing the room in impossibly high-heeled boots. "I didn't mean to scare you, love. Why don't you come give your mama a kiss?"

Melody stared at her mother for a long stretch—it could have been ten seconds or ten minutes for the questions that flew through her mind. Finally, she drew in a deep breath and let it out with a prayer for patience. She kissed Janna's proffered cheek and then stepped back from the cloud of perfume. "What are you doing here, Mom? And how did you get in?"

"You gave me a key, remember? Last time I was here."

A key that she was supposed to have returned when she left. Melody hadn't made a fuss, because her mother's dismay over her living arrangements had made it clear she wouldn't be coming back short of hell freezing over. Melody barely kept herself from inquiring about the temperature of hades.

"That answers the last part but not the first. I know you didn't come all the way from Nashville just to visit me."

Part of her waited for her mother to deny it, but instead Janna reached out one cool, slender hand to grasp Melody's and drew her over to the sofa. "Sit down, sugar."

Melody's heartbeat quickened again, this time from dread.

"There's no easy way to say this. Grandma Bev is dead."

"What?" Melody stared at her mother, unable to comprehend what she was saying. "That's not possible! I just talked to her a couple of weeks ago."

"Apparently, she had been having some heart issues that she didn't want anyone to know about. She had a stroke. They think it was a blood clot.

She called 911, but she died on the way to the hospital."

Melody felt like the ceiling had caved in on top of her. No, it would have been easier to breathe with a ton of bricks on her chest than through this news. "I can't believe it."

"I know you were still close to her. That's why I wanted to tell you in person."

Melody fell back against the cushions, tears welling in her eyes and spilling down her cheeks. *Close* was an understatement. Her grandmother Beverly had raised her, homeschooled her, done all the things that her mother was too busy to do because of her country music career. She was the one who had wiped Melody's tears and kissed her scrapes and taught her all the things a young girl should know and quite a few things she shouldn't. But that was her grandmother. She'd been an unusual mix of traditional and modern: a university literature professor, twice married, who nonetheless attended a conservative church and gave up her career to raise her only granddaughter. She had been the one to encourage Melody's love of art and baking, even while she insisted on a thorough classical education.

"I know this is a huge shock. I only hope you're this broken up when I die."

Melody turned incredulously to her mother. "For the love, Mom. Could you give it a rest?

This is the one time in our lives when even you can agree it's not about you."

"Why, I never—"

"No, you never do." Melody pushed herself to her feet, hugging her arms to her chest protectively. "When is the funeral?"

"Tomorrow. I thought we could drive up together for the service."

Once more, she was stunned nearly speechless. "Tomorrow? How long have you known about this?"

"Since Thursday morning, but—"

"Thursday? And you're just now telling me?" Melody stared in disbelief. "How could you keep something like this from me?"

Janna stood, her unnaturally sculpted body stiff. "Don't act like that. She was *my* mother, you know."

"And yet somehow your career was always too important to come visit her."

Janna jerked like she'd been slapped, but she smoothed it over with the ease of long practice. "I'll come by and get you at nine. It's a bit of a drive to Longmont." She brushed past Melody toward the door and paused with her hand on the knob. "I know you don't want to believe this, but I loved her. I love both of you."

Melody stared as the door shut behind her mother, guilt creeping in to mingle with the grief. Maybe she hadn't been fair. Of course Janna loved Beverly, and of course she would be upset. But she also wouldn't put it past her mother to turn this tragedy into some sort of publicity op, a chance to play the grieving daughter before cameras, where she would weep prettily beneath a netting-veiled hat and dab her eyes with a lace handkerchief. No doubt her albums would get a boost from playing on the public's sympathies. It was an uncharitable thought if ever there was one, but Melody had been a prop in those publicity stunts too often to not be cynical.

She walked numbly to her bedroom, crawled beneath the duvet fully clothed, and sobbed until it was time to go to work.

CHAPTER FOUR

Justin Keller always liked to say that the best pilots were problem solvers. And right now he had two problems.

One, his Mustang was still stranded in a snowdrift on a Capitol Hill street.

Two, he'd neglected to get the phone number of the beautiful blonde baker who had rescued him.

Actually, the second one wasn't really a problem, or at least not the true problem. The biggest problem was that, despite every good reason to let it go, he was still thinking about Melody Johansson.

A blisteringly hot shower and half a cup of coffee did what six hours of sleep had not—restored him to his usual pragmatic self. He picked up his now fully charged cell phone and wandered to the boxy contemporary sofa in his living room, holding down the power button to start it up. As soon as it acquired a signal, a notification flashed onto his screen to alert him of two missed calls.

The first was from his sister, making sure he was still coming to dinner tonight as planned.

The second instantly filled him with dread. A sweet female voice poured from the speaker:

"Hey, Justin, it's Claudia. I was wondering if you were going to be around this weekend. I'm in Denver for a few days, thought we might grab a bite or see a movie. . . ."

Claudia. He racked his brain. Daughter of a client he'd transported to Denver a few weeks ago. Exotic, stylish, expensive handbag and shoes. He'd chatted her up a bit, which was his job. Okay, fine, maybe he'd flirted. But how had she gotten his personal number?

Right. There had been a quick repair needed during a scheduled refueling stop, so she and her father had gone to the airport restaurant for lunch. Justin had called when the repair was completed. She must have swiped his number from Daddy's phone.

Justin rubbed the back of his neck ruefully, considering, then deleted the message. She was young, barely twenty-two, and he hadn't dreamed she'd read anything into the banter. He'd just been trying to smooth over her irritation at the delay.

Besides, it had only taken that short conversation to know he had nothing in common with a twenty-two-year-old socialite. Unlike Melody, with whom he'd chatted as if they'd known each other for years. If the baker had read anything into his flirting, it was because he'd meant every word.

Justin scrubbed his hands through his hair

and tried to push away the memory. He could never go there. Not because he wasn't attracted to her—he'd have to be blind and stupid not to notice the attraction that had hummed to life the instant she put her hand in his. He was simply certain that the last thing she needed was a guy like him. About the only thing they had in common was a passion for their careers that went far beyond punching a clock. She was most definitely a romantic; he had dismissed that nonsense a long time ago. She was probably looking for a boyfriend; he was just looking for a date for the rare Saturday night he spent at home. She seemed to have some religious faith; he . . .

Well, he didn't so much know where he stood. It would be a lot easier to be an atheist and dismiss God entirely than to be mired in his current ambivalence. There was most certainly a God up there, but it seemed like He and Justin were no longer on speaking terms. And it hadn't been Justin's doing.

He shoved his well-worn resentment away and instead pulled up a number from his contact list. Since problem number two wasn't going anywhere, he might as well address problem number one.

Pete picked up on the first ring. "Hey, Justin. You're back, I take it. What's up?"

"I need a fa—" Justin broke off as the strains

of classical music reached him from the background. "Where are you?"

"At Abby's ballet lesson. Why?"

"No reason. Doesn't Jessica usually take her?"

"She's at Andrew's soccer game. You know your sister wouldn't give up a chance to coach the Rapids' future star forward."

Justin grinned. He'd known Pete Costa for a decade, ever since they'd both worked at the same airport, Justin as a flight instructor, Pete as an aircraft mechanic. Despite the fact that Justin was several years younger, they'd hit it off immediately. He hadn't expected, however, for Pete to fall in love at first sight with Justin's older sister, marry her a few short months later, and pop out two kids with her in the space of three years.

"I made the mistake of driving the Mustang to the airport last week and got it stuck in the snow on the way home," Justin said.

Pete began to laugh. "That car has caused you more trouble than it's worth."

"So you always say. Can you take me to get it when you're done?"

Pete sobered, though amusement still laced his tone. "We'll be finished in twenty. I'll text you when I'm outside your building."

"I'm in no hurry. Thanks, Pete." Justin clicked off the line and poured himself a cup of coffee. He'd already slept half the day away, but picking up the car would take up precious little of his afternoon. He gave another fleeting consideration to Claudia's call, then dismissed the idea. He'd probably just hit the gym and catch up on one of his neglected DVR recordings until it was time to go to Pete and Jessica's house for dinner.

A glamorous life indeed.

When Pete's text came in thirty-five minutes later, he grabbed his jacket, keys, and a collapsible snow shovel and headed downstairs to where his friend's white Volvo was parked. Justin had given him all sorts of flak when he'd traded in his sporty coupe for the wagon, but Pete had just smiled like he knew something Justin didn't.

"Hey." Justin slid into the passenger seat and twisted immediately around to the three-year-old girl in the backseat. "Hello, Princess Abigail."

"Hi, Uncah Justin." She favored him with a toothy smile, beaming out from beneath a cap of brown curls. "What'd you bwing me?"

Justin put on a surprised look. "Bring you? Why would you think I'd bring you anything?"

She cocked her head with a knowing smile. "Not funny."

Justin grinned at Pete. How his friend managed to resist her, he'd never know. He reached into the pocket of his jacket and pulled out a small plastic bag, which he passed to the little girl. She dug into it with all the excitement of Christmas morning and pulled out a handful of refrigerator magnets.

"Do you know what they say? That one says—"

"Texas." She held up the one shaped like a cowboy hat. "See?"

Justin glanced at Pete, surprised.

"I know. One day she just started reading the cereal box. I'm thinking we might have our hands full with this one."

"What does 'hands full' mean, Daddy?"

Pete grimaced. "It means you're a smarty-pants and you're going to be in college way too soon."

Justin settled face-forward in his seat. "I'm still getting used to the idea of being an uncle. Let's not rush things."

"You're telling me. But one day they're born, and then you blink and they're starting school." Pete shot Justin a look. "You're what, thirty-four?"

"You know I am. And no, I'm not dating anyone. Not seriously, at least. Did Jessica put you up to this?"

Pete's lack of response said it all. Lately his sister's sole mission in life seemed to be marrying him off.

"Tell my sister that if and when I decide to settle down, she'll be the first to know. And no, that does not mean setting me up with one of her single friends who says she doesn't mind my weird work schedule. They always say that and then in the next breath ask how long I intend on flying."

"You know she worries about you. She wants you to be happy."

"I know she does. But I didn't work a decade just to pay off eighty thousand dollars of flight school and certificates that I'm not going to use anymore."

"What about Sarah?"

"Four months in and she wanted to talk about a future in which I no longer fly and I get an office job that would have me home at five thirty every night." A shame too. He'd actually liked Sarah. She was pretty and funny and smart—all reasons he'd broken his own rules on commitment to date her for six months. She was an assistant district attorney for Boulder County, and her long hours had made him think maybe he could do the long-term thing after all. Then she'd started talking about moving to a private practice that would give them more time together, hinting around about him considering another line of work, and that illusion had shattered. Sooner or later, they all wanted to change him.

"Anyway, you can tell Jessica that you did your duty and I shut you down as usual."

Pete just grinned and kept his eyes on the road. Maybe it wasn't only Jessica who was plotting against him these days. Justin caught a glimpse of his car where he'd left it. "There I am. You can pull in behind."

His brother-in-law did just that, crunching down a huge hill of snow in the process. Sure enough, plows had pushed mountainous drifts up against the driver's door of the Mustang. Justin reached for the door handle to get out, but Pete grabbed his arm.

"Wait a minute. I wanted to show you something." Pete pulled his phone from his cup holder, brought up a web page, and passed it over.

Justin's brow furrowed until he recognized a businesses-for-sale site. "You found something?"

"Charter out of Fort Lauderdale-Hollywood. Multiple planes; pilots and staff already in place. One and a half million in revenue."

Justin whistled softly and took the phone, scrolling down the listing. "How much do they want?"

"More than we have. But there's always loans. And once you're vested . . ."

"What kind of equipment?"

"Two Baron G58s and a Pilatus PC-12 turboprop."

Justin exhaled a breath he hadn't realized he was holding. "Not bad. Send me the link?"

"I'll text it to you. Look it over. If you're interested, we can set up a trip to go check it out."

"Sounds good."

Pete fell silent for a moment. "Don't tell Jessica. I don't want to get her hopes up."

There was something in Pete's voice that struck fear into Justin's heart. "Is she okay? Is there something I should know?"

"Same as usual. She fell the other day but insists that she just tripped. I don't know if it's true or not."

Justin nodded slowly, telling himself not to jump to conclusions. He changed the subject. "Jessica left me a message about dinner. Are we still on?"

"Of course."

"Good." Justin twisted in his seat. "All right, Princess Abby, time for me to rescue my loyal steed. I'll see you later, okay?"

His niece looked up from her new magnets long enough to wave good-bye, then back she went, reading the state and city names to herself. Justin shook his head as he climbed out. Definitely too smart for her own good.

He extended the shovel and cleared the snow away from the Mustang's door, then started digging behind both the front and rear wheels until they were down to bare pavement. With any luck, that would give him enough traction to get moving and onto the cleared street. And then the poor Mustang would remain garaged in any weather except blinding sunshine. For all he knew, the next time he'd drive it was when he packed up his life and moved to a new home. Which was beginning to look like it might be in Florida.

Justin unlocked the door of the Mustang, climbed inside, and turned the key in the ignition. The engine immediately rumbled to life. He let it run for a minute to warm up and then put it into gear. A few squirrelly, fishtailing moments later, he was out onto clear pavement and moving forward once again. He let out a breath of relief and glanced in the rearview mirror to see Pete and Abby pull out behind him.

He made a left at the next street, Pete heading straight toward his own home. Justin may or may not have glanced down the alley to look for the presence of a blue Jeep he already knew wouldn't be there. And he may or may not have felt some disappointment when he was right.

Just after five, Justin pulled up—in his SUV this time—in front of the Costas' house, a 1930s cottage in Denver's East Colfax neighborhood. Neatly trimmed evergreen hedges marked the front path, the house's shutters recently painted. Only the security bars covering the windows indicated it was in an "up-and-coming neighborhood," a real estate euphemism for a formerly bad area experiencing a burst of popularity because of high prices elsewhere.

Five o'clock seemed like a ridiculously early

time for supper, but the kids had a seven o'clock bedtime and turned feral if their dinner stretched much past twilight. Justin grabbed the glass bottle of soda off the seat beside him along with a can of gourmet hot chocolate and crunched up the snowy walkway to the front door.

The screech of kids inside reached him before he set foot on the front steps. He loosed a half-smile/half-grimace and knocked on the door. Pete answered, Abby clinging to his back, while five-year-old Andrew ran circles around him in a Darth Vader mask and cape. As soon as Justin stepped inside, the little boy thrust out his hand, evidently using his Sith powers on him.

Justin set down the soda and cocoa, clutched his throat, and sank to his knees.

"Okay, that's enough," came a feminine voice from the room beyond. "No more strangling your uncle with the Dark Side. Go get washed up for dinner."

Andrew scampered off immediately, though not in the direction of the bathroom or the kitchen, so his obedience to the command was debatable. Justin popped back up to his feet in time to see Jessica emerge from the kitchen.

"Hey, Jess." He gave her a hug and kissed the top of her head. "You're looking well. Don't tell me your no-good husband is finally pulling his weight around here?"

"On occasion." She winked at Pete, who just

72

shook his head. "When he's not rescuing you, that is."

"He told you about that, did he?"

"Of course he did." She held out her arms for Abby. "C'mon, girlie, let's find your brother and get both of you washed up."

"Let's go open that soda. It's that small-batch artisanal nonsense your sister likes, isn't it?" Pete gestured for Justin to follow him to the kitchen, where the smell of roast chicken and potatoes emanated from the oven. Justin leaned against the counter while Pete got out mismatched glasses and filled them with ice. "What did you think about the link I sent you? I know it's out of our price range, but Jessica really believes being at sea level will help, and at this point, I'm willing to try anything."

Justin sighed heavily. Jessica had been diagnosed with relapsing-remitting multiple sclerosis several years ago, but in the last couple, her symptoms had become more frequent and more concerning. Which was why this potential move out of Colorado was so critical. She'd noticed that almost all her complaints went away while visiting Pete's family in Miami, and they came right back upon returning to Denver.

Justin circled back to his thoughts on the charter listing. "It's pretty high, but if his fleet has been maintained well and he can back up his revenue figures, it's worth exploring. Buying an existing charter is going to get us in the black much faster than starting one from the ground up. No pun intended."

Pete poured soda into three glasses and tasted his experimentally. "You know I'm not one for sentiment, but I really appreciate you doing this. You're leaving your whole life for Jess and me. That's not something most people would do, even for family."

Justin brushed off the thanks. "What life? Denver's just a crash pad at this point. You're giving me an excuse to check out of the grind, live someplace sunny, and fly to some of the most beautiful islands on earth. Besides, you know I've been wanting to do something like this for years."

"Yeah, I do." Pete clapped his hand on Justin's shoulder. "Just brace yourself. Jessica's already trying to figure out how to meet some women in Florida to set you up with."

"You weren't supposed to *tell* him that." Jessica rolled her eyes as she reentered the kitchen, two newly cleaned children in tow. "This husband of mine is a traitor."

"You're really not going to give up, are you?"

"Not until I see you married off to a gorgeous, kind, funny woman and settled with a bunch of children. I'm thinking four or five."

Justin snorted. "You are worse than our father. He's only asking for three."

"I'll settle for three." She grabbed a pot holder off the counter and took a roasting pan from the oven, revealing two beautifully browned whole chickens. "Tell me about this business you and Pete are considering."

Justin went to the table, pausing to help Abby into her booster seat, then settled into his own chair. "So much for keeping it quiet."

Pete shrugged. "Your sister is a mind reader. She knows when I'm hiding something."

Justin grinned, knowing it wasn't far from the truth. "We'll know more when the broker responds to our inquiry. It's a small fleet, but they've got the range to service the Bahamas, the Keys, and Cuba. There's also the possibility of regularly scheduled service to Nassau."

"And what do our parents think about this whole thing?"

"I haven't told them yet. But if I had to guess, Dad's going to try to talk me into interviewing with United, and Mom is going to act all disappointed that I haven't given this up yet."

"To be fair, she has legitimate reasons to feel that way."

"Maybe, but she's our mother, not my wife, so she doesn't have a say in the matter. You know me . . ."

"I know you're not getting any younger." Jessica gave him the side-eye but apparently decided not to pursue the topic further, for which he was grateful. When their parents split, Jessica had sided with their mom, and Justin had gone with their dad. Which wasn't as dramatic as it sounded, considering their mom had moved into a rental house right down the street and they ran between the two as if the neighborhood were simply an extended hallway. It hadn't stopped Jessica from resenting Rich Keller's career as an airline pilot for being the deciding factor in the divorce, though.

Jessica went back to the topic at hand. "So what happens if everything checks out?"

Pete jumped in. "Then we make a written conditional offer, hire a lawyer to check out the books, apply for licenses, and get a loan."

She looked between them. "How long do you think?"

Justin hesitated. "If all goes well . . . early summer."

"Wow, that soon."

Pete reached across the table to squeeze Jessica's hand. "If you're not sure—"

"No, no, it's not that. It's good timing too, since our lease is up in July. It's just hard to leave Colorado."

"I'm pretty sure the first time you take the kids to the beach in December, you're going to feel okay with the choice," Justin said.

Pete laughed. "And that first winter without shoveling snow is going to make *me* okay with it." His expression softened. "It's what we have to do for your health. I'll go wherever it takes."

Tears welled in Jessica's eyes, and Justin looked away, feeling like he was intruding on a private moment. He might like to tease Pete, but it was clear that he adored Justin's sister and their kids. Their happy little family was almost enough to make him regret his near-permanent vow of bachelorhood. He'd always said that he would never make the mistake his dad made, marrying a woman who didn't know what she was getting into. Because like his dad, he knew that he would never be able to give up flying, not even for someone he loved. It was what he'd always wanted to do, what he'd trained for, what he'd paid a fortune to achieve.

But in Florida, maybe he wouldn't have to make the decision. He'd be doing day trips on his own schedule, as often or infrequently as he felt like flying, coming home each night to his own bed. That kind of lifestyle could be compatible with settling down.

And now he was turning into a big sentimental idiot. He reached for the drumsticks on the platter and served them to Abby and Andrew, then took a couple of thighs for himself. "I've been dreaming about your roast chicken since the last time you made it, Jess."

"Liar," she said, but at least the tears were gone and she was grinning at him. He didn't like to think about what would happen if this move didn't work, if her condition continued to get worse.

Fortunately, they didn't touch on serious topics much longer, instead turning toward the US's World Cup prospects and various other soccer-related topics that Justin pretended to care about. When they were done, the two chicken carcasses were picked clean, only a scattering of roasted potatoes left in the pan. Justin rose, preparing to clear the table, but Jessica waved him down.

"No, don't. I've got it. You two have things to discuss."

"Actually, I'm going to rack out early. It's been a long couple of days."

Justin pushed in his chair, but Jessica caught him. "Are you coming to church tomorrow? Abby's class is singing with the worship team."

Justin shot his sister a look. "Really? You're going to use my niece as bait?"

"We miss you," Jessica said levelly. To her credit, she was persistent. "Just come with us. You promised you'd go if you were home on Sundays."

Justin sighed and gave his sister a quick squeeze. "Say a prayer on my behalf. Maybe God listens to you better than He does to me."

"Justin—"

This time it was Pete who gave her the warning

look, and Jessica surrendered with a helpless shrug.

Pete saw him to the door. "So you'll send the e-mail?"

"First thing tomorrow."

Pete clapped him on the shoulder and squeezed. "Thanks, brother."

"Don't mention it. I'll let you know what they say."

On the way out to his car, Justin's phone dinged in his pocket. He pulled it out with a frown and checked his notifications. Facebook.

A friend request from Melody Johansson.

Justin almost missed a step but recovered right before he pitched down his sister's icy walkway. He stared at the phone for a moment before he clicked Accept. What did he do now? Post on her timeline? Say hello?

No, she was the one who had sought him out. If she wanted any more contact with him, she could take the initiative. He shoved the phone back in his pocket like it burned his hand and strode to the car, where Melody and that little point of social media contact needled him the whole way home. Normally, he wouldn't hesitate: he'd message her, invite her to meet him for coffee or a drink. But he'd already decided she wasn't a casual date, and now he was actively looking to move away from Denver. It was a waste of time. For both of them.

Instead, when he got home, he went straight to his computer and began to compose an inquiry letter to the charter's broker. By this time tomorrow, they'd know whether the purchase was a possibility or if they'd have to go back to their long search. For Jessica's sake, he hoped it was exactly the deal they were looking for.

CHAPTER FIVE

Melody should have called in sick, but the restaurant work ethic was too deeply ingrained in her psyche. Besides, had she stayed home, all she'd have done was wonder why Grandma Bev hadn't let on that she was sick. They'd always been so close, even if they only saw each other every few months. Why wouldn't she have given Melody the chance to say good-bye?

With the help of Hugo, the other weekend baker, and Melody's furious determination to work instead of think, they plowed through their tasks ahead of schedule, giving her just enough time to grab two hours of sleep and get ready for the funeral. Her exhaustion was a blessing—her grogginess would let her move through the day wrapped in a fog, insulated from her grief.

It also made it much easier to deal with her mother. When Janna had said she would drop by to pick her up, Melody had assumed she'd rented a car upon her arrival in Denver like a normal person. Oh, she'd rented one all right, but the glossy black town car came with a driver. Janna couldn't arrive at her mother's funeral in a rented Ford Focus, apparently.

"You look awful," Janna commented when the driver opened the door for Melody to slide in.

She, of course, looked very elegant in a black suit and pillbox hat covered with, predictably, black tulle.

"I just worked an overnight shift and got two hours of sleep. Oh, and the woman who raised me just died. Of course I look awful."

Janna looked stung by the comment, but she let it pass. "I don't know why you stay on at that awful restaurant, considering the hours they make you work."

"The 'awful restaurant' was Rachel's place, a very good restaurant, and I haven't been there for over nine months. This is a bakery, and bakers always keep terrible hours. We discussed this."

"No, we didn't. But we would have if you ever answered my phone calls."

Melody heaved a sigh. They had this same conversation every time they were together. "That's because I turn off my ringer at work and while I'm sleeping, Mom. Call when I'm awake and I'll pick up."

Janna waved a hand. "I couldn't possibly keep track of all that."

"Between 2 and 8 p.m. It's not that hard." But in order to remember, Janna would have to actually listen in the first place. "It doesn't matter. I'm going to sleep on the way. Wake me up when we get there."

Melody leaned back against the black leather seat, turning her head toward the window. When she closed her eyes, though, the racing of her thoughts prevented any actual slumber. How ironic that even sitting here next to the woman who had given her life, her grandmother's death made her feel like an orphan.

Eventually, she must have fallen asleep, because she awoke to a firm hand shaking her arm. She straightened abruptly, disoriented, and untangled her tongue with difficulty. "Are we there?"

"Here." Janna thrust a small mirror at her, but her tone seemed almost sympathetic. "You might want to fix your makeup."

Melody took it and found her mascara had trailed down her cheek as if she'd been crying. She wiped her cheeks with a tissue and then dropped her hands. "I don't want to do this."

"Me neither, sugar." Janna put her arm around Melody and held her close for a moment, then seemed to be bracing herself for what came next. "But she deserves a proper good-bye."

It was a kind of truce in honor of a woman they both loved. Even so, Melody spent the service in a daze. She was relieved that there was no casket or viewing, just a beautiful glazed urn beside a wreath of flowers and a framed portrait from her grandmother's younger days. Most of the attendees were from Beverly's church and the hospital where she'd volunteered for the past several years.

It was only when they'd accepted the condolences of the attendees and were left in the empty sanctuary that Melody thought of what she should have asked earlier. "Who organized the service?"

Janna's mouth compressed into a thin line. "She did."

"What? How?"

A sigh eased from her mother's lips. "It was her lawyer who called me, not the hospital. He said she'd been very specific in what she wanted to happen. She'd prepaid her cremation and the church as soon as she knew she was ill. Even wrote out a list of people to invite." Janna shook her head. "Independent to a fault and determined to run things even from the afterlife."

Melody resisted the urge to say she seemed to have passed on a good deal of that to her daughter as well. "So what now?"

"I suspect we'll find out soon enough. We're due at the lawyer's office in less than two hours."

"On a Sunday?"

"Well, darlin', you know I'm performing at the Ryman tomorrow night. Surely you wouldn't expect me to cancel."

And like that, they were back to their old dynamic. No need for comfort herself, so why would she think Melody would need it either? Probably for the best. Janna had never been the nurturing sort.

They left the church and let the driver choose their restaurant for lunch since he claimed to be familiar with the area, landing them in a nice-enough café with overflowing plates and nothing to say to each other. Melody tried to make small talk a few times, but the conversation quickly petered out. Other than arguing over Melody's life choices, they had nothing to discuss.

Melody blessed the clock when it finally turned over to two o'clock, time to go to the attorney's office. He was located in a small business park in a three-story professional building, the directory showing a long list of doctors, financial advisers, and lawyers. Benjamin B. Harrison, Attorney at Law. They rode up the elevator in silence and emerged into a beige hallway on the second floor.

Janna took the lead inside the small office and marched straight to the receptionist. "Janna Leigh and Melody Johansson to see Mr. Harrison."

"Yes, Mrs. Johansson, I'll let him know you've arrived."

Janna's expression soured a little—she'd never taken Melody's father's last name despite their short marriage—but to her credit she didn't correct her. She instead sat primly in one of the leather chairs while Melody wandered around the room, looking at the mediocre modern art on the walls.

"Ms. Leigh? Ms. Johansson?"

Melody turned at the male voice and did a

double take. She'd expected the lawyer to be a distinguished older gentleman with graying hair, not a good-looking guy barely approaching forty, fit and dressed in a stylish, slim-cut suit. He crossed the room to shake their hands.

"I'm Ben Harrison. Would you like to step into my office? I'm sure you have a lot of questions for me."

"That's an understatement," Melody muttered, earning a nudge from Janna. She slipped into the farthest chair before the big mahogany desk and surreptitiously perused the room. Typical attorney's office—a wall full of bookcases containing law references, the usual boring art. She noted a photo of Harrison with a red-haired woman and a preteen girl. Nice family. Traditional. Like she even knew what that meant.

"I want to start by saying that I advised Beverly to talk to you as soon as she learned that she was seriously ill. But she was very adamant that this was the way she wanted to do things."

"That's my mother," Janna murmured. "Stubborn to the core."

Melody stared at the attorney. He sounded far more familiar with Beverly than mere legal counsel suggested. "How did you know my grandmother?"

Harrison looked a little sheepish. "She played poker with my grandmother. I've known her for a few years."

Melody couldn't help but smile. Not bridge or canasta, but poker. No doubt Grandma Bev could bluff a high roller in Vegas if she wanted to—no one ever seemed to guess at the sharp woman beneath the sweet granny exterior.

Harrison continued. "She asked that I act as the executor of her estate. She didn't want to be another point of contention between you two, nor did she want to be a burden. She said that she had her church family and friends around her, so she wasn't lonely, and she didn't want you to mourn her before her time. Hence making all her arrangements early. She insisted that we do this the same day as the memorial as well, so as not to drag out the process."

Melody felt a pang of guilt. Maybe her mother hadn't arranged it to suit her schedule after all.

Harrison took a file folder from a desk sorter and opened it. "Right. The documents are fairly involved, so if you'll allow me to summarize, it will be a bit easier. Janna, to you, your mother has left the contents of her home, as well as her car. She believes you might wish to keep her jewelry, art, and family albums. But she suggests you hire a firm to liquidate the rest. She didn't want you stuck in Colorado while you oversaw it."

Janna smothered her surprise. "Let me guess. She had a suggestion on who to use?"

Harrison smiled reluctantly. "She did. Melody,

to you she left in trust her liquid assets, her home, and her late husband's car. Because you're named as the sole beneficiary and successor trustee, those items are yours, today, without going through probate. I can help you navigate the trust details if you want. Janna, your items are outside the trust, but we'll just need to complete some notarized paperwork to avoid court."

It was all Greek to Melody, these legal terms she'd rarely heard, and her head spun from the implications. Her grandmother had left her all her money, her house, and her husband's car? It was almost too much to believe.

"She left letters for each of you explaining her choices." Harrison passed them each a sealed envelope, which Melody took with trembling fingers. "Now before we get to the paperwork, there's a few more things we should discuss. . . ."

After they signed the papers—Melody too dazed to know exactly what they were—they left the office, each with a folder of additional information in their hands. Melody barely registered her mother's stiff posture. She was still too busy processing what had just happened, the envelope like a beacon in her hand, impossible to ignore. Had Grandma Bev explained why she hadn't told Melody she was so sick? Apologized for not letting her say good-bye? She wasn't sure she was ready to find out, especially with her mother looking over her shoulder.

"I should have known," Janna muttered in the backseat of the sedan.

"Should have known what?" Melody knew better than to give her mother an open invitation like that. She was obviously in shock.

"Oh, don't pretend you're surprised. I shouldn't be. It's just that after all I've done for her—"

"Wait. All *you've* done for *her?*"

"You were too young. You have no idea . . ."

"I know that she quit her job as a professor to raise your daughter when you were too busy to do it yourself. I know she hated being on the road as much as I did, but she did it so you could have me and your career at the same time. And here you're begrudging the fact that she left me more than you? Have you not seen where I live?"

"Darlin', you know I would gladly pay—"

"I know you would. Just like I know your money always comes with strings. Or have you forgotten about my college tuition?"

Janna sniffed and turned away, a hurt expression on her face. "I don't know why I try. You've made up your mind that I was a horrible mother, and nothing I do will ever change that."

"No, Mom, you're wrong. You weren't a horrible mother. For that you would have had to be around in the first place."

Janna looked genuinely stricken then, but she shoved on her glasses and turned her head toward the window.

The usual flood of regret and guilt rushed in. "Mom, I'm sorry—"

"No, you're right. And you've done just fine without me. Assuming you don't get killed coming home to that ghetto apartment of yours."

And like that, the guilt evaporated. Melody sat back and stared out the opposite window, willing the car to go faster and deliver her from this uncomfortable reunion. There was too much water under the bridge, too many hurt feelings. Even when mourning the death of someone they both loved, they couldn't put their differences aside.

Maybe Beverly knew them best after all.

CHAPTER SIX

Melody almost regretted that Sunday was her night off, but when she crashed early and slept thirteen hours straight, it became clear that she'd needed the rest. The next morning, she groggily squinted at her phone, still tangled in her bedcoverings. She had a handful of missed calls and group texts from Rachel and Ana, timestamped the night before.

Are you okay? Call us if you want company.

Thinking of you. Let us know how you're doing.

And from Rachel: Brunch at my house tomorrow. No excuses.

Melody glanced at the time and saw it was just past eight. She typed a reply: I'm there. What time?

Immediately, Rachel came back, as if she had been waiting for the text. 10:30?

Done. Melody put her phone aside and pushed herself up in bed, testing her body, her emotions. She felt wrung out and hollow from the grief of the last few days, and tears lingered beneath the surface, waiting for the least provocation.

Melody shoved them back, pushing them down with a deep, shuddering breath. Her grandmother wouldn't want her to weep. She was in the arms of her Savior, after all. If Bev were here, she'd get that stern, half-chiding look on her face and say, "Melody Anne, you have so much to be grateful for. Do you think God wants you to focus on what you've lost or what He's given you?"

She'd lost her grandmother. But she still had friends who loved her, and now she had the means to make her own choices. She owed it to Grandma Bev to be appreciative.

Melody stumbled to the kitchen to start the coffee, bleary-eyed and aching in a way no force of will could completely assuage. She needed something to do before her restlessness made her stupid. Something to occupy her hands and mind. Something to honor Grandma Bev's memory and the way she'd blessed her only grandchild even through her death.

Which meant baking, of course. Preferably something complicated, even tedious. A dessert Grandma Bev loved.

Macarons.

Melody had long since perfected her recipe, which was no small feat considering the difficulties involved in making meringue at high altitude, but that had happened under the tutelage of a pastry chef, not in her grandmother's kitchen. Try as Bev might—and she'd loved them, so she'd tried often—she'd never managed to achieve the fine-textured, perfectly proportioned *pieds* and crisp-tender bodies that characterized the French sandwich cookie. The first time Melody had achieved a perfect result, she'd swiped some from the bakery and FedExed them to her grandma.

So chocolate macarons it would be. Melody methodically took out the ingredients—almond flour, cocoa, powdered sugar, granulated sugar, and eggs—and preheated her oven. Despite being a tiny electric range with a ridiculously small cavity, it heated evenly and consistently— perhaps the only reason she hadn't fussed over the fact that two of the burners no longer worked. Should she complain to the landlord for a replacement, she'd have to learn all the quirks of a new appliance.

She carefully separated the eggs one at a time into the bowl of her KitchenAid mixer, added the granulated sugar, and flipped it on, then sifted the almond flour and powdered sugar together into a bowl. By the time she got to the step of piping the batter, now chocolate colored and flavored, onto parchment, the fist in her stomach had begun to ease its grip. Baking might be an art, but it was predictable and scientific in a way life could never be.

While the macarons were baking, she put together the chocolate-hazelnut buttercream filling, a simple process that took her mere minutes and had her wandering her small kitchen in circles while she waited for the second batch of cookies to come out. Then there was the seemingly endless wait for them to cool on the baking sheets before she could peel them from the parchment.

When at last all the cookies had been paired up with a neat dollop of filling in the middle, she stacked them artfully on a creamware platter and started building her photo. This time, she chose a matelassé covering that she'd cut down from a damaged antique bedspread and stretched it over the table. One of her teapots and a pretty china cup later, and all that was left was to select a book.

It didn't take much thought. She moved into the bedroom and came back immediately with a slim English translation of Henrik Ibsen's *A Doll's House*. Grandma Bev had taught the play for years, but she'd always insisted that the *makarons* Nora nibbled must surely be the French variety and not the more likely Scandinavian coconut type—because who would waste so many calories on coconut? The recollection gave Melody a smile.

She nestled the book into the composition and then snapped several photos, the best of which she uploaded immediately. And then she paused, stumped for a caption. Tears clogged her throat while she typed and discarded various ideas.

Finally she just put, *In loving memory of Beverly Patricia Keene* and tapped Post before she could break down.

"Well," she said aloud, clearing her throat to rid it of a sudden lump. "I guess it's time to go."

She quickly packaged the macarons in a plastic container and put it in the fridge, where they'd age to perfection in a few days, and went to put on real clothes. By the time she'd pulled up in front of Rachel's house, she had herself mostly under control.

Her friend opened the door and immediately enfolded her in a hug. "Mel. How are you?"

Melody soaked up the comfort for a moment, then pulled back. "I'm okay. Really. I'm just a little stunned. So much has happened, I don't even know where to begin."

Ana appeared in the hallway, dressed for work in a tailored sheath dress and high heels, her glossy dark hair twisted up at the back of her head. Of the three of them, she was the only one who held an actual corporate job, but she worked such long hours in her new position that she routinely slipped out to meet them. She squeezed Melody into a tight hug. "The only reason I'm not mad at you for not letting us come over is because I'm betting you were asleep."

"I was. I needed it." Melody instantly felt better flanked by her two best friends. After nearly ten years of friendship with Ana and seven with Rachel, the women felt more like family than her actual blood relatives.

For one thing, they didn't breeze in and out of her life as it suited them.

"So how was spending the day with your mom?" Ana asked as they walked into the kitchen. Something smelled amazing already—a quick peek into the oven showed that Rachel had bacon cooking on a sheet pan.

"It was strained, as you might expect. The woman shows up at my door the day before the funeral, not even having had the decency to tell me what happened as soon as she found out? That's a low, even for her."

"I've never quite understood your mother," Rachel said. "But then again, I guess her career is pretty self-focused."

"That's putting it mildly." Melody seated herself at the table and accepted the mug of coffee Rachel put in front of her. "She had the gall to pull a guilt trip on me for not being more enthusiastic about seeing her."

Rachel sighed sympathetically and went back to chopping vegetables at her kitchen counter. Her relationship with her own mother was even less existent than Melody's, but maybe that was easier. It was hard to move on when someone popped into your life as they wished, disrupted everything, and then bailed when they actually had to account for their actions.

"That's not even the weirdest thing, though. My grandmother had planned her own service and cremation. She even dictated that we meet with her lawyer the same day as the funeral. I had no idea she'd been ill, but obviously she saw it coming. Why wouldn't she have told me?"

"Maybe she didn't want to upset your life like your mother does?" Ana suggested.

"Maybe. She left me a letter, but I haven't been able to bring myself to read it."

In the kitchen, Rachel poured eggs into one pan while simultaneously sautéing something in another. Even at home, she multitasked with ease, her movements quick and economical. Melody smiled. Definitely missing the restaurant.

A couple of minutes later, Rachel slid a plate in front of Melody. "French-style omelet with sautéed mushrooms for Madame." She glanced at Ana. "Veggie, right?"

"You know me so well." Ana smiled and turned back to Melody. "Do you want me to read it?"

Melody pulled the envelope from her pocket and smoothed it out. Then she slid it across the table. "You better or I'll never get to it. Wait for Rachel, though."

"Give me a minute. Ana, will you grab the orange juice from the fridge and put the butter on the table?"

Ana rose gracefully, smoothing down her dress, and did as Rachel asked. Somehow she could make carrying orange juice look elegant. There were times when Melody envied her poise.

Rachel and Melody lived in a different world completely, spoke a similar language, accepted the strange culture of the food service industry. Ana knew plenty about it, having done publicity for a number of restaurants, but she wasn't part of it. When Melody thought of regular hours and a decent paycheck, she wondered if Ana didn't have the right idea after all.

As if she were reading her mind, Rachel asked, "Did your mom give you the third degree about your career choices again?"

"Of course she did. She also referred to my neighborhood as the ghetto."

"That's a little harsh," Rachel scoffed. "Though I wouldn't exactly keep my doors unlocked at night."

"Well, I suppose there's a chance to change that, if I really wanted to."

Rachel looked questioningly at her as she delivered Ana's veggie omelet. "Oh?"

"It looks like I inherited my grandmother's house, her husband's car, and the whole of her liquid assets. Which was not a small sum."

"And you're just now telling us that?" Ana asked. "Talk about burying the lede."

"It feels ghoulish to be thinking about my inheritance. She just died on Wednesday and already I should be figuring out what to do with what she left me?"

"No, of course not," Rachel said. "But being

happy about that doesn't mean you didn't love her or you don't miss her. She knew how hard you work and how difficult things have been for you over the last few years."

"I know. I'm just not ready to deal with it all."

Melody fidgeted with her coffee cup until Rachel came back to the table with her own omelet, the bacon, and a plate of brioche toast.

After Rachel said a brief prayer, asking for God's blessing for the food and comfort for Melody, Ana looked between them. "Are you ready for me to read this?"

Melody set her fork down. "Go ahead."

Ana unfolded the letter and scanned it quickly before she began.

"Dear Melody,
"If you're reading this, then my fears were correct and I really didn't have much time left. I'm sorry I didn't tell you in advance. My heart condition came on so fast and progressed so quickly that I was still trying to decide my course of action. I didn't want you to worry and I certainly didn't want you to drop your life to come to me. Don't say that you wouldn't have, because I know you better than that. I raised you, remember? I know the lovely young woman you've become. I know

99

how you habitually put others before yourself and delay your own dreams for the future.

"If you expected mushiness from me for my last words, you seem to have forgotten all the tough love I've dished out over the years. So take this to heart: stop putting off your plans. Do you remember when you first told me that you no longer wanted to study literature and you wanted to bake? You said you'd rather fail at something you loved than succeed at the wrong thing. You've been waiting for your chance. That time is now.

"I've left you my house in Longmont, Grandpa Ralph's car, and my remaining investments. You may do whatever you wish with these things. Please don't look at them like time capsules or antiques that need to be kept to honor my memory. They were tools to live the life that I wanted, the life that I wanted to give you. Your mother is probably going to have strong opinions on the matter, but don't let her sway you. I've always known that God has a plan for you that doesn't look anything like hers or mine.

"Sell what you need to fund your dreams. If that's going back to Paris to further your education as a pastry chef, do it and have a crepe in my honor in Le Marais. If it's traveling the United States and working with the best bakers you can find, do that too. It will make me happy that I've been able to launch you into the next phase of your career and give you some independence. If there's one thing I've learned about artists from raising two of them, it's that the need to make money from your art is the quickest way to kill inspiration. So take chances knowing that your future is at least somewhat secure. Make things that feed your soul and not just your body, whether it's your fabulous custard or the perfect loaf of bread.

"Whatever you choose to do, give your plans to God and He will give you all you desire. Know that I support you and I'm more proud of you than I can say. I love you. Don't waste time grieving . . . I'm finally home where I belong. Honor my memory by making yourself an amazing life.

"Your loving grandma, Beverly."

Ana lowered the letter, looking just as shaken as Melody felt. "Are you okay?"

Only then did Melody realize silent tears were streaming down her face. "I'd forgotten that conversation. My mother was furious that I had spent four years and a lot of money on my literature degree, only to decide I wanted to make bread and cakes for a living. She couldn't understand that I loved creating things far more than I liked analyzing them."

"So what are you going to do?" Rachel asked softly.

"I can't sell the house." She knew the truth as soon as the words left her lips. "Regardless of what she says, it was the closest thing to a real home I had. But I don't want to live in Longmont either."

"Maybe you can rent it," Ana suggested. "Let some family begin their life together there. It would be enough to pay your rent on a nicer place in the city, I'd think."

"I think Grandma Bev would like that," Melody said. "I don't need or want the car. It's a classic, but she wasn't ever really attached to it. I don't feel bad about selling that."

"Then maybe you can find someone to appraise it and help you unload it."

Melody nodded slowly. It was still hard to think about disposing of her grandmother's possessions, but she felt better having the decision made. Renting the house felt right; maybe it was delaying the inevitable, but at least she could keep it in the family while still benefiting from her inheritance as her grandmother wished her to. The car was just a task to be done. But the money . . .

When she said as much, Ana said quietly, "You don't have to decide right this second. If you'd like help deciding how to invest it, I can recommend someone."

"I know what I want to do with it. I've been thinking about this for years." Melody's stomach tightened. Dreaming about it in the abstract was one thing; taking steps to make it a reality was something else altogether. "I want to open my own place."

Rachel smiled. "I thought you might."

"There's only one problem. Even with the inheritance, I don't have enough money to do it myself. I think I'd need a partner."

Rachel's expression turned serious. "Are you sure you want a partner? You know how well that worked out for me. There's a reason I'm still sitting on the idea."

"Because you're waiting for the *right* partner. Say, a best friend?"

Rachel looked genuinely startled.

Melody reached across the table and grabbed Rachel's hand, the first tendrils of enthusiasm beginning to push through the layer of grief. "Think of it. The two of us, in business together. You've been looking for a restaurant that would allow you to express your point of view as a chef without taking over your entire life. I've been wanting to create my own pastries and bake traditional breads like I used to. We already know we work well together. Why shouldn't we pool our resources and do something together?"

The corners of Rachel's mouth lifted. "A bakery-café. Open early, closed by six . . . enough for the morning coffee stop, the lunch rush, and the commuters picking up dinner on the way home."

"A bakery section for retail sales. Your amazing food, not just the normal diner fare. High-end. Like you used to serve at Paisley, just a little . . ."

"More casual and accessible. A community gathering place." From Rachel's face, she looked like she was catching the excitement. "Of course, there would be a lot of things to be decided before we even started looking at locations. Ownership, decision-making. I don't want this to harm our friendship. You know I'm used to being in charge."

"Easy," Ana said. "Rachel handles the kitchen; Melody decides all the baked goods and desserts; you guys use me for marketing, publicity advice, and general referee skills. I have five younger siblings. I've had lots of practice."

Melody looked between her two friends, for the first time in the last two days feeling something other than the crushing weight of grief. "This isn't just talk. We could really do this."

"We could," Rachel said softly. "I wish it didn't take something like this to make it happen, but think how proud and happy Grandma Bev will be looking down on you."

Melody gripped Rachel's hand, then grabbed Ana's with her other one. Her heart squeezed with both anticipation and sadness. "How do we get started?"

"Way ahead of you." Ana held up her notebook. A list of bullet points already filled the page. "You didn't think I'd be left out of all the excitement, did you? Of course, there's lots to be done before we even get to this. I would get the house and the car rolling first, just so you don't have to deal with it at the same time you're signing commercial leases and hiring contractors."

"Alex could help you out with the house," Rachel said. "He knows quite a bit about real estate because of his own investments. Let's all have dinner one night and talk it through. That just leaves the car."

An idea surfaced, a memory Melody had forgotten in everything that had happened over the last few days: a classic Mustang half-buried in snow. "I can take care of that one myself, I think. I know just who to ask."

She opened the Facebook app on her phone and saw that, indeed, Justin Keller had accepted her friend request, but he hadn't posted anything to her timeline. Before she could think better of the idea, she tapped out a private message.

You said you owed me one. Did you mean it?

CHAPTER SEVEN

Melody pulled up in front of Justin's building and sat in her Jeep for a full five minutes, second-guessing her decision. It had seemed so logical when she was talking it over with her friends yesterday. She'd done him a favor; he was willing to do her a favor in return. Simple quid pro quo.

The only problem was, she was having trouble convincing her mind of the fact. Once the stupor of grief had begun to lift in the excitement of new plans, she remembered the sharp, instant spike of attraction to Justin. And that wasn't a good thing, considering her track record with men.

But she was here now, and it was too late to change her mind. She hopped out of the Jeep and crunched her way through the snow that still piled his street to the clear sidewalk. As was typical in Colorado in the spring, the storm had blown through and the sun had immediately come out, now pounding down with an intensity that made it feel much warmer than the thermometer's thirty-four degrees. Already, snow was dripping from trees and melting off roofs, causing a steady drum of water in the rain gutters.

Melody marched up to the front door of the apartment building and tried the door. Locked. She turned to the intercom panel, expecting to see names in the slots beside the buttons, but instead they only showed apartment numbers. She pulled out her phone to see if he'd told her which apartment he was in when he suggested she come over today to chat. He hadn't.

Just as she was about to message him, a young woman appeared on the other side of the door and pushed through. Melody grabbed the handle so it wouldn't close behind the woman, startling her. She looked barely twenty-four, but she was pretty, the type of girl a guy might chat up at the mailboxes or help carry in groceries.

"Hey, you wouldn't know where Justin Keller lives, would you?"

The girl looked at her blankly. Melody prompted, "Good-looking, light-brown hair, blue eyes, yea tall? Pilot?"

Understanding lit her face now. "Ahh, that's his name? He lives on my floor but he's always in a hurry." She gave Melody a crooked smile. "Nice going."

"Um, thanks. Do you know his apartment number?"

"Yeah, he's in 202." She looked her up and down. "Good luck."

Melody slipped inside the building. There was a small elevator, but it looked about the same age as the building, so she bypassed it in favor of the door marked Stairs. When she emerged from the stairwell into the second floor hallway, her heart was pounding for reasons other than exertion. Maybe she should have told him why she was coming rather than just saying it was easier to explain in person.

But then she wouldn't have been able to see him again.

Stop being stupid, she told herself sternly. She found apartment 202, not too difficult considering there were only six on this floor, and knocked sharply.

No answer.

She raised her hand to knock again when the door swung open under her hand. She blinked dumbly. "Hey."

"Hey yourself." Justin stood in the doorway, just as handsome as she remembered, only more casual in a pair of loose-fitting jeans, a faded gray T-shirt, and bare feet. Apparently she'd been right about what lay beneath that uniform. Definitely a gym body. Or good genes. *Really* good genes.

She gulped down an awkward rush of attraction and dragged her eyes upward before her perusal could get embarrassing. It didn't help. His hair was far more messy than it had been the other night, like he'd just rolled out of bed at 10 a.m., and it was clear he hadn't shaved since she last saw him. The scruff made him even more appealing.

Melody regained the power of speech and forced words from her suddenly dry mouth.

"I know I'm a little late. Is it still a good time?"

His mouth widened into a smile. "Of course. Come in. Unless you'd like to talk in the hallway . . ."

Melody let out a breathless laugh, realizing that she was clutching her handbag nervously. "Sure, thanks."

She stepped inside, finally getting her jitters under control. The apartment was old, but it seemed freshly painted, with a small living area and a kitchen sporting outdated appliances and oak cabinets. The furniture was a step up from black-leather bachelor stuff, at least, and he had a normal-size television, not one of the seventy-inch behemoths single guys seemed required to own.

"Have a seat." He gestured to the sofa, a nice gray tweed. "Can I get you something to drink? Water? Coffee? I'd offer you a beer, but it's not even eleven o'clock and you don't really strike me as the beer-drinking type."

"Not usually," she said. "Coffee would be great, if you don't mind. Cream, two sugars."

"Coming right up." He walked back to the kitchen, unperturbed, clearly comfortable with the fact she'd shown up at his apartment on a Tuesday morning with some mysterious request.

She took the time to study the rest of the place. Simple mass-produced furniture, but with a decent amount of style—a mix of streamlined midcentury he'd probably picked up from CB2, a couple of throw pillows. But the overwhelming impression was that the place was almost obsessively neat. No newspapers spread on the coffee table or remote controls plopped on the couch. Not even a single water glass. For goodness' sake, there were still vacuum lines on the rug. When he came back with her coffee, he placed a coaster beneath it.

Who was this guy?

He took a seat in the armchair situated perpendicular to the sofa, a safe distance away, and turned those startling blue eyes on her. "So how can I help? As you reminded me, I do owe you one."

Melody fished an envelope from her purse. "My grandmother died last week."

Instantly, his expression shifted to one of sympathy. "I'm sorry. Were you close?"

Melody nodded, but thankfully the tears stayed behind her eyes. "Very. She practically raised me. She didn't tell anyone she was sick, so it was a shock to us all. Anyway, she left me most of her stuff, including her car. And she left me a letter telling me to sell whatever I didn't want, so since she never really liked the car anyway . . ."

Now Justin looked curious. He reached forward to take the envelope that Melody held out and slid a couple of photos from inside. He let out a low whistle. "AMC Hornet. I haven't seen one of these in years. It's not a very grandmotherly car, is it?"

"It was her second husband's car," she said, "but she hated the thing. Said it was uncomfortable and noisy and hot. It doesn't have air-conditioning. I guess he was kind of into racing, which she thought was ridiculous, and yet she held on to it for more than thirty years after he passed. I have no idea what to do with it. Is it worth anything?"

"Depends on the condition and the model. They made regular Hornets and a lot of them for quite a few years, which drives the price down. If it's got the bigger engine, it might be worth more. Between ten and twelve thousand dollars, I'd guess." He put down the photos. "Then of course it all depends on how long you want to hold on to it looking for the right buyer. This isn't something I'd put up on Craigslist, especially if it's completely intact."

"I don't have any sentimental attachment to it. I don't even know if it's running."

"If it doesn't have a lot of rust, it will be more valuable since there aren't sheet metal reproductions available for most AMCs. But I couldn't tell you without seeing it."

"I'd love to show you, but it's in Longmont right now."

"I don't mind the drive."

Melody blinked at him. "Now?"

"Why not? I'm off this week. I'm assuming neither of us has anything better to do. If you drive, I'll even spring for lunch."

Melody studied him. He looked completely sincere, truly interested in the car, which was pretty much the opposite of what she'd expected. Maybe she'd thought he'd flirt, tease her, do that annoyingly effective smoldering thing again. But right now, he was throwing it out there as a way to kill time.

Well, what did you expect? That he'd answer the door and sweep you into his arms and say he'd thought about you every moment since you parted? Don't be an idiot. You don't want that anyway. You don't even know the guy.

She sipped her coffee while she considered. "Okay. I just have to be back by six or so. I've got things to do before I head into work." Those things being dinner with Rachel and Alex to talk about her grandmother's house. Maybe since she would be up there today, she could take a few photos.

"Okay. Let me get my shoes and we'll go. Do you like Mexican food? I know a great restaurant in Boulder." He wandered back into what she assumed was his bedroom without waiting for an answer.

Melody stared after him in confusion. He acted like she was an old friend, not just someone he randomly ran into when he got stuck in the snow.

112

And this drive to Longmont felt like much more of a favor than the one she'd done him initially.

Justin emerged from his bedroom a minute later wearing a pair of snow boots, a shearling-lined leather jacket, and a knit beanie not unlike her own. "I'm ready if you are."

Just crank the ruggedly handsome dial up another two notches, why don't you? Melody smiled and stood. "Let's go."

So maybe he'd been a bit overenthusiastic in his offer of help. Melody had seemed surprised by the fact he was willing to drive to Longmont to look at the car. No more surprised than Justin himself when the words floated out of his mouth.

He'd pretty much convinced himself that he'd never see her again and that it was for the best. Especially since the business broker had responded with the information he requested. They were currently sending messages back and forth, trying to find a convenient date for Justin and Pete to fly to Florida to check it out. Even when Melody had messaged him with a mysterious request for help, he'd been sure he'd be able to keep it strictly friendly.

And then she had shown up looking equal parts gorgeous and vulnerable, and all his best intentions had gone out the window.

He followed her down to her Jeep and climbed into the passenger side. Melody waited until he was buckled in and then pulled away from the curb. "So how'd you get into classic cars?"

Excellent. A safe topic of conversation. "I don't know. I guess I was a typical little boy, fascinated with planes, trains, and cars. After my dad and I built the plane, cars seemed pretty straightforward."

"Right, the plane. No big deal. Everyone builds planes on the weekend, don't they?"

Justin chuckled. "When you're both pilots and live and breathe aviation, I suppose you do. If you want, I'll show it to you sometime."

Melody threw him a sidelong glance, as if judging the intent behind the offer. "Maybe. We'll see."

"Anyway, my dad—who is about to retire from United after thirty-five years, incidentally—had this old Plymouth Barracuda that we fixed up. I learned to do everything but major transmission work. After that, we restored a 1974 Dodge Challenger. And then we got busy with work. Five years ago, I picked up the Mustang in rough shape, and I've been tinkering with it ever since."

"So nothing on this Hornet should be a big surprise to you?"

"I'm not that familiar with AMCs, but I should be able to tell you what kind of shape it's in, yes."

"I really appreciate it. I know it's weird asking you for help when we barely know each other."

I'm glad you did. Nope. *I was hoping for a reason to see you.* Definitely not. "It's really no trouble. I'm happy to help." There. That was friendly and noncommittal.

She glanced his direction again. "So what else do you do, besides help people you don't know?"

"If you'll recall, you're the one who did that. And really, I'm pretty boring. When I'm not working, I'm being as lazy as possible. Sleep late, work out, play a little soccer in the park when the weather is good. Like I said, boring." He studied her profile. "What about you? What do you do when you're not baking or rescuing strangers from certain death?"

Melody laughed, a throaty sound that did strange and not altogether welcome things to his insides. "I don't think you would have died out there. But to answer your question, I'm pretty boring too. I go to flea markets, restore antique furniture sometimes. My friend Rachel hosts this thing called the Saturday Night Supper Club at her house. So I do the baking for that."

"That's hardly boring. How does one get an invitation to such a thing?"

"Why? Do you want to come?"

He grinned at her. "I thought you'd never ask."

"That was pretty smooth. We'll see. It's very exclusive. You have to earn a spot on the guest list."

"Seems I'm going to have to work extra hard to make myself indispensable, then."

A flicker of a smile crossed her face, but she kept her eyes fixed on the road. He'd take it as a positive sign that she didn't immediately attempt to make this into a one-time thing.

No. Wrong line of thinking. This had to be a one-time thing.

"So. Tell me about this flea market obsession of yours."

"Obsession? Who said it was an obsession?"

"Just a guess. Tell me I'm wrong."

This time, he caught a glimpse of a barely there dimple. "You're not wrong exactly. I would call it an enthusiastic hobby, not an obsession."

"What kind of things do you buy?"

"Anything that catches my fancy. You'd have to see my apartment to really understand. All this beautiful furniture, either cast off on the curb or sold for a fraction of what it's worth. All they really need is some TLC. I saved an old Queen Anne side table, for example, that was damaged and stained almost beyond repair, filled in the gouges, and covered it in chalk paint. It's now my entryway table. A Chippendale sofa, which I refinished and reupholstered with vintage fabric I found on eBay. That sort of thing. And then of course, there's my book collection."

"You collect books? I didn't expect you to say that. What kind?"

"Classics, mostly, 1800s to mid–twentieth century. And I look for various editions of my favorites."

"Do you read them all?"

Melody laughed. "Of course I do. I also photograph them." She pulled out her phone and tapped an icon before handing it over.

It was an Instagram profile called Books in the Bakery, populated by a collection of pastry-and-book photos. He was no judge of photography, but they did give him a sudden craving for a huckleberry muffin, if not the urge to reread *Huckleberry Finn*.

"This is pretty impressive, Melody."

"I don't know about that, but it's fun." She held out an open palm and he placed the phone in it. "Keeps me from giving in to the mind-numbing boredom at work."

He hadn't understood what she'd meant when she said her work wasn't really baking, but after seeing photos of her elaborate, varied pastries, it seemed obvious her talent was wasted in her current situation.

They drove in comfortable silence until Melody turned off Highway 36 onto Highway 287 toward Longmont.

"So this is where you grew up?" he asked.

Her knuckles whitened on the steering wheel. "Kind of. When we were in Colorado."

Something in her tone warned him to tread

carefully. "You moved around a lot? Like the military?"

"No. Definitely not like the military." Her laugh sounded brittle, and the openness she had shown earlier shut like the slam of a prison door. He would take the warning to back off, even if it made him even more curious than before.

They were proceeding into Old Town Longmont now, a charming historical district filled with late-1800s buildings and period houses. Like any other city, the outskirts had suffered from sprawl and not a little bit of blight reflecting its poorer-neighbor status to nearby Boulder, but this part of the city was intact. The kind of place that families moved into with dreams of riding bikes down tree-lined streets and walking the dog to get a Saturday morning cup of coffee. The image of suburbia made even his relatively friendly neighborhood seem downright urban.

Near the city center, Melody pulled up to the curb in front of an older house. It was modest, with a sunroom addition on one side of the walkway and a detached garage on the other. She put the car in park, switched off the ignition, and sat, staring at the front for a long moment. "Okay then. Let's take a look."

She seemed to be bracing herself as she grabbed her handbag—some woven thing that looked like a rug—and hopped out of the Jeep. He trailed behind her on the walkway as she fished keys out of the purse and unlocked the front door. When he finally caught up, she was standing in the middle of the living room, her arms hanging by her sides.

"Melody?" he asked softly.

She turned and he saw the tear streaks on her cheeks. She swept them away quickly. "I didn't expect this to be so hard."

He resisted putting his arm around her, instead rubbing her shoulder in what he hoped was a comforting way. "Of course it's difficult. We don't have to do this right now."

"Yeah, we do." She wandered around the living room, trailing a finger over the furniture. Some of it was antique, but most of it was typical disposable 1980s stuff that had seen better days. She stopped at an end table and lifted a silver-framed photograph. Even at a distance, he could see it was an older woman and a little girl. Melody and her grandmother.

She slipped the frame into her purse and then threw a wry look over her shoulder. "Don't tell anyone."

"Tell who? This is yours anyway, isn't it?"

"The house is. The stuff inside belongs to my mother. She won't come back to look at it before she sells it off."

"Surely she won't mind you taking photographs."

That look again. "You don't know my mother."

Justin moved up beside her and peered at the frames still left on the table. There was a photo of three women: one he presumed was Melody's grandmother, one who was definitely Melody, and one who surely must be the mom in question. Why wouldn't Melody have taken that one too?

He lifted another photo, which was of the middle-aged woman alone, wearing a stunning evening dress. Squinting, he racked his memory for where he'd seen her before. "This is your mom? I swear I know her."

She said nothing, simply took the photo from his hand and replaced it on the table. "She's a country music singer."

"That's why your grandmother raised you then? Because your mom was so busy with her recording career?"

"And touring. And publicity." Melody's shoulders sagged in resignation as she turned to face him fully. "We lived on the road when she was on tour, and Grandma Bev and I came back here when we weren't. Mom, of course, had her house in Nashville and just came out here to visit me."

An odd arrangement to be sure, especially with a little girl, but at least her mom had attempted to see her. He said as much and got a bitter laugh in return.

"You would think so, wouldn't you? I'm not convinced it wasn't all a publicity stunt. You

120

know, being a devoted single mother. Oh and look, she brought her daughter up on stage tonight in front of twenty thousand people to sing a duet."

Melody shook her head as if she could shake away her memories. "Anyway. That doesn't matter now. I'll find the car keys."

Justin grasped Melody's wrist before she could move away. "It's okay to be angry, you know. That your grandmother left you. It sounds like she was the one sure thing in your life."

"Yeah," she said softly. "She was."

"It might help to talk about her. They say that's the best thing after a loss."

"Who is *they?*" Already, Melody was pulling herself together. The woman was tough.

"*They.* You know, the people that go around studying these things so *they* can write articles about it."

Melody cracked a smile, but she didn't seem to be inclined to take his advice. "Come with me. The keys are probably in the kitchen."

CHAPTER EIGHT

Melody escaped the living room and Justin's empathy before she could break down completely. She'd known it was going to be difficult to come back to this place, this house that had been her refuge for as long as she could remember. She just hadn't expected to be slammed with memories, good and bad, the minute she walked through the door.

She slipped through the old-fashioned swinging door to the kitchen and proceeded straight to the junk drawer. It only took a minute to find the keys to the car, attached to a green plastic dinosaur keychain. Her grandmother's idea of a joke, probably, considering she called the car Godzilla.

"Follow me." She nodded to Justin, who lingered in the kitchen doorway, then unlocked the back door and cut across the yard to the garage. The leaves didn't look to have been raked the previous fall; she'd have to get someone out to do that before she put the house up for rent. She unlocked the garage with her keys and stepped aside for Justin.

It was a single bay, its edges packed with tools and boxes, the main floor space taken up by a chamois-covered vehicle. "May I?" Justin asked.

"Sure. Let me open the garage so you have

some light." She pushed a cracked button and the heavy slab swept upward, flooding the space with sunshine. Justin grabbed the edge of the cover and gently pulled it back to reveal a metallic green compact car.

Justin rubbed ancient dirt from the fender and whistled. "Original paint job, and in good condition. Nice."

Melody tossed him the keys. "Be my guest. I don't even know where to begin."

She pulled out an old shop stool and dusted it off with a nearby rag, then plopped herself down while she watched him. He circled the car, taking note of every detail, occasionally leaning down to rub at some perceived flaw in the paint. Then he unlocked the driver's door, popped the hood, and bent over the compartment.

"What does it look like in there?" she called.

"Like an engine." He poked his head around the hood. "Come look."

She hopped off the stool and circled around to the front of the car. He had his hands braced on the front edge of the engine compartment. "It's clean."

"Yeah, he obviously took care of it, if it looks like this now. How long has it been sitting?"

Melody shrugged. "Twenty, thirty years? She never drove it. She might have taken it out a few times to clean the garage in the time I lived here."

Justin nodded and pointed to a couple of

black hoses. Even she could see the rubber had deteriorated. "The hoses and belts are in bad shape. Those will all need to be replaced. But I'm wondering . . ." He frowned and then returned to the driver's side, where he bent down and peered at something on the inside edge of the door.

"What are you doing?"

"Following a hunch." He pulled out his cell phone and started typing something in. His eyebrows lifted. "Let me check one more thing." He got down on his hands and knees and slid under the car until only his feet were sticking out beneath the front. She cringed to think of him on the filthy ground beneath the vehicle.

He scooted out with a smile on his face. "You're going to like this, Melody. There were a couple of different models of this car made. One of them was high-performance, the SC/360. The pinstriping and the hood scoop came standard on that one, but they were also options on lower models, so that doesn't necessarily tell us anything. However, I just looked up the details on an enthusiast forum, double-checked the casting number on the engine and the model number on the door tag, and it looks like you've got an SC/360 with an original V8 and four-barrel carb."

Melody blinked at him. "What does any of that mean?"

"It means that this car is extremely valuable to

the right collector. There are probably only about a hundred of these left, and most of them won't be in nearly this condition without restoration. Original is worth money."

"How much money?"

"Keep in mind you'll need to put a little cash into it first. I'd need to get it started to know how much, and the carburetor's probably gunked up with varnish. It's going to need to be taken apart and cleaned before it will start."

"Assuming we do all that . . ."

Justin held up his phone. "According to what I've found so far, maybe twenty grand."

"You're kidding me. For this old thing?"

"There's a strong secondary market for American pony cars, and AMC collectors tend to be pretty obsessive. This is far rarer than my Mustang, I'll tell you that."

A smile lifted her lips. Twenty thousand dollars. Her grandmother had left her enough money to put in an even amount of capital as Rachel, split the business fifty-fifty, but this would ensure that she could afford to eat and pay rent while they were waiting to turn a profit.

But there was a catch. "How hard will it be to find someone to fix this up? And how much would it cost?"

"Well, assuming I did it myself, a few hundred for the parts. Plus new tires. Less than a thousand total, I'd think."

She caught her breath. "Justin, I can't ask you—"

"You didn't. I just volunteered." He grabbed a rag from a nearby shelf and wiped his hands. "It'll be fun. The Mustang's pretty much done, so I've been thinking I could use a new project anyway. Unless of course you don't want me to. I won't be insulted if you don't want to trust something this valuable to a stranger."

Melody bit her lip and felt tears prick her eyes. She usually wasn't a crier, but her emotions floated dangerously close to the surface right now. "No, I would be grateful if you would. Thank you. You have no idea what this means to me."

Justin's face broke into a smile, as if he'd been hoping she'd agree. "We'll have to get the car down to Denver, of course. It'll go to my dad's, where I keep all my tools. Pretty sure he's not going to be able to resist helping."

"I'll arrange for the tow, whatever you need. This is amazing, Justin. Thank you."

He was looking at her seriously now, gave her a little nod. "You're welcome." Then he cleared his throat. "Should we lock up and go grab lunch? I'm starving."

"Yeah, let's do that." Melody closed the garage door while Justin put down the hood and slipped the cover onto the car. Then they walked together back into the house. Melody pocketed the car keys and pulled out her cell phone.

"I need to take some pictures first. I haven't decided what to do with the house." She started with the kitchen, snapping photos from every angle. As she lowered her phone, her eyes lit on her grandmother's KitchenAid mixer on the counter, its white enamel nicked from years of use but the stainless-steel bowl gleaming as bright as ever. Impulsively, she hefted it off the counter and handed it to Justin.

"Let me guess," he said. "I never saw this."

"I'll claim a small-appliance burglar got to it." There was no way she was letting her mom liquidate the mixer that represented the time she'd spent with Grandma Bev. The mixer in which Melody had made her first dough, the one that had cranked out batches of Christmas cookies in February after they'd missed cookie season because they'd been on tour.

The soft look in his eye said he understood, and she avoided that expression as she sped through the photos in the rest of the house.

"I know it might sound silly to want to keep this old place," Melody said when they were settled back in her Jeep. "I mean, I definitely don't want to live here. But—"

"It has a lot of sentimental value."

Melody pulled out on the street, following the directions on Justin's GPS app. "It's more than that. See, I only went to real school in second and third grade. The rest of the time, my grandmother homeschooled me. It was easier, more flexible, and we could travel with my mom. But there were times that we lived here for a few months at a time, and it felt . . . normal." She threw him a self-deprecating smile. "Nowadays, I'd take *normal* as an insult, but back then it was my highest goal."

"Every kid wants to fit in. It's only when you get older that you realize it's boring."

His understanding lifted her heaviness. "It is. Maybe that's why I never seem to keep a job for more than a couple of months. I get restless. Once upon a time, I thought I was going to be a literature professor like my grandmother. I went to Saint Mary's College outside San Francisco— my mom's choice, to be honest—but even with her picking up the tab for tuition, the Bay Area is an expensive place to live. I needed a job, so I got a position as bakery assistant at Noelle Patisserie." She paused, waiting for his reaction. When he just stared at her blankly, she said, "It's arguably one of the best bakeries in the country, even if back then it was still making a name for itself."

"Ah." She could tell it still meant nothing to him.

"Anyway, by the time I got through my undergrad degree, I realized that critiquing literature was destroying my love for it, and I was just getting through the day so I could go work at the bakery. I'd intended to go straight into a master's/PhD program, but instead, I shredded my acceptance letters and went to work full-time at Noelle."

"I'm sure that went over well."

"My mom was furious, of course, especially considering Saint Mary's costs upward of forty grand a year."

Justin's mouth dropped open.

"I know. I graduated ten years ago, and I just recently paid her back the last dime."

Had the memory not still been so painful, Melody would have enjoyed the horrified look on Justin's face. "She actually made you pay her back?"

"Oh no, nothing so obvious. She just liked to throw it in my face as one of the ways I'd disappointed her. So I said I would repay it and she 'generously' agreed not to charge me interest."

Justin's mouth pursed into a low whistle. "I'm sorry, Melody. That's . . ."

"That's my mother." She cleared her throat. "I really can't blame her for being angry. Had I realized my passion for baking earlier, I could have saved all of us a lot of time and money."

Justin's brow furrowed. "You said you graduated ten years ago. You're what? Twenty-eight? Twenty-nine?"

"Thirty."

He seemed to be doing calculations in his head. "But that would make you sixteen when you started college."

Melody shrugged. "Homeschooled, remember?"

"Yeah, but you were a kid. At sixteen no one knows what they want to do for a living."

"You did."

"That's different. I was raised by a pilot and I've always been excellent at math, but I'm not brilliant like you. What else was I going to do?"

A flush heated her cheeks. "I'm not brilliant."

"You started college at sixteen."

"You flew a plane at sixteen. I just read books."

Justin paused. "Okay, you're right. We're both brilliant."

His matter-of-fact tone caught her off guard. She started laughing and continued laughing hard enough that she missed the turn to the restaurant and had to follow the GPS's rather testy-sounding instructions to return her to the parking lot.

She switched off the ignition. "Well, while we're showing off, I might as well tell you that my restaurant experience has given me the ability to order *five whole things* in Spanish."

"I'm very impressed. I can basically order a *cerveza* and salsa."

"Don't worry; I've got your back as long as you like tamales, tacos, or enchiladas."

"You said five."

"That included the salsa and beer."

He laughed too, and as they went inside, the melancholy she'd felt at her grandmother's house ebbed away. As it turned out, neither of them had the opportunity to use their Spanish even if they'd wanted to, because the server was a pale Irish-looking girl even blonder than Melody. The food, however, was some of the most authentic she'd ever had. They gorged themselves on nopales and sopapillas and enough hot salsa to turn their tongues numb.

Melody pushed away her decimated plate and fixed her attention on Justin. "So I'm curious. How does this pilot thing work that you get entire weeks off at a time?"

"Jealous, are we?" Humor sparkled in his eyes, and she couldn't help but smile in return.

"Maybe a little. But mostly I'm curious."

He folded his napkin and tossed it on the table. "The FAA has all sorts of rules on how many consecutive duty hours we can perform and how many flights we're allowed a year. Different companies offer different schedules. I'm on an eighteen-day fixed. I know which eighteen days a month I'm on duty, but I don't get my actual schedule until the night before."

"So you have no idea where you're going to be at any given time?"

"Nope. And it could be one long flight or a bunch of short ones depending on scheduling.

But that's what makes it fun. Last tour, I flew into nineteen different cities, ten of which I haven't been to this year. I went to the top of the arch in St. Louis for kicks. Lost twenty bucks on a riverboat casino in New Orleans just to say I did it. Of course, there were also overnights in Omaha, Nebraska, and Riverside, California. They can't all be glamorous."

"I admit, I am jealous," Melody said. "I love to travel, but it's been a long time since I've even been out of Denver city limits."

His expression turned serious, legitimately curious. "Why don't you?"

"Money, for one thing. My schedule, for another. I work every night but Sunday. Until someone invents a Star Trek transporter thingy that can zap me to Europe and back in a single day, I think I'm out of luck."

"Is that where you'd go? Europe?"

"I went with my mom on a world tour when I was nine. Four continents in sixty days. My favorite, of course, was Paris. I got back there as soon as I could. Lived there for almost a year, in fact, staging at some excellent patisseries. Would have stayed longer if I could have." She didn't say that the reason she'd made a hasty departure back to the US had blue eyes almost as brilliant as Justin's and a sexy French accent. To be fair, Luc hadn't promised her anything; she'd read into that herself thanks to his natural Gallic romanticism and her shaky grasp on the French language.

"Hey, where'd you go?"

Melody snapped back to the present, somehow having fallen into that memory like it was yesterday. "Sorry. Just reminiscing."

He cocked his head to study her, an indication her casual tone hadn't been completely successful. "Good memories or bad ones?"

"Depends on the day." She tossed her own napkin on the table and began to scoot out of the booth. "Shall we go? I've got to work tonight, and traffic is bound to be awful."

Justin didn't seem perturbed by her slip of attention, just settled comfortably into the passenger seat of her Jeep like he belonged there. She stole a quick look at him as she backed out of the parking lot. If she were being honest, her initial interest in him had been almost wholly physical. She made no apologies for enjoying that pull of attraction even when it threw up warning flags. But today had proven that she actually liked him. He was funny, intelligent, perceptive. Surprisingly humble, which was not a trait she'd have associated with a guy who was practically the template for a romance novel hero.

"What?" His head turned in her direction, and she flushed, realizing she'd been staring. A dumb idea, especially considering she was supposed to be watching the road.

"Nothing." She searched for something to fill the suddenly awkward space between them. "You said your dad is a pilot. What about the rest of your family? Do you have siblings?"

It was the right thing to ask, apparently. She learned that his parents had divorced relatively amicably. He had an older sister, who was married to his good friend, and a niece and nephew. Once he got on the subject of Abby and Andrew, it was pretty clear he adored them.

As if the guy wasn't appealing enough before, he liked kids. How was he still single? Not that she could ask that question without seeming like a crazy woman on the hunt for a husband. And she wasn't crazy. Not really.

Forty-five minutes of stop-and-go traffic later, Melody pulled up in front of Justin's apartment complex and shifted to neutral, letting the engine idle. "Thank you, Justin. That was fun, and it could have been really hard."

"It's my pleasure." He smiled and reached for the door handle. "Let me know when you can have the car towed over and I'll text you the address. I leave on my next tour Monday."

"I'll do that." Melody smiled back, but disappointment sparked in her faster than she could quash it. What was she expecting anyway, a good-night kiss? It had been a surprisingly enjoyable day, but never had he given her any indication he thought of it as more than a favor.

Maybe the attraction was one-sided. Considering how many women he must have fawning over him, a literature-loving baker probably wasn't high on his list.

And then he turned back, bracing a forearm against the Jeep's doorframe. "Would you like to go out to dinner with me sometime this week?"

Her thoughts had spooled out so far along the "never gonna happen" lines that it took a second to reel them back in. "Uh, sure. But my only night off is Sunday."

"Sunday works for me. Should I pick you up at your place?"

She nodded, transfixed by his direct aquamarine stare. "I'll message you my address. Say six?"

"Six it is." That knee-weakening smile flashed. "I'll see you soon."

"Yeah, you too." Her brain stumbled over itself in a pathetic attempt at coherent speech, but before she could redeem herself, he slammed the door and turned up the walk to his building.

Melody glanced at the clock. Two hours until her dinner with Rachel and Alex. She couldn't wait to tell her friend what had happened.

She just didn't know whether she meant about the car or Justin himself.

CHAPTER NINE

Melody intended to use the time before she had to head to Rachel's house to do . . . something productive. Instead, she found herself wandering aimlessly through her small apartment, fluffing pillows, rearranging tchotchkes on her living room side tables, sliding hangers around in her closet. She finally connected her phone to her Bluetooth speakers and selected her favorite old-school U2 album, letting the sounds of eighties rock fill the silence in her apartment while she scanned her bookshelf. Her fingertips touched her well-worn college edition of Thomas Hardy's *Far from the Madding Crowd*. She'd read it at least a dozen times, and she knew it so well she could probably recite passages by heart. Whenever she needed to escape reality, she could envelop herself in fictional Wessex, England. She'd never admit it aloud, but she'd thought it was a real place until her sophomore year in college.

And yet even Bathsheba Everdene and her hapless attempts at romance couldn't hold Melody's attention for long. Maybe it was because she didn't know how to cast Justin in this melodrama of her life. She didn't want to believe he was yet another Sergeant Troy, dashing and handsome but ultimately unreliable, but she couldn't picture him as a long-suffering Farmer Oak, either. Justin was unquestionably a man who knew what he wanted and went after it.

Then again, Melody knew even less about sheep farming than she did about aviation, so it was far from a perfect analogy.

No, things couldn't be so simple. She'd have to go on real-world experience here, not literary advice. In her experience, the smoothest, best-looking guys were the least trustworthy. Add the pilot career and the classic cars, and he was almost too good to be true. Which meant he was absolutely too good to be true.

And yet she hadn't been able to keep herself from accepting his invitation to take her out on Sunday. She was, in fact, breathless just thinking about seeing him again.

Melody sighed and set down her book, instead wandering into her kitchen. Fine. Literature might have failed her, but baking never did. She began pulling buckets of ingredients from the cupboards while she considered.

She had an arsenal of fancy French desserts at her disposal, ones that she made frequently as an attempt to keep up her pastry skills while she languished in a commissary bakery. *Crème brûlée. Croquembouche.* Any number of elegant desserts that required tempered chocolate, a particularly precise operation at high altitude.

And yet none of those called to her today, the marks of mastery of her profession. After being in her grandmother's house, she was craving memories. Which meant her version of Grandma Bev's butterscotch bars.

Just because they were homey didn't mean they were ordinary. Most versions of this recipe relied on butterscotch chips, waxy little chunks of hydrogenated oil and synthetic butterscotch flavor. Bev's used malted milk powder and a truckload of butter, relying on the interaction between the oven's heat and the milk powder to give that toasty, caramelized flavor that suggested rather than screamed butterscotch. Melody's version also subbed brown sugar for some of the white with a healthy shot of molasses to add a deep, earthy note. At the last moment, she added some chopped hazelnuts from a little glass jar in the cabinet for extra texture and flavor.

Thoughts of Justin faded as she mixed and spread the batter, then slid the shallow jelly roll pan into the oven where it would bake into a sheet of butterscotchy, nutty deliciousness. When it came out dozens of minutes later, fragrant and golden brown, she inhaled the aroma, basking in her sense of accomplishment at a perfect result. There was nothing like taking basic ingredients and transforming them into something both beautiful and tasty. As soon as they were cool enough to cut, she carefully portioned the bars into even squares and loaded them into a pastry box, a supply of which she kept in the space between her cabinet and refrigerator.

Melody packed the dessert into the Jeep with twenty minutes to spare and began the short drive across town to Rachel's house. She let out a sigh of relief when she saw that Alex's car was nowhere in sight. Maybe that meant she would have a few minutes with her friend before they got down to business.

"What's this?" Rachel asked as soon as she opened the door. "You didn't have to bring dessert."

"I was bored." Melody handed over the box and shrugged off her down parka. She shut the door behind her and followed Rachel into the kitchen. "Where's Alex?"

"He'll be here in a bit. I asked him to pick up a bottle of wine on the way, but knowing him, he'll come back with six."

Melody smiled. Alex was a perfectionist, and if Rachel didn't give him very specific instructions, he'd return with multiple options just to make sure one worked. "What are we having?"

"Chicken primavera pizza. I'm going to grill it on the barbecue on the back porch."

"That sounds amazing. Apparently we were both going for comfort food, because I made Bev's butterscotch bars."

"Alex is in for a treat, then. He's never had the

famous butterscotch bars." Rachel maneuvered herself over to her cutting board, where she was in the middle of slicing paper-thin rounds of vegetables to go on top of the pizza. "What would you think about doing some rustic pizzas for the café? I always wanted to put them on the menu at Paisley, but Dan and Maurice thought they were too lowbrow."

"I love that idea. And now we might even be able to afford a pizza oven."

Rachel caught the leading tone in her voice and raised an eyebrow.

"Justin thinks Grandma Bev's old Hornet is worth about twenty thousand dollars."

"You're kidding."

"I guess it's rare. He says he can do the minor restoration for a thousand and then help me find a buyer. Though I should probably use it for living expenses while the bakery gets underway, not a pizza oven."

Rachel just stared, as if she wasn't sure how to respond. Then she set down her knife and threw her arms around Melody. It was such an uncharacteristic show of enthusiasm that Melody laughed out loud.

"I'm so excited!" Rachel squealed. "Does this mean we can get started for real?"

"That's exactly what it means."

"I've got so many ideas rattling around my head, you have no idea." Rachel went back to her slicing. "Don't think I missed the part about Justin."

"I didn't think you did."

Rachel's knife never wavered, but she was clearly waiting.

"He went to Longmont with me today to look at the car. We had lunch on the way back."

"And?"

"And we're going out on Sunday night." Melody held her breath, waiting for the warning.

But Rachel just nodded. "I want to hear all about it, after."

"You're not going to tell me to be careful? I mean, you of all people have seen what I've gone through with guys."

"I don't need to tell you to be careful. You've been doing that for the last year. Ever since Micah."

"Micah." Melody almost snarled his name. "Please don't remind me."

"Maybe it's time to take a chance. But you have a type, and you know I don't mean hair color."

"Right. Why do I even keep trying when my track record is so bad?"

"Because you know that not all men are like that," Rachel said. "Just . . . be careful."

"There it is." Melody laughed. "I knew you couldn't resist."

The front door rattled and then creaked open.

"Rachel, I'm here." Alex appeared in the kitchen, carrying a box under his arm.

"Did I tell you?" Rachel shot a meaningful look toward the bottle tops sticking above the cardboard. "And I don't even drink."

"You just said dry white. That covers a huge amount of ground." Alex glanced Melody's way and smiled. "How are you? Want a glass?"

"I'd love a glass."

A quick discussion with Rachel on the wine pairing ensued, and Alex went in search of a corkscrew. He seated himself across from Melody and began to work the cork out of the bottle. "Did you bring the photos with you? Rachel says you want to rent instead of sell."

"I do. I went there today and it's in pretty good shape."

"I looked it up, and it's a good area for an income property. You still may want to fix it up to command a higher rent. If that doesn't feel too sacrilegious."

"No, I think Grandma Bev would be fine with it." Melody pulled up the photos she'd taken and passed her phone across the table to Alex.

"Five minutes!" Rachel called as she swept by them to the gas grill standing at the back door. A warning not to get too deep into discussion. Food never waited in this house; it was always the main event.

Alex swiped through the photos, nodding

slowly. "It's a cute little place. Perfect for a young family. Does everything seem structurally sound?"

"Oh yeah. She took care of it. It's just a little outdated. Everyone likes new, modern kitchens and open floor plans."

"They do, but they also like character." Alex's mouth tipped up into a wry smile. "Or so I'm told."

Melody chuckled. Alex's penthouse condo was a showplace of contemporary architecture; "full of character" didn't describe it as much as "stylish and spectacular." He'd overseen the renovations of two units on his floor himself, renting out one so he could live in the other. Maybe he wasn't quite the hands-on construction type, but she'd take his contact list any day.

"So what do you think?"

"Honestly, Mel, from what I know of you and how you feel about this house, I'd just do a new coat of paint, refinish the hardwood floors, sink some money into granite or quartz countertops in the kitchen, and call it good. Anyone looking for an eight-hundred-square-foot house in Old Town is looking to live small and leave a light footprint. Play up all the original features; fix what's broken. Otherwise it's just another soulless gut job and you'll never forgive yourself for it."

"Are you sure you're not a real estate agent in disguise?"

"Told you," Rachel said through the screen.

Alex passed the phone back. "I just don't want you to be unhappy with what you've done to a place that holds so many memories."

He was an uncanny judge of character if he could tell that about her in the little time he'd known her. Part of the reason she hesitated to sell the house was because she knew someone would come in and do a massive renovation and destroy all the house's original charm. If she could update it while keeping its integrity, she'd sleep better at night. Or during the day, as the case might be.

Rachel reappeared with a wooden peel holding a free-form pizza heaped with vegetables, its edges blackened by the flame. Melody's mouth practically watered at the sight of it. The moules on Saturday had been amazing, but after the day she'd had, pizza and wine and butterscotch bars—hopefully with good coffee—would feed her soul as much as her body.

Her friend cut the pizza into diagonal strips with a dangerous-looking mezzaluna, and then it was a free-for-all to grab the crispiest slices.

Melody closed her eyes to savor the perfectly tender vegetables on top of the crisp pizza crust and sighed with happiness. "You did a garlic Parmesan cream sauce."

"I figured I was allowed to deviate from traditional primavera since it's pizza."

"It's good Parmesan."

"Local. Makes up for the fact it's not Italian."

Alex was looking between the two of them with amusement. She supposed to someone who didn't habitually deconstruct every item in his head, their food banter probably was funny. It didn't take them long to polish off the pizza, and then Rachel made coffee while Melody transferred some of the butterscotch bars to a plate.

When they finally dug in, the bars earned a wide-eyed look from Alex. "These are really good."

"They are," Rachel said with a nod. "I can imagine them served warm with a scoop of vanilla ice cream. A twist on a brownie sundae."

"Mmm," Melody agreed. "With a drizzle of homemade caramel on top?"

"That would be divine. You should make that happen."

"Don't you think it's a bit . . . homey? It's straight-up Americana, and we both usually gravitate toward French. Or at least European. I figured our place would be along those lines. Fresh-baked pastries in the mornings, European-style breads in the afternoon."

"Both of us are grounded in French cooking, but I don't want to be theme-y. We call it something like La Maison and the first time I want to do an udon bowl as a lunch special, everyone loses their minds. Suddenly the menu is unfocused and the reviews say 'award-winning chef falls flat.' "

Melody didn't blame her for being wary. After all, an unfair restaurant review started the debacle that lost her Paisley. "It doesn't have to be that on-the-nose. And I don't want to replicate Paris. I was just thinking if we're going to do this, let's open a place that really reflects the things we love."

"I agree. We may be French at heart, but I'm not going to turn down a really good home-cooked lasagna. And Dutch apple pie à la mode is one of life's great summer pleasures."

Melody held up a hand. "I trust you absolutely on the food. And the business decisions."

"And I trust your baking and design vision."

"Trust is great, but you need to nail down your concept," Alex said. "It's going to determine your location. Different neighborhoods will embrace different concepts."

"Alex is right," Rachel said. "I'll start working on the menu so you'll have an idea of what I'm thinking and what kind of baked goods I'm going to need to go along with them . . ."

". . . and I'll start working on the dessert and bakery menu. What do you think? Meet back at the end of next week?"

"In the meantime—" Alex tapped something into his phone, and Melody's cell beeped a moment later—"call my contractor and see what he says. Maybe a real estate agent, too, for some advice on fixing the house up as a rental."

"Thanks, Alex. I'll check it out." For the first time, Melody realized what she had taken on. Fixing up a house to rent, selling a classic car, all so she could start a risky business with her best friend. It made her question whether she was up to the challenge. After all, her track record for sticking with a single project was woefully poor. What if she couldn't do it all? What if she let Rachel down?

No, she wasn't going to think that way. Focusing on the negative would only distract her from the positives—finally, she'd be getting the thing she'd always wanted. Not just the chance to be her own boss, but the opportunity to remedy the lack that had been hovering at the edge of her consciousness her entire adult life.

Roots.

CHAPTER TEN

Temporary insanity.

That was the only way Justin could explain how he'd managed to keep things friendly and platonic with Melody, only to blow it at the last minute by asking her to dinner.

Not that he didn't want to take her to dinner. She was . . . magnetic. That was the only word he could think of that came close. Beautiful, smart, funny, sensitive. He was acutely aware of wherever she was in relation to him, like the pull of a compass needle toward north. By the end of the day, worn out from pretending he had no intentions beyond friendship, it had been all he could do not to kiss her. So he'd asked her out instead.

And then he'd gone upstairs to find an e-mail agreeing to the date he'd proposed for a tour of the charter business and realized what an utter nitwit he really was.

But what was done was done. He wouldn't back out on the car project because he really did owe her one, and besides, even if it wasn't a car he'd personally chosen, it would be fun. He would do some research this week and play off the dinner as an informational meeting. Kind of a jerk move, but not as much a jerk move as getting involved with a woman he'd have to bail on in a few months.

He did still need to clear the whole car idea with his dad, though, and he hadn't even mentioned the Florida plan. So on Thursday morning, Justin made the trip across town to his father's house.

The painted-brick bungalow was located in Washington Park West, bought by his parents long before the neighborhood became one of Denver's hottest and most expensive districts, maintaining a quiet family feel with large lots and well-kept homes. Justin pulled up on the street and stepped out of his SUV, pausing at the curb. He'd grown up here, but it had been years since it felt like home. He strode up the front pathway to the door and knocked before letting himself in with the key.

"Hey, Dad, are you home?"

"In here." The voice came from the living room, and he heard the faint drone of the TV in the background. Justin moved through the hallway, jingling his keys in his hand, until he came to his dad sitting in a recliner, a cup of coffee in one hand and the newspaper in the other. Still in his pajama pants and a white T-shirt.

"I thought you'd be back. When did you get in?"

"Last night. I'm only back until Saturday, though." Rich Keller, though he might not look like it at the moment, was a senior pilot at United

Airlines, where he'd flown for the last thirty-five years, his seniority granting him the ability to dictate his lines and his schedule. Unlike his son, who pretty much went where the company routed him.

Justin wandered toward the coffeepot in the kitchen. "You mind?"

"Help yourself."

Justin poured himself a cup, then plopped onto the sofa placed diagonally to his dad's chair. "You have a final flight scheduled yet?"

Rich gave him a pointed look. "You didn't come over early on a day off to talk about my retirement. What's up?"

Justin pulled up the charter listing on his phone and passed it to his dad.

"Florida, huh? They're asking a lot of money."

"About five hundred thousand more than we're willing to pay."

Rich let out a low whistle. "Revenue justify the asking price?"

"Not sure yet. It depends on their liabilities. We're going there in a couple of weeks to check it out in person, look over the aircraft, meet the staff."

"You have a lawyer yet?"

"Pete's taking care of that. There's a lot to like about this company. The owner's willing to stay on for six months for the transition. And he's had it up for sale for over a year, so we think he might be willing to make a deal for the right buyers. It's just all dependent on the timing. I don't want to quit AvionElite until my stock is vested and I can take it with me."

"If you're that desperate to get out of fractional flying, it's not too late to start a career in the majors. Internal recs still mean something, you know. With your hours and qualifications, you would have no trouble picking up an airline job."

"And I'd be starting over as a junior first officer, at the mercy of the worst lines and schedules. No, thank you. If I were going to do that for another ten years, I'd stay where I am."

"If that's your choice . . . I just never thought of you being happy with day charters." Rich shrugged. "I did get my official retirement date."

"They're finally prying your hands off the controls?"

Rich grinned. "April 21. Minneapolis-Denver. You want to ride along?"

It was a tradition on an airline pilot's last flight to invite family and friends to come along, where they usually had some sort of celebration with cake and balloons at the gate. "I think I'm working, but I'll have to check."

"If you can make it, do. If not, no big deal."

"I'll do my best. I did want to ask you something, though. I found another project car. Fixing it up for a friend. I wanted to make sure you were okay with me keeping it here before I arrange to have it towed."

Now Rich's interest was piqued. "Oh? What is it?"

"A 1971 AMC Hornet SC/360."

"Who is she?"

"What do you mean?"

"I know you. You wouldn't give that car a second look, no matter how rare, if there wasn't a girl involved."

He'd give his dad this: he didn't miss anything. "Just a woman I met over the weekend. She did me a big favor, so I'm happy to do one in return. It'll be easy. It's in great shape."

"She know what it's like to date a pilot?"

"It's not like that—" not yet anyway—"and she works in food service, so she knows weird schedules."

"Food service?" Rich lifted an eyebrow. "She's a waitress?"

"Pastry chef."

"Ah. It's fine if you want to keep it here. No other use for the extra bay in a three-car garage."

"Thanks. I already ordered the carb kit and hoses, but I haven't been able to start it to know how it runs. She's just going to sell it, but I'd like to give her a chance to make as much as she can off it."

"Let me know if you want help." Rich drained

his coffee cup and set it aside. "If the weather stays good, I was thinking about taking up the RV-7 tomorrow. Feel like coming?"

"Absolutely." It had been months since they'd gone up together in their plane; both of them flew it independently when they had free time, but Justin always liked to fly with his dad. It reminded him of the days after his parents had gotten divorced when he was struggling through the changes in his life. Somehow things always seemed better in the air, less urgent, as if the intensity of his troubles faded as the distance from the ground increased. Even now, he felt a clarity in the left seat of a plane that he rarely felt anywhere else.

"You know, you'll have a lot more time for recreational flying when you're retired. How does it feel to be leaving it behind?"

"I'm not going to lie. Fantastic." Rich grinned and pushed himself out of the chair, then carried his empty cup to the kitchen. "Now about this girl . . ."

"I told you, there's nothing going on with this girl."

"And I told you, I don't believe you." His expression turned serious. "If you're really leaving Denver in a couple of months, you'll leave her alone. Help her out, since you've already agreed to work on the car, but don't get involved."

"I've already thought of that, Dad. That's why I called her a friend. She seems fun, but I've got this sense that deep down, she's probably the relationship type. Maybe if I were going to stick around—"

Rich pegged him with a stern look. "Don't kid yourself, Justin. If that were really the issue, you would have stayed with what's-her-name—"

"Sarah."

"You would have stayed with Sarah. It's okay. No one is forcing you to do things the traditional way. I've got plenty of nephews to carry on the Keller name. Better that you know what you want now than find out fifteen years after you're married."

Justin shrugged. "If we get this charter, I can fly as much or as little as I want. Who knows? Maybe I'll decide family life is exactly what I want."

"Whatever you say." His dad clapped him on the shoulder and then stood. "I'm going to get dressed. Feel like walking to Kimball's for lunch?"

"Sure." While his dad was changing, Justin went to the garage and began sorting through his tools, organizing the already-organized collection in its big black chest. The whole time, his mind turned over his dad's words, his warning. He wanted to believe his dad was wrong, that he was simply letting his own bias color his outlook. But

Justin's own experiences had proven that outlook correct too many times.

Which left him perpetually single with a string of first and second dates to pass the time. He simply wasn't willing to give up the thing that made him . . . *him,* no matter how great the woman might be. And yet he didn't want to get to his dad's age and realize he had no one to spend his retirement with. Maybe this Florida thing was exactly what he needed to break him out of this no-win cycle.

A fresh start.

CHAPTER ELEVEN

Work had always been somewhat tedious, but now that Melody knew she was on borrowed time, it was downright torturous. Every batch of dough became a mental critique: what she would do differently when she made it in her own place, how she would improve upon the breads in her current routine. The easy rhythm she usually found in the scraping and kneading of dough and the physical labor of lugging sacks of ingredients eluded her. Now that she and Rachel had decided to move forward with the café, she wanted it here now. She longed to be testing recipes for their own place, overseeing construction, finalizing menus and design decisions. Never mind the fact that she was getting way ahead of herself—they didn't even have a name or a location—she was still living firmly in the future.

But that didn't mean there wasn't work to do. She spent her non-baking hours downloading menus from restaurants she admired, regardless of whether they were in San Francisco, New York, Austin, or London. She flipped through her pastry books, brainstorming ways to transform traditional confections into something new and exciting. She spent hours on Pinterest pinning images of residential and retail spaces that inspired her.

Fortunately, Rachel seemed just as enthusiastic. The recipes that appeared on their shared Pinterest board expressed that clearly enough, just as her pins to the design board showed that they had very different tastes. Rachel gravitated toward the clean and industrial, while Melody liked soft and classic. There was an intersection in there somewhere, hopefully something different than the vintage-industrial look that had taken over the city's cafés. Something that implied the established overlaid by the modern. That sent Melody in search of photos of contemporary decor in historic spaces from all over Europe.

By the end of the week, she was pretty sure her eyes were permanently crossed from staring at a screen.

She dragged herself in from work on Saturday morning, intending to grab a few hours' sleep before she headed over to The English Department for brunch with Rachel and Ana. She was just pulling off her boots when a text message vibrated her phone.

Hey, it's Justin. Just confirming tomorrow night. Do you like Asian food?

The jitters she had suppressed all week came rushing back. Even though he was merely words on the screen right now, he might as well be standing next to her considering how breathless she felt. She typed and deleted her response until she had something suitably casual. I do! Looking forward to it. Still picking me up at 6?

If that works for you. Address?

She typed her address in quickly and waited. And waited. But her text remained the last one on the screen. She pulled off her flour-dusted clothes and yanked on a pair of threadbare yoga pants and an old T-shirt with the collar cut out. Still nothing. She broke down and texted back, Dress code?

This time, little dancing dots appeared, indicating his reply. Sorry. Spilled coffee all over my kitchen. Dress code is casual.

Melody laughed. At least he was secure enough to admit when he did something stupid. But the casual dress code . . . that meant they weren't going anywhere fancy. She wasn't sure if that was a relief or a disappointment. Either way, she wasn't going to let on. See you tomorrow.

Sounds good. I've got info on your car to discuss. Makes more sense to do it in person.

Okay, that was a little . . . odd. Maybe he thought she was in a big rush to get the car finished? If that were the case, she'd already have had it towed instead of waiting on Justin to give her the thumbs-up.

She plugged in her phone and climbed into bed, where she tossed and turned, her bone-deep exhaustion unable to keep her from replaying the text exchange with Justin. Had she misread him after all?

No, she was overthinking things as usual. He was the one who had asked her out. Were he having second thoughts, he would have canceled. She just had to keep her expectations low. Dinner didn't mean he was looking for a long-term commitment, just a night out. So for now, that's where Melody would start.

Her calm conviction lasted as long as it took to get ready the next evening. She'd have liked to pretend that she pulled the first thing her fingers touched out of the closet and put it on, but the truth was, she began planning her outfit when she woke at 2 p.m. and didn't make a final selection until a quarter to six, when she had to either choose something or show up at the door naked. Somehow she figured the latter might give him the wrong idea of her intentions.

The weather had swung back to the warm side of the thermometer, presenting them a string of sixty-degree days and melting all but largest snow piles in the corners of streets and parking lots. As soon as the sun went down, the temperature would rapidly drop thirty or forty degrees, but at least she only needed to give a nod toward the weather rather than bundle herself up head to toe.

She finally settled on a pair of black skinny jeans and a loose-cut black T-shirt beneath an Aztec-patterned cream-and-black blanket cardigan. Ankle boots and a floppy felt hat completed the outfit. It was cute but casual, stylish without trying too hard. Comfortable. Unpressured.

Who was she kidding? She'd spent two hours doing her hair and makeup. "Comfortable and unpressured" was the last thing she would call herself.

She was about to change her clothes again when the buzzer on the intercom rang. She moved quickly to the door and pressed the button. "Hello?"

"Hey, it's me. Can I come up?"

"Sure. Number six. But you already knew that or we wouldn't be talking on the intercom." She let go of the button and banged her head against the doorframe. Brilliant.

His laugh came over the speaker. "Then buzz me up."

Shaking her head at her own idiocy, Melody pressed the button that would release the latch on the front door and went to find her handbag, a tan leather satchel that could fit half of her earthly possessions. By the time the knock came at the door, she had pulled herself together.

At least she'd made the right wardrobe decision. Justin was wearing a light sweater under his shearling coat with a pair of dark jeans and boots, his hair artfully mussed, a day's growth on his jaw.

He looked her over with open admiration. "You look great." His attention transferred to her surroundings. "Wow, this place is amazing! You'd never guess from outside."

"Being inspired is better than keeping my security deposit."

He wandered around the room, hands in his coat pockets. "You did all this yourself?"

Melody trailed him, looking at the decor through his eyes. "For the most part. The furniture is either thrift store finds or curbside cast-offs that I refinished. I did have the Louis XVI settee professionally reupholstered. It's just a reproduction, but it was too complicated to do myself."

"Impressive. And here I was congratulating myself for buying a sofa that wasn't black leather. I didn't even give in to the call of recliners."

Melody laughed. "It was worth the effort. Your place reads more gentleman bachelor than aging frat boy."

"Thanks. I think." He stopped in front of her bookshelf. "This is your collection?"

"This is a quarter of my collection. My bedroom is lined with bookshelves." She cleared her throat before he could ask to see them . . . or not. "Should we go?"

He pulled his hands from his pockets and

checked his watch. "I guess we should. Our reservation is at 6:15."

Melody nodded and grabbed her purse, then locked her apartment door behind them. "Where are we going?"

"Have you ever been to Soyokaze?"

"I went there with Rachel when it opened and haven't been there since. The food's great."

"And here I thought I was going to surprise you."

Melody smiled, her earlier nervousness melting away. "Between Rachel and me, we've either worked for, met, or eaten the food of every chef in Denver. But I admire your taste. It's a very good restaurant."

"Thank you for throwing me a bone." He held the front door open for her, then led her down the walkway to the street where his Mustang sat. In the waning light, she now saw the car was charcoal gray with black racing stripes, reflecting back the pink-orange rays of sunset. No worse for the wear after its adventure, apparently. He unlocked the passenger door and held it open for her. Nice. What a change to go out with a gentleman.

Justin circled to the driver's side, giving Melody a moment to inspect the interior. It had a stripped-down, hard-edged masculine quality, all black upholstery and shiny silver accents. It was every bit as neat as his apartment, not a speck of dust on the dash, not a single stray leaf or smudge of dirt on the floor mats.

She watched him approach the driver's side, trying to reconcile all the disparate things she knew about him. The jet career, the flashy classic car—both suggested he'd have an ego to match. He certainly had plenty of confidence. And yet he was also kind, calm, and courteous. Which side was an act?

He climbed in the driver's seat and stuck the key in the ignition. "Tell me the truth: What do you think?"

She felt her cheeks heat before she realized he was talking about the car. "It's gorgeous. You did all of the work?"

"Mostly. I had the upholstery done by a pro and some parts rebuilt by the factory. Like you, I know when to leave things to the experts." He flashed her a quick smile as he pulled away from the curb with a throaty rumble of the engine. "I always intended to turn it around, but when I was done, I couldn't part with it."

"That's a relief. You were starting to strike me as disturbingly practical."

"Not entirely. Though I did remember to check the weather forecast before I left tonight. Wouldn't want you to have to rescue yourself this time."

"It would be the most exciting thing to happen this week. The most variety I've had was having to reduce the water in my doughs to compensate for the humidity."

"At least the bar is set low. Makes it easy on me." He threw her a mischievous look before his eyes went back to the road, and she found herself smiling.

She liked this guy. A lot.

When they got to the restaurant, he once again did the chivalrous thing and opened the car door for her, holding out his hand to help her out of the low-slung seat. His fingers closed around hers and held them for a second; then he swept his hand in the direction of the restaurant down the block. It was a former auto garage in an untrendy residential neighborhood in Stapleton, complete with the original glass-inset roll-up door.

"You'd never know this was here, would you?"

"Proof the food is excellent," Melody said. "If you can survive tucked away here, you can survive anywhere."

Justin held the door open for her and then gave his name to the hostess, who grabbed two menus and led them to a small table in the corner. Despite the plain commercial exterior, the inside was moody and atmospheric, with the original brick walls, dark paint, concrete floors, and an abundance of quirky lighting. It had changed since the last time she'd been here, more on trend, and she instantly liked it.

Their server approached as soon as they were seated, a tall, tattooed guy with a sleek ponytail and a nice smile. "Welcome to Soyokaze. I'm Donovan. Can I get you something to drink while you look at the menu?"

"I'll have some ice water and a glass of Kubota," Melody said.

"And you, sir?"

"Water for now, thanks." As soon as the server left, Justin leaned forward across his folded arms and said, "Tell me you didn't just order sake by name."

"I did. You're not going to have anything?"

"Not tonight. I've got an early flight, and my contract states twelve hours bottle-to-throttle."

"I've never heard that term before. But I guess I'd feel better knowing my pilot hadn't been drinking. Do you always follow the rules to the letter?" The question came out with a tinge of flirtation.

He smiled. "Always."

"Why?"

"Because I like my job. Because there are good reasons for the rules, especially when it has to do with my passengers' safety, not to mention my own and the plane's." He cocked his head and studied her. "I take it you're not much of a rule follower."

"I wouldn't quite say that. It's more that I see them as guidelines that should be followed where possible. It's just not always possible. You should be glad I'm not such a stickler or I would never have let you in."

Justin chuckled. "But you're a baker. Isn't that precise? All chemistry and physics? Unalterable natural laws?"

"Well, I'm never going to make water boil higher than 202 degrees at this altitude, however convenient it would be. But everything else is negotiable. You change one thing, you compensate with others. It's all about manipulating the environment to get a desired outcome." She pegged him with a stare. "And don't start reading into that. We were talking about baking."

"Somehow I have a feeling that isn't limited to baking." Now that definitely had a flirtatious sound to it. "Considering how persuasive you are, I'm surprised you haven't convinced the bakery to let you take over the place."

"I might not need to."

"Oh?"

"Rachel and I are opening a restaurant together."

Before he could respond, Donovan returned with Melody's sake and a bottle filled with ice water to share. "Are you ready to order?"

Justin looked down at his menu as if seeing it for the first time. "I haven't looked yet."

Melody took it out of his hand and handed both

166

to the server. "We'll let the chef choose for us tonight."

"We will?"

She smiled at him and looked back to Donovan. "We will."

The server seemed amused at Justin's bafflement. "Very well."

Justin leaned forward and pitched his voice low. "He better not bring me something that's still alive."

"Oh, relax. When you let the chef choose, you get the best thing on the menu . . . or even off the menu. I've known them to make something special when they aren't busy, just because they can. You do eat fish heads, don't you?"

Justin's eyes widened, and Melody broke into laughter again. "Sorry, I'm kidding. I promise."

"You're mean."

"Just testing to see how adventurous you are," she said.

"I'm pretty adventurous, but I draw the line at things that can look back at me." Justin folded his hands. "Now, did I imagine it, or did you just say you and Rachel are opening a restaurant?"

A twinge of insecurity bit into Melody's insides. "Is that so hard to believe?"

"No, but a week ago, you were talking about it like a distant dream, and now you're doing it. How did that happen?"

Melody shrugged, still self-conscious. "I admit,

it did come about fast. But my grandmother was very specific about me using my inheritance to follow my dreams, and this has always been my dream, so . . ."

"You're gutsier than I gave you credit for."

Something in his tone gave Melody pause. "You think it's too risky?"

"You already know it's risky. I'm just impressed. Most people say they want something, but when they're presented with the opportunity, they're too scared or set in their ways to take it. I admire the fact you're going for it."

The look on his face as he leaned back in his chair, a mixture of fascination and respect as if *she* were suddenly the mesmerizing, adventurous one, made her heart drum against her ribs. She averted her eyes and fiddled with her flatware, suddenly not sure what to do with her hands, while she scrambled for a new topic.

"Tell me the craziest thing that's ever happened on a flight."

That look vanished, and she could breathe again. "Passenger-wise or pilot-wise?"

"Both."

Justin thought for a second, then launched into a story about a time he was ferrying a married couple between their home in Connecticut and their house on Nantucket. "At some point in flight, the wife figured out the husband was having an affair, and she clocked him with a decanter. So they're literally rolling around on the floor of the jet, the wife screaming obscenities the entire time. Since I was acting as the F/O on that flight, I had to get up and physically break them apart. Then the husband took a swing at me for putting my hands on his wife. . . ."

"What happened?" Melody asked, simultaneously fascinated and aghast.

"I had a black eye for a week. And the worst thing is, I couldn't hit him because he was an owner. Not for long, though. He was 'encouraged' to sell his shares by management in return for me not pressing assault charges. My copilot was ticked because while I was restraining the idiots in the cabin, he had to be on an oxygen mask in the cockpit. And then there was the matter of getting blood out of the carpet before the next leg."

"No, really?"

He held up a hand. "Scout's honor. I am a whiz with a carpet cleaner when the situation calls for it."

Melody laughed. He kept surprising her. "Why do you do it, then? If you flew for an airline, you wouldn't have to deal with crazy passengers and carpet cleaning."

He smiled. "You sound like my dad."

"Not pleased you didn't follow in his footsteps?"

"Nah, he just started back when airline pilots

were treated like gods. Doesn't understand why I'd want to be a 'glorified limo driver.' His words, not mine."

"That seems a little harsh."

Justin shot her a mischievous look. "I tell him at least I'm driving a limo. He's driving a bus. It's in the name."

It sounded like he had a good relationship with his dad if they could joke around like that. If she tried something like that with her mom . . . well, she'd never try that with her mom. Melody could barely breathe without offending Janna as it was.

"Why do *you* do it?" he asked. "The bad hours and the hard work and, you implied, low pay?"

"Because I love what I do. I love baking bread especially, because even though it's the simplest, most basic form of nourishment, when it's done right, it's a revelation."

"Almost biblical," he teased.

"Exactly. And then on the pastry side, it's an utter indulgence. No one *needs* dessert. People order it to celebrate special occasions or to brighten up a bad day. And there's nothing better than seeing the delight on a guest's face when they order something unexpectedly whimsical or taste something that's better than they could have imagined."

"That's a good answer."

Melody raised her water glass. "To good answers for difficult jobs."

He clinked his own glass to hers. "Cheers."

Almost as if he'd been waiting for the lull in the conversation, Donovan returned to the table with two bowls, both heaped with noodles and seafood, balancing a third plate on his forearm. "Tonight we have for each of you an udon bowl with mushroom dashi and halibut collar, topped with crispy fried shallots. These are soft steamed pork-belly *bao* with scallions and ginger to share. Enjoy."

Melody smiled at Justin. "No eyeballs in sight. You first."

Justin picked up his chopsticks—expertly, she noted—and levered some of the udon into his mouth. His eyebrows flew up. He dipped a spoon into the bowl of broth and sighed at his first sip. "That's really good."

"Go ahead and say it."

"You were right. Melody Johansson, will you be my culinary guide from here on out?"

Melody threw her head back and laughed. "Okay, smart aleck. I deserved that."

Justin smiled and went back to his meal, and Melody dug into hers. It was every bit as good as the rapturous look on his face had suggested, and she was quite sure this wasn't on the menu. Score one for insider knowledge.

As the night wore on and went from supper to a dessert of strong coffee and *daifuku*, mochi balls filled with fruit-flavored cream, the conversation turned into a good-natured contest to tell the best story. Justin told tales of unruly passengers, unexpected weather, and even an emergency landing because of a small fire on his jet. Melody countered with stories of being lost in foreign cities, having to fill in for a pastry chef when she was still barely competent as an assistant, and a small fire in one of her ovens. And then she decided to pull out the big guns.

"I sang in the Grand Ole Opry."

Justin blinked at her. "What?"

Melody nodded. "I was twelve. Touring with my mother. She was a guest performer, and she pulled me up on stage to sing a duet."

"No kidding." Justin looked fascinated. "I didn't know you could sing."

Melody lowered her voice. "That's the thing. I can't. It was a total disaster. Somehow my mom missed the fact that what was cute when I was eight was no longer cute when I was a pimply, awkward almost-teenager."

Justin cringed and covered his eyes with his hands. "Oh, that's just painful. Did you disappear afterwards?"

"I tried, but of course it made the newspapers. Most of the reporters were kind because I was just a kid, but a few made snide comments about how I was certainly not going to follow in her footsteps." Melody sighed. The memory no longer held embarrassment, just the recollection of how out of touch her mother had been with anything but her own life. Still was, for that matter.

"So you know I have to ask—who is your mom anyway? She'd have to be a big deal to sing at the Opry. Would I know her?"

"You'd know her. Her publicist makes sure of that. As far as who she is . . ." Melody shrugged. "Beats me. At this point, I doubt she even knows herself."

It was a dodge, but the last thing Melody wanted to do was insert her mom any further into what had been a thoroughly enjoyable night out. The thoughtful look came back to Justin's eyes, and then he deliberately folded his napkin and set it beside his plate. "You win. That is definitely the best story of the night."

Melody caught her bottom lip between her teeth. "What do I win, exactly?"

Something intense lit in his blue eyes, setting the jitters back in her midsection. Her fault, because she had stirred it up. She didn't feel sorry.

"I'll have to think about that," he said finally. "Make sure that it's a suitable prize."

"Okay then." Melody tossed her napkin on the table and rose. "Will you excuse me for a moment?" She slung her big handbag over her shoulder, resisting the urge to glance back and see if he was watching her. But as she rounded the corner to the restrooms, she dared a look his direction. His eyes were locked on her.

She escaped to the ladies' room and went straight to the sink to wash her hands, even though they didn't technically need washing. When she caught a glimpse of herself in the mirror, she saw what Justin had no doubt noticed: her flushed cheeks, her bright eyes. Oh yeah, he had to know she was into him. She fluffed her hair, settled her hat at a slight angle, and replaced her lipstick in her bag without applying it. Presumptuous maybe, but she was taking no chances.

Once she had herself together, she returned to their table, where Justin was signing a credit card receipt. He thrust it into the little folio before she could get a glimpse of the total and smiled at her. "I hate to call it an early night, but I do need to be at the airport by five tomorrow."

"Totally fine," she said. "I don't want to be the reason you're flying tired."

He escorted her out of the restaurant, and she could feel the warmth of his hand where it rested on the small of her back, though that was likely just her imagination. He opened the door for her, held out his hand for support as she climbed in. She pretended not to notice how his touch lingered.

"So where are you headed tomorrow?" she asked, just to fill the silence.

"No idea yet. There should be an e-mail waiting for me with tomorrow's schedule when I get home."

"That has to make it hard to pack. How would you know whether to bring your swimsuit or your snow jacket?"

Justin laughed. "Doesn't matter. Even when I overnight someplace good, I get in too late to enjoy the beach. I hear corporate pilots get laid over in horrible places like Maui and Nassau for days while they wait for their passengers."

"Must be terrible for them," Melody said. "I'm told that some people actually sleep during the nighttime and work during the day. Which seems like a pretty revolutionary idea to me."

Justin didn't look at her, but she caught his grin. Funny that they should have such disparate jobs and still be able to commiserate over the lack of regularity.

They reached Melody's apartment far too soon, and she was surprised just how disappointed she felt that the night was coming to a close. "If you don't mind," he said, "I'll walk you up."

"You know, the neighborhood really isn't that bad, despite what my mother seems to think."

He held up his hands. "I didn't say anything. I'll just feel better knowing that you're safely in your own apartment."

Nope, he definitely thought she was going to get mugged on her way up to her place. But instead of irritating her, like her mother's assumptions did, the gesture warmed her.

Justin followed her into the building and up the stairs to her apartment, where he paused outside her door.

"Are you sure you don't want to come in? Have a cup of coffee?"

"Thanks, but I shouldn't."

"Next time, then." Melody realized it sounded like she was fishing for another date. Probably because she was.

"That's a guarantee." His voice went deep, resonated with promise, but he didn't reach for her. He did the opposite, in fact, thrusting his hands into the pockets of his jeans.

Disappointment washed over her as she turned around and put her key in the door. Maybe she had somehow offended him or turned him off . . . which was a shame, because she'd really thought there might be something to that spark between them.

So much for being gutsy and mesmerizing. That girl wouldn't wait for a guy to make the first move. That girl knew what she wanted and acted on it.

So why couldn't she be that girl?

Melody dropped her hand from the doorknob and turned. Before she could talk herself out of it, she pulled off her hat and stretched up to kiss him.

It didn't take long for Justin to recover and draw her closer, his hands going to her waist. If he'd been surprised by her forwardness, now he was in no hurry to move away, every brush of his mouth becoming a question, an inquiry, an exploration. When he teased apart her lips, she somehow lost her balance, melting into him until nothing remained but that moment: his scent, his taste, the feel of his muscular body against her soft one.

He finally broke the kiss and stepped back, leaving her shaken and unsteady. "I really have to go. I'll call you when I get back."

Melody watched him walk away, unable to form a farewell or do anything but stand there. Tonight had confirmed what she'd known the first time she laid eyes on him—if she fell for him, she would fall hard. A smarter, more sensible woman would quit this now before he could permanently embed himself in her silly romantic fantasies. But even as she thought it, she knew the truth: she was neither that smart nor that sensible.

CHAPTER TWELVE

He was a first-class jerk.

Justin practically fled the building, berating himself for his lack of restraint. What had he been thinking? He'd promised himself that he would keep this thing with Melody businesslike, despite his decidedly unbusinesslike interest in her. He was leaving, after all, potentially moving across the country. Only a total loser would start something with a woman like that and have absolutely no intention of seeing it through.

It didn't even matter that *she* had kissed *him*. He could have kept it sweet and simple. Instead, he'd pulled her to him and responded like it would be the first of many to come. And it wouldn't be. Couldn't be.

Melody was a knockout, though, and not just her looks. Her confidence, her enthusiasm, her sense of humor. The fact she had no problem bossing him around or making the first move, but clearly appreciated chivalrous gestures like opening doors and pulling out chairs. The way she savored everything, felt so passionately about her career. Her very presence had him doing the exact things he said he wouldn't.

He needed to put an end to this right now. For both their sakes.

Easier said than done, considering he still had the car to deal with. The parts should be waiting for him when he got back. As soon as she had the Hornet delivered to his house, he could fix it up, introduce her to his auto-broker friend, and gently extract himself from the situation.

His reluctance to do so had no relevance to the matter.

His conviction should have made leaving on his next tour easier, but his mood ran toward stormy when he woke early Monday morning and made a quick breakfast in his dark kitchen, slamming pans and mugs with far too much vehemence. Probably not the right frame of mind for dealing with owners and their guests. He was paid not only to get his passengers safely from point A to point B, but to communicate that he wanted to be doing nothing more with his time.

Even in his head, the thought took on a slightly sarcastic cast. He might have told Melody that he had taken the job for variety and quality of life, but he hadn't told her that it often wore on him. Multiple short flights a day, multiple cities, a variation on the same hotel room, restaurant, and gym eighteen days a month. He spent more time in strange beds than he did his own. It was the reason he'd always had an exit strategy, always planned to move on when he found the right situation, regardless of what he told his dad.

"Suck it up, cupcake. Three more months and

it's blue waters and white sands all the way." He grabbed his roller case from where it waited in the hallway, draped his overcoat over one arm, and headed out to begin what would no doubt feel like a long, one-hundred-twenty-hour day.

The navy-blue sky had begun to transition to dawn silver when he parked outside one of the general aviation terminals at Centennial Airport and made his way through the tiny building to the crew lounge, not much more than a glassed-in closet with a couple of computer stations and a handful of chairs. His first officer—whoever it would be today—hadn't arrived yet, so he took the opportunity to go over his flight plans, the fuel orders, and the manifests before he headed out to the plane.

"You Keller?"

An arrogant voice intruded on his thoughts and he lifted his head from the clipboard.

"You must be—"

"Adam Cole, your first officer." Something in the man's tone suggested the words rankled.

Justin sized the man up. Early fifties, slightly graying hair, in good shape. He immediately pegged him as a defector from the majors, one of the pilots who had bailed on his airline after the last contract negotiations. Great. The guys who had had seniority at their last job, especially the Airbus and 777 captains, tended to resent guys like Justin who joined the company early and climbed the ranks at a young age. Not to mention the general culture clash between captains and first officers that existed everywhere he'd ever flown. Justin got along well with all but a handful of the company's F/Os, but with the way dispatch routed planes and distributed crews, he'd probably never fly another tour with this guy. Not worth setting things straight for the sake of five days as long as Cole did his job.

Instead, Justin picked up his bag, indicated with his head for Cole to follow, and walked through the glass doors across the apron where their Citation XLS waited, already moved from its hangar and hopefully loaded with catering by the line crew.

Justin left Cole to do the walk around as he climbed into the narrow cockpit and began his preflight setup—entering waypoints into navigation, calculating anticipated passenger and baggage weights, estimating fuel load. For the first time since he'd woken that morning, his foul mood lifted. Odd as it might seem, he enjoyed the minutiae, the process of readying the plane for its flight. The routine was comforting, necessary. Got him in the right frame of mind to pilot a metal tube through the sky at four hundred miles an hour.

Cole appeared in the cockpit and handed over his clipboard. "You might want to take a look at the tires. I'm comfortable with the wear, but it's your call."

Justin nodded. If there was any resentment, Cole wasn't letting it get in the way of his job. Justin climbed out of the plane, agreed that the tires were fine, and signed off on the walk around. Time to start the engines and taxi the jet to the terminal entrance where they'd meet their guests.

Fortunately it was just the owner and his wife, who brought only small bags and a tiny dog that looked far more like a rat than a canine to Justin. She yipped at him when he neared, the pink bow on her head bobbing and making her look even more ridiculous. Justin struggled against a laugh as he led them to the plane.

"They have a dog," Justin murmured to Cole when he returned to the cockpit.

"Lord have mercy," Cole muttered. "I could tell you stories about flights with the little ankle-biters."

Justin grinned, his opinion of the man shifting. "Rochambeau for cleanup duty?"

"All right." Cole seemed amused by the idea. "On three."

Cole threw rock, as predicted; Justin threw paper. "For your sake, I hope the stupid thing doesn't have a small bladder."

"I hope the FBO in St. Louis has a carpet cleaner. I once flew a leg with a Great Dane who got motion sickness. There are just some things you can't forget."

Justin chuckled. They ran through the last of the preflight checklists and began their slow trip down the taxiway toward the runways. When they were finally off the ground in Denver and pointed toward Missouri, he glanced over at him. "So how long have you been with the company?"

"Almost two years," Cole said. "Just relocated from Tulsa to Dallas. My wife's an AA pilot and the commute was getting to her. At least this way it cuts a few hours off her day."

"Kids?" Justin asked.

"One, but she lives with her mom. How about you? Married?"

He shook his head. "No."

"Good move. No reflection on my wife, of course, but it's my third marriage. Got smart and married someone in the industry this last time. The job's too hard for anyone who isn't in it to understand."

"Right." Justin didn't say he had seen that firsthand with his own parents. That it was one of the major reasons he was thirty-four and hadn't had a relationship that lasted longer than six months. That he wished the obstacles weren't so well-documented now that he'd met someone new.

Because that was ridiculous. Obviously.

But the thought didn't leave, just buzzed

around the back of his head as they made the stop in St. Louis, then repeated the whole procedure again, plus a repositioning leg at the end of the day that took them to next morning's departure city of Madison, Wisconsin. He was just trying to convince himself that he was doing the right thing by backing off. It wasn't as if he'd known Melody very long. He wasn't arrogant enough to assume she'd be crushed by being dumped— which implied that they were actually dating, which they weren't. It was simply that were he planning to stay in Denver for the foreseeable future, Melody seemed like the type who might be okay with his crazy schedule. She understood what it was like to have a job that required long and irregular hours. She hadn't even blinked when he said he'd call her in a week.

And yet, by the end of that week, he was already counting the minutes until he could see her again.

The last leg of his tour landed him in San Francisco at midday. He and Cole were flying commercial back to their domiciles, leaving a handful of hours to kill. How was he going to pass four hours in a city known for its traffic?

The idea struck him with a measure of guilt, almost as if he were doing something illicit. He was mapping out his destination on his cell phone when Cole approached, his hand outstretched.

"I'm meeting a friend at the concourse bar until

my flight leaves. It's been a pleasure flying with you."

"Likewise." Justin shook his hand. "I'm going to take the courtesy car. Do you want me to drop you at the terminal on my way?"

"Yeah, thanks." Cole seemed surprised, but he shouldered his bag and followed Justin out to the battered sedan reserved for crews on layovers.

Justin navigated away from the general aviation center toward SFO and dropped Cole at the departures deck, then made his way from the airport into the city. Technically, he wasn't supposed to take the car for too long, but assuming traffic wasn't terrible, he could do the round trip in ninety minutes.

Forty minutes later, through surprisingly light northbound traffic, Justin found street parking in the Inner Sunset neighborhood and hoofed it three blocks to his destination.

As soon as he pushed open the heavy oak door of Noelle Patisserie, the tinkling of bells enveloped him, along with the sweet, earthy scent of bread and pastries. A handful of customers lingered over coffee and croissants at small round tables. A couple, each carrying a paper bag laden with bread, brushed past him out the door.

A middle-aged woman looked up from where she was wiping down a stainless-steel counter behind the cases. "I'm sorry, sir. We're about to close."

"Please." He held up a hand. "You wouldn't happen to remember Melody Johansson, would you?"

The woman stopped and gave him her full attention, expression surprised. "Melody? Yes, of course I remember her. One of our best apprentices. I haven't seen her since she decided to move to Paris. Why? Something didn't happen to her, did it?"

"No, nothing like that. She was just telling me about this place the other day and how it made her realize her calling as a baker. I'm in San Francisco for a few hours, thought it would be nice to bring something back for her."

A knowing smile came over the woman's face. "Boyfriend?"

"No, just a friend."

"Long way to come from the airport for just a friend."

Justin frowned, puzzled, until he looked down at himself and remembered he still wore his uniform.

"I'm Marin." The woman offered a hand, which he shook the best he could over the top of the case. Justin offered his name in return. "As you can see, we're pretty much cleaned out for the evening. Just a few loaves of bread left."

"I'll take them. She waxes rhapsodic about bread, so I know she'll be thrilled."

There went that knowing look again. She pulled

them out of the case one by one and slid them into individual paper bags. "What's Melody doing these days? I take it she's back in the States?"

"She was a pastry chef at a restaurant in Denver for a while. She and a friend are about to open their own place."

"Really! Good for her. I can't say I'm surprised. She took to baking like she was born for it."

"Are you responsible for all this?"

"Only the pastries," Marin said. "The bread is my husband's domain. He's already gone home for the day. Here, I'm going to wrap up a couple of croissants for you to take for yourself. Don't try to save them; they won't be good for much longer."

"Thank you." Justin took out his wallet, but she waved him off before he could pull out any money.

"No, it's my pleasure. Tell Melody that Jeff and I said hello and good luck on her new place. If we ever make it out to Denver, we'll come by and see her."

It was polite fiction and they both knew it. Owners were tied to their bakeries; sole proprietorship didn't come with vacation time. But he smiled anyway. "She would love that, I'm sure. I'll let her know."

"Please do. It was nice meeting you, Justin. I'm glad Melody has found someone who appreciates her *and* her talent."

His smile faltered, but he waved good-bye and stepped out onto the cold, windy street. He'd only been thinking about the coincidence that he was in San Francisco so soon after Melody had talked about this place; he hadn't been thinking of the message the gesture would send when he was trying to cut ties.

No, he'd been thinking about that kiss and how he'd really like to experience it again. The exact opposite of cutting ties.

Too late now. The deed was done, and he had two croissants to eat while he waited for his flight to leave, assuming he didn't have to surrender them to the FBO desk in apology for having the car gone so long. He pulled out his cell phone when he climbed back into the warmth of the borrowed sedan and texted Melody a quick message: Flying home tonight. Deliver the Hornet tomorrow?

There. That was neutral and noncommittal. As was her response: Okay. Do my best.

Justin drove back through the deepening evening, focusing on the long line of brake lights in front of him while he tried to figure out how to spin this into a friendly and decidedly nonromantic gesture.

Too bad that thinking made him not only a jerk, but also a liar.

CHAPTER THIRTEEN

Melody pretended like she wasn't counting the days until Justin returned, but in truth, she was watching the calendar like a child waiting for her birthday to come. Not so much because she was dying to see him—though she was—but because this was her first chance to find out who he really was. He'd said that he would call her when he got back. Either he would or he wouldn't. And that would tell her whether or not she had been harboring romantic fantasies about him for no reason.

Fortunately, between her usual work schedule and putting together a sample menu for the bakery-café, she didn't have much time to obsess over the potential beginning of a new relationship. When she finally met her friends to go over her progress on Friday night, she had an electronic folder full of research and a Pinterest board full of inspiration photos.

Rachel opened the door for her, a mug of coffee in hand. "Come in. Ana is on her way."

"She managed to escape from the office before seven o'clock on a Friday? I'm impressed."

"*Escape* is right." Rachel shut the door and walked with her into the kitchen. "I think she had to make up some excuse about why she needed to leave."

"Her job is insane. No promotion or paycheck would make that worth it to me."

Rachel laughed. "She would say the same thing about our jobs, I'm sure."

"I could never imagine Ana working in a kitchen, but if she did, she'd probably end up bossing everyone around by the end of the day."

"True. Even I do what she says." Rachel went to the large French press on the counter and poured Melody a cup of coffee, stirring in milk and sugar just the way she liked it.

She murmured her thanks and sipped it while she booted up her laptop. "How has the menu planning been coming along?"

"Slowly. I have too many ideas, and we both know I'm going to be tinkering up until the day we open."

"That's okay. Mine is provisional too. We just need something for the business plan and to make sure we both agree with the direction we're taking. If the size of my bread menu is any indication, we're going to need a lot of space."

"You do realize we're going to have to operate on a skeleton crew, right? We won't be able to afford assistants when we begin. We'll be lucky to have a cashier."

Melody hadn't thought that far. "I think you

underestimate how well-known you are. After all the press you've gotten, I imagine there's going to be a lot of people watching to see what you'll do next."

Rachel looked unconvinced, but Melody had a sense about these things. This wouldn't be a slow start. As soon as word got out—helped along by Ana's promotional genius—people were going to flock to their place. Denver was always enthusiastic about restaurant openings. All it would take was a couple of good reviews in publications like *5280* and *Westword*, and word of mouth would do the rest.

"Anyway, I'll wait until Ana is here to tell you about it."

"No need; I'm here." The slam of the front door punctuated the words as Ana clicked down the hallway. Say whatever you wanted about their friend, she had an instinct about making entrances. Today she was wearing slim-cut slacks with her ubiquitous high heels, a simple cashmere sweater, and a fur-trimmed coat that Melody could only call "couture ski bunny." She plopped herself down in a chair, shrugged off her coat, and gave a long exhale like she was in a yoga class. "You have no idea how happy I am to see you two."

"Long day?" Rachel asked, sliding a third cup of coffee in front of her.

"Understatement. Honestly, the amount of

the raise should have been a tip-off when I took the job in the crisis management division. I just figured I was already dealing with crises all the time, might as well be paid better for it." She made a face. "Wrong. These clients take dysfunctional to a whole new level. I'm starting to dream of a simple product liability scandal."

Melody chuckled. That was Ana's most scathing criticism, the implication that someone didn't have it all together. It was somewhat amazing that they were all friends. Rachel was relatively structured, but by design, Melody operated in a near-permanent state of controlled chaos. Simply listing all her jobs in the last five years would have Ana breathing into a paper bag.

"Okay, Ana's here. Let's see the menus."

Rachel seated herself beside Melody and across from Ana, shoving a piece of paper at each of them. Melody pulled two folded sheets from her purse and distributed them as well.

Rachel's list was restrained, refined, and written like a menu. She might think this was a rough draft, but Melody would be willing to bet that the final version would be strikingly close. A handful of sophisticated yet comforting egg dishes, which would be accompanied by house-made toast. High-end sandwiches, soups, and salads, with some unusual pastas. And then there was a separate weekend brunch menu that selected the best of both breakfast and lunch. She must have been working on this in every bit of free time she had.

By comparison, Melody's was rambling, expansive, and maybe a touch overoptimistic. The breads alone topped out at a dozen, plus a dozen more pastries, each with their own variations. She was most certainly going to need to narrow down the selection.

Despite that, however, the menus seemed to work together. Melody had already planned breads to accompany the breakfasts; others like the briny olive loaf would be perfect for Rachel's sandwiches. Enthusiasm welled up inside her. Already their ideas were jibing, like they had at Paisley.

"I like this," Ana said when she was finished reading the sample menus. "Secondary to this would be good coffee—the small-batch, locally roasted sort. Though you might want to start with something recognizable like Lavazza and grow your coffee menu over time."

"That's a good idea," Rachel said. "I'd like the food to be the focus to begin with and just make the coffee complementary to the menu. Maybe we can offer espresso drinks and pour-overs by the cup."

"No one expects more from anything but a coffeehouse," Ana said.

"I know mine needs to be edited," Melody

said. "As it is, if I don't want to work around the clock, I'll need an assistant in the morning. I'm planning on having a constant supply of fresh pastries until about ten o'clock. After that, we'll do the lunch desserts. And I'm thinking fresh, warm bread should be available after 2 p.m. every day."

Rachel was nodding. "That seems like a good plan. Maximizes staffing hours and oven real estate and still lets you go home with only a twelve-hour day."

Melody chuckled. Only restaurant veterans would be happy with a twelve-hour day. The difference was, this time it was their own place. They were investing in themselves and not someone else's business.

"So I guess the next step is for us to get with a real estate agent and look for a space. You know this could take us years. It took me ten months to find the space for Paisley, and there I just got lucky."

"That gives me time to get my grandma's house settled and sell the Hornet," Melody said. "I'm not in a huge hurry."

"Good," Rachel said. "I want this to be right, not rushed. In the meantime . . . I was thinking I might just throw together a quick pasta. Are you guys hungry?"

"You had me at *pasta,*" Melody said.

"All right," Ana said. "But I'll be cursing

you the entire time I'm at the gym tomorrow."

"You're best friends with two chefs," Rachel said. "Embrace the fluffiness."

"You have no idea how tempting that is, but I've spent too much of my life in the gym getting this body to give up now. Besides, aren't you supposed to wait until after you get married to gain weight?"

"Alex seems to think so. Poor guy's been hitting the gym every day to work off my cooking. Though I don't see him giving up his workout routine just because he's married."

Melody looked closely at her friend. "Is there something you're not telling us?"

A wash of pink rose to Rachel's cheeks.

"There is!" Ana gasped. "Tell us everything. Are you engaged?"

The flush deepened to bright red. "He hasn't officially proposed or anything. He knows that would freak me out. But we've been talking about whether a wedding would be too stressful before the café opening or if it would just make everything easier. We'd see each other a lot more since we'd be living together, and he works at home . . ."

Melody squealed and clapped her hands together. "You're getting married!"

"Not yet." Rachel couldn't repress her smile. "But . . . someday soon."

Melody couldn't help it. She leaned over and

hugged her friend hard around the neck. "I'm so happy for you. It's been a long time coming."

"You can't say anything," Rachel said. "Alex would flip out if he knew I was telling you about this."

"No, he wouldn't." A smile played at Ana's lips. "He'd probably be thrilled. Anyone who sees the two of you together knows that he adores you. He would have married you six months ago had he thought you'd go for it."

"You're probably right." Rachel looked as shy and excited as a little girl daydreaming about her storybook hero. Melody sighed. It almost made her believe in fairy tales after all.

"Where is Alex, by the way?" Ana asked. "It's Friday night and you're not spending it together?"

"Doing a climbing clinic in Arizona with Bryan. Apparently he's good enough now that Bryan's bringing him along as an assistant. Second set of hands and eyes."

"Which means that he's still procrastinating on his book?" Melody asked.

Rachel laughed. "Exactly. I can pretty much guarantee he'll come back with all these new ideas and then disappear for a few weeks to write them. Which isn't a bad thing since we're going to be pretty busy ourselves."

Melody's phone beeped and she pulled it out of her purse to check the notification. Her heart started beating harder when she saw it was from Justin.

Flying home tonight. Deliver the Hornet tomorrow?

Her excitement faded. That was a very cold message. But maybe he was between flights and didn't have much time.

How much time did it take to write something like *Can't wait to see you tomorrow?*

Unless the week he'd spent away had made him realize he wasn't as interested as he thought he was. Or maybe he'd never been interested. She had kissed *him,* after all.

"What's wrong?" Rachel asked from the kitchen. "You're frowning at your phone."

Quickly, Melody tapped back an equally vague answer. Okay. Do my best.

"Wait, that's Justin!" Ana gasped. "I can't believe we forgot about your date! How was it? What happened?"

Five minutes ago, Melody would have gushed over him and how much fun they'd had. But now? "I don't know, guys. I thought it went really well. He seemed really into me. Insisted on walking me to my door."

"Ooh," Rachel said. "He kissed you good night?"

The flush was back. "I kissed him. And he seemed into it. But then he just left."

"That's good, though," Rachel said. "Remember

what you and Ana told me when I first got together with Alex? Not to confuse respect with lack of interest?"

"That's what I figured, and then I get this." Melody showed them the text.

"That's . . ." Ana trailed off. "Maybe he's just not good at text messages. You know, some people hate communicating any way but face-to-face."

"Or maybe he's regretting the fact that he agreed to help me. He said he'd call when he got back, like that was a good thing."

"You're overthinking it," Rachel said. "Again. He wants you to have the car delivered tomorrow. So go with it and see him. You'll get a pretty good idea of what his intentions are."

"Look who's the expert now," Melody teased.

Ana shrugged. "She's the only one who's actually managed to get and keep a guy lately."

"No new candidates?" Melody asked.

Ana made a face. "God needs to drop one from the sky or put him in my path in the grocery store."

"Or deliver him in a snowstorm to your place of business," Rachel said.

"Hopeless romantic," Ana muttered. "I never thought I'd see the day when you two traded places. Rachel used to be the cynic in our group."

"I'm not being cynical. I'm just . . . overthinking. Again." Melody sighed. "Okay, you're right. I'll see him tomorrow morning. I need to make sure the car gets to the right place anyway. I'll go from there."

Ana studied her closely. "You really like this guy, don't you?"

"I do." Melody sighed. "He's normal, but in a good way. No crazy hobbies or weird religion or bizarre fetishes that I know of. Except for the job, he's pretty much perfect. And except for the job, *I'm* pretty much perfect . . . so that makes us perfect together, right?"

Rachel laughed. "There's my girl. I was starting to worry for a second."

"I guess that means I need to call for a tow. Got anyone you like, Ana?"

Ana pulled up her contact list and pushed her phone toward Melody.

"Of course you do." Melody laughed. "What do you need a tow truck for anyway?"

"Clients. You'd be surprised."

By the time Rachel was finished with the pasta, Melody had arranged for a flatbed to transport the Hornet from Longmont to Justin's dad's house in Washington Park. It was decided. She'd follow the truck over there and settle this matter once and for all.

CHAPTER FOURTEEN

Melody left the bakery a few minutes before six the next morning and started the forty-minute drive north to her grandmother's house. On a weekday, traffic would already be stop and go—Highway 36, the main artery between Boulder County and Denver, hadn't been expanded even though the population had doubled. But on a Saturday morning, it was downright sleepy. Today, that wasn't necessarily a good thing. Eighteen hours awake after a marathon planning session with her friends and a full shift at the bakery left her struggling to keep her eyes open. She turned the Jeep's stereo to a rock station and cranked the volume high enough to make her ears bleed.

When she arrived at the little house, the tow truck looked to have just arrived and was backing into the driveway. Melody parked on the street and hopped out of her Jeep, meeting the driver just as he stepped out of the cab of the truck. "Give me a second to open the door for you. I'll warn you, though, it's not drivable."

"Not a problem," the guy said easily. "I'll wait here."

Of course it wasn't a problem, Melody thought, rolling her eyes at her own comment. Why would someone need a tow truck if their vehicle was drivable? She fished the keys from her pocket and unlocked the front door, intending on going straight through the back again. And then she stopped, frozen, her chest too constricted to take a full breath.

Bare floors stretched in every direction, squares of shiny varnish showing where area rugs had once protected them. The furniture was gone. Art had been taken down, leaving only nails in the walls. Even the antique chandelier had been removed from the ceiling, its wires dangling from the center of the plaster medallion.

Every bit of evidence of Grandma Bev's life, everything familiar from Melody's childhood . . . vanished as if it had never existed at all.

Melody dragged in a lungful of air, barely aware that it came on a sob. She wrapped her arms around herself as tears rolled down her face, the reality of her grandmother's death washing in after being suppressed for weeks. When she finally came to herself and remembered the tow truck driver waiting outside, she went to the bathroom to splash water on her face and then reached for the empty space where one of Grandma Bev's eyelet-bordered guest towels would have hung.

They were gone. Just like Bev was gone. And pretty soon, her car would be gone too.

Doubt crept in for a bare second before Melody

dismissed it. If Bev was looking down on her right now, she was probably scolding her. Things were just things, she would say. They didn't have souls. They didn't have memories. They were simply tools that should serve their lives. And the car hadn't even been sentimental to her. Grandma Bev had bequeathed it as a stepping-stone for Melody's next adventure. She wouldn't want her to feel guilt, only gratitude.

By the time Melody pressed the button to open the garage door, she had her emotions under control, though there wasn't anything she could do about her tear-streaked face and red-rimmed eyes. The tow truck driver was waiting impatiently on the other side of the door, but his face changed when she swept back the chamois cover. He let out a low whistle.

"My grandmother's husband's," Melody explained. "It's time to put it in the hands of a collector instead of languishing away in a garage."

"Don't worry. I'll take good care of it."

Melody handed him the keys and returned to her Jeep to watch from a distance as he hooked chains to the axle and winched it onto the bed of the tow truck. In the morning light, she could see how the paint had oxidized in places, but beneath the layer of dust and faded wax, she could tell it would gleam. And if Justin could get it running . . .

Her heart jumped again at the thought of Justin and didn't stop its pounding the whole way back to his dad's house. She focused on the Hornet's bumper on the truck in front of her, tried to convince herself there was nothing to be nervous about. But she hadn't seen him or really heard from him in the week since their kiss—since she'd thrown herself at him.

She didn't have long to wait. When she pulled up behind the tow truck in front of a brick bungalow in a nice, old part of Washington Park, Justin was waiting on the front step with a steel travel mug in hand. He rose to his feet, and even at a distance, his presence put jitters in her stomach.

He met her halfway down the driveway as the truck driver let down the back end of the bed with a whirr of motors. "Hey there. Car looks better than I remembered."

She smiled. "I know. It gives me some hope for it."

He smiled back but kept his distance. "I've got what I need to get it started, I think. I'm anticipating finding some surprises once it's running. Hopefully it won't be too expensive."

"Give me the total of what you've already spent and I'll reimburse you right away."

"That's really not necessary."

"It's very necessary. You're doing me a favor, and you're already donating your time and energy. I'm not going to let you float the cost of the parts."

He looked like he still wanted to protest, but he finally nodded. "I'll total up the receipts and let you know. Two or three hundred so far."

"If we can get even close to twenty thousand from it, I'll consider that an excellent investment."

They watched the tow truck driver unload the vehicle close to the third bay of the garage in silence, but it wasn't a comfortable silence. Tension practically poured off Justin. This wasn't the flirtatious, fun-loving guy she'd been out with last weekend.

This was a guy who was blowing her off.

"I've got something for you," he said.

She blinked. "You do?"

"Yeah, hold on a minute." He turned and went back into the house, then came out with a big twine-handled paper bag. He passed it to her.

"What is this?" She dug into it and found half a dozen loaves of bread. Beautiful bread. Strikingly familiar bread.

"I ended my tour in San Francisco last night. You'd mentioned Noelle Patisserie, so I thought . . ." He shrugged. "Marin insisted on sending you these. I told them about your new place and they said they'd come by and see you if they were ever in Denver."

Melody inhaled the scent of fresh wheat and

yeast, immediately transported back to her time at Noelle Patisserie. They were more than a day old already, but she knew they would still be better than anything she had baked in the last several years. Jeff was a genius; she could only hope to approach his level of skill someday.

Impulsively, she set the bag down and threw her arms around Justin's neck. "Thank you. You have no idea what this means to me."

His arms went awkwardly around her, barely touching her. She drew away, confused. He'd done something incredibly nice for her, gone to a lot of trouble even—the bakery was nowhere near the airport—and now he didn't want credit for it? There was a guilty look on his face that made her stomach quiver again, this time not in a good way.

"It was nothing," he said. Almost like he was begging her to believe it.

Melody gathered herself and stepped back, hurt building inside her. Not that she had any reason to be hurt. He had never promised her anything. Never said he wanted to see her again. He hadn't initiated that kiss, even though he'd been fully committed to it.

Now he was realizing that it had all been a mistake. As was she.

She cleared her throat. "I appreciate it. Both the bread and the help with the car. Let me know when you have the total and I'll get you the money right away."

"Melody—"

"I've got to go. I've been up for twenty-one hours. Can barely keep my eyes open." She threw him a halfhearted smile, took her bag of bread, and walked to her Jeep without looking back.

When she passed through the door of her apartment a few minutes later, her eyes were still dry, but the weight in her chest had only grown. After her grandmother's empty house, Justin's rejection was one too many blows to her emotions. She pulled a bread knife from her drawer and carefully sliced the heel off one of the country loaves, then slathered it with good European butter. When she sank her teeth into it, she sighed.

She hadn't been exaggerating when she told Justin there was something elemental about good bread. Closing her eyes and savoring Jeff's creation took her back to a time when she was so filled with excitement about finding her calling that she would have rather worked than slept, and there were many times when she'd made that choice. It had been worth the sacrifice to find something that clicked. Something that she could stick to. Something that proved she wasn't the flighty, distracted screwup her mother made her out to be, but someone with real skills and talents.

A tear trickled from her lower lashes, and she

swiped it away angrily. She wouldn't cry over Justin. All this proved was that he wasn't the one for her, and he'd done her the favor of letting her know that early on. If Grandma Bev were here, she'd fix a stern glare on Melody for letting a temporary setback skew her perspective. *"When we let ourselves cry over things that weren't ours in the first place,"* she used to say, *"it's like telling God that we don't appreciate what He's actually given us."*

Melody rubbed her eyes dry and drew herself up with a deep breath. No more self-pity. She'd never been promised someone to spend her life with, someone to fill her heart. Maybe that's why she'd been given this passion for baking. Maybe that's why every relationship she'd had so far had ended in failure—because it was a distraction from her true life's work.

She ate one more slice of bread before she replaced the loaf in the bag and stumbled to her bedroom. In a couple of weeks, Justin would be out of her life. The car would be sold to a collector, and she'd be neck deep in her new venture. It was time for the hopeless dreamer to settle down and build something real and lasting.

It took several minutes to fall asleep, but by the time exhaustion took her, she almost believed it.

"Another one bites the dust." Melody slid into a seat at one of their favorite breakfast joints near

Coors Field late the next morning, a false note of perkiness in her voice.

Ana and Rachel stared at her. Both of them were still dressed for church, from where she assumed they'd just come. Melody had gotten off work at six, slept about four hours, and then dragged herself out for an emergency brunch meeting. It didn't matter. She'd slept on and off all day yesterday until it was time to go to work and throw herself into making the best bad bread she could.

"We have no idea what you're talking about," Ana said finally. "What bites the dust?"

"Another man. Justin. I think that's over."

Rachel sighed, her expression twisting in sympathy. "What happened? Things looked so promising."

"I think I read too much into it. And as usual, I rushed things. Kissed him. Figured the fact he kissed me back actually meant something." Melody picked up the menu and scanned it, even though she wasn't really seeing the words.

"What did he say exactly?" Ana's tone indicated she was going into full deconstructionist mode.

Melody told them about the bread and Justin's uncomfortable reaction. "It was weird. He's been so smooth and flirtatious from the moment we met. And all of a sudden it's like he found out something terrible about me."

"What a jerk," Ana said. "Talk about mixed signals."

"That's exactly what it is. Mixed signals." Melody shook her head. "Where is our server? I really need some coffee."

"Maybe he's just reluctant to get involved with you because you've got so much going on. Starting a restaurant and everything . . ."

Melody waved a hand. "Whatever. It doesn't matter. I'm over it."

Ana and Rachel exchanged a look.

"What? I am. It wasn't like we were together or anything. I'm fine."

Rachel leaned forward over her folded arms. "It's okay to be sad, Melody. Or upset. Or angry. You know you don't have to put on a brave face for us."

"Who's putting on a brave face? I've got much better things to worry about right now. Like the café."

"If you say so," Ana said, looking unconvinced.

"I do. If I'm going to be upset, I have much better reasons. Get this . . . my mom's already emptied out the house."

Now her friends got serious. Rachel's tone changed. "No. Are you okay?"

"I was shocked and a little hurt. I mean, it's not like she did anything wrong. That's what Grandma Bev told her to do, even gave her the contact information for a liquidator. I just wasn't expecting everything to change so fast."

"If there's one thing I've learned in the last year," Rachel said softly, "it's that change feels terrible at the time but can be really good in the end. I thought my life was over when I lost the restaurant. But you know what? Now I'd rather have a smaller, lower-profile place with one of my best friends than any fine-dining restaurant or big award. And I wouldn't be getting that if everything hadn't fallen apart."

The server finally arrived and took Melody's coffee request as well as their food orders. As soon as the woman bustled away, Melody picked up where they'd left off. "That's what I've been telling myself. I've always been so restless, I've been reluctant to commit to something like this. There's always the 'what if.' What if I want to travel? What if I meet a great guy? What if I want to do something else? But none of those things have happened. So why am I spending all my effort *not* having a life in case I get a life later? It's stupid."

Rachel smiled sympathetically. "It's human nature."

"It's stupid human nature. So I'm done with that. I'm excited about this café. It may not be Paris, but you know what? You guys aren't in Paris. So I'll bring a little Paris to Denver and we'll be feeding the souls of all those other people who dream of Europe and can't get there. That sounds like a worthy endeavor to me."

"Hear, hear," Ana said.

The server sped by long enough to leave Melody's coffee, and she raised her mug. "To new adventures, close to home."

"To new adventures," Rachel and Ana echoed, clinking their coffee mugs together. The pain in Melody's chest eased a degree. She didn't need anything else. She had her friends, and now she had a purpose. And if she kept putting one foot in front of the other, everything would work out the way it was supposed to in the end.

CHAPTER FIFTEEN

The next week passed with a steady, measured gait. Despite the brave face Melody had put on for her friends, Justin's rejection still stung. Not a deep wound; more like a paper cut she forgot about until she had to squeeze lemons, startling her that it still existed. Surprisingly, her feelings about her grandmother's passing were similarly dim; most days the grief was a shadow, lingering in the background.

So she did what she always did when she was avoiding something: she baked.

Not the fancy French pastries she was supposed to be testing for her future menu, but the comforting sweets of her childhood. Her Instagram feed filled up with gorgeous photos of her creations displayed alongside books, some of their links tenuous at best. Double chocolate cookies made with huge chunks of Valrhona chocolate found their American-Parisian mash-up reference in Alcott's *Little Women*. Currant cinnamon rolls as big as a baby's head were paired with *The Secret Garden*. Her lemon-blueberry muffins posed alongside a favorite childhood picture book, *Blueberries for Sal*. And while her Tumblr expanded in length, she carefully avoided the scale, sure that her emotional baking had expanded her in width as well.

When on Thursday afternoon she hit bottom on the big Cambros that held flour and granulated sugar, she decided enough was enough. She needed to do something else before she went into diabetic shock or stopped fitting into her extensive wardrobe.

Twenty minutes later, Melody stepped out the front door of her apartment building, dressed in jeans and a flowy crocheted sweater, her hair plaited in a thick braid over one shoulder. She hopped in her Jeep and headed to her favorite time-killing distraction—the section of South Broadway known as Antique Row. She found street parking a few blocks away from her favorite cluster of shops and climbed out of the Jeep, her oversize bag tossed over her shoulder. The warmth of the sun on her face cut through the cold air and began to evaporate her sullen mood.

She had to admit, she loved the hunt, even if items that had once been available for a bargain now climbed in price as the young, hip urban dwellers in the surrounding neighborhoods snapped up midcentury and Danish modern pieces to furnish their eclectically designed homes. Melody, fortunately, was far more interested in transformation than restoration.

The first two stores were a bust, yielding

nothing but mass-produced furniture from her mother's era. When she entered the third, the owner, an older woman named Georgia, popped up from behind the register. "Melody! I was hoping you'd come in. I have something to show you."

Georgia waddled out from behind the counter and gestured for Melody to follow her deeper into the dark shop. Melody smiled when she saw today's outfit: a long purple T-shirt and leggings printed with sunglass-wearing penguins. Georgia had dozens of pairs—lips, Christmas trees, rainbows, you name it—always combined with a tunic-length T-shirt that might or might not match. Today she'd paired the ensemble with neon-green running shoes.

"Here we go," Georgia said proudly, spreading her hands wide before a chandelier hanging from one of the shop's overhead beams.

Melody blinked. "That's . . . hideous."

"Isn't it?" Georgia could barely restrain her delight, clasping her hands to her ample bosom.

Melody circled to view the abomination from all sides. It was a five-armed chandelier with elongated lines and candle-style bulbs, none of which were particularly special. But the entire thing was covered in crawling vines and flowers and hanging naked baby cherubs, all painted garish shades that made her think of an *Alice in Wonderland*–style acid trip.

"It's perfect," she said. "How much?"

"Seventy-five."

Melody shot Georgia a look. "Fifty."

Georgia thought for a moment. "Okay. But just because it's you."

"Thank you." Melody fished two twenties and a ten from her wallet. "Can I pick it up on my way back to the car?"

"Of course, dear. And I want a photo when you're done. The moment I saw it, I thought, *If anyone can make over this monstrosity, it's Melody.*"

Hopefully Georgia's confidence wasn't misplaced. In her mind's eye, Melody could see it transformed by layers of pastel paint, rubbed off wet to show the different colors. . . .

She was halfway down the next block before she realized she'd missed her stop. She swiveled on her heel and returned to the little niche in the long building. But neither it nor the next several stops yielded anything even close to her earlier find, and all she really wanted to do was haul it home and begin the process of cleaning and stripping the varnish from its exterior.

Her stomach rumbled, reminding her that she'd eaten nothing but a leftover mini quiche when she left the bakery that morning. She turned off Broadway onto an intersecting street, one side of which were commercial spaces, the other side the backyards of houses. There were a few restaurants on South Broadway, but she had a particular destination in mind, just a couple blocks over on Old South Pearl.

Five minutes later, she pushed through the door of one of the quirkiest establishments in Denver: Gibraltar Mediterranean Bakery. The owner, Agni, was Greek, but her baked goods ranged from baklava to tiramisu. If you came in on the right day, she even had fresh Turkish delight under glass, fragrant with rosewater and lavender and pistachio, so far from the jellied abomination that passed for the sweet in most Western countries.

Agni was behind the counter when Melody entered amid the jingling of bells. She brightened as soon as she saw her. "Melody! I haven't seen you in weeks! Look, we have *kolache* today."

Melody chuckled. "Ran out of pastries from the Mediterranean, so you're moving north?"

"No, no. Customer request. Sweet Czech grandmother misses the tastes of her home. I said I would give it a try." Agni gave a shrug, her dark eyes sparkling.

"I'll have one then. And a cappuccino, please."

"Of course." Agni retrieved one of the jammy pastries from the case and put it on a plate, then turned away to pull the shot for Melody's cappuccino. Melody perused the rest of the selection behind the glass. Agni was a talented baker, with an uncanny ability to reproduce

216

traditional sweets from anywhere in the world. Except French. The simple—and yet utterly complex—croissant was the only thing she didn't do well.

Melody moved to the cash register, looking over the little baskets of tea balls and candied nuts. And then her eye fell on a printed sign in a plastic holder:

Thank you for your support of Gibraltar Mediterranean Bakery. I regret to say that because of family responsibilities, we will be closing permanently on May 1st. Please join us for a farewell party between ten a.m. and two p.m.

"You're closing?" Melody asked, unreasonably stricken by the news. "Why? How?"

"My mother is ill." Agni glanced over her shoulder. "I wanted her to move to Denver so I could care for her, but she refuses to leave. Says she was born in Greece and there she'll die."

"Is it that bad?" Melody asked in a hushed voice.

"Oh no. My mother is just dramatic. I think she is lonely and wants me to come back. But she is legitimately ill, so . . ." Agni shrugged again, the gesture holding volumes of meaning.

"That's such a shame. You can't hire someone to run it while you're gone?"

Agni brought the cappuccino in an oversize cup and saucer and placed it before Melody. "I am the baker. Who else would do this?"

Melody reached for Agni's hand and squeezed it. "I'm so sorry. You'll be missed. I know your customers must be heartbroken. You've been in the neighborhood for years."

"Life moves on. You must be ready to change with it or be crushed beneath it, yes?"

"I suppose you're right." Melody took out a ten-dollar bill and handed it over, then waited for her change. A guilty thought struck her. "What about the building?"

"The building." Agni's face screwed up in disapproval. "Three years left on the lease and I'm still negotiating an early release with my landlord."

"Could you sublet it?" Melody asked.

"Yes, but in less than a month? It's nearly impossible."

"How much is your rent?"

Agni cocked her head. "Why? Are you interested?"

Melody's pulse quickened. "Maybe. A friend and I are planning to open a bakery-café together and this could be a good location for us."

"Then come. Look." Agni waved Melody behind the counter and held the swinging door to the kitchen. "See for yourself."

Melody followed her in slowly. It was large and pristine, with clean cement floors and subway tiles stretching to the ceiling. Several ovens marked one wall; the walk-in stood opposite;

218

cooling racks waited alongside a massive Hobart mixer at the back; one long stainless-steel table stretched through the center of the room.

It was almost exactly how she would have set up her own space. "Does it have ventilation for a gas range?"

Agni shrugged. "I was told it could be put in over there. I use induction burners for anything that needs heated, so I never had it installed."

"How much is the rent?" Melody asked again.

Agni thought and then named a figure that was far less than what Melody had expected. She nodded coolly. "Let me call my friend and drink my coffee, and we'll talk more."

Away from Agni, she could barely contain a tremor of excitement. She took her kolache and cappuccino and found a table in the corner, then dialed Rachel. "You're never going to believe what just dropped into my lap. How fast can you get to Gibraltar Bakery?"

Rachel walked into the bakery exactly thirty minutes after Melody had called her, her expression puzzled. "I'm here. What's the urgency?"

Melody gestured to the table where she was drinking her second cappuccino. "This place is closing."

"That's too bad. I like her baklava." Rachel broke off a piece of the kolache on Melody's plate and took a bite. "I thought it was doing well."

"It is. But she has to go back to Greece and she's still got three years on the lease."

"Really." A hint of interest crept into Rachel's voice, even though her face remained blank. Melody had forgotten how implacable she got when she was in business mode. "It's a big space, probably bigger than she needed. Does she have a lunch menu or anything beyond sweets?"

Melody shook her head. "Just the bakery, though she does do a lot of corporate catering."

"Can we look at the kitchen?"

Melody caught Agni's eye, where she was ringing up a customer at the counter. She nodded and gestured with her head for them to go in. They slipped past her into the kitchen space, and Rachel began wandering around the room.

"We'd have to add a range. I need six burners and a flattop, plus whatever you need."

"Induction is better for me," Melody said. "More precise than gas."

"Is she willing to sell off her equipment at a discount?"

"Sounds like."

Rachel looked surprised, but continued her inspection: the ovens, the walk-in, the prep sinks. "We'd need a bigger dishwashing sink and probably a dish machine."

"Agreed. And I'd put in two more ovens,

especially if you're going to be using them in the morning."

"How much is the rent?"

Melody told her, and Rachel scowled. "What's the catch?"

"No catch that I can tell. The corner location has good traffic flow—I've been watching out the window while I waited—and she's already got an established clientele. If I keep her most popular sellers and then we add in the food, plus the bread, I think we'll easily do four thousand the first month."

"That seems low." Rachel fell silent, thinking. "Is she willing to let us look at her books? We're not buying her business per se, but if we're subletting the space and hoping to inherit her customers, I want some hard numbers to work from."

"You can look at whatever you like." Agni's voice came from behind them. She walked to Rachel and held out her hand. "Agni Christakis."

"Rachel Bishop."

Agni smiled. "I remember you. What do you think?"

"It's a nice space. We'd want to build out the kitchen a bit more so we can serve a hot menu and redesign the front of the house, but I can see it working for us. I'd want to talk to the landlord before we sign anything, see what his long-term plans are."

While Agni and Rachel were going on about leases and landlords and P&L statements, Melody studied the space, visualizing the changes. There was plenty of room for her breads and pastries. The walk-in was large enough to hold her pre-ferments and fillings without encroaching on Rachel's supplies or violating food safety regu-lations. She'd want a dedicated space by the ovens for proofing her dough and a sizable hardwood butcher block for working breads. Not inexpensive additions, but if they could get the equipment at a discounted rate from Agni . . .

". . . get back to you in a week or so if that's all right with you?" Rachel was saying.

"Absolutely. I leave for Greece on May 15, so I would prefer to have everything in place by then." Agni shook Rachel's hand, and Melody turned back to the duo. Agni smiled. "Somehow it feels like I would be leaving my neighborhood in good hands."

Her neighborhood. That's exactly the feel Melody had envisioned for her dream bakery: something that would be part of the community, woven into the fabric of the neighborhood's daily life. The thought of coming here to work every day, getting to know the customers and making new ones, sent a thrill of anticipation down her spine. Melody gave Agni a hug good-bye, then walked with Rachel out onto the sidewalk.

Rachel stepped off the curb and backed

away so she could view the entire storefront. Melody held her breath while she waited for the pronouncement.

"It's perfect," Rachel said finally. "Good location, but not overly trendy. Plenty of foot and drive-by traffic. And if we can sublet, we'll get a head start on our profitability. A place like this would cost us much more if we were to lease direct."

Melody let out her breath in a long exhale. "I think it's perfect too. I can just imagine us working here together."

"Let's not get ahead of ourselves. We've got the landlord to meet, a business plan to write up, and if we decide to go forward, all our permits and licenses to acquire before we can even get working on the build-out. I gave Agni my card, and she said she was going to e-mail me some information on her receipts and put me in touch with the landlord. I think I'll have Alex ask Mitchell's opinion on it too. That is, if you don't mind me running point on this."

"No, not at all." Rachel had the restaurateur experience, not to mention access to a big-time real estate developer friend of Alex's.

Her mind buzzing with the new possibilities, Melody picked up her chandelier from the antique store and went home to clean and prime it for its first coat of white. Too bad Rachel's taste leaned toward the modern-industrial vibe;

this would make a great piece for the entryway of the bakery. Who knew? Once Rachel saw it finished, maybe she'd be just as taken with the quirkiness of the piece and relent. After all, wasn't that what typified what they loved about European bakeries: the charm, the odd angles, the juxtaposition of modern and antique?

As she spray-painted the chandelier on a bed of newspaper on the front walkway of her apartment building, Melody imagined how she would make over Gibraltar's design. Vintage-inspired floors. Reclaimed-wood shelving along the far wall when you walked in, filled with locally made preserves. The quirky chandelier over the entryway, casting light on a marble-topped counter. Agni's place was nicely designed, but it could be so much more, an oasis from the city bustle.

While she waited for the primer to dry, she started compiling a new Pinterest board on her phone, pulling in some of Rachel's favorite industrial pins and combining them with a more rustic-vintage vibe. She sent her friend an invitation to join the new board and then sat back and smiled.

For the first time since her dreams about Justin had crashed and burned, she felt a spark of excitement. This creative outlet was exactly what she needed: the hard work, the knowledge that she and Rachel were building something beautiful and useful and worthwhile. Really, anything else in her life—men especially—was just icing, and contrary to popular opinion, she'd always been about the cake.

CHAPTER SIXTEEN

"So this is new." Melody slid into the tiny corner table of the unfamiliar coffee shop where Ana and Rachel waited. When she'd gotten the text with the name of the place, she'd drawn a blank, and she'd thought she knew every place to get caffeine in the city. "Are you in witness protection or something? Having to avoid our usual hangouts?"

Rachel laughed. "I'm between classes and this is close to campus. Besides, their coffee is pretty good."

"Right. I forgot. You're a college girl now. So what's the occasion? Sounded urgent."

"Not so much urgent. I just have news. Alex talked to Mitchell about the Gibraltar space."

Melody leaned forward. "What did he say?"

"He said Platt Park is a reasonably good location. Maybe fifty thousand impressions a day. Warned me not to get too secure in the lease rate we assume from Agni because he thought it might double by the time we go to sign a new one. Property values have skyrocketed in the last few years; the east side is already out of control with new development. He's predicting the southwest will be the next to go."

Melody lifted her eyebrows. "So that's added pressure for us to be profitable as soon as possible."

"It is," Ana said, "but it's also encouraging. Young professional homeowners with dual incomes mean lots of discretionary spending. Those are the ones who don't think twice about dropping ten bucks every morning on coffee and pastries on their way into work. Regulars like that keep a business afloat."

"On that note, this is what I've put together for sales estimates." Rachel pulled a printed sheet from a folder and passed them each a copy.

Melody's eyes widened. "These are some serious projections, Rach. Are you sure we can manage this? They seem optimistic to me, and you know I'm the biggest optimist of us all."

Ana was running her finger down the columns of numbers. "They might be aggressive, but Rachel's regained quite a following. We're still promoting the Saturday Night Supper Club on Instagram and Twitter, and even though it's not open to the public, it's spawned similar clubs all over the country." She pulled out her own file folder from her handbag and passed them each a stapled stack of papers. "Here's the competitive analysis."

Melody flipped through the papers. "Ana, this is thorough."

Rachel looked equally surprised. "You shouldn't

have done all this work. Or at least you have to let us pay you for it."

Ana waved a hand dismissively. "Nonsense. You're my friends, and I'm happy to do it. Besides, I had my assistant help me with the research."

"You won't get in trouble for using company resources?" Melody asked.

Ana snorted. "With the hours we work? No. One of the partners makes his assistant do his grocery shopping. Daphne is just grateful I'm capable of buying my own kombucha."

Melody scanned the section that listed all the competitors in the area. Ana had identified all the coffee shops, bakeries, and restaurants in a five-mile radius of Gibraltar, along with their menus, relative strengths and weaknesses, operating hours, and even somehow managed to come up with estimates of their annual revenue—no doubt the work of her hardworking assistant. There were several pages of summary at the end, clearly Ana's doing, that identified the current unexploited segments of the retail food market and how she thought their restaurant might be able to fill them.

"I think you've both missed your callings. And I'm beginning to feel like the dumb one in this trio."

"Yeah, but the dumb *pretty* one," Ana said with a wink.

Melody jostled her friend's arm. "Thanks a lot. And you're a liar because you're both prettier than I am." She held up her hand. "No arguing. It's a fact."

"Whatever." Ana rolled her eyes. "I just wanted to get these to you before you made your decision on the retail space. It's a big investment."

"It is. And now that Justin and I are on the outs, I have no idea when the car might be done. If it might be done."

"That's your property," Ana said with a frown. "If he's not going to work on it, he needs to give it back."

"No, I'm sure he will. I'm just being grumpy." She shouldn't have said anything. It was simply that he hadn't been far from Melody's mind, even as she worked on supply costs for the bakery. "So what's the next step?"

"I was going to ask you the same thing," Rachel said. "You've got the numbers. I laid out what our investments are going to be at each phase if we're splitting the business fifty-fifty. I need to know if you're in. If you are, we form our LLC, apply for business licenses, and begin negotiating the lease so we can start the renovation."

It had been one thing to talk about their business in terms of menus and design, another to talk about the legal tasks on the business side. Melody was suddenly, uncomfortably aware that she was putting every dollar she had—even if she hadn't had it for very long—into this venture.

"Mel, if you don't feel good about this—"

"No, that's not it. It's just a lot to process. It seems like it's moving so fast."

"It is moving fast," Rachel said. "This should have taken a lot longer, but that space you found is too good to pass up."

Melody let out a long, slow breath. "Okay. Let me look at it tonight and I'll get back to you."

"Great." Rachel rose and picked up Ana's folder. "I have to run and meet my group. This is going to be our accounting project. The advantages to going to school with a bunch of nineteen-year-olds—they do whatever I say." She saluted them with the folio, a wicked twinkle in her eye, and strode from the coffee shop with purpose.

Ana looked at Melody. "She's a little scary sometimes."

"And you've never worked for her." Melody looked around the coffee shop. "I think I'm going to grab something to drink. Can you stick around for a little bit?"

"Unfortunately, no. This is my lunch hour. I've got to get back." Ana hiked her purse over her shoulder and rose as well. "But I'll see you on Saturday."

"You know, some people actually eat lunch on their lunch hour."

"I'll eat when I'm dead."

"That's not how that saying goes!" Melody called after her, but she was already vanishing out the door. She looked back at the two reports in front of her, her heart slamming into her ribs. This was really happening. Her dream was coming true. Not the romantic, Pinterest-worthy fantasy she'd toyed with for years, but the real blood-sweat-and-tears, hard-work sort of dream. They would deposit huge chunks of money into a joint bank account. They'd sign a lease. They'd hire a contractor and watch that sum begin to dwindle. And then hopefully, if all Rachel's projections were right and they understood the neighborhood and came up with the perfect menu and worked Ana's promised marketing and promotion plan, maybe that account would start filling back up and they'd be able to draw decent salaries.

She pored over the paperwork for the rest of the afternoon. Weighed her options.

She could back out, take some of that money and travel like she'd considered doing just a few weeks ago.

She could bank it, use the money to help her get out of this apartment into something nicer, maybe fix up her grandmother's house.

Or she could trust Rachel's experience and her own instincts that said this would be a big hit. Put her inheritance into this risky venture. Plant roots here in Denver.

Should she do this, the part of herself that liked to keep her options open, dream about future possibilities, would have to take a backseat. She'd be committed.

It wasn't until she was in the third hour of her shift, shaping dough to bake bread she didn't even like, that she made her decision. She punched the buttons on her cell phone with floury fingers.

"Rachel, it's Melody. I'm in."

CHAPTER SEVENTEEN

After years of talk, they were actually doing this.

Justin knew he should feel more excited when he boarded the commercial flight in Denver; after all, he had always planned on owning his own company, and buying an existing charter was a shortcut through years of groundwork. But the closer they flew to the southernmost mainland state, the more knotted his stomach became.

Florida was beautiful; he could admit that. Their approach brought them over sapphire waters and white-sand beaches—not the worst scenery to call home. The seventy-degree weather certainly had an edge over Denver, which had flipped back into the thirties the day before they left. Of course, it was only April. He knew from past experience that by the time summer arrived with its oppressive humidity, he'd be missing the dry climate of Colorado.

But one couldn't have everything. While Colorado had its own thriving charter tourism industry, ferrying skiers and visitors from Denver into the high mountain ski resorts, it wasn't at sea level. And despite the fact they weren't talking about it, that was the primary reason both he and Pete were hoping this business worked out.

Pete had brought Jessica, not so much to

help evaluate the business as to evaluate her potential new home. That was one thing Justin didn't have—someone in his life with veto power. But when they met him on the jetway after disembarking from the 737, Jessica's eyes sparkled with excitement. "I've always loved Florida. Did you know that we're only a three-hour drive from Disney World?"

Justin chuckled. "Let's not get ahead of ourselves. It's not a cheap place to live, and we don't even know if this charter is a good buy."

"I know. And I will be telling myself that while I'm lying by the pool today, getting a tan." Jessica grinned at him, and Justin couldn't help but laugh again. It was nice to see her excited about something, acting like the woman he remembered. She had always been relentlessly upbeat, but he still could see the toll that keeping up with daily life took on her. At least, this trip would be a much needed vacation. At best, it would be a totally new start.

They rolled their carry-ons out to the ground transportation area, the warm, gently moist air enveloping them. Pete turned to his wife, reiterating a conversation they'd obviously had earlier. "You'll be okay going to the hotel by yourself? It doesn't make any sense for us to leave the airport, just to come back in an hour."

Jessica rolled her eyes and then stretched up to kiss Pete lightly on the lips. "I'm fine. Seriously.

If you can't find me when you come back, look at the pool or the bar. I've been craving a piña colada all week."

Justin grinned at Pete. "We may have to drag her away kicking and screaming tomorrow."

"No kids and nothing to do? You better believe I'm going to live it up." She turned her attention to the curb, where a white Hyundai was pulling up. "This is my Uber. Let's see if he can drop you at the FBO."

They piled their suitcases into the trunk, and Pete negotiated the extra stop with the driver in rapid, confident Spanish. Justin only caught a handful of words—he'd naively studied German in high school and college, which so far had only come in handy for reading labels on imported beer.

The charter company was headquartered on the other end of the airport from the commercial terminals, separated by a fairly significant distance. All things considered, it wasn't much different than Centennial or any of the other GA airports he visited for work.

The FBO—fixed-base operator, the company that provided services to private and corporate pilots alike—was a huge, modern building that looked more like the headquarters of a tech company than an aviation facility, all stucco and glass with tropical landscaping. The Uber driver dropped them off in front of the double glass doors, pausing barely long enough for Pete to kiss Jessica good-bye and make her promise to have the bellman help her with all the suitcases.

The FBO's interior was just as posh, with soaring two-story ceilings held up by columns and walls of windows looking out onto the runways. Seating areas screened by potted plants gave passengers a quiet place to sit and relax while they waited for their flights. Justin knew from passing through here for work that there was also a gym, a crew room, and sleeping areas for pilots, not to mention the adjacent customs facility for travelers going to and from the islands.

Pete walked to the customer service desk, where a pretty, professionally dressed Latina sat behind the high counter. "We're here to see Luis Garcia at South Beach Charters."

"They're at the end of the building, upper floor. But I'd be happy to call up for you." She smiled, her gaze lingering on Justin. "Names?"

Pete cleared his throat. "I'm Pete Costa; this is Justin Keller."

The woman picked up the phone and spoke softly into the handset, then hung up and smiled at both of them this time. "Mr. Garcia will be down in a couple of minutes. You can have a seat over there while you wait."

"Thank you . . ." Justin leaned over to check the name tag on her blouse. "Alicia."

"You're quite welcome, Justin." She gave him a flirtatious look before going back to her computer monitor, but he saw her dart a few more glances their way while they moved to the leather sofa.

"You're unbelievable," Pete said, more admiring than annoyed. "You just can't turn it off, can you?"

"What do you mean? I'm just being friendly."

"The kind of friendly that has her thinking about slipping you her number."

"Not interested," Justin said. And meant it.

Pete stared at him. "Are you feeling okay?"

"I'm fine. I just didn't come here to pick up women. Business trip, remember?"

"Never stopped you before."

"It *always* stopped me before." Justin scowled at Pete, not sure why he was so irritated by the exchange. He did tend to flirt. It came as naturally as breathing, and it smoothed his way in daily life. Need to ask a heinous favor from the CSR? Make her feel like the only woman in the world; smile while looking into her eyes. Late returning the courtesy car? Bring back lunch. Of course, the lunch thing worked with the men, too, but the women tended to be more appreciative.

Did that make him shallow? Or just pragmatic?

No wonder Melody hated him right now. He'd done the exact same thing to her, then switched off just as easily, even though he hadn't actually been trying to manipulate her.

"Hello? Where'd you go?"

Justin started back to the present. "Nowhere. Why?"

"You're thinking about that girl, aren't you?"

Justin went for evasion. "What girl?"

"The Hornet girl. Dad told Jessica, who of course speculated all night about who she might be."

"She's just a friend," Justin said. "I'm possibly moving to Florida. Doesn't make sense to get involved with someone right now."

"But you would get involved with her if you knew you were staying in Denver?"

"I'm sorry, Jessica, what did you say?"

Pete chuckled. "Fine, fine. I'll back off. But you're awfully defensive about someone who's just a friend."

Justin was preparing a retort when he was saved by the approach of a man wearing pressed slacks and a button-down shirt, his salt-and-pepper hair and sun-weathered face putting him somewhere in his sixties. This must be Luis Garcia. Justin already knew he was a retired airline pilot himself who had gone to the charter side nearly two decades ago after making his fortune in south Florida real estate. The e-mails from the broker had given him the feeling that the charter was more of a hobby than anything else.

"Justin, Pete, I'm Luis. Pleasure to meet you both. Pleasant flight from Denver, I hope?"

Justin smiled and shook his hand. "It was, considering I wasn't flying the plane."

Luis chuckled. "And it bothered you the entire time. Follow me, if you would. We're supposed to go over the paperwork, but we both know you really want to see the fleet. I figured I'd just send you back a packet to review with your lawyer, if that's all right with you."

"Fine with me," Pete said.

It was definitely the more interesting part of the trip, but Justin knew there was far more to the viability of the business than just the equipment. "Before I go, I'll want to talk to your pilot-in-charge about scheduling and routing and the flight planning system."

"That would be me. I can answer any questions you have. In the meantime, let's go to the hangar."

For the next four hours, they combed over the two planes housed in the charter's leased hangars, accompanied by Luis and his chief mechanic. The third was currently in flight, leaving a Beechcraft Baron G58 and the Pilatus turboprop. From everything that Pete and Justin could tell, they were impeccably maintained, with upgraded flight decks and newly refurbished interiors. Luis was going after the luxury charter market and, if his numbers checked out, succeeding at it. He easily recited figures and statistics from the top of his head in answer to Justin's questions.

It quickly became obvious that Luis wasn't part of the company—he *was* the company. Only then did Justin begin to understand the full scope of his responsibilities should they go forward.

They parted ways with the promise to return early the next morning for a test flight and a look at the remaining G58 before they returned to Denver, then made their way back through the FBO to where another Uber waited out front.

"So what do you think?" Pete asked as soon as they were headed to the hotel.

Justin answered slowly. "I can't find anything wrong with it. The planes are gorgeous. An easy sell to customers. If you think they've been properly maintained . . ."

"From what I can tell, they have been. The chief mechanic knows what he's doing. Everything tells me that it's on the up and up."

"But it's still overpriced," Justin said. "We need to get our lawyer to dig into the books. Do some more research. Probably one more trip."

"Right." Pete visibly deflated. Guilt washed over Justin, but he wasn't about to ignore what a huge undertaking this would be. Then again, he wasn't watching his wife's health slowly decline with each passing day. Pete had a big reason for wanting to make this work, even while Justin had his own for wanting it to fall through.

Melody.

Somehow it always came back to her. He'd

known her for a couple of weeks; they'd seen each other exactly four times. And yet he couldn't stop thinking about her. Her easy laugh. The way her brown eyes sparkled when she got excited about something. The feel of her in his arms. Even now, as the car slid along the highway, the sunset drenching the coastline in warm color, he couldn't help but wonder if she liked the beach, what she would think about living in a place like this.

He'd dated Sarah for six months and never once had she distracted him like this.

But Melody was different. Freer. More alive. When he was with her, he felt like he'd known her forever, and yet he knew he'd barely scratched the surface.

He was preoccupied at dinner, and he begged off the excursion to check out Fort Lauderdale's nightlife, instead sitting in front of the TV in his room, remembering the hurt look on Melody's face when he'd blown her off. Right now she was either hating him for being an indecisive jerk or wondering what she'd done to cause such a rapid-fire flip of his attentions. He'd been completely unfair to her.

There was only one answer. When he got back, he had to tell her everything.

CHAPTER EIGHTEEN

Rachel wasted no time getting started on their new project. They hadn't yet decided on a name for their restaurant, so after a half-dozen calls yielded no progress, she registered their new business as "RM Ventures LLC" with the idea that it could encompass their initial bakery-café plus any expansion they did in the future. That same afternoon, they opened a joint checking account for the business, each making an initial deposit of five thousand dollars.

The next step was to secure Gibraltar's retail space. Melody was happy to leave that job to Rachel, who began the process of talking to Agni, the landlord, the agent brokering the deal, and the lawyer she'd worked with when she secured Paisley's location. Melody assumed this project would be on hold while they sorted out the details, but to her surprise, less than two weeks later, she was sitting in the leasing agent's office, signing her name on the dotted line beneath Rachel's.

"That was anticlimactic," she admitted to her friend minutes later as they waited for the elevator to the bottom floor. "It seems like there should be more to signing your life away."

Rachel just laughed, beaming with excitement.

"This isn't the first time I've done it, so it doesn't feel like a huge deal. When we signed for the space for Paisley, I just about panicked. Maurice had to hand me a paper bag."

Somehow Melody couldn't imagine Rachel panicking over anything restaurant-related. She stepped onto the elevator and waited for her friend—and now partner—to follow before she punched the ground floor button. "So, what now?"

"We'll want to get the contractor out there to take a look at the space and get us a bid on the changes, particularly the ventilation. I'll coordinate that with Agni. Then we'll need to get our building permits, start the build-out, get our certificate of occupancy and final business licenses. I'm assuming we're going to forgo the liquor license?"

"Right. I don't see any reason to serve alcohol if we're closing at six. And it's one less element to worry about."

"Good. Let me make some calls and I'll e-mail what I need you to do." Rachel's smile turned a little crafty. "It wouldn't hurt to have you work up some design ideas in the meantime. . . ."

Melody's own smile returned. "I'll make you some sample boards. I've already pinned hundreds of ideas on Pinterest. It's just a matter of what's going to look best in the space."

"Better get to it. Not to mention narrowing down your menu—"

243

"Already on that. I've had to throw out some of my best recipes because they're just too expensive."

"Thinking like an owner. I like it."

The elevator delivered them to the bottom floor, and after a quick hug, Melody and Rachel went their separate directions. It was still only two o'clock, which meant if she didn't delay, she would have enough time to test another recipe or two before she went to work.

Melody had been toying with the idea of putting éclairs on the menu ever since they came up with the bakery-café idea. It was a traditional pastry that didn't get much love from serious chefs—the sweet equivalent of the iceberg salad, tired and uninspired. But it didn't have to be.

Not that this was solely her idea. She might currently be mired in mediocrity, but she'd kept up with the pastry trends on the coasts and overseas. New York was exploding with exciting variations on traditional patisserie, most of which had not yet made their way west to the Rockies.

By the time she got home, she was already planning out her afternoon for maximum efficiency. She dropped her purse on the sofa, changed out of her professional clothes, pulled on an apron, and got to work.

The pastry came first. If cooks had their mother sauces, pastry chefs had their mother doughs, and *pâte à choux* was the grand dame among them. It was one of the first things she'd learned to make and still one of her favorites. There was magic in the way the dough went together, butter and flour and salt, cooked until the raw flavor of the flour disappeared, but not so much that it went dry and crumbly. Then four or five eggs got added one at a time until it transformed into a thick batter. It was traditional to beat it by hand, but Melody had learned long ago she got more consistent results with far less effort by using a stand mixer. Then she spooned the batter into a piping bag fitted with a star tip and piped long, uniform lines of dough onto a parchment-lined baking sheet.

As soon as those went into the oven, she began to concoct her flavors. A maple-and-vanilla crème that would be topped with a maple glaze and bacon bits. A lemon curd topped with toasted meringue, the filling for which was already prepared and jarred in her fridge from her lemon bar experiment earlier that week. A cardamom-scented custard paired with a brûléed sugar glaze. She had so many ideas that she could conceivably make a different variation every day.

Which, when she thought about it, wasn't a bad idea. Daily specials could build their roster of regulars. Croissant of the day in the morning, and then éclair of the day in the afternoon. She jotted the idea on a notepad and peeked on the shells. They were beautifully puffed and browned, an undulating light-dark pattern on the exterior from the ridges of piped dough. She shut off the oven and propped open the door with a wooden spoon to cool. If she let them sit in their own steam, they'd get soggy and lose that beautifully crisp exterior.

She was filling and glazing her second set of éclairs when her phone jangled to life several feet away. Justin's number flashed onto the screen, and she looked down at her sticky hands in dismay. Finally she answered the call with the clean knuckle of her ring finger and tapped the speaker icon.

"Hey, Justin." She bent over the countertop so he could hear her, proud that her tone sounded so steady and nonchalant.

"Did I catch you at a bad time?"

"Not really. I'm testing recipes. What's up?"

"I have the first-round totals for you. It's a bit more than I originally thought. With the parts I've already purchased, including the new water pump, it's going to be $362. I know that's a little high—"

"No, no, it's okay. It's well worth it. Can I drop it by your place later? I'm in the middle of something right now."

"Would you rather I come by your apartment and pick it up? It's no problem."

The unexpected offer made her breath catch. She'd already abandoned any real hope of romance with him, but that didn't sound like an offer a guy would make when he was anxious to get rid of her. Unless of course he just wanted to ensure he got his money quickly. She wasn't sure which was worse—how fast her hope deflated or the fact it existed in the first place.

But she managed not to let those thoughts surface in her voice. "If you wouldn't mind? You'd save me some time."

"Sure. I'll be over there in a bit. See you then."

Melody ended the call and stared at her phone for a minute. "Don't get your hopes up. Don't have any hopes in the first place. And whatever you do, do not go change your clothes for him."

She was totally going to change her clothes for him.

But first she was going to finish the maple éclairs before the rapidly hardening glaze became unusable. When she'd finished piping flavored whipped cream into the pastry and dipped each oblong into the glaze, she scrubbed her hands and practically ran to the bedroom to change out of her sweatshirt. The leggings could stay, but she pulled on a more figure-flattering top, a knit tunic that slid off one shoulder. She quickly braided her long hair over one shoulder and secured it with an elastic.

She had turned to the lemon variation when the intercom buzzed. She rushed to the door and pushed the button. "Hello?"

Justin's voice came through the speaker. "It's me."

Two simple words that sent her heart fluttering like a demented butterfly. She punched the button to unlock the front door and paced until his knock came. She didn't even play it cool by waiting a couple of seconds to open the door. "Hi."

"Hi yourself. Something smells good."

"I'm experimenting. You're just in time to taste test." She went back to the kitchen like she didn't care if he followed, even though every nerve ending was on alert, attuned to his presence.

"I take it that means plans for the restaurant are moving along?"

"We've got an LLC, a bank account, and a really expensive lease for a large and intimidating retail space."

He smiled. "I'm so happy for you. When do you open?"

"Early summer, I think. Everything is just falling into place. It's a little unsettling, actually."

"That's great." He stood awkwardly in the middle of her kitchen, and she remembered belatedly why he was there.

"Right, the money. Hold on."

He started to protest that he was in no rush, but she was already in her bedroom, digging into the lining of the suitcase under her bed where she kept her emergency stash. Call her paranoid or just used to being on the move, but she hated the idea of not having enough cash to escape town at a moment's notice. She came back and pressed four hundred-dollar bills into his hand.

"This is too much—"

"No arguing. Call it a tip. Have dinner on me one night as my thanks for the favor."

He nodded and shoved the money in his pocket, but his eyes never left her face. She shifted uncomfortably and nodded back toward the kitchen. "Got a minute? I could use your opinion."

He relaxed. "Sure. What are you making?"

She explained the traditional éclair recipe and her plan to spin off modern variations inspired by classic sweets. "I want you to tell me what you think of when you taste them."

She led him to the counter and handed him one of the maple éclairs. He took a bite and sighed, a slight smile tipping up the corners of his mouth. "This is good. Maple bar donut, right? But so much better . . ." He took another bite and then finished it with a third. "I would happily eat those all day long."

"Pace yourself. These are like a billion calories." She handed him the crème brûlée next.

"Mmm, this is good too, but it tastes like a regular éclair. Except the crunchy topping. What is that? Sugar? Like those things you burn with a torch?"

"Crème brûlée, yes." He got it, but the words

regular éclair had her crossing those off the list immediately.

"I haven't finished these last ones. You need to taste this all together." She cut a piece of unfilled éclair with the side of a spoon, then scooped it up with a bit of the cold lemon curd and the fluffy, not-quite-set meringue. She lifted it to his mouth, and his fingertips rested on her hand to steady the spoon while he tasted it.

"That's what lemon meringue pie tastes like in heaven," he said.

"I'd hoped you would say that. This is easily my favorite out of the three."

His fingers were still holding her hand, and their eyes locked with a sudden hum of energy. Melody slowly lowered the spoon to the counter, but he didn't let her go.

"Melody, I'm sorry about the other day. I handled it badly. I didn't mean—"

She shook her head. "It's okay. I'm sorry. I read too much into our date. And that kiss."

"No," he said softly. "You didn't." He reached out and tucked a stray piece of hair behind her ear, sending tingles across her skin. The impulse to step closer was almost irresistible, the pull of two magnets together, but she refused. She'd rushed things before. She wasn't going to be the one to make the first move this time.

But he made no move at all, and the way his eyebrows drew together suggested worry. "I thought I was doing the right thing for both of us. Putting an end to things before anyone could get hurt." He paused, and his voice came out husky when he spoke again. "But no matter what I do, I can't stop thinking about you."

She looked up at him, simultaneously thrilled by his words and utterly confused. "I don't understand. We haven't really even gotten started. Why would you want to end things already?"

He dropped his hand and looked away. "Melody, I need to tell you something."

The words sent chills, not the good kind, straight down her spine. Her chest tightened on the inhale. "Please tell me you're not married."

"No. No! Nothing like that."

"Okay," she said, moving toward her dining set. "Then tell me."

As soon as they were seated across from each other, safely separated by an expanse of table, Justin began to tell her about his sister who had multiple sclerosis and his plan to buy a charter business in Florida with his brother-in-law. Melody struggled to keep up, having been sure that this was going to be a way of letting her down easy or telling her why they couldn't be together.

Which she supposed it was, but when he was done, she just stared at him. He hadn't blown her off because he wasn't interested. He'd been trying to do the right thing. It would have been easier to just tell her from the start, of course, but she gave him points for truthfulness now. And then, unexpectedly, a smile split her face. "You're *buying* a charter business to the *Bahamas?* That is unbelievably cool."

He blinked at her. "It is, but . . . it's in Florida. Not here."

"I know."

"So you see why it's a bad idea for us to get involved. I can already tell you take dating seriously, and if there's no future for us . . ."

Melody leaned back against her chair. "Do you like me?"

"Yes, of course I like you. I more than like you, if that kiss didn't tip you off."

Hope bloomed in her chest, unreasonable and thrilling. "Then why overcomplicate things? You're here for three months or however long it takes to get your business under way. We could end things now, or we could enjoy the time we have together and see where it takes us."

Justin frowned. "That's really not what I expected you to say."

"Listen, I figure one of three things will happen." Melody held up her hand and ticked off points on her fingers. "One, our odd schedules will become a problem and we'll fizzle out naturally. Two, one of us will discover a deal breaker and the time frame won't matter anyway. Or three, we're still going strong when it's time for you to leave and we have to decide what to do then."

"And that's really okay with you." Justin stared at her like he couldn't quite tell if she was serious or not.

"No, it's not *okay* with me. But it's better than walking out of each other's lives right now, don't you think?"

A smile tugged on the corner of his mouth. "I've never met anyone quite like you, Melody."

"That's exactly why you shouldn't let me get away so easily."

"Believe me, I don't intend to. I am, however, wishing I'd talked to you sooner. I'm leaving tomorrow for a week. I don't suppose I could talk you into spending the rest of the afternoon with me?"

Melody cast a doubtful look at her kitchen. "Right now, I need to get back to my éclairs."

"Are you sure?" He leaned forward and took her chin in his hand, then brushed his lips against hers in a feathery kiss she felt down to her very toes.

"No fair," she whispered.

"Who said I played fair?"

She wavered for a long moment. It wasn't like she needed to finish the éclairs. They were simply a test, and she already knew which ones had made the cut.

"Okay," she said finally. "If I get to choose."

He smiled again, his eyes crinkling at the corners. "Lead on."

CHAPTER NINETEEN

"A bookstore?" Justin didn't mean for his dismay to show in his voice when he pulled up in front of the address Melody had given him, but it escaped all the same. When she told him she wanted him to experience one of her favorite spots in the city, he'd thought a restaurant, a park, maybe even a museum . . .

Melody laughed, though, apparently unoffended. "Not just any bookstore. Rare books."

"So you're saying I'm not going to find any Clancy or Child here?"

"No, but they do have a pretty impressive aviation section. . . ." Her voice trailed off enticingly. Okay, so that did sound interesting. It wasn't as if he didn't read—he usually had a magazine or a nonfiction book in his flight case for layovers. It was just that bookstores typically frowned on patrons stealing kisses in dark corners, and that idea had figured prominently in every variation of this afternoon he'd considered.

But if this was how she wanted to spend her day, he wouldn't complain. She'd accepted him back without any question after he'd been a total jerk. He'd do anything she wanted to prove he was sorry. He sent her a wink. "I'll follow you, then. You can broaden my horizons."

Pink rose to her cheeks, a sign she'd taken his flirtation exactly as he'd intended, and she levered the door open before he could circle around to do it for her. He took her hand, found it cold, and pulled it into his coat pocket, forcing her to move against his side. When she threw a smile up at him, he amended his earlier judgment. This might not be so bad after all.

Justin followed her into the charming square of small boutiques, surrounded by what would be a greenbelt were it later in the year, then down a set of cement steps to the lower level, where the bookstore lay. He pulled open the heavy wood door with the tinkle of bells and let Melody precede him into the warm interior.

An older gentleman in a fisherman knit sweater looked up from his book at the counter, his face breaking into a smile. "Melody! You're back! So nice to see you."

"You too, Thomas. I brought a friend today. Justin, this is Thomas. Thomas, Justin."

Justin smiled and nodded hello, aware the man was looking him over critically. Apparently Melody spent a lot of time here if the shopkeeper was acting like a grandfather vetting his favorite granddaughter's new boyfriend.

Melody stepped in quickly. "Justin's a pilot. I thought he might be interested in those books you bought last time."

255

"You know where to find them, dear. Nothing in particular for you today?"

"Not unless anything new has come in. . . ."

Thomas shook his head. "Came across a Harper edition from 1967, but it was in pretty poor shape. You're not interested in reprints anyway."

Melody shook her head. "I'll just browse then, thanks."

Justin's brow furrowed as they walked deeper into the bookstore, and he pitched his voice low. "What was that about?"

"A personal quest, I guess. I've been after a yellowback edition of *Far from the Madding Crowd* for years now. It's become my white whale."

"Okay, that reference I got. But what's a yellowback?"

"It was a fiberboard-bound book that they used to sell at Victorian railway book stalls. They had these amazing illustrated covers and some sort of advertisement on the back. They're exceedingly difficult to find now. Thomas has been on the hunt for a while. Of course, it would cost me a couple months' rent if he did actually find one. It would be a bit like finding your paperback Lee Child a hundred and twenty years from now."

Melody wandered past a little reading nook with antique wingbacks and an Oriental rug. Despite its modern exterior, the store had the feel of a private library in some crumbling manor home. He could see why Melody liked to escape into the store's paper-scented hush.

"How did you get into all this anyway?"

"Raised by a lit professor, remember? As a kid, I didn't read *The Magic School Bus*; I read the Grimms' and Perrault's fairy tales. Other teens read these high school romance paperbacks, and I was reading Victorian and Gothic classics. It stuck, I suppose." She paused in front of a shelf, ran her fingertips along the spines, and tipped one out for a moment before replacing it.

"So why is this particular book your white whale out of the hundreds you've read?"

She looked back at him. "I don't know. It's completely contrary to itself. It's a tragedy with a happy ending. It's pastoral and macabre at the same time. The heroine is an independent woman, but it's hard to call her feminist when she's constantly at the mercy of men and her own poor choices." Melody shook her head. "I think my reading of it has changed over the years. Maybe that's why I still love it. It's not the same because I'm not the same."

The flush came back to her cheeks, and she averted her eyes. "And now you're sorry you asked."

Justin smiled and tilted her chin up so she had to look at him. "I'm actually thinking I might be too dumb to date you."

That pensive expression disappeared in a flash, and she laughed. "Don't worry. I still waste afternoons watching cat videos on YouTube." She grabbed his hand. "Come see this. . . ."

She dragged him confidently through the shop, winding around shelves and past more reading niches, then stopped. Justin perused the titles: mostly modern warplane encyclopedias, but Melody went straight to several slim, cloth-bound volumes and pulled one out.

Spanning the Pacific by John Prentice Langley. He cracked the cover and saw the publication date: 1927. "This is kind of cool. These are novels?"

"Yes, I think so. There's a whole series of them. When I was in here last, Thomas was buying these from a private collector."

Justin knelt by the shelf and pulled out the other matching volumes. He wouldn't say it to Melody, but these books weren't really his thing. His dad, on the other hand, had a ridiculously extensive aviation library. He'd get a kick out of vintage dime-store novels. "I'll get them. They'll make the perfect retirement gift for my dad."

"I didn't mean to pressure you into it. . . ."

"You didn't. Now, I somehow don't believe you're done browsing."

She grinned. "Not remotely. Are you game?"

"I'm good. Don't let me stop you."

She didn't, winding her way through the

shelves, oohing and aahing over different editions of books she already owned, which apparently included seven copies of *Madding Crowd*. "What can I say? I know what I like."

Justin just watched her, cataloging the expressions flitting across her face from delighted to disappointed. He should be bored, but he wasn't. He felt like he was seeing the real Melody Johansson for the first time, the one who would be content to curl up with a book for hours and lose herself in stories. When she came across a copy of a first-edition paperback of Goldman's *The Princess Bride* and clasped it to her chest, he thought for a moment she had found her white whale. The look on her face when she replaced it on the shelf said it all.

"You really want that, don't you?"

Melody just gave an embarrassed shrug. "It's not what I came here for."

Justin pulled it off the shelf and added it to his stack.

"Justin, you can't! That's an eighty-dollar paperback!"

"Eighty?" He barely managed to keep his eyes from bugging out. "That's okay. We'll just be having tacos for dinner instead."

"No, I'm taking you out someplace good after this." She paused. "Seriously, Justin, you don't have to do this. I'll survive. It's not like I don't already have two copies at home. Of course neither of them are first editions, but . . ."

"Really? That's supposed to be persuasive?"

Melody caught her bottom lip between her teeth. "Well, maybe I'm not trying to be *that* persuasive."

He laughed. "Come on. I better pay before your guilt overcomes your collecting frenzy."

When they returned to the counter, Thomas again put down his book and studied them over the top of his glasses. "That was quick. I figured you'd spend another hour vacillating over your purchases."

"She would have if I'd let her. But who am I to argue with a first-edition paperback of a modern classic?"

Thomas's expression turned approving. "Forget diamonds. Books are this girl's best friend."

"I'm finding that out." He shot Melody an amused look and handed over his credit card. Once again he managed not to flinch at the total— apparently this was a pretty substantial gift for his father, too—and waited while Thomas wrapped each book in tissue paper and sealed it with a gold foil sticker. All except Melody's book, which he handed directly to her, unwrapped in a second bag.

"Thanks, Thomas. You know me too well."

"And now I'm beginning to," Justin murmured as they made their way out the door. They hadn't made it two steps before she turned and tugged him to face her.

"Thank you," she said quietly. "That was very extravagant."

"Call it an apology for being an idiot."

A smile tipped up the corner of her mouth. "You seem to have a talent for grand gestures. First the bread and now the book?"

"As long as you don't tell me you also have a passion for exotic sports cars, I think we're good."

"No worries on that account. You're the one with the car problem. So consider this my thank-you." She stretched up and pressed a light kiss to his lips, but when she tried to back away, he held her fast. It didn't matter that they were standing in a public walkway or that the air was cold enough to make his fingertips numb. He brushed a stray tendril of hair behind her ear and looked into her eyes for a long moment.

"What?" Her voice came out breathless, anticipatory.

In response, he bent to cover her mouth with his own, gently, far more patiently than he actually felt. The last thing he wanted to convey was that he was after the perks of a temporary relationship. No, if their first kiss was heated, this one was sweet, as if they had all the time in the world to discover each other.

When they parted, she looked up at him with an expression verging on wonder and cleared her throat. "Hungry?"

"I most certainly am." It came out huskier than

he intended, laced with an unintended hint of innuendo.

That little spot of pink appeared on each cheek again. "I know just the spot for dinner, then."

And when she took his hand and interlaced her fingers with his, he was surprised once again to find how much he liked it.

CHAPTER TWENTY

Melody directed Justin through the city to one of her favorite restaurants just off the 16th Street Mall, a long outdoor promenade with a full complement of stores and restaurants. The warmth of Justin's hand and the filtered afternoon sunshine drugged her with a drowsy feeling of well-being. She marveled at how simply, uncomplicatedly happy she felt at this moment. She had always felt everything intensely; hadn't she come to fear that fast, fierce attraction to a man as a sign things would burn out just as spectacularly? But never had she met someone who could light her up with his touch and still make her feel this safe and comfortable.

Justin pulled up at the valet stand in front of the restaurant she indicated. "Asian again?"

Melody blinked. She hadn't intentionally stayed away from her usual European and American picks, but now that she thought about it, she was craving something other than the food she'd been immersed in for weeks. "If you'd rather go somewhere else . . ."

"No, this is fine. I just thought you might be trying to feed me fish heads for real this time."

Melody laughed as the attendant approached

and opened her door. "Nothing that can look back at you, I promise."

Inside, the restaurant was just beginning their first seating, half the tables already filled. The hostess led them to a spot by the window in the far corner, close to the kitchen. Melody took that to mean it was one of the few unreserved tables, the worst in the house, but she didn't mind the location. The faint clatter of cooking was oddly comforting, and from here she could watch both the patrons coming in and the passersby on the street.

Which was a silly thought: when Justin was seated across from her, he filled all her attention. The restaurant around them might as well not have existed.

Melody did know the restaurant, but she didn't take control of the ordering this time. Instead, they chose a handful of small plates to share. When Justin ordered a cocktail, she blinked at him. "Don't you have to fly tomorrow?"

"I pick up my plane in Detroit, so I'm technically not on the clock until noon."

"So you have until midnight until you turn into a pumpkin?"

"Something like that."

The food came out soon after their drinks, but they lingered over the dishes, almost unconsciously stretching out the meal. "So I'm curious," Melody said finally. "You talk about your dad all the time, but you never mention your mom. What's the story there? I know you said they were divorced. Do you see her?"

"Not often. They co-parented pretty amicably when my sister and I were kids. When I was seventeen, she got married and moved out of state. We don't really talk much now. I haven't seen her in years."

Melody sensed there was far more beneath those words than he was willing to tell, but she didn't press. Instead, she said lightly, "If only I could be so lucky. My mother likes to show up randomly, criticize everything about my life, and then run back to Nashville so she doesn't have to deal with the fallout."

"What does she get out of it?"

"Beats me. My mom never really got the nurturing gene. That was my grandmother. Most of the time I felt like a photo op to my mom. Not now, of course. An underemployed adult baker is a lot less cute than a little girl with ringlets and missing teeth. I mean, for heaven's sake, she named me *Melody*. From the start, I was meant to be an accessory."

Justin watched her with a sympathetic look. "Are you ever going to tell me who she is?"

"You mean you haven't googled it? My name would probably bring her up."

"It felt invasive. I figured if you wanted to tell me, you would."

Melody sipped her cocktail and considered. What did it hurt, really? "My mother is the incomparable Janna Leigh."

Justin stared at her blankly.

"She's a platinum recording artist? Hosted this year's Academy of Country Music Awards on TV?" And half a dozen other things, for good reason. Janna Leigh might not have been a great mother—or any kind of mother at all—but she was a talented songwriter, a gifted singer, and an engaging performer.

Justin simply shrugged. "The name sounds familiar, but I'm not sure it's because of her music."

Melody laughed. "Wouldn't she love to hear that."

"What about your dad? Is he around?"

"My father lives in Sweden and I haven't seen him since I was thirteen. He sends me flowers on my birthday and a piece of jewelry or something at Christmas."

Justin reached for her hand. "I'm sorry."

"I'm not. Hard to miss something you've never had. Honestly, the idea of two artists in one house was doomed to failure." At his quizzical look, she said, "My dad is Magnus Johansson. You've probably seen some of his films."

His eyes got wide. "He made *Stockholm*. It was an amazing film."

"It was. There's a reason why everyone calls

266

him the Swedish Roman Polanski. Minus the nasty proclivities and flight from prosecution, of course."

"You didn't really have a chance, did you?"

Melody laughed, hearing her bitterness reflected back at her. "At being normal? Not a single one."

"At being anything but an artist. Passionate. Creative. Exciting."

Melody's thoughts froze in their tracks. "You think I'm exciting?"

"I think the way you approach life is exciting. You make me wonder what I've missed around me while I've been so focused on my goals."

His smile warmed her straight through, but it started an uncomfortable squirm there too, as if what he said didn't match up to the truth. "You're the one flying off to multiple cities every day and rubbing elbows with celebrities and moguls."

"Trust me, it sounds more glamorous than it is. Regardless of who's sitting in the cabin, the routine is the same. I mean, I do love my job, but you're the real risk-taker here."

"Says the man who flies a home-built plane."

He waved a hand. "That's just aerodynamics. There's nothing risky about science."

Melody laughed, the spell broken. Their server came to the table and asked about dessert, but Justin glanced at his watch. "Don't you have to work tonight?"

An uncomfortable feeling came over her at the thought of ending this night so abruptly, just when they were really connecting. She hesitated to call it desperation, but it clawed into her all the same. "I'll call in sick."

He stared at her.

"I've never missed a shift. And the pastry chef here is a bona fide genius. Totally worth it."

Justin held up his hands. "Far be it from me to stand in the way of a pastry chef crush. I'll have the five-spice donuts."

The server looked amused by the whole exchange. "And you, miss?"

"The banana *lumpia*, please. And coffee."

The server moved away, and Melody pulled out her cell phone to dial the store manager. "Robert, it's Melody. I'm not going to make it in tonight."

Silence came through the line and Melody checked her screen to see if it was still connected. "Robert?"

"I heard you. I just didn't believe it."

"Something important came up. Hugo can handle things without me. I've covered enough for him that he owes me one. Five, in fact."

Robert cleared his throat. "I heard you're going to open your own place."

Melody's thoughts ground to a sharp halt. What did that have to do with anything? "Not for a couple of months."

"But you are leaving? It's not just a rumor?"

Now Melody was beginning to feel a little unsettled. "No. It's not a rumor. But I'd planned on giving plenty of notice."

"Except you're calling in tonight with no notice."

Justin caught her eye and made a gesture toward the door. She shook her head and turned her attention back to the phone. "You're going to bust my chops for calling in *once* when there's already a second baker scheduled? After all the times I've done this shift myself?"

"Melody," Justin hissed. "It's okay. We can go."

But the tenor of the conversation had already gotten her back up. Someone had overheard a phone conversation and tattled to the general manager, who now wanted to make her life difficult, despite the fact she'd been the most experienced and dedicated employee they'd ever had.

"The thing is, Melody, we need reliable employees to uphold the standards of our bakery."

The whole conversation suddenly struck her as completely laughable. "Robert, we both know the only thing it takes to do this job is the ability to read directions and watch an instructional video. Consider this my resignation." And she clicked off the phone.

Justin stared, slack-jawed. "You just quit your job."

"Robert's an insufferable blowhard who lets everyone else off the hook because I take up the slack. It was two months overdue. At least." She grinned. "And the banana lumpia really are that good."

A disbelieving laugh slipped from Justin. "You're insane."

"Not insane. I just know what I want. And right now, I don't want this night to end."

The statement hung there for a moment, and she realized how it might be taken. But Justin saved her. "I'm wishing I didn't have to leave tomorrow. And before you say anything, I don't have the option of calling in sick."

"I'd never dream of asking. Look, here come our desserts."

Melody was right: the lumpia—Filipino-style eggrolls stuffed with banana and drizzled with caramel sauce—were worth losing a job over, especially a job she didn't even like. As was the feel of Justin's hand gripping hers as they waited in the chilly night for the valet to bring the car around. Her heart swelled with something she hesitated to call happiness. It was more like . . . contentment. As if a switch had been flipped, turning off her restlessness and her over-thinking. Tonight, she couldn't find it in herself to worry about the future. She would just enjoy this perfect moment to the fullest.

Justin didn't seem to have that ability. "I can't believe you quit your job."

Melody waved a hand. "*C'est pas grave.*"

He looked at her quizzically.

"It doesn't matter. Sometimes I think the French have it right. Americans worry so much."

"Did you drink more than I thought?"

No, but she definitely felt intoxicated. With her sudden freedom from a job she hated. With him. With life. The feeling lasted all the way home in his car, where he walked her up to her apartment. They turned to each other in front of her door.

"Do you want to come in?" she asked, nervous again. About what, she couldn't articulate.

"I probably shouldn't. I'm leaving early and I haven't packed yet."

"I understand."

"I don't think you do." The look he gave her made her tingle down to her toes, caused her breath to catch. "I won't be back until next Saturday. But I want to take you someplace. Sunday morning?"

"I thought I might go to church since I don't have to work . . . ," Melody said slowly.

"Afterward, then. Let's say noon." His hands found her hips, steadying her in place while he lowered his mouth to hers. The first time they'd kissed outside her door, it had been a flash fire, a lit match touched to a pile of kindling,

271

unexpected and powerful. But now, he kissed her softly, sweetly. Tenderly. All too briefly.

Her fingertips drifted to her lips as she watched him walk away, wondering if she'd been mistaken.

For all their talk of wait and see, that kiss tasted like a promise.

Chapter Twenty-One

Melody spent the next day reliving every detail of the date: every word, every touch, every kiss. Especially the kisses. The practiced and assured way Justin kissed made all the warning flags pop in the back of her mind; it clearly spelled *player*. And yet he seemed to deliberately stay out of her apartment at the end of the night. That suggested something else entirely.

Her cell phone beeped, and she snatched it up, hoping for a message from Justin. Instead, it was Rachel, a message on their running group-text thread. We need to come up with a restaurant name posthaste.

Posthaste, huh? Rachel was stressed if she was getting formal. Time to lighten the mood. Melody tapped out some ideas. Cut the Cake? Gluten Maximus? The Bun Also Rises?

Almost immediately, Rachel's response: Ugh! No!

And then Ana's: Are you on drugs?

Just high on Justin. She deleted that message before she could press Send. That was definitely an in-person conversation. For now, she just wanted to enjoy the happy flutter that remained from their amazing day together.

She couldn't let Rachel off the hook, though.

I take it that means Flours for Hours and For Goodness Cakes are out too?

Rachel sent back a string of angry face emojis, and Melody burst out laughing.

Okay, fine. I'm heading out to collect material samples for the bakery. You and Ana keep working on it.

It was a quirk of Melody's that she rarely visualized a space and then filled it. She needed something, whether it be building materials or textiles, to inspire her, which meant visits to the design centers and showrooms that dotted the southwest section of Denver. Three hours later, her Jeep's backseat was stacked full of tile and paint samples, her brain crammed with just as many design possibilities. She stopped by Gibraltar for a cappuccino and a piece of Agni's amazing baklava and sat in the corner with a small sketch pad, outlining the dimensions of the room and the current placement of the fixtures. They'd have to get exact dimensions from the contractor, but right now it was unnecessary. She just needed the basic feel, the shell of the place, so she could overlay her own ideas on the existing layout.

She and Rachel had already agreed that the kitchen was much too big for their needs, compared to the rest of the space. They were used to working in close quarters, and since they planned on having a maximum of five kitchen staff in there at one time, they could get by with a little more than half. That would open up an entire section of the room for seating that was currently just a blank wall.

Melody's pencil scratched across paper, at first just the suggestion of shapes, then bolder strokes to define walls and lighting and furniture. A long, high bar went into the new space reclaimed from the kitchen, adjustable wood-and-iron stools beneath, a cool multi-light fixture over the length of it. They could hire a local craftsman to make it and install power strips on the underside for people to plug in their laptops, maybe run the electricity up the hollow leg of the table. That meant they'd need a power fixture under-neath—that note got scribbled on the back of the sketch.

Then some square tables with slim metal chairs to maximize the number of seats they could fit while giving enough space to pass in the aisles. It was a balancing act between making it inviting but not too comfortable. Maybe they could do some soft seating up front in the bakery and orchestrate the back to turn tables over quickly.

She held the sketch at arm's length, comparing her vision with the current reality in front of her. They looked nothing alike, each choice diverging further from Agni's warm Mediterranean style.

She loved it.

The question was if Rachel would agree. She

laid the sketch flat and snapped a photo of it, then texted it to Rachel with a question mark as the only caption.

Her response several moments later: Wait. That's not our place?

It is if you want it to be.

I LOVE IT.

Melody smiled and let out a sigh of relief, Rachel's approval easing the knot of nervousness inside her. Amazing how quickly their dream bakery had taken shape beneath her pencil. Grandma Bev was probably looking down on her and smiling.

I'm going to work up some mood boards tonight. Meet tomorrow?

Ten? I have an early class and then I'll be home. I'll invite Ana too.

Perfect. Melody wasn't entirely sure if she meant the class she was teaching at the culinary school or one she was taking at the university, but either way, Rachel's schedule was enough to make Melody's head spin. In fact, she'd barely heard from her friend since they'd signed the lease, unless abbreviated notes on inspiration pins counted as communication.

She packed up her sketchbook and pencils and drove her samples home, where she immediately got to work on the inspiration boards. She'd had the home improvement center cut a thin sheet of plywood into four-foot squares to serve as the base, upon which she'd adhere all the different materials.

As the evening wore on, she sorted out the pieces that weren't going to work and narrowed down the design schemes to two: one light and bright, the other industrial and moody. She checked the clock reflexively, preparing herself to clean up and head to work before she remembered she had no place to go.

Had she really quit, just like that? She'd been intoxicated, no doubt, but not from alcohol. Justin's influence over her was far headier than any substance she could ingest. It wasn't like she hadn't planned on putting in her notice anyway. The lease went into effect in a few days, and the contractor would be out to take measurements sometime next week. The idea of trying to juggle everything along with a night job was laughable.

Plus it would have meant seeing a lot less of Justin.

She thumbed through her contacts before she shut off her phone's screen with an irritated shake of her head. He was working. She wasn't going to be the girl who needed to check up on him.

Melody put away her supplies and leaned her two finished mood boards against the dining room wall, then drew herself a bubble bath. Changing from a night owl to a day dweller would take time. When she was relaxed and warm and a little pruney, she wrapped herself in her coziest pajamas, made a mug of steamed vanilla milk, and climbed beneath her cloud-like duvet. For good measure, she shook out a melatonin tablet and a prescription sleep aid. She wasn't big on pills, but she knew transitioning her body clock was going to take more than warm drinks.

She reached for *Madding Crowd* on her nightstand, but instead her fingers touched the leather-bound Bible her grandmother had given her at her baptism when she was thirteen. She hauled it into her lap and turned the fragile pages. It had been too long since she'd read it, too consumed with work and grief and, for the first time in a long time, hope.

Highlighters turned the pages into a colorful rainbow of reminders, not Melody's doing but Bev's. As she turned toward the back, her eyes lit on one verse illuminated in pink and starred with a ballpoint pen. Romans 8:28: *"And we know that in all things God works for the good of those who love him, who have been called according to his purpose."*

Was that what God was doing now? Working things for her good—Grandma Bev's death, the new restaurant, even Justin? She'd heard the verse nearly every day growing up, accepted it without question. It was the automatic answer any time she questioned her mother's absence or the long stretches in a tour bus or anything else she didn't particularly like about her life. And so it had taken on the quality of a well-worn meme, something spoken so often it started to lose its meaning.

Melody replaced the Bible on her nightstand, feeling guilty for even thinking such a thing. Good things were happening now. Of course this was God's doing. She didn't have to understand it to accept it. She just had to trust.

Melody awoke the next morning late but feeling more alert than she had in days. She made herself presentable, gathered up her mood boards, and headed to Rachel's without even her customary pot of coffee. When she arrived, Ana's familiar black Mercedes was missing. She hefted the inspiration boards and trundled up the front steps, where Rachel opened the door before she could knock.

"I come bearing gifts," she announced as she edged by Rachel and headed straight for the kitchen table. "I can't believe I beat Ana."

"She just texted. She can't come. Work crisis."

"All her work is crisis. Literally. Should we be worried?"

"I don't know. I don't think so." Rachel stopped in front of the boards where they sat on the table. "Wow. I loved what you put together in the sketch, but these are . . ."

"Aren't they?" Melody smiled. Both color schemes used a healthy dose of gray, black, and white, but the one on the right was moodier, more industrial, as suited Rachel's taste: hand-scraped plank floors, lots of stainless steel and slate and glazed gray tiles against a pale dove-gray wall. The one on the left was lighter, more classically European: tiny coin tiles for the floor, reclaimed wood counters, elongated white subway tile set in a herringbone pattern. And of course she'd included a snapshot of the almost-finished cherub chandelier.

Rachel rubbed a finger against the tile samples and examined the colored-pencil sketches Melody had done to try to communicate the differences between the two. "I don't know how we're going to decide."

"I thought for sure you'd go for the one on the right," Melody said.

"I thought I would too; it reminds me so much of Paisley. You really nailed my taste."

"But . . ."

Rachel glanced at her, a smile forming on her lips. "The one on the left looks more like you. And I kind of love it."

"Really?" Melody threw her arms exuberantly around Rachel. "I mean, I would have been fine if you picked the other one, because I like it too, but—"

"This one merges Paris and Denver. It's sophisticated, but in a more relaxed way. I think our customers will love it."

Melody flipped over the board to display a piece of paper taped on the back. "Then here are all the manufacturers and style numbers to give to the contractor. As soon as we can get in there, I can show them exactly which walls will be which finish so they can do the measurements."

Rachel was still looking over the rejected design. "You know, Melody, you are a talented baker, but I think you could have just as easily been a designer."

"And now I can be both." Melody sobered. "Do you think it would be inappropriate to drop in on Gibraltar's good-bye party? It's been part of the neighborhood so long, it feels wrong not to celebrate, but I also don't want Agni to think we're vultures, waiting to swoop on her misfortune."

"I think it would be nice. We are doing her a favor in a way. And I haven't started anything for breakfast yet. Why don't we have a pastry there to say good-bye?"

"Perfect. I'll drive." It would give Melody something to do with her hands and attention while she told Rachel that she and Justin were together . . . and about the looming separation on the horizon.

Except Rachel started talking about having the contractor come out to start the measurements and draw up plans, and Melody couldn't find a place to smoothly segue into her love life.

Instead, she just nodded and said the right things and tried to be as interested in certificates of occupancy and building permits as Rachel was.

And then she was parking on Old South Pearl and her chance was blown. Only then did she realize that not only hadn't she told Rachel about Justin, but she'd forgotten to mention that she'd quit her job as well.

CHAPTER TWENTY-TWO

It took a Herculean effort to keep his mind on his flights and off Melody on his seven-day tour, but Justin managed . . . until his plane touched down in Denver. The desire to see her built from the moment the "fasten seat belts" sign went off and only grew the closer he got to downtown Denver. He resisted it. For one thing, she'd said she was adjusting to her new daytime schedule slowly, early bedtimes interspersed with long periods of insomnia. For all he knew, that meant she was still asleep.

Instead, he made a quick stop at his apartment to drop his bags and change into some grungy clothes, then headed to his dad's place.

Rich's car was missing from the driveway, so Justin didn't bother to unlock the house, just went directly to the garage and punched the code into the keypad. The door slid open with a low hum, gradually revealing the chrome and green front end of the Hornet.

It was coming along. He'd only gotten as far as cleaning the carburetor, which as he'd expected was varnished shut with the residue of old gasoline. Today he figured he'd change the sludgy oil and see if the beast would start.

The garage was even colder than the outside

air, untouched by the spring sunshine spreading over the city, so he pulled on the flannel coat he left here expressly for that purpose and slid under the car on a padded roller board. He'd just gotten the old oil drained from the pan and a new filter installed when he heard the hum of an engine abruptly cut off.

He slid out on the board to see Pete walking up the driveway.

"Hey," Pete said when he was within speaking distance. "I thought you'd be here. I dropped by your apartment earlier."

Justin wiped his greasy hands on a rag and pushed himself to his feet. "I needed to make some headway on this car. What's going on?"

"I finally got the paperwork back from the lawyer; thought you might like to take a look."

Justin automatically reached for the sheaf of papers, then thought better of it. "You can put it on the bench and I'll look over it when I'm done."

Pete dropped the paperwork on a clean spot on the workbench and took a slow circle around the car. "She must be a knockout."

"Why does everyone keep saying that? It's a classic. You know, this thing will actually trounce my Mustang on the quarter-mile."

"We all know that's not your style. You're a collector, not a racer. And you only drive the chick magnets."

"Then it's a good thing I'm only fixing this and not driving it."

Pete shook his head. "Tell me about this woman."

Justin sighed and cocked a hip against the open engine compartment. Pete wasn't going to let it go. "Same one as before. The baker."

"And?"

"And nothing. We're seeing each other."

"She know about the business?"

Justin nodded once.

"And she's still okay with it?"

"So she says. I was ready to break it off with her, but she wanted to wait and see where it goes."

Pete made a face. "I don't like the sound of that. That usually means she thinks you'll fall in love with her and change your mind. Like . . . what was her name? The redhead. The one you met at the car show."

"Becca." Justin unscrewed the cap from a plastic bottle and began to funnel motor oil into the car's empty reservoir.

"Right, Becca. Either that, or she figures you'll invite her to come along with you. Or marry her."

If only it were that easy. "She just invested her entire inheritance into a bakery here in Denver."

"So what are you doing? You know this isn't going to end well."

Justin tossed aside the empty bottle and

reached for another one. "Thanks for the vote of confidence."

"I tell the truth. You're usually the one keeping things light and meaningless. What's the deal?"

Justin sighed and straightened. "I don't know, okay? It's probably going to go bad, but I can't bring myself to break it off, even if it's for her own good." He narrowed his eyes. "Why all the interest in my love life? Jessica again?"

Pete plopped himself on a stool at the work-bench and watched Justin finish filling the oil reservoir. "She's worried about you. Feeling guilty, I think, about having you move away for us."

"Tell her she has nothing to feel guilty about." Justin wiped away excess oil with a rag and then screwed the cap back on. "This was my idea, remember? No matter what I tell my dad, I'm starting to get tired of the fractional gig. At first the waiting and the cleaning and the kowtowing didn't bother me, but . . ."

"But now you really are feeling like a glorified chauffeur," Pete finished for him. "You sure you're not going to feel the same way shuttling vacationers to and from the islands?"

"The key word there is *islands*." Justin flashed a smile. "I can soothe my bruised ego with my ocean view."

"Funny you should say that. If this guy accepts our offer, we're going to need to go out there again, sign the paperwork, and get the ball rolling on business licenses. Jess and I thought we'd take the opportunity to look at houses. You want to come?"

"I'm stuck with AvionElite until at least the end of the month, remember? I don't want to be signing leases until I've let my place go."

"I know that. Just thought . . ."

"Jess is giving me my last chance to get out before it's too late."

Pete nodded.

Justin clapped a hand on Pete's shoulder. "Listen. You guys are family. We're doing this for Jess. It's okay. I knew what I was getting into. It's going to be great."

"And the girl?"

Justin shrugged. "You know me. Probably lose interest before it ever becomes an issue."

For the first time since Pete arrived, he seemed to relax. "Let me know what your schedule looks like, and we'll work around you."

"I'll e-mail you. And I'll look over the paperwork later and let you know what I think."

"Good." Pete gave him a half slap, half handshake and turned on his heel. "Good luck with that beast."

Justin waited until Pete was back in his car and pulling away from the curb before he climbed into the Hornet's driver's seat and pushed the key into the ignition. Here went nothing.

The engine struggled to turn over, the starter whining in protest. He gave it a little gas, and the engine finally caught and rumbled to life. The whole car shuddered as the cold motor pulled in new oil, lubricating the neglected cylinders, and gradually settling to a throaty rumble. A smile came to his face. Ugly as it might be, this beast would be fun to drive. It was almost too bad that Melody was selling it.

He kept the clutch in and pressed the accelerator, listening to the engine as it revved. There. A misfire in one of the cylinders. He tried again, watched the RPM. Not a big surprise, given the age and history of the car.

Justin shut the engine off and climbed out to remove a spark plug. He hadn't included it in his estimate for Melody, but they weren't so expensive that he felt like he needed her approval. He shrugged off his jacket, took the plug with him as a sample, and hopped into his Mustang, aware that he was avoiding the larger problem.

He'd told Pete that he was all in with the Florida move, but it was a complete lie.

CHAPTER TWENTY-THREE

This past week had been the longest of Melody's life. She told herself that Justin's absence was convenient, considering she and Rachel had spent every free moment discussing design and business issues, but she didn't believe it. The leap in her heart when he called on Saturday to tell her to wear snow boots and a warm jacket belied every protest to the contrary.

Melody had fully intended to get up early to go to church with Rachel and Ana, but when she pried her eyes open at 11 a.m. on Sunday morning, she saw that she'd slept through her alarm so many times that it had given up on her. As had her friends . . . after half a dozen missed text messages. She dragged herself from beneath her duvet and stumbled into the bathroom.

The going-to-bed thing was never a problem. It was the waking up between three and six every morning that was killing her. She'd been getting a lot of reading done this week, but the fact she'd been sneaking contemporary romance novels, so far from her usual literary bedtime preferences, didn't help her sleeplessness. She found herself glued to the pages, desperate to reassure herself of the characters' happily ever after.

She showered, primped, and dressed as quickly

as she could, leaving enough time to down a full pot of coffee. When Justin buzzed at the building minutes before noon, she was slipping on her boots with her mug in hand.

She opened the door to him before he knocked. "Hey! Give me a second to put this in the sink and we can go."

"You're looking much more alert than I expected." He put his hands in his pockets and watched her with a half smile.

"I'm fine as long as you don't ask me to make any witty conversation. I'm still running on autopilot this morning. Afternoon. Whatever." She poured the rest of her coffee in the sink, grabbed her handbag, and moved to the door.

"Wait." Justin grabbed her arm and tugged her back around to him. Then he took her face in one hand and kissed her slowly and thoroughly.

Melody sighed and wound her arms around his waist with a dreamy smile. "I missed you."

"I can see that." His voice, pitched low, held all sorts of promises she was suddenly a little too anxious to explore. "However, we need to get going."

"What's the hurry? Are we going to be late for something?"

He checked his watch. "Kind of. You feel up for an adventure?"

The dare in his voice broke through her sensual haze. "You bet I am."

Despite her sassy words, Melody had been telling the truth when she warned him not to expect conversation—it was all she could do to stare out the window of Justin's perfectly nice Nissan SUV and shake the fog of a midday awakening. She was coherent enough to know he was heading out of the city into the southern suburbs, sprawling communities of newer houses connected by highways, interstates, and toll roads. When he exited the freeway and headed east up Arapahoe Road, a six-lane highway that connected the Denver Tech Center to the city's suburbs, she couldn't stay quiet any longer.

"Where are we going exactly? Last time I checked, there was no longer any snow in the tech center."

"You'll see. I guess I should have asked you this before—do you like the mountains?"

"Yes." Though they were going the wrong direction through suburban sprawl for the mountains. Then she saw the signage on the right side of the road for Centennial Airport. "Where are we going?"

Justin chuckled. "The airport, obviously. After that, wait and see."

He turned down an adjoining road, then up to a gate, beyond which an array of business jets stood in a neat grid. He swiped his card and the gate slowly slid back.

"That's a Citation XLS," he said, pointing

at one of the smaller jets through her window. "That's what I fly for work."

"It's so . . . small," she said, surprised. "Somehow I always envisioned them being like airliners."

"More like a fighter than an airliner. At least that's what we like to tell ourselves. Speaking of, look . . . an F-18." He pointed at a military jet parked straight out front of one of the terminals.

"What, did the guy just stop in for lunch?"

Justin chuckled. "Maybe. The airport restaurant is pretty good. But this airport handles a lot of military traffic too."

He navigated slowly across the expanse of concrete, then drove up to what looked like a huge self-storage facility. She supposed it was, in a way: the rows of long rectangular buildings no doubt held planes that ranged from little two-seaters to corporate jets like the ones Justin flew. After a couple of minutes, he pulled up in front of an end unit with a small entry set beside a huge corrugated metal door.

"This is it?" she asked inanely. "There's no security or anything?"

"Nope. There aren't any commercial flights from Centennial, so it's the crew's job to make sure their passengers pass muster." He fixed her with a mock serious stare. "There isn't anything I should know, is there? You're not secretly on some Homeland Security no-fly list, are you?"

Melody laughed. "No, but I haven't been anywhere interesting in so long, I'm not sure I'd know if I were."

"Good enough for me." He pushed open his door and paused on the running board. "Stay here for a sec."

Melody watched while he fumbled with his keys, then unlocked the smaller door and disappeared into the hangar. A moment later, the corrugated panel began to sweep upward, folding in half like an accordion to reveal Justin standing behind it. He grinned and waved her over.

Melody hopped out of the SUV and slowly approached the hangar. It really was a giant garage, filled with toolboxes and parts and things she couldn't name. But instead of a car, the interior housed a gleaming blue-and-white airplane. Its wings were low below a bubble cockpit, with a single prop in front.

She didn't know what she'd expected from a home-built plane, but this sleek, professional-looking thing was not it. "You actually built this?"

"My dad and I, but yes. What do you say?"

Excitement built in Melody along with a little apprehension when she saw the word *experimental* emblazoned across the back of the cockpit behind the seats. "Is it safe?"

"As safe as flying a small plane can be." When Melody hesitated at that unhelpful comment, he sighed. "Look, I totally get it if you're not comfortable with this. If it makes you feel any better, this plane just had its annual inspection, so I know it's in perfect condition. I've logged over five thousand hours, several hundred of them in this plane. I'm completely confident in our safety."

She recalled her early cocky answers and nodded. "Okay then. Where are we going?"

"It's a surprise."

"You know, I think they call that kidnapping."

"Only if you're not coming willingly." He grinned. "Now I just need to pull it out."

"And how do you do that?" She looked around, but there was nothing resembling tow machinery in the hangar.

He disappeared and came back with a piece of metal that looked like a two-pronged pitchfork. "You might want to stand back." He attached the tow bar to the plane's front wheel, then after checking to make sure Melody was clear, tugged the plane forward. It rolled easily.

Her stomach did a flip-flop. Planes were supposed to be huge, heavy things that could withstand storms and turbulence. Not something barely bigger than a car that could be pulled by a garden tool.

Where's the adventurous risk-taker now? her own thoughts mocked her.

They must have shown on her face because

Justin called, "I won't think any less of you if you want to back out."

Melody straightened her spine. "No, I'm good. It will be fun."

Justin didn't look completely convinced, but he didn't say anything more, just climbed into the SUV and moved it into the hangar space the plane had just occupied. "Let's close this up, and then we'll get going."

He led her to the right side of the plane and boosted himself up on the step to slide back the canopy. Then he hopped down and offered her a hand. "Climb on up."

"On top of the wing?"

"Yep. Be careful. Only step in the spots that are marked."

Gingerly, she climbed up with his help, avoiding the flaps, and settled herself into the right-hand seat, the leather cushion split to make room for the control stick between her knees. Justin was doing something outside—maybe giving the exterior a check, she thought. Finally, he climbed up beside her and settled into the left seat. He reached behind him and slid the canopy closed, then twisted the handle to secure it.

"Your seat belt is behind you, five-point harness." He demonstrated with his own, pulling the V over his head and fastening it to the buckle between his legs. "Push-button release. Exits are above and to your right and left. To open the canopy, you twist the handle counterclockwise and then slide it back." He demonstrated again to make sure she understood, then picked up two headsets with boom mics attached and indicated for her to put hers on. As soon as she did, he twisted a knob on the radio in the panel in front of them, and his voice came out of the earphones, slightly tinny. "Can you hear me?"

"I can hear you." Her stomach did a backflip. Being strapped into this tiny cockpit with the bubble canopy above her felt a little like being trapped in a hamster ball.

Her apprehension must have shown because Justin reached over and placed his hand over hers. "We don't have to do this. The last thing I want is for you to feel pushed into something."

"No. No, it's just my first time in such a tiny plane. I'll be fine, really." She smiled at him, and he nodded.

He went through his start-up procedure, checking panel switches and electronic instrumentation against a checklist on his knee. A series of buttons and switches later, he started the engine, giving a disturbingly sputtery start before it settled into a steady hum. After a couple of minutes, Justin seemed satisfied by whatever he was monitoring and threw her an encouraging smile. "Here we go."

The plane moved slowly forward down the small road between hangars and then out toward the regular part of the airport, all connected by yellow lines that Melody assumed made sense to him. Then he stopped and went through another series of checks on instrumentation, flipping on switches and adjusting . . . she couldn't imagine what he was adjusting, but his confident attitude at least steadied her nerves.

"Centennial Ground, Experimental RV One-one-one-four-Quebec, with ATIS Alpha, departing northwest bound. We require a run-up."

A pause and then a female voice returned, "RV One-one-one-four-Quebec, taxi to north run-up area and monitor tower."

Justin repeated back the instructions, and then they were moving again. Even on Sunday afternoon, aircraft of all sizes surrounded them, some moving back to parking areas, others taxiing toward the runways as they were.

Melody waved a hand toward the radio. "So this is all routine to you?"

Justin flicked her a quick look. "There's nothing routine about any flight. When I started out, though, I had a major case of mic fright. I bungled it so bad one time I swear I could hear the controller laughing at me."

Melody grinned. "I find that hard to believe."

He shrugged, but his lips twitched into a smile. "I was only sixteen. I couldn't even talk to girls, let alone air traffic control."

When they finally made it to the run-up area,

along with several other planes, Melody fell quiet and let Justin do his checks on the engine and whatever else he was verifying. He transmitted his readiness to depart, getting a reply that amounted to "wait." A few minutes later, they got their taxi clearance and were moving toward the runway.

"I didn't understand any of that," she said when the radio went silent.

Justin grinned. "Don't worry. I did." He gave her a play-by-play and tried to help her unravel the nearly indecipherable communications from the control frequency. She'd never realized this little airport was quite so busy. How did he possibly keep it straight?

She sneaked a sideways glance at him while he wasn't looking. Despite her best efforts, it was getting a bit difficult to resist the pilot appeal.

The tower came on again with their call sign, giving them departure clearance on runway 17L. Justin followed instructions and moved the plane toward the white-striped portion of the airfield.

"Ready?" He glanced at Melody, a questioning look on his face as they began to taxi again. It was a purely rhetorical question, but she nodded anyway.

Justin made one more transmission, ending with "good day," which was evidently a sign-off of some sort, and then they were speeding down the runway. Or maybe slowly building up speed was more accurate. The prop seemed to blur and shift at the front of the plane, barely visible through the windshield, until the aircraft lifted off the runway. As they bobbed into the air like a cork in a glass of water, Melody's stomach dropped out beneath her, then righted itself as they climbed into the sky.

The runway still stretched out beneath them, the surrounding fields already growing smaller. Justin was talking on the radio again, but she wasn't paying attention, too fixed on the shrinking landscape beneath them. Office buildings looking like nothing more than tiny boxes set beside postage-stamp parking lots. A main road—the expressway, she thought—with cars crawling by. A smile widened on her lips and a laugh of delight escaped her mouth.

When she looked at Justin, he was smiling.

"What?"

"You're not afraid anymore."

"I wasn't afraid!"

"Sure you weren't."

Melody stuck her tongue out at him, earning a laugh, but went right back to her fascinated inspection of the landscape below them. They made a wide left turn, and then they were heading northwest toward the mountains.

After a few minutes, she asked, "How high are we now?"

"About eight thousand feet."

She peered out the window again. "It doesn't look that far up."

"That's because the land below is over five thousand."

Melody sat back in her seat and gave a happy sigh. "You do know how to make an impression, I'll give you that. This must go over with the women."

He slid her a funny look. "I've only taken one other woman up in this plane, and that was my sister."

"I don't believe you."

"No, really. I guess I didn't figure any of the others had your sense of adventure."

The fact that she was set apart gave her a warm feeling in the center of her chest. Even though she didn't want to know the answer, she couldn't resist the chance to ask about his dating history. " 'Any of the others'? Just how many are we talking about?"

"Many," he replied sheepishly. "Most of them didn't last past the third date or so. The ones who did . . . they figured out pretty quickly that I'm never going to be around for the office Christmas party or the brother's wedding or any of the other normal events that they want a boyfriend for."

Melody cast around for the proper response. "I think they were shortsighted."

"Oh yeah? Why?"

"The souvenirs, of course. I know you said you

don't fly to Europe, but if you ever make it to Paris, there's this bakery called Pierre Hermé on rue Bonaparte. Bring me back some macarons?"

Mischief glinted in his eyes. "You and my niece would get along well. She doesn't care about having me back; she just wants the refrigerator magnets I bring her. Even though I think my sister wants to kill me. She's running out of space on the fridge."

"A girl after my own heart. Why have five when you could have fifty? In case you hadn't noticed from my apartment, I'm a hopeless collector." She would have said more, but she was too distracted by Denver's landscape creeping by beneath them. The view was pretty spectacular. She took her headset off for a moment out of curiosity, but the roar of the engine put an end to that thought. Instead, she turned her attention on Justin. He looked completely relaxed and comfortable, like he was cruising along a freeway, but she noticed he was keeping an eye on the electronic gauges and GPS screen, minute adjustments of the stick keeping the wings level and the speed constant. At least that's what she thought he was doing. She asked him to fill her in on how everything worked, which was all the encouragement he needed.

Her attention was coaxed away from his thorough descriptors by their gentle upward climb, the terrain beneath them turning from city to foothills to mountains, their craggy peaks covered in snow. He seemed a little more attentive to the outside view and the GPS now, even though he was as relaxed as ever. And then they began to descend.

"So, I don't want to scare you or anything . . ."

Melody jerked her head in his direction just as a shudder vibrated through the plane. "I don't tend to like sentences that begin like that."

He grinned. "The approach to the airstrip looks worse than it is. It's a cool day with no wind, so it should be pretty smooth. Just giving you a heads-up."

She breathed in and out, realizing that her laid-back approach to life might not follow her this high up in the air.

She could feel them slowing down, and then they were descending, seemingly right into the mountains. Vibrations traveled through the plane, and she grabbed the edges of her seat with her fingertips.

"You okay?" he asked.

"I'm fine."

"Liar."

They were dipping lower and lower to the ground, the jitters smoothing out. Only then did she notice the big log structure set in the middle of a wide, snow-covered field, beside which lay a long flat strip of newly cleared dirt.

"Wait, that's where we're landing?" She didn't

expect an answer and didn't get one as they continued their steady descent. Justin throttled back the engine until it felt like they were barely moving, floating above the dirt, their shadow flying before them on the snow beside the airstrip. Then they touched down with a delicate bounce.

Melody let out her breath and started laughing.

Justin turned to her. "I'll take it that means you don't hate me."

"I don't hate you. I'm actually pretty impressed."

"I'm good with that." He taxied around the end and positioned the plane facing the way they'd come. They sat there for a minute, the engine idling, before he started flicking switches, shutting down the engine and all the electronics. "Brace yourself."

She didn't have to ask for what—the frigid air hit her face as soon as he twisted the handle and slid back the canopy. She fumbled for her jacket and zipped it up against the sharp breeze.

Justin hopped out, chocked the wheels, and then was at her side, offering her a hand down.

"Welcome to Silverlark, the best little mountain town no one has ever heard of."

CHAPTER TWENTY-FOUR

Melody breathed deeply, the scent of evergreens riding along with the singe of cold air to her lungs. She might live in Colorado, but there was a huge difference between living below in the city and being up in the high country, especially during transitional seasons like spring and fall. Down below, the day would be practically balmy; up here, it was like winter hadn't yet left.

She accepted Justin's help to climb down and began moving toward the lodge with him. They'd barely made it halfway across the snowy field before a woman appeared outside, waiting for them.

When they got close enough to make out details, Melody could see she was pretty, around her own age or a little older, with hair so black it took on a blueish tinge in the sunshine. Her only nod to the cold was the unzipped down jacket she wore over jeans and a black T-shirt.

"Reggie, hey." Justin stepped forward and gave her a brief hug.

Reggie turned from him with a warm smile and held out a hand. "You must be Melody. Welcome to Jasper Creek Lodge. I'm so glad you came prepared. We'll only need to find you some snow pants. Come on inside."

Melody looked at Justin. "Snow pants?"

"You'll see."

They followed Reggie up the stairs into the lodge, pausing beneath the wide eaves of the porch to knock the snow off their boots. By the door hung a hand-carved sign with the name and a faithful reproduction of the lodge. Below it read *Jewel of Silverlark* and the altitude, 8,225 feet.

The inside was everything Melody could have wanted in a rustic mountain lodge: a log structure lit with massive iron chandeliers, hand-scraped wood floors, woven Navajo rugs, and heavy leather furniture. A fire burned in a gargantuan stone fireplace. It hardly mattered what else Justin had planned—she'd be content to sit in one of those big armchairs in front of the fire for the rest of the afternoon.

"This way," Reggie threw over her shoulder, gesturing for them to follow her through a side hallway.

"Is this a hotel?" she whispered, trailing behind.

"Used to be. It's an event center now. Corporate retreats, that sort of thing. Reggie runs an outdoor adventure business situated here. It's kind of a long story. . . ."

"It's a very long story," Reggie said, but the words were accompanied by a kind smile. She gestured for them to enter a large room, half the size of the great hall, packed with rack after rack of outdoor gear and clothing. She sized up both of them with narrowed eyes and then went straight to a rack of snow pants. She pulled a pair of black ones and handed them to Justin, then gave a pair of bright-pink ones to Melody.

"Unless you'd prefer black," Reggie said. "I do."

Melody grinned. "I like the pink. Where can I go put these on?"

Reggie showed her to a little dressing cubicle with a solid door at the back of the room, where Melody stepped out of her boots. She hesitated only a moment before stripping off her jeans as well. Reggie was a good judge of sizes, because the pants fit her perfectly.

She could just barely catch their conversation outside. ". . . good sport. You really didn't tell her what you were doing?"

"Nope . . . sure she was going to go for the plane . . . in the Jeep?"

Melody smiled. So this was something he'd been planning for a while. When she decided she'd eavesdropped long enough, she opened the door and emerged.

"Perfect!" Reggie exclaimed. "Why don't we get you some gloves while Justin changes?" She pulled Melody over to an old-fashioned chest of drawers and opened the second drawer to reveal dozens of pairs of gloves, extracting a white pair. "Now a hat."

"Oh, I came prepared." Melody reached into

the inside pocket of her jacket and pulled out her knit beanie. "It's usually cold in the bakery at night, even with the ovens going, so I always have one on hand."

Justin emerged, already changed, his jacket zipped up and a hat pulled onto his head. Reggie reached into her pocket and dangled a pair of keys. "GPS is programmed in case you don't remember how to get back."

"Thanks, Reg. You know I owe you one."

"Yeah, yeah, I owe you like ten, so it'll be a while before we're even." She smiled at Melody. "Have fun. There's some snacks in the back if you get hungry before you get home."

Melody still felt slightly baffled as she left the outfitting room and followed Justin to an exit opposite the one they had come in. Like the back porch, the front had been cleared of snow, and a swath had been cut through the driveway out to a gate several hundred yards down the road. Justin jingled the keys and made for a black Jeep— a newer, nicer version of her own. "Want to drive?"

"Not since I don't know where we're going yet." She climbed into the passenger's seat and twisted around to see if she could find the snacks Reggie had been talking about. They must be in the old-fashioned picnic basket on the backseat. She was about to peek inside when she glimpsed the two inner tubes shoved into the cargo area.

"We're going tubing?"

"Yep. There's a great place not far from here. You're going to love it. And we'll probably have it all to ourselves."

"But it's Sunday and the weather is beautiful. People would be crazy to pass it up."

"What people?" Justin asked with a grimace. "Silverlark used to have a population of about three thousand, but a few years back, the only bridge connecting the town to the highway collapsed. They tried to get government funds to help with the rebuild, but it took so long to get under way that most of the small businesses had to close. The lodge is the only thing that's remained open, but they lost all their tourist business. Reggie had the idea to open it for corporate events and fly the guests in."

"Which is why she owes you ten?" Melody guessed.

"Exactly. She rented the plane; I flew the charter as a favor."

"Why not use yours? Did your dad not like the idea?"

"Experimental planes can't be used for anything but personal flying. This would technically be considered commercial since she was arranging the flights for guests, even if I wasn't charging her."

"That's really nice of you, Justin. How do you guys know each other in the first place?"

"We went to college together. She was my calculus tutor."

"You must have been really bad at calculus if you were willing to do that kind of favor." When Justin didn't say anything, she narrowed her eyes at him. "You were dating. I can't believe you just asked a favor of an ex-girlfriend to take another girl on a date!"

He laughed. "It's really not like that. We dated for a while, but there just weren't any sparks. On either side. Decided the only reason we lasted as long as we did was because we were good friends. Didn't seem any reason to ruin that."

Now Melody couldn't help but look at Reggie in a different light, and she wasn't sure if she liked the twinge of jealousy that surfaced. "I don't believe you. She's gorgeous."

He tugged a lock of Melody's blonde hair. "Not my type."

It was clearly a dodge—Reggie would be any guy's type—but the fact that he made the attempt was flattering. She relaxed into the neoprene-covered seat and watched out the window. They had to be somewhere remote, because not even a cursory attempt at clearing the snow had been made—only the red-and-white-striped stakes on either side marked the margins of the road. Justin navigated it as surely as he flew his plane, glancing occasionally at the GPS to make sure they were on the right track. And then he pulled over to the side and pointed out her window. A wide, white field stretched out beside the road, a mountain meadow ringed with trees, steep undulating slopes like a kid's wavy slide smoothing the tree line down to the open area. "This is us."

Melody climbed out of the Jeep and sunk into snow nearly to her knees, suddenly glad for the loan of snow pants. The cold air bit into her skin and seared her lungs, and she tugged down her hat tighter over her ears. Justin pulled the two black inner tubes from the back of the Jeep and tossed her one, which she barely caught in midair. It was heavier than she expected, with handles and a tow strap attached.

"Ready?" Justin asked.

"I'm ready. In fact, I'll race you. Go!" Melody took off before he could react, plunging into the snowy field. It was an ill-considered race, the furious pace she'd imagined more like a slog through molasses. She heard Justin's laugh behind her, clearly amused at the attempt, but she refused to admit defeat, even when the altitude and the cold made her breath come hard and fast. By the time she reached the top of the hill, she was thoroughly winded.

Justin climbed up beside her, not even out of breath. "I knew you were competitive, but I didn't know you were crazy."

"There's still a lot you don't know about me."

"Like what?"

"Like my mad tubing skills."

He threw back his head and laughed. "We'll see. I'll race you down."

"And what do I get if I win?"

"A kiss." His eyes sparkled with mischief.

"And if you win?"

"A kiss."

Melody narrowed her eyes. "Somehow I think you come out ahead in both these scenarios."

"If you really think *I'm* the one who comes out ahead, then I've been falling down on the job." He flipped his tube over. "Ready?"

"No, no. If I win, you have to haul me back up the hill in my tube."

Justin sighed. "Okay. Fine."

"Good. Set, go!" Melody threw herself onto the tube and let out a little scream when she took off far faster than she was expecting. The inner tube raced down the hill, getting air at the edge of each undulation. She gripped the handles for dear life, the grin on her face threatening to split her cold skin. When she reached the bottom a full second ahead of Justin, she threw her hands up in victory. "I won!"

"You cheated."

She gave him her most innocent look. "I have no idea what you're talking about. I don't cheat."

"Sure you don't." He winked at her and reached for the leash in the snow. "But lucky for you, I'm feeling charitable toward my little snow bunny today."

She gaped. "Snow bunny?"

"If the pink pants fit . . ."

Melody crossed her arms over her chest in mock petulance. "I was starting to feel bad about tricking you, but now I think I'll just sit back and enjoy the ride."

He jerked the tube forward, and she grabbed on to the handles before she could tip. "Hey, be careful with the merchandise!"

His laugh trailed back to her as he slowly climbed the hill, pulling her behind him without any seeming effort. The guy must spend all his free time working out on the road if he was this unaffected by exertion and altitude.

"Okay back there, my queen?" Humor—and more than a little sarcasm—tinged his voice.

"I was just thinking that those snow pants do absolutely nothing for your butt."

"But you *were* checking out my butt."

"I was trying, no thanks to you." When he turned around in surprise, she just grinned and crossed her arms over her bulky jacket. He narrowed his eyes and hauled her the last dozen feet up the hill.

And unceremoniously overturned the tube to dump her in the snow. She came up spluttering, covered in powder, ice crystals clinging to her hair. She wiped her face with the back of her hand and narrowed her eyes at him. "Oh, it's on now."

He crouched down, like he was expecting an imminent snowball to the face, but she just smiled. "No, that would be too easy. I want you to wonder when I might get my revenge."

"You have a sadistic streak; do you know that?"

"So I've been told. Because I'm going to enjoy trouncing you on this next run."

"This is supposed to be fun, Melody. It doesn't have to be a competition."

"Then how would it be fun?" She grinned at him and dragged her tube over to the place she'd just slid down. The snow was packed already, meaning it would be slick and fast. Justin, on the other hand, picked a new line. Poor sap. He really didn't know what he was up against.

Justin watched her suspiciously, but she wasn't going to jump the gun this time. She waited until he called "Go!" and shoved off on her tube. It sped down the hill even faster than before, but she saw Justin creep up beside her and then overtake her, hitting the bottom a split second before she did.

She sprang off the tube in disbelief. "What? How did you manage that?"

"You forget that I'm a lot bigger than you. More weight, more speed." He moved to her side and pulled her to him by the cuff of her jacket. "Now my kiss."

She turned her face and tapped her cheek. "Right there."

"You're a little cruel."

"You already said I was sadistic."

He pressed a chaste kiss to her cheek. "That's ascetic, not sadistic. You're really just denying yourself."

Melody rolled her eyes and turned away, bending over as if she were going to pick up the leash to her tube. Instead she gathered a handful of snow, turned, and launched it directly at Justin's head.

He was quick. He jerked to the side so it clipped the edge of his hat instead of colliding with his self-satisfied smirk. His eyes glowed with mischief. "Now you've asked for it." He bent down and scooped up an enormous handful of snow.

Melody flipped her tube on its side to use as cover and the snowball smashed across its bottom. She fired back another snowball before he could recover; it hit him squarely in the chest.

"C'mon, hotshot," she taunted. "You can do better than that." She gathered up another one, but when she peeked out to launch it, a handful of packed snow hit her in the face. She spluttered but didn't hesitate, throwing her own.

He ducked and it sailed over his head.

"Now you're going to get it." She crouched behind her tube and began to make snowballs, one after another. She peered around the tube, ready to launch the next one, but Justin was nowhere to be seen.

A snowball crashed into the back of her head. She whirled and a second one hit her in the face.

"I give!" she shouted, wiping snow from her eyes. "Stop. You win!"

Melody knelt, head bent, trying to clear the rapidly melting snowball from her face. When she didn't get up, Justin rushed to her side and knelt beside her. "Are you okay?"

"Sucker." She popped up and shoved a handful of snow down his jacket. The look of shock on his face was worth the fact that her hair was turning into a mass of curl-sicles from the onslaught.

He grabbed her wrists before she could retaliate further. "That was just mean."

"No, I just like to win." She grinned at him, out of breath and shivering. "I'd have thought you already knew that about me."

"And what else should I know about you?" His voice seemed to drop an octave, his tone transforming into something intimate.

She swallowed, suddenly out of breath in a way that had nothing to do with the snowball fight. He was teasing, but the urge to be completely honest bubbled up inside of her. "I know I come off all confident, but I haven't had the best luck with men in the past."

His teasing smile faded. "How so? Is there someone I need to go beat up for you?"

Melody laughed, but even to her own ears, it sounded fragile. She plopped down on the edge of her tube. "Ana already tried. She's barely five foot two, but I had to keep her from going over to my last ex's house with a baseball bat."

Justin crouched beside her. "I like her already. I do not like the fact your ex did something baseball-bat worthy."

"Yeah, well, I should have known better than to get involved with my chef. The worst thing was, I loved him." She laughed humorlessly. "You know that saying about no one buying the cow when they can get the milk for free? Turns out it's right, at least when it comes to me. He was seeing someone else the entire time. They got engaged a week after I found out."

Justin shook his head in disbelief. "Well, first of all, you're not a cow, so let's get rid of that insulting metaphor. You're a kind, beautiful, interesting woman. That was 100 percent about him. It was no reflection on you. I feel sorry for his fiancée, honestly."

Of course he was going to say that. But his words were sincere, his blue eyes so earnest that she could feel his gaze penetrate directly to the soft, vulnerable parts she tried to keep hidden. She'd told him this much; she might as well put it all on the table.

"When I said we should keep seeing each other, I didn't think I'd like you this much. I don't want you to leave."

His expression softened. He pulled off his gloves, then combed the crusted snow from her hair with his fingers. "It's all I've been able to think about. I don't want to leave you either, Melody. You're like no woman I've ever met."

Her heart thudded against her rib cage, a drumbeat in the quiet. "I've heard that before."

"I'm sure you have. But I promise you, I mean it." He brushed cool fingers across her equally cold cheek, then brought his lips to hers. Her breath came in a sharp inhalation as she wrapped her arms around his neck, giving herself over completely to the kiss, heat blazing through her body in the cold. He tightened his arm around her, burying his other hand into her hair. She wanted to hold something back, that part of her that had been hurt before, but deep down she knew it was futile. Her head might warn caution, but her heart was the one in charge, and it sought nothing more than the way he made her feel. Wanted. Adored.

When they parted, they were both breathing hard, little puffs hanging in cold air. Justin smiled. "I'm surprised the snow isn't melted down to the ground around us."

She laughed quietly. "I'm sorry for shoving snow down your coat."

"I'm sorry for . . . Sorry, I can't do it. I'm

really not." Justin pulled her to her feet. "What do you think? A couple more runs, or break for snacks?"

Only then did Melody realize she was shivering. "I wouldn't mind something hot in the Jeep right now." At his smirk she said, "I meant something hot to drink."

"I'm glad you specified. I was starting to think I'd read you completely wrong." He winked, then took her gloved hand in his bare one. "Come on, snow bunny. I happen to know that Reggie packed us some of the lodge's famous hot chocolate."

A couple of minutes later, ensconced in the warmth of the Jeep, its heater pumping out lukewarm air from the vents, Melody studied his profile, the ache in her chest intensifying. She was at the edge of a precipice, one she couldn't afford to tip over. Not when their respective businesses would pull them in opposite directions mere weeks from now.

"Here you go." Justin poured hot chocolate from a thermos into a frigid stoneware mug, then handed it to her. "There's some shortbread in here too, if you feel like it."

She felt shy and surprisingly fragile as she took a cookie and bit into the buttery square. "This is amazing. From the lodge?"

"Probably," Justin said. "The cook, Eloise, has been there since the lodge opened in 1973.

She must be . . . seventysomething? She's partly retired, just comes back to cook for guests. And that's fewer and farther between these days."

"That's such a shame. It's beautiful up here. Every time I go to those quaint little mountain towns, they feel overrun with tourists. This is like going back in time. You'd think people would be flocking to the quiet and seclusion."

"You'd think, but there just isn't the infrastructure to support tourism anymore. The lodge is no longer open to the public because they can't afford the full-time staff. Reggie just hires event staff as needed. There isn't a gas station in town because there's not enough people to justify trucking in the fuel. The nearest grocery store is twenty miles through the pass, same with restaurants. The only people who live up here are hermits and recluses."

"Sometimes I can understand the inclination. Of course, I'd go a little crazy without people to bake for. You'd find me in my little cabin, bread stacked up to the rafters."

"Instead of the crazy cat lady, you'd be the crazy bread lady?"

"Something like that." She fell silent, looking out at the pristine, peaceful landscape for a long moment before turning back to him. "I can't believe you did this. No one's ever done anything like this for me."

"Now that, I cannot believe. Or at least I think

it's a shame. You are the kind of woman a man goes all out for."

Melody smiled into her cup, warmth blooming in her chest. "What do you think? Should we do a few more runs?"

Justin checked his watch. "I think so, and then we should probably head back for an early dinner. We need to be off the mountain before sundown."

"Then we're burning daylight. And I'm still looking for a rematch. Unless you're too scared of getting beat by a girl?"

Justin leaned over and kissed her softly on the lips. "Bring it on, snow bunny."

CHAPTER TWENTY-FIVE

Justin followed Melody from the Jeep to where they had left their tubes on the slope, a smile on his face. She was a complicated woman, equal parts tough and vulnerable, smart and playful. He was never sure which side was going to surface at any given moment, which only played into his fascination. And contributed to the constant desire to grab her and kiss her senseless.

It was why he couldn't fathom how he was going to leave her behind.

They'd gotten themselves into a royal mess. He'd been just as sure as she was that this relationship would fizzle out like all his previous ones. That one or the other of them would get tired of the struggle to see each other amid his travel and her night schedule. And yet she was fast becoming the best part of his day, his month. He used to live to fly, and now he flew simply so he could return and see her. The idea of coming home, even to blue waters and sandy beaches, and finding her absent held absolutely no appeal.

A gust of wind peppered his face with grains of powdery snow, causing him to cast a concerned eye to the sky. It was still mostly blue with a wispy covering of clouds. An errant gust, hopefully. The weather report, which he had checked this afternoon before leaving, showed clear conditions with gusts of no more than seven miles an hour. But he knew how quickly things could change in the mountains.

Justin managed to beat Melody two of the next three runs, citing his heavier weight as the deciding factor, then convinced her to ride the rest of the time with him. Really it was just an excuse to have her nestled against him, her back against his chest with his arms wrapped around her. The sweetest kind of torture. But within the hour, the wind had picked up in a way that was starting to make him nervous.

He didn't let on. If they took off with this wind, she'd be nervous enough; no need to put the potential dangers into her head now. "Let's go back. Believe it or not, I'm getting hungry."

"I'm pretty happy where we are right now." She didn't move from the tube, instead twisting around to kiss him.

He groaned. "You're killing me, Melody. Seriously, Reggie is expecting us back, and I'm not going to make Eloise hold our dinner for us."

"Okay, okay." She levered herself up with his help, and he reluctantly followed. Then they collected their tubes and dragged them back to the Jeep. When he turned on the ignition and turned around on the road, the wind threw a crackle of hard snow up into the windshield.

"Just in time," Melody said. "It's really getting windy."

"Mountains." Justin kept his tone bland, but he was starting to get a bad feeling about this.

By the time they reached the lodge, he couldn't ignore the truth. The report had been wrong about the afternoon conditions, and he'd been too distracted by his gorgeous companion to do as he ought and check the forecast a second time when they arrived. The wind sock on the edge of the airstrip stuck straight out.

Reggie met them at the door with a bright smile. "Did you two have fun?"

Melody beamed. "It's been ages since I've been tubing. I can't remember the last time I had so much fun." She cast a look at Justin, and he swore he saw a tinge of pink on her cheeks that had nothing to do with the cold. Reggie lifted her eyebrows at him and he sent her a warning glare.

"Why don't you come inside and thaw out. I've opened a couple of rooms on the second floor. You can shower and get warmed up before dinner. You're still a little early."

"Go ahead," Justin said to Melody. "I'll meet you back here when you're done. I need to file our return flight plan."

"Okay." Melody smiled, unaware of the thoughts rattling around his head. She accepted Reggie's directions to room eight and climbed the wide stairs to the second floor, giving him a little wave before she disappeared down the hallway. He watched her go, smiling at the upper hall long after she left.

"Wow, you've got it bad. I've never seen you like this over a woman."

"She's different," he said without thinking, then cringed. "Reg—"

"How long have we been friends, Justin? I assure you, as tempting a specimen of manhood as you are, I'm not secretly pining over you. If I recall, you made a pretty terrible boyfriend."

He grimaced. "I'm sorry. You know—"

"But you make a pretty good friend." Reg socked him in the arm, surprisingly strong considering her willowy frame. "I'm happy for you. But I also know that was a blatant excuse to get her out of the room. What gives?"

"I need an internet-connected computer if you don't mind. My phone doesn't get any data up here, and I need to check the weather."

"I was wondering if that was going to be a problem. You can use the one in my office."

He followed her to the small space off the outfitting room, dark-paneled and filled with heavy log furniture. Her desk was covered with paperwork. He sat down at the computer, trying not to notice the big red *Past Due* stamp on the bill sitting by the mouse.

"Is that wind sock outside fifteen or twenty miles per hour?"

"Fifteen, I think," Reggie said. "Why?"

"We might need to cut dinner short if there's a break in the wind. Technically, I can still take off, but . . ."

"I wouldn't blame you for not risking it."

He pulled up the weather radar for the area, saw nothing out of the ordinary. Then he looked up the Aviation Weather Center to check the wind aloft reports and swore beneath his breath.

"Bad news?"

"Not good." He drummed his fingertips on the desk. "I'm going to file my flight plan, but if the winds don't calm by six, we're stuck here for the night."

"You're always welcome here. Or you could try driving down and come back for the plane tomorrow."

"No, it's bumper-to-bumper on I-70 the whole way because of road construction. We wouldn't get back until midnight the way things have been lately. You might say some prayers for good weather if you wouldn't mind."

"You've got it. But really, what's the harm? You can fly out at dawn, have her back in time for work or whatever. Melody doesn't strike me as the high-maintenance sort."

That was true. And really, a night at a romantic mountain lodge wasn't the worst date scenario, as long as he was careful not to let it get *too* romantic. The last thing he wanted her to think was that this was all a setup, especially after what she'd told him about her ex.

"You're right. I'll be finished in just a minute. Don't say anything to Melody yet, though."

"My lips are sealed. I'm going to check on dinner and see if we can't speed things up. If you catch a break, you'll want to go immediately."

Justin nodded, but he knew that it was wishful thinking. The wind aloft reports showed speeds that were far too high for such a light plane, not to mention the potential for dangerous downdrafts over valleys and passes. He wasn't going to risk their lives and his aircraft to get home on time in dangerous conditions.

He wanted to kick himself for not being more conscientious. He knew better. Had he checked the forecast, he would have turned them straight around and gone back to Denver while the getting was good, even if it meant missing this afternoon with Melody.

He filled out the flight plan with a new departure time, which gave him a two-hour window before it had to be refiled. By then, it would be too dark to fly under VFR rules anyway.

He went upstairs to room seven, a large bedroom decorated with the same combination of leather, fabric, and hand-woven rugs as the great room, and stripped off his wet snow clothes. The sweater beneath his jacket was slightly damp, thanks to Melody's sneak attack, but at least he had jeans to change into. He showered in water as hot as he could stand to chase the chill from his bones and then dressed again. He was just emerging from his room when Melody exited the one next door.

Her face was scrubbed clean of makeup—though it had been so subtle, until now he hadn't realized she'd been wearing any—with her hair braided in a long plait down her back. Her sweater and jeans hugged every generous curve, making his throat instantly go dry.

"I left my coat in the bathroom to drip dry. I hope that's okay."

"I'm sure it is." He glanced around to make sure they were alone and then tugged her to him for a kiss.

"What was that for?"

He dipped his head and murmured in her ear, "I just can't seem to help myself."

Footsteps below told him that Reggie or Eloise was back, so he released her reluctantly and took her hand instead. "Dinner awaits."

Reggie had had their meal set up in a small dining room off the great hall, near the window overlooking the airstrip. For such an out-of-the-way place, the arrangement was elegant: white tablecloth, gold-rimmed tableware, graceful wine and water glasses. He pulled out Melody's chair for her and then settled into the one opposite. He was wondering how to broach the subject of their possibly changing plans when Melody glanced out the window and said, "Wow, I thought it was supposed to be clear and calm today."

"So did I," Justin said darkly.

Her eyebrows rose and then understanding dawned in her expression. "It's too windy to leave."

"Possibly," he said, even though he'd all but given up on the winds calming. The last thing he wanted to do was leave in a lull and end up buffeted by high winds above the ridges. "I can take off in anything up to twenty, but it gets sketchy at higher altitudes. Do you have anything planned for tomorrow?"

"Not since I became officially unemployed."

Eloise appeared then with two plates in hand. She looked like everyone's grandmother, gray hair twisted up in a bun, her plump form draped in slacks and a button-down shirt, with a plain apron over her clothes. She set the plates down in front of them and said professionally, "Butter-basted brook trout over barley, apple, and lima beans. I'll be back out with the bread." She winked at Justin.

"Oh, no you don't. Come give me a hug." He stood and held his arms out. The woman laughed and pulled him into a tight embrace. "Don't think you're going to get away from me."

"I was just trying not to compete with your young lady," Eloise said with a sassy smile.

"This young man is my favorite. Just don't tell my sons. They'd disown me."

"My lips are sealed." Melody's lips quivered against laughter. When Eloise left, Melody looked at Justin. "Competition?"

"If I were forty years older, maybe. When I was doing the charter flights for Reggie, Eloise would insist on feeding me and then sending enough back with me for two days. For a bachelor who hates to cook, it was something of a godsend."

"Everyone needs a bossy grandmother." Melody's smile faded, sadness creeping into her expression.

He reached across the table and captured her hand, sending her an understanding smile. "You miss her."

"All the time. Most of the time it's just a dull ache, but occasionally—"

"I understand." He squeezed her hand. "I never met your grandma, but somehow I have a feeling she'd be incredibly proud of you right now."

"I think she would too. She'd probably say, 'Melody Anne, it's about darn time.'" She smiled, then picked up her fork and tasted a piece of fish. "This is wonderful. I can't believe the lodge wouldn't stay open based on the food alone!"

"Hard to come here for dinner when you can't get to it. Plus, most people living in the area aren't looking for fine dining. A shame, too, because Eloise is amazing. She used to cook in San Francisco before she married a Colorado man and came out here."

"That must have been before there were many women working in kitchens," Melody said. "I'm impressed."

They worked their way through a dinner that was indeed very impressive, followed by a blueberry crumble that more than met Melody's standards.

Justin cast a regretful look out the window, where the winds had only increased. "I'm calling it. We're going to have to stay here tonight."

Melody sent him a small smile that did dangerous things to his insides. "I'm not exactly complaining. It's beautiful up here."

Easy there, he told himself at the leap of anticipation in his gut. He wasn't going to take advantage of the situation, no matter how much he might want to. He'd determined long ago that he wouldn't be that sort of man, regardless of the shaky state of his faith. He was pretty sure God wouldn't strike him down for sleeping with Melody, but it would most certainly break the trust they enjoyed. He wasn't going to be another guy in her life who only wanted to use her.

He found Reggie to let her know they would be staying the night, and then returned to the dining room, where the table had been cleared. He found Melody sitting in one of the huge leather chairs in front of a roaring fire, staring pensively into the flames. He plopped in the chair beside her. "Scrabble."

She glanced at him. "What?"

"I just passed a stack of games in the other room and saw Scrabble. I don't suppose you'd like to play."

She straightened, that competitive gleam coming to her eyes. "I don't know. I have to warn you that I'm pretty good at it. Did you notice my extensive collection of Victorian novels?"

"Contrary to what you might think, I am no slouch myself." He grinned. "What do you say?"

"Up to you. I play Scrabble like I snowball fight."

He lowered his voice and gave her a significant look. "I like the way you snowball fight."

She blushed again, then rose from her seat. "You're on. Just remember, I warned you."

Justin had been telling the truth—he was no slouch at Scrabble. But he quickly found how difficult it was to match a girl with thousands of books. She came up with rare words like *aumbry* and *cumbrous,* sending him to the dictionary more than once to challenge her plays. He had plenty of lesser-known aviation terms, *dihedral* and *yaw* among them, but it was *longeron* that she challenged. He smiled smugly when she found it in the dictionary. "See, you're not the only one with a vocabulary."

331

"Good-looking, capable, *and* intelligent," she teased. "You're the whole package."

And teasing or not, he rather liked the pronouncement.

They moved on to rummy, which she played like she did everything else: on the edge of vicious competition. But she looked so adorable he couldn't feel bad about losing to her over and over. To be honest, his mind wasn't completely on the games anyway. The planner in him, the problem solver, wanted to talk about their situation and break it down until they came to a solution that wouldn't end with either or both of them miserable. But every time, he pulled the words back. It was always possible they'd find no solution, and that was something he wasn't ready to accept.

The clock's hands crawled past ten, but Melody seemed to be as reluctant as he felt to end the night. Eloise had left them a vacuum carafe of hot chocolate before she retired for the night, so they poured another cup each and collapsed on the deep leather sofa nearest to the waning fire.

Melody didn't hesitate to scoot up against him, legs tucked beneath her, and he draped his arm around her shoulders.

"I'm sorry I messed up today's plans."

Melody peered up at him. "I'm not. It's been ages since I've had so much fun with a guy."

"Honestly, me too."

"It's been ages since you've had this much fun with a guy?"

He huffed out a laugh. "Be quiet. You know what I mean."

"I do." Melody's smile faded. "So what's the story with Reggie?"

He shifted so he could look at her better. "Are you jealous? I meant it when I said we were just friends."

"I'm not jealous. I'm . . . curious. I know you said you used to date, but it seems like there's a lot more than that."

Justin drew in a breath and then exhaled it slowly. He should have known Melody was perceptive, that she'd pick up on the fact he and Reggie weren't merely old friends. She just waited, her expression patient, while Justin wrestled with how much to tell her.

"Reggie and I became friends our freshman year of college. She was a math major, and I was business. She, her roommate Allyson, and I became inseparable." He threw her a grin. "It helped that we were in most of the same courses, because I was working my way through school and I usually had to choose between my flight students and going to class. Reggie and Allyson took notes and brought me up to speed on what I'd missed."

"Hence the calculus tutoring."

"Right. Our junior year, Allyson started seeing

this man she'd met at her barista job. He'd come in and see her practically every day on his way home from work. Reggie was worried that the relationship was getting too serious, but I told her she was overreacting. Ally seemed happy. She was in love. She said they were talking about getting married as soon as she graduated.

"And then one night, Ally called Reggie. She was helping me study for a test in the library, so she let it go to voice mail. We didn't check the message until we left a few hours later. Ally was in hysterics. Turns out the guy was married and his wife caught them together. Reg and I rushed back to the dorms, but she wasn't there. We waited up all night for her and she never showed.

"We didn't know what to do. She wasn't answering her phone. None of her friends had seen her. In the morning, Reggie insisted on calling the police. But we were too late."

He swallowed hard at the recollection. "Sometime after Ally called us, she'd lost control of her car and wrapped it around a tree. They think she died instantly."

"Alcohol?" Melody asked softly.

"It was in her bloodstream, but she wasn't even close to drunk. The cops ruled it an accident, but we've always wondered . . . There were no skid marks, you know?"

Melody took his hand, interlacing their fingers and shaking him out of his memories.

334

"After that, Reg and I kind of turned to each other. No one else understood what it was like for us, the guilt we felt for not answering the call. Even today, I wonder if things would have turned out differently if we'd talked to her."

"You can't do that to yourself. You don't even know what really happened. It might have been just as they said. An accident."

"I know." Justin dragged his eyes away from the fire and back to Melody's face. "Anyway, it didn't take long for us to realize that we were together for the wrong reasons. We were better as friends than anything else, and that's how we've stayed for the last twelve years."

Melody stretched up and kissed the corner of his mouth. "I'm so sorry. It's terrible to lose someone you care about that way. I can understand why you don't get serious about anyone."

Justin's brow furrowed. "That's not why. My job—"

"—is no more difficult on relationships than mine, even if that's not saying much. You never wanted to be the kind of guy to lead a woman on."

He stared at her, momentarily at a loss for words. She was absolutely right. He'd never thought about it in those terms. "I saw how my parents' marriage ended and never wanted to experience that. And if I'm not going to get married and settle down and have kids . . ."

". . . you should only date women who don't expect too much from you," Melody finished. "I get it, Justin. It's totally reasonable. I mean, it's a lonely way to live, but I understand why you'd feel that way."

And yet somehow he'd gone ahead and dated Melody, who he'd pegged from the beginning as the kind of woman who wanted, needed, and deserved a commitment. He'd broken his own rules, thinking that the time limit on their relationship would keep things from getting too serious.

"Hey." She reached up and turned his face toward hers, looking deep into his eyes. "I knew what I was getting into. I'm not going to do anything drastic if this doesn't work out. Have a little faith."

Faith. As if that had done him any good before. As if God had bothered to heal his sister or reconcile his parents or keep Ally from speeding full force into a tree. He had no doubt God existed, had even prayed to turn his life over to Him as a teen with several other members of his youth group. And yet in the ensuing years, he'd begun to wonder if sending a Savior to earth had been God's last attempt to help His creation. The world often felt like a cosmic windup toy, set down and left to career wildly on its own, unhinged, without direction.

"I'm not sure I know what that means anymore," he said quietly. "I'd like to believe that there's some bigger pattern at work, but so much seems to be just rotten chance."

Melody leaned her head against his chest. "Trust me, it's not always easy. There are things in my life that made me wonder where God was, why He didn't step in when He could have. But then things like this bakery make me realize that there has to be a plan in there somewhere. Every step of this venture has fallen into place far too easily. I can't help feeling like God orchestrated it all to come together because this is what He wants me to be doing. And if that's the case, who am I to argue? It doesn't feel like coincidence."

"You know what I like most about you?"

She smiled up at him. "No, but I can't wait to hear."

"Your unshakable optimism." He chuckled and kissed the top of her head. "However, I do not feel optimistic about flying groggy tomorrow, so I think it's time that we call it a night." He carefully extracted himself from Melody and held out his hand to help her up.

Melody followed him silently up the stairs to their adjacent rooms. Away from their cocoon by the fire, he began to regret telling her about Allyson and interjecting that heavy note into what had been an otherwise-lighthearted day. He stopped in front of the door marked eight, and Melody turned to him.

"I'm sorry if I ruined the mood." His hands went to her waist of their own accord, drawing her nearer. "This was supposed to be fun."

"It was," she said softly. "It was better than fun."

There was that warning again that they were straying into dangerous territory: the softness of her voice, the way she looked at him with shining eyes. He should turn around and leave her, but he stayed rooted to his spot.

Like their very first date, she was the one to move first, stretching up to press her lips to his. The sweetness of her lips teased at the edges of his self-control, begging him to deepen the kiss. But they were alone in an otherwise-deserted lodge; there would be nothing to stop them from falling into her room and letting the electricity that sparked between them lead to its natural conclusion.

And he wouldn't. For one thing, it would be wrong. For another, it was just plain unfair. They had yet to determine their future together. He wouldn't make a tacit promise to her that he might not be able to honor.

Justin disentangled himself, seeing his own desire mirrored in her expression, and pressed as chaste a kiss as he could manage to her lips.

"Good night, Melody. I'll see you in the morning."

He turned to his own room before he could

change his mind and shut the door behind him, telling himself he'd done the only honorable thing. God might not care how His creation broke one another, but at least Justin still did.

CHAPTER TWENTY-SIX

Melody threw the lock on her door and paced the length of her room, both relieved and confused. It had been a magical day. The flight, the snow, the amazing meal. The way Justin focused on her like she was the only woman in the world. There was no shortage of chemistry between them—that kiss in the snow had proven that—but he seemed determined not to take advantage of the convenient opportunity that the weather had provided.

She sank onto the edge of her bed. Micah—or any of the other men she'd dated recently—wouldn't have shown the same kind of restraint. Hadn't, in fact. The only conclusion she could draw was that she'd finally broken her streak of bad choices.

And yet Justin was an even worse variety of bad choice, because she could no longer pretend her interest was temporary. When he left, it would be a pain that didn't compare to the betrayals she'd experienced.

"You're so stupid," she whispered, the resignation in her voice surprising even her. How could she have thought she was getting out of this intact?

Melody stripped off her jeans and sweater

and climbed between the cool, smooth sheets, but sleep wasn't going to come easy. Not considering her slow-adjusting body clock, and not considering how thinking of the future wound her in knots. She finally slept before sunrise and woke up just after 9 a.m., no more refreshed and every bit as troubled as she'd been three hours earlier.

She dressed in yesterday's clothes, washed her face, and went down to the dining room, where Justin was already sipping a cup of coffee and making notations on a clipboard. She paused just outside his notice, watching how his ridiculously handsome face creased in concentration, and felt the little leap of her heart that meant something wonderful and absolutely no good at the same time.

"Good morning," she said finally, walking over to the table.

He looked up, his face breaking into a beaming smile. "Good morning. Sleep well?"

"Okay, I guess. Are we leaving?"

"Just need to file the flight plan. I was waiting for you to wake up."

"Sorry. It took me a while to fall asleep last night. I'm used to shift work. It's still hard to sleep when normal people sleep."

"I forgot about that. Had I remembered, I would have kept you up and continued to kick your butt at Scrabble."

Her jaw dropped. "You did not kick my butt. You beat me by one point, and I still think that *longeron* is not a valid word."

"It's in the dictionary. I know you're used to winning, but so am I." He leaned forward and pitched his voice low. "I will say, that killer instinct is pretty irresistible."

Melody wrestled down a flush and plopped herself into the seat across from him. She tapped a half-empty French press. "Coffee?"

"Help yourself." He slid a clean mug across the table to her. "Or I'm sure Eloise will brew a new pot. She said to let her know when you woke up so she can bring breakfast."

Melody poured the remainder of the coffee into her mug and took an experimental sip. It was already lukewarm and slightly too strong, but it was caffeinated, and it slid into her like a magical elixir. "I'm going to need a couple more of these before I can have a conversation."

"You're in luck, then." He pointed to the doorway, where Eloise was bustling through with a basket of baked goods and another French press. The woman either had hearing like a dog's or she had them under surveillance.

"Good morning, Melody," Eloise said cheerily. "I hope you don't mind a cold breakfast. I didn't know when you'd be up and I know that Justin wants to get going as soon as possible."

"This is wonderful, thank you." There were

house-made blueberry muffins, carrot bread that looked suspiciously like cake, and a small bowl of fruit. Melody would never find fault with baked goods and coffee.

Justin put aside his clipboard and rose from his seat. "You eat; I'll be right back."

Melody waited until Eloise bustled back to the kitchen and then slid the clipboard around to face her. When Justin returned, she was frowning at a chart filled with numbers and abbreviations in his neat block penmanship.

"What is this?" she asked.

"It's a flight log." He pulled his chair closer to hers so he could look over her shoulder, his nearness sending shivers through her. "These are waypoints, minimum altitudes, course headings." He flipped to a chart beneath it and showed her a line that connected their location to Centennial Airport.

"Isn't that why you have a GPS?"

"Electronics can fail. This is a short flight, and I'm familiar with the route, but I always have a hard copy and navigational charts just in case." He shot her a sideways grin. "It's a good idea to avoid peaks and ridges and other obstacles."

"I would think so." She looked closely at the chart, which was basically a topographical map with overlapping concentric circles and little square boxes with numbers in them. Frequencies for the control towers, she thought. "This actually makes sense to you?"

He moved his chair back around to his side and reached for a blueberry muffin. "I'd be careful asking too many questions or I'm going to be tempted to wow you with my incredible aviation prowess."

"And here I was just thinking how humble you were for a pilot." She stuck her tongue out, earning a grin in return from him.

"In all seriousness, I'm careful flying into and out of the mountains. It takes specific training and experience and a lot of attention. If you hadn't noticed, by the way, there's emergency equipment behind the seats, including food to last us three days."

"In case we crash?" That wasn't a comforting thought.

"In case we make an 'unexpected, off-airport landing.' " Justin made air-quotes with his fingers and went back to his muffin, completely unperturbed.

Well, if there was one thing she'd learned about him, it was that he was cautious. She could appreciate that when he had her life in his hands at ten thousand feet. She watched him from beneath her lashes while she sipped her coffee. She'd misread him so badly on their first meeting. He wore the good looks and the flirtatious manner as a mask, a costume. It took time to realize he was as cautious and methodical about life as he was in the captain's seat.

They polished off far more of the baked goods than was good for them, then moved out the back of the lodge toward the airfield. Melody remained in one of the rocking chairs, watching as he did his preflight walk around.

Reggie emerged from the side door and approached slowly before sinking into the chair next to Melody's. She watched Justin for a minute too before saying, "He's a good guy."

"I'm getting that feeling."

"He must like you. He doesn't do things like this for just anyone."

Melody shot her a searching look. "He did for you."

Reggie gave a little laugh and shook her head. "We have a different relationship than you probably think. He helped me through a tough time in college. I needed a friend, and he was there when no one else was."

"He told me about Allyson. I'm sorry."

"He did?" Reggie seemed genuinely surprised. "He doesn't talk about it with anyone. Not even me. Not anymore."

"He said you two got together for a little while after it happened."

"We did. We had shared something terrible. I think we both assumed that meant we should be in a relationship, before we were mature enough to understand that there's more than one kind. But honestly? It was like kissing my brother."

Melody arched an eyebrow, and Reggie pressed her hand to her forehead. "Right? How could that be? Look at him. He's probably one of the most attractive guys I've ever seen in real life. And there was just . . . nothing."

Melody looked out toward Justin, who was still going over the plane's mechanics with every bit of thoroughness she'd come to expect from him. The tightening in her chest was almost painful. When she turned back, Reggie was watching her with a knowing smile. She pushed herself to her feet. "It was nice meeting you, Melody."

Melody shook Reggie's outstretched hand. "Same here. Good luck to you."

"Thanks. I'm going to need it." She smiled without elaborating and walked out to Justin, giving him a quick and completely platonic hug. When she came back, she tossed Melody one more smile. "He's about ready to go."

Melody crossed the snowy field to the plane, where Justin waited to help her up onto the wing and into the passenger compartment. He disappeared for several minutes, then climbed into the left seat and pulled the canopy forward.

"Ready to go?"

"Absolutely." She stayed quiet while he flipped through his notes on the clipboard, went through the preflight check, and started the engine. They put on their headsets, tested to make sure they could hear each other, and then they were taxiing into position on the airstrip.

He throttled the engine up to maximum power and fiddled with a bright-red knob for a moment; then they hurtled down the narrow airstrip. Melody's stomach dipped when the wheels left the ground, but Justin didn't climb immediately, instead hovering what felt like inches above the dirt as they picked up speed. Then the plane nosed up into a steep-angled climb, and she couldn't stop herself from digging her nails into the leather upholstery. The sensation of weightlessness made her head spin, and she purposely focused on the instrument panel in front of her rather than the steeply pitched view out the side. Only when they finally leveled out did she release her death grip on the seat and dare a peek out the window.

They were already above the nearest mountain peak. Justin reached over and rested his hand on her arm. "Are you okay?"

Her breath came out in a rush. "I'm fine. Now."

"Sorry. I should have warned you. It's a pretty hard climb."

She let out a shaky laugh. "Now you know the truth. I'm a total coward."

"You are not a coward. I'm honored by your trust in me."

"I don't have much choice if I want to get

home." She shot him a smile so he knew she was kidding, then slid on her sunglasses against the glare of the rapidly rising sun.

They flew in relative silence, the muted hum of the engine in the background. And then Justin asked, "What were you and Reggie talking about?"

She turned to him. "You."

"That's not unsettling at all."

"I think you probably know what she had to say. She was reassuring me that there was nothing between you two."

His tone was calm but curious. "Did you need reassuring?"

"Not really. I know you're friends, and I also know that you wouldn't have gone to all this trouble for me if you were still interested in her. I believe her when she says she's not attracted to you—"

"Ouch."

"Which is good for me, since I most definitely am."

He gave her a look that made her heart beat a little faster. "Good save on the ego crusher there. Does that mean you've forgiven me for stranding you here overnight for the sake of some snowballs?"

Melody laughed. "I already told you this was the best date I've ever had. I'm so glad you managed to drag me away for a while."

"I guess now would be the time to tell you I've got to leave at the end of the week."

"I expected as much. We're about to begin construction, so I'm going to be busy anyway."

"You know, this is the first time I've ever had this issue. Usually women want more of me and not less."

Melody gasped. "I didn't say that! And seriously, could you try for at least a little humility?"

He grinned. "I could try, but I wouldn't succeed. Like you said, I've got the whole package going on here—"

"You're impossible, you know that?"

He pulled her in and planted a quick kiss on her lips, taking just long enough to look into her eyes. "You wouldn't like me so much if I weren't."

It was true, but she wasn't going to tell him that. "Eyes on the . . . air. Or whatever you call it."

"Yes, ma'am." He winked at her and turned forward again, pausing to check the flight log on his knee.

"I have been meaning to ask you: Are you going to be home two Saturdays from now? The eighteenth?"

He glanced at her. "Pretty sure. I think I get home the day before."

"Then would you like to come to the Saturday Night Supper Club with me?"

"Meet your friends, you mean?"

Melody just nodded, holding her breath.

"I'd love to. I've been wondering when I might get to meet everyone."

"Good. It's a date, then." Which meant she needed to actually tell Rachel and Ana that she and Justin were together. She hadn't meant to keep it from them—not exactly—but it was way past time to come clean.

Melody peered out the window, watching the mountainous terrain turn more developed as they passed over the Front Range foothills and then breached the borders of the metropolitan area. As he had on their way there, he skirted the edge of the city and then turned back toward the airport. She stayed quiet as he contacted the Centennial tower and made adjustments to their heading to get on the airport approach, focused, relaxed, and absurdly handsome. How had she ever thought she could resist him?

Compared to the high-mountain landing, their return to Centennial was uneventful. She tuned out the tower frequency chatter, only paying attention when Justin transmitted, and that was mostly because she liked the sound of his voice. Their descent was gradual and smooth, and they touched down on the concrete runway with scarcely a shimmy or bump. It was literally coming back to reality, being set down on the edge of a city where her life would resume as normal, where he'd be leaving again for over a week. And despite the fact she'd meant what she said—she really did need to focus on the restaurant—it wasn't without a twinge of regret.

"Safe and sound," Justin said. "Almost a day late, but who's keeping track?"

It was almost the same procedure as takeoff, just in reverse. They taxied back to the hangar, where he shut down the engine and started his final checklist. Justin tossed her his car keys so she could move the SUV out while he pushed the plane back in.

"Back to your house now?" he asked when he'd gone through his whole postflight routine.

"Probably a good idea. Thanks again, Justin. I had fun."

"So did I." He smiled at her as he moved to open the passenger door. As soon as he shut the door behind her, her phone beeped. A missed message. The call must have come in when they were still too high for a cell signal.

Melody punched the button to dial voice mail and held her phone to her ear.

Rachel's voice poured through the line, tense and frazzled. *"Melody, where are you? I'm in the middle of a class and the contractor just called to tell me you never showed up! Are you okay? What happened? You were supposed to be there to let him in at nine! Call me."*

The blood drained from Melody's face, and

351

she swayed along with the sudden, dull thrum of her pulse. Justin stared at her. "Melody? Is everything okay?"

She hung up and pressed her hand to her forehead. "I'm in so much trouble. I was supposed to be at the bakery first thing this morning to let in the contractor."

Justin winced. "Is Rachel furious?"

"When she finds out I wasn't hit by a car, yeah, she's going to be mad." Melody let her head fall back against her seat. How had she let that slip her mind?

Because she'd been completely focused on Justin, that's how. When she was with him, everything else took a backseat.

"Mel, I'm really sorry. I had no idea. It's my fault."

She shook her head. "No, it's not. It was my responsibility, and I completely forgot. I would have rescheduled or had Rachel make other arrangements."

"She'll understand, though, won't she? It's not like you planned to be stuck overnight in the mountains."

"Maybe." But Rachel never forgot things like this, not when it had to do with work. Only Melody would blow off the important first step in their renovation because she was out with a guy.

Justin reached over and squeezed her hand, but he didn't try to reassure her. When they pulled up in front of her apartment building, she said, "You can just drop me off here. I'm going straight to my car. Rachel should be home by now. I have to go see if I can grovel my way out of this."

"Call me later and tell me how it turned out." He leaned across the console and kissed her gently. When he lifted his head, he was looking at her with an expression that made her want to sigh with happiness, even through her dread. He meant it. He wanted to hear the outcome of a disagreement with a friend because it mattered to her. Was it any wonder that she was falling for him?

"Wish me luck."

"Good luck."

She threw him a smile and climbed out of the car, slinging her bag over her shoulder, then half-jogged to her Jeep parked a few spots in front of his. As she levered herself up into the driver's seat of the vehicle, Melody couldn't shake the feeling that her coach had just turned back into a pumpkin.

CHAPTER TWENTY-SEVEN

Melody made the drive to Rachel's house in frustratingly slow stop-and-go traffic, praying that this wasn't a waste of time. For all she knew, Rachel wasn't even there, and Melody would have to sit on the front porch and wait.

But when she climbed the steps of the Victorian house and rapped on the front door, the blurry figure of her friend appeared behind the stained-glass panel almost immediately.

Rachel swung the door open, her eyes wide. "Melody! There you are! I was getting so worried. First you didn't show up at the restaurant and then you didn't return my call? What happened?"

Melody rushed inside and shut the door behind her. "I am so sorry, Rachel. I swear to you, I didn't mean to flake out. Justin flew me to the mountains for the day yesterday, but the winds came up—"

Rachel's expression shifted. "You were with Justin? I thought you two had called it quits."

"We did, but we sorted it out. He wanted to take me someplace special, but we were supposed to be back last night. And then it got too windy to take off, so we had to stay the night and come back this morning."

"Then why didn't you just call me? I could have

had Ana go over and open it . . . or I could have had someone cover my class. Or something."

Melody grimaced. She didn't even have a good excuse. "I'm so sorry. I completely forgot. I know that's a horrible reason, but it's the truth. Were you able to reschedule for later this week?"

"No, I couldn't." Rachel made her way to the couch, where she curled her legs up beneath her. "The soonest he can get out is next Thursday. You have no idea how much I had to beg to get him here today in the first place. This is going to set us back at least two weeks."

Melody sank into a chair adjacent to the sofa. "I'm sorry, Rachel. I never meant to let you down."

Rachel fixed her with a hard stare. "Melody, this isn't a game. We've got a lot riding on this, and every week we delay costs us more money. I need to know you're committed and you're not going to just throw me over for some guy."

Guilt flooded her. Rachel was right. She had dropped the ball. But it wasn't Justin's fault, and it wasn't like she'd intentionally bailed to go on a date with a random man. "Rach, he's not just some guy. I think I'm falling for him."

"And you decided this after how long? A couple of days? A week?"

Heat rushed to Melody's face. Put like that, it sounded insane. Her feelings at the beginning of a relationship were always intense, but this was different. For the first time in longer than she could remember, she could be herself. She wasn't stressing over whether she was being interesting enough or pretty enough to keep his attention—he seemed fascinated with her all the same. That had to mean something, didn't it?

"I know it sounds crazy, Rachel, but he's amazing. He makes me happy. When I'm with him—"

"You forget everything but him. Just like Micah. You thought he was the one, too, and you practically threw away your career over him."

"Justin is not Micah."

Rachel sent her a pointed look. "Are you sleeping with him?"

Guilt transformed into anger in the face of Rachel's interrogation. "That's none of your business."

"It *is* my business because I'm your friend. Had you not gotten in so deep with Micah, you would have seen him for what he was. I don't want to see you get hurt again."

Melody jumped to her feet. "No, you just don't want my life to mess up your perfect plans. Rachel, I supported you when you met Alex. For heaven's sake, we practically coached you through the first two months with him. Why can't you be happy for me?"

Rachel rose and reached for Melody's shoulder. "Because I know you, Melody. Every time you have to make a commitment to something true and real in your life, something that would actually move you forward, you sabotage it with some guy. And now that we finally have the chance to have our own place, you're screwing it up. You're flying off to the mountains with someone you barely know when you should be focusing on opening the restaurant."

Melody sucked in a deep breath, feeling her vision go blurry around the edges. Whether from fury or from welling tears, she couldn't tell. She shrugged Rachel's hand off her shoulder. "This isn't about you."

"Yes, it is about me." Rachel looked hard into her face. "I've been waiting for this chance, Melody. Do you think the concept is what I would have chosen for myself? No, it isn't, but you're my best friend. I wanted to do this with you. I wanted to work alongside you every day, make something really special that we can be proud of."

"And I want to do the same thing!"

"Do you? Really? I need to know for sure. Because if you back out on me and this fails, I'm done. I've put every dime I have into this. I don't get a third chance." Rachel looked away, but not fast enough to hide the tears that slid down her face. She swiped at them angrily. "You know what? You should go. I need time to think. You can let yourself out." She strode into her bedroom and shut the door firmly behind her.

Melody remained in the middle of the living room, her chest tight, a knot twisting up her middle. She'd made Rachel cry. Rachel never cried.

She wanted to go and apologize again, beg Rachel to forgive her, but there was nothing she could say to change what she'd done. It wasn't that missing an appointment was unforgivable. It was that by trying to explain away her mistake, Melody had said Rachel's dreams were unimportant, that *she* was unimportant. She was choosing not seven years of friendship but a few weeks of acquaintance with a guy who, for all she knew, would be gone just as quickly.

Looking at it from Rachel's perspective, Melody couldn't blame her. Especially when the relationship really did have an expiration date.

She let herself out the front door, twisting the lock on the handle behind her before she stepped outside. For a moment, she considered going to Justin's place, but that wasn't the answer either. Any decisions made with his arms around her would not necessarily be the correct ones.

Instead, she drove back to her apartment, climbed the dingy stairs, and let herself into her soothing cocoon. If ever there was a time she needed Grandma Bev, it was now. When she'd broken up with Micah, it wasn't her friends she'd run to but her grandmother, spilling out the sordid details without editing. How he'd found her weakness, her need for love and connection, and exploited it. How she'd been so infatuated she hadn't realized he was just using her for sex. How she felt so stupid and ashamed and more than a little shattered when she learned it was all a lie . . . that he was committing to someone else.

She remembered Rachel's half-pitying, half-judgmental questions about Justin and felt another flush of anger. At least Bev had never used her past mistakes against her. She'd said there was no use wasting her life on regrets; Melody had learned an important lesson, and all there was left to do was repent and move on. Her grandmother had never brought up the topic again.

Melody wandered into her kitchen and flipped through her collection of old recipe cards, looking for an activity to settle the sick feeling in her middle. She finally selected a card in Bev's neat handwriting: honey whole wheat bread. She mixed the ingredients by hand, turned the dough out on a floured cutting board, and poured all her frustration into kneading it. What would her grandmother say about Justin? She'd no doubt understand why Melody was so taken with him. Both Bev's husbands had been handsome charmers. For that matter, so was Melody's father. Seemed that particular weakness ran in the family.

Bev would say that any man who required her

to give up the people and things she loved wasn't the one for her. That when push came to shove, anyone who truly loved her would make the sacrifice without being asked.

She would say that Justin wasn't the man for her if she had to give up the bakery.

Melody swiped the back of her hand across her cheeks before her tears could drip into the dough. Making Bev's recipe, she could almost imagine her grandmother was here, giving her tough-love advice in that no-nonsense way of hers. She was always urging Melody to be independent, make her own decisions instead of letting them be made for her. She'd probably tell her to break things off with Justin.

And yet Bev had been enough of a romantic to try again, even after her first marriage had failed. *"You can't decide that just because one man was no good, the next one will be too,"* she'd said once. *"I guess I just decided to have a little faith."*

And that must have been where Melody had gotten her unflappable, irrational hope. That was why she wasn't going to call Justin right now and end their relationship. Even if she couldn't see how things would work out, she wasn't ready to give up the possibility that they might.

The dough had become soft and elastic while absorbing her frustrations and worries, so she shaped it into a ball and dropped it into an oiled bowl to rise. Then she picked up her phone and texted Justin.

Rachel is really mad. And she has every right to be.

A moment later, the reply. I'm sorry. Everything okay between you two?

It will be. I just need to make it up to her somehow.

You will. You want to come over?

Yes; yes, she did, but that was why she couldn't. Thanks, but I have bread dough rising. Besides, I really have to call Rachel and work things out.

You've got this. Call me later.

She smiled, buoyed by his confidence. Then she took a deep breath and dialed Rachel's number. Her friend picked up on the third ring, but Melody rushed to beat her to the greeting.

"Rach, it's me. Don't hang up, please. I have some things I need to say."

A long pause. "I'm listening."

Melody gathered her thoughts. "You were right. No matter the reason, I had a responsibility and I failed. I've only been thinking of myself. I haven't considered what you're giving up to work with me, what it would do to you if I pulled out. I hope you can forgive me."

She fell silent, waiting for a response, but it didn't come. "Rachel?"

A sniffle. "I'm sorry I reacted the way I did. I shouldn't have thrown Micah in your face.

I know how much he hurt you. But I'm still concerned about how fast this is going with Justin, especially if you felt the need to hide him from me. I know you want me to love him, but I love you more. I don't want you to get hurt again."

It was as close to a full apology as she was going to get, and Melody couldn't fault Rachel for her caution. Their relationship was more like sisterhood than friendship, and Rachel wasn't going to back down on what she thought was in Melody's best interests.

Which was exactly why she had to tell her the whole truth. "Rach, there's something else you should know. . . ."

She poured out the whole situation: the looming departure, the reason Justin had turned cold on her. Her own decision to continue seeing him.

When she was done, Rachel let out a long exhale. "Oh, Mel. What are you going to do?"

"I don't know," she said simply. "I think he could be the one. No matter how crazy that sounds. Were it any other time, I'd just go with him. But I'm absolutely sure I want to do this bakery. How can I possibly make this choice?"

The silence stretched on the other end of the line. "Is it wrong that I really want you to choose the bakery?"

Melody laughed and blinked away the start of tears. "It's not wrong. Selfish, maybe . . ."

Rachel snorted. "Shut up." Her tone sobered. "If you're serious about this guy, I guess you should bring him to supper club so Ana and I can check him out. Make sure he meets our high standards for you."

"It's good you said that, since I already invited him."

"Well then, that's settled. Just don't expect us to go easy on him."

"I would never expect you to." Melody's voice softened. "This whole thing is just so bittersweet. Had you not lost Paisley, had my grandmother not died, we wouldn't even get to do this. And now, add in Justin . . . I just don't know how to feel."

"I know." Rachel fell silent for a long moment. Then she said suddenly, "That's what we should call it."

"Call what?"

"The café. We should call it Bittersweet."

"Bittersweet." Melody tried the word out on her tongue, imagined it displayed across their awning, stamped onto pastry boxes. Her favorite kind of chocolate, just a touch too sharp to be completely sweet. Just like life. Just like the genesis of the business. "It's perfect."

"So where does this leave us? Are you still in? Tell me now, Melody. I promise, whatever you decide, I'm behind you."

Melody's heart squeezed in her chest. As much

as it might be pointing her to Justin, she was equally sure she was supposed to do this bakery with Rachel, even if she had no idea how she was going to make this work.

"I'm in, Rach. No matter what." She just hoped the name didn't become too much of a self-fulfilling prophecy.

CHAPTER TWENTY-EIGHT

If Melody had her way, she'd be spending every minute Justin was in Denver with him. But since she'd renewed her commitment to Rachel, she was determined to prove she was dedicated to their newly named Bittersweet Café. Somehow Rachel had sweet-talked the contractor into coming back to take measurements so they could get the architectural drawings going, and Melody had spent every moment since then working on the design for the interior, ordering supplies and appliances, and basically proving her commitment to the venture.

Justin seemed to understand, even if the schedule meant only quick suppers and some hastily stolen kisses. Neither of them said aloud what they were thinking—that time was growing short. As much as Melody wanted to save up moments with him for later, the more a part of each other's daily life they became, the harder it would be when he left. The fact they even continued on, Melody could only attribute to her faith. If this relationship was meant to be, they'd be provided with a solution. She held on to that belief like a lifeline.

And then he was away on an eight-day tour,

removing the temptation of shirking her duties to be with him. Instead, they fell into the habit of talking late every night when he got settled in his hotel, even if half the time Melody was barely coherent. She was still relying on a combination of warm milk, melatonin, and sleeping pills to reset her body clock, which was stubbornly hanging on to its old schedule.

The Thursday before Justin was scheduled to return, Melody was desperately trying to stay awake for his call, but three more chapters into *Madding Crowd* and her blinks were getting longer and longer. Disappointment crept in when she realized he wasn't going to call. It happened sometimes; he'd get in late and decide not to wake her up.

Just as she set her book aside, though, her phone rang.

She didn't even look at the screen before she answered, a smile on her face and in her voice. "Hey there."

"Hey. Did I wake you up?" His voice, as smooth and warm as melted chocolate, poured over her.

She snuggled deeper into the covers, phone pressed to her ear. "No, I was just about to go to sleep. I figured you got caught up somewhere."

"I did. Delays because of weather in the upper Midwest. How was your day?"

"Mmm." It suddenly took too much effort to

form the word *good*. Was she mumbling? She felt like she was mumbling. "Where are you?"

"Lansing, Michigan. In the tiniest, most ill-equipped hotel I've ever seen. It doesn't even have a gym."

"That's a shame." Vaguely, Melody knew Justin working out was a good thing, something she'd probably enjoy watching, even if she couldn't quite grasp why.

"Melody, are you okay? You sound a little off."

"I'm feeling a bit sleepy right now. I'm still trying to adjust to . . . to . . ." Where was she going with that?

He laughed softly, and the sound covered her like a warm blanket. "Why don't you go to sleep, then, and I'll call you tomorrow."

"Night, Justin," she mumbled. "I love you."

The last thing she remembered was her phone falling from her fingers, but she was too sleepy to catch it before it hit her pillow.

Justin stared at the phone in his hand, stunned speechless. Which didn't matter, because if he wasn't mistaken, Melody had just fallen asleep on the phone without hanging up.

After she told him she loved him.

He clicked off the phone and swallowed hard. She sounded so sleepy, it had probably been a reflexive answer, like she would end a call with her mom. Or maybe not, considering the shaky nature of that relationship.

Either way, it didn't mean anything. It couldn't. What if it did?

Justin set his phone on the tiny hotel nightstand and started unbuttoning his uniform shirt with shockingly clumsy fingers. They'd been careful not to make promises, not to talk about any feelings they might have for each other. If they remained unspoken, it was like they didn't exist. He and Melody would enjoy each other's company and go their separate ways. Sure, it would hurt for a little while, but they'd get over it. They'd both be so busy that they wouldn't have time to think about it.

But if Melody loved him, that changed things, didn't it?

Naturally, he couldn't ask her. If it had been a slip, the question would embarrass her and inject awkwardness into an already difficult situation. If she'd meant it, it would demand a response he wasn't quite ready to consider. His only option was to pretend she'd never said it.

Forgetting it was an entirely different matter.

The next morning, settling into the first segment of his tour's last day, he glanced at his copilot. "You married?"

Marilyn Terayasu quirked an amused look at him. "I am, but even if I weren't, I think you're a little young for me."

Justin grinned. Unlike some of his other first officers, he'd taken to Marilyn right away. She had to be at least fifty, a former Air Force C-17 pilot who had jumped to the civilian world when she hit twenty years in and a full military pension. In addition to her sarcastic wit, she was sharp, attentive, and disciplined. Didn't seem to mind that her captain was twenty years her junior or that she'd be lucky to see a promotion by the time she hit her second retirement.

"I'll try to get over it," he said wryly. "What does your husband think about this?"

"My husband is just happy I'm not flying supplies in and out of Bagram. We never came under fire on a single flight, but he was sure that I was just lying to him so he wouldn't worry. Ferrying corporate types is a big step up in his mind."

"Would you have? Lied so he didn't worry, I mean."

She smiled. "Of course. I take it you aren't married."

He shook his head.

"Girlfriend?"

"Something like that."

"Let me tell you something about women. They like relationships to be defined. If you want to hold on to this one, you need to decide what she is to you."

Justin darted a glance at her. "Up until now,

369

she's been the one to keep things casual. She's about to open a bakery with a friend, doesn't need the complications, but now I wonder . . ."

"Do you love her?"

It was the question he'd been chewing on since Melody's accidental admission the night before. Did he? Would he even know what it felt like if he did? After all, his greatest relationship accomplishment to date was staying on speaking terms with women he'd seen a handful of times without any intention of seeing them again. He was the master of the polite brush-off. And yet the thought of doing any such thing with Melody was unimaginable.

"I don't know," he said finally. "Too soon to tell."

"Then let me give you a word of advice: when you know for sure, tell her. Don't play games. I know you young people are big on hooking up and moving on, but life's too short. When you find someone special, you hang on to them."

Justin shot her a smirk. "You're not *that* much older than me."

"Oh, believe me, sometimes that twenty years feels like a lifetime." She winked at him. "You seem like a nice guy. Don't be a cliché."

Don't toy with Melody's heart, she was saying. Suddenly, their agreement felt cruel. It was one thing to accept Melody's irrepressible optimism when they were just casually feeling things out.

It was another if she'd truly fallen in love with him.

If he were still a praying man—or rather, if he thought God was interested in anything he had to say—he would plead for some sort of sign, an indication of whether to move forward or let her be.

But since he wasn't, and God remained an implacable mystery, he'd just have to figure out this one for himself.

CHAPTER TWENTY-NINE

Justin was still mulling over the matter—okay, obsessing—when he returned to Denver late Friday night. He managed to hold himself back from calling Melody until noon Saturday, just in case she'd had another rough night, but when she answered, he heard hammering and power tools in the background.

"Hello? Melody?"

"Justin! Hold on. Let me go outside." A couple of moments passed and the construction noise faded. "Sorry. I'm at the restaurant. By some miracle, our permits got expedited. I'm telling you, there has to be divine providence involved, because things never move this fast in Denver."

The words were like a knife in the gut, however unreasonable. She wasn't acting as if she knew she'd dropped the L-bomb on him the last time they'd talked, though, which meant he needed to play things cool.

"I'm so glad to hear that! I just wanted to check if we're still on for the supper club tonight."

"If you still want to go. . . ."

"Of course I do. Why wouldn't I?" Melody stayed quiet, and a disturbing thought occurred to him. "You're afraid they're not going to like me."

"No!" Melody exclaimed. "Or not exactly. I'm just afraid . . . I don't know."

"That they think I'm just messing around with you. That I don't actually care about you."

"Do you?" The question was teasing, but he could hear the real need beneath the words.

He took a moment and made his voice steady. "Of course I do, Melody. Do you have any idea how much it kills me every time I leave?"

"It kills me too," she whispered. "See you tonight?"

"Wouldn't miss it. Melody, I want them to like me, but the only opinion that really matters to me is yours."

She didn't immediately reply, giving his heart a little jolt and reinforcing exactly how important tonight's supper club was to her. He lightened his tone and tried again. "Don't worry about it. Whole package, remember? They won't be able to resist me."

"Or your awesome humility. See you soon."

"Can't wait." He clicked off the phone and stared at his apartment wall pensively. This was make-or-break for them. These women were Melody's family. If they didn't like him, it was over. Maybe not immediately, but how could she resist their disapproval?

Up until now, Melody had been the one who believed things would somehow miraculously work out for them, while he braced himself for their inevitable separation. But for the first time, Justin realized he was anticipating a future in which the opinions of their friends and family mattered, a future that stretched out ahead of them, unbroken. Maybe Melody's optimism had begun to rub off on him. Or more likely, he was just fooling himself.

He'd never wanted to be proven wrong so badly.

Justin showed up at Melody's apartment a couple of minutes before six o'clock that night and slid in behind a resident before the door closed behind him. He rapped sharply on her door and stood back from the peephole, hands thrust into his pockets, pretending a confidence he didn't currently feel.

Meeting the best friends was more serious than meeting the parents. And then there was the surprise that was waiting down below.

She swung the door open, a startled look on her face. "Did you buzz?"

"Nope, surfed in behind someone." He stepped inside and shut the door behind him. Before she could say anything, he kissed her. All the tension he hadn't realized he'd been holding melted from him now that he had her in his arms. She tasted as sweet as whatever concoction she'd been working on earlier, the scent of vanilla floating around them. If there was any advantage to their long stretches of separation, it was that every time he kissed her hello, it felt like the first time.

"I missed you," he murmured in her ear.

"I missed you too." She rose on tiptoes to plant another quick kiss on his lips, then twisted away. "I told Rachel we'd be there a little early."

"The better to interrogate me?" He rocked back on his heels, crossing his arms over his chest and watching while she bustled around the kitchen. A bowl of something went in a crate along with a paper bakery box. Then she slid her bag onto her shoulder, hefted the crate, and crossed the room toward him. He took the crate from her and nudged open the door.

Melody grinned. "I never said that."

"You didn't have to. I just want to know whether to expect a lie detector test or Chinese water torture."

Melody locked her door behind them. "Depends on whether Ana had time to pick up the polygraph."

Justin chuckled and followed Melody down the stairs, but she didn't laugh. "Wait, you weren't serious, were you?"

Melody shot him an unreadable look. "You'll just have to wait and see."

"That's mean. Now I'm wondering if you deserve your surprise."

She stopped just before the building's exit. "You got me a surprise?"

"Not unless you call off the polygraph."

"Now I'm curious what you've got to hide." She threw a grin over her shoulder as they moved out the front door and down the walkway to the street. Then she stopped short in front of the classic automobile parked at the curb. "Wait. That's not my car."

"It certainly is." He watched as Melody moved to the Hornet's side, swiped a finger against the fender. Gone was the dirt and oxidation, the original green paint now buffed to a high shine, even though the original white stripe was nicked and scratched and the chrome bumpers pitted from the years. It was still an impressive machine . . . at least compared to its former self. Regardless of how nicely it had cleaned up, he knew he'd never have given it a second look were it not for Melody.

He fished the keys out of his pocket, popped the trunk, and deposited the crate inside, then handed the keys to Melody. "Looks like you're driving."

An expression of delight surfaced on her face and she practically skipped around the car. She slid into the driver's seat and waited for him, alight with quivering anticipation. "Even the inside looks new!"

"I had my detailer come by this afternoon and polish it up."

"Justin, you shouldn't have."

"Of course I should have. Now start her up."

Melody carefully inserted the key into the ignition and twisted it. The engine roared to life with a throaty rumble, vibrating straight into their bones. It turned out to have needed more than just a new set of spark plugs, but after a full tune-up, it practically hummed.

"I can't believe you got it running. You're a miracle worker."

He waved off her amazement. "It was fun."

She smoothed her hands over the steering wheel, speechless. Might as well give her the news. He handed over a sheet of paper.

"What's this?"

"My friend's appraisal. If you're interested in listing the car with him. I took it over this afternoon for him to look at."

Melody read over the paperwork. "Twenty-three thousand?"

"Apparently, the V8 engine and the four-speed tranny add about 20 percent to the top price. He said it could go for as much as twenty-five, but at twenty-three, he thinks he can get a buyer within a few months."

Melody lowered the paperwork. "I don't know what to say."

"If that seems too low, we can try for the full twenty-five. But I told Dean that you needed the money for your business, and he thought this was your best bet."

"That's not what I mean." She turned to him with a quavering smile. "You did all this for me. On your time off."

"It's nothing, really. I expected it to be much more work than it was."

"No. It's huge." She slid her hand up his arm and leaned forward to kiss him. "Thank you."

He studied her face in the dim light from the street, felt the answering tug in his chest. "You're welcome." He reached for his seat belt and buckled it on. "Now, let's take her for a spin."

Melody pressed in the clutch, put it in first, and pulled away from the curb. He watched her silently. If he'd thought she was sexy driving her Jeep, it was nothing compared to her behind the wheel of a restored muscle car. Then again, he practically thought the way she breathed was sexy.

After a few seconds, a smile crept onto Melody's face. "I have to admit, it's fun to drive."

"Don't tell anyone, but it's a couple seconds faster on the quarter mile than my Mustang. And since they made fewer than eight hundred of these in the early seventies, it's far rarer."

He was so focused on Melody and the car that he didn't pay attention to their route. She parked on a crowded street in a mixed residential neighborhood, put it in neutral, and pulled the parking brake, but she didn't switch off the engine. Justin let the silence stretch until he couldn't stand it. "You know, you don't have to sell it. I won't feel bad if you decide to hold on to it."

She shook herself and glanced at him, her eyes clear. "It's not that. It's just . . . I didn't expect it would be hard to let it go. It wasn't even my grandmother's car."

"From what you told me of your grandmother, she wouldn't want sentiment to stand in the way of your dreams. I think she'd tell you to sell it without batting an eyelash. In fact, she pretty much did."

"You're right. I've just managed not to think about her . . . all this . . ." She let out a long, shaky breath. "It kind of sneaks up on me sometimes, even when I'm happy."

Justin found Melody's hand on the seat between them and interlaced his fingers with hers. "She was important to you. It's okay to miss her. But letting the car go doesn't mean letting her go. You'll remember the contribution she made to your bakery every time you step through the door."

"You're right." Melody squeezed his hand, and it was all he could do not to kiss her again, even though this wasn't the right time. "Now no more stalling. It's time to face the music."

"I'm not the one stalling, sweetheart." He winked and climbed out of the car to retrieve the crate from the trunk. He curled one arm around it, then pulled out a small gift bag.

"What's that?" Melody asked, peering over his shoulder.

"Hostess gift." He shrugged. "What can I say? My mom was big into etiquette."

Melody tried to peek inside, but he whipped the bag out of her view. "Come now, it's not nice to open someone else's gift."

"Fine, but I'm not going to call off the polygraph now."

Melody let herself into the house and was immediately greeted by exclamations of excitement. Justin followed more cautiously, closing the door and wandering down the hall of Rachel's Victorian house. It was low-key and furnished with a mix of modern and vintage decor, giving him his first clue into Melody's best friend and business partner.

"Justin, come meet Rachel and Ana." Melody poked her head around the corner and waved him in.

Slowly he moved into the kitchen. It was already half-filled with people, mostly women. Melody took the crate and directed him first to a tall brunette dressed in jeans and a simple button-down with a black apron tied around her waist. "Justin, this is Rachel."

"Nice to meet you, Justin." Rachel gripped his hand hard. Intentional or not, it was his second clue about her. But she gave him a friendly smile before looking to the man next to her. "This is my boyfriend, Alex."

Justin shook Alex's hand as well, picking up a vaguely sympathetic air. Obviously the other man knew what he was being subjected to—or he'd been through the process himself. Belatedly, Justin remembered the gift bag in his hand and handed it over to Rachel. "Thank you for the invitation. This is for you."

Rachel's brow furrowed as she dug through the tissue paper and pulled out two small glass jars. "Blueberry jam?"

"I was in Maine this past week, thought you'd probably enjoy it. Plain blueberry in one and blueberry-rum jelly in the other."

Rachel smiled. "Thank you, Justin. That's very thoughtful."

Melody slid an arm around Justin's waist and looked up at him through narrowed eyes. "You brought Rachel jam and you didn't bring me anything?"

"I gave you a running and fully detailed car!"

"Okay, you get a pass." Melody slipped away from him. "This is Ana."

Ana was even shorter than Melody, but the four-inch heels on her boots gave her a boost of height. She gave him a very distinct once-over, top to toe, before looking him straight in the eye and offering her hand.

Justin took it briefly and gave her a nod. "Ana."

It seemed to be the right response, not fumbling for her approval, because after staring him down for a moment longer, she said, "Glad you could make it. We've been looking forward to meeting you."

"Same. It's pretty clear from the way Melody talks about you two that you're practically sisters."

"That they are," Alex said from across the room, offering a reprieve. "Wine?"

"Sure." Justin edged away from the girls to the only other male in the room as Alex poured him a glass of white wine. After a moment, he said, "Melody told me you're a writer?"

"I am. Working on a new collection of essays right now, couple of magazine pieces. You're a pilot, I understand?"

Justin nodded.

"Tough gig, schedule-wise. So you probably understand the crazy that's their lives, huh?" He nodded toward Melody and Rachel, who were setting the table together.

Justin sensed this wasn't just idle conversation—he'd probably been nudged by Rachel to see what Justin thought about the venture. "I'm not sure anyone completely understands it unless they live it. But I get doing what you love even when it doesn't fit into banker's hours."

"I'm glad they're doing this. Rachel says

she's happy teaching and going to school, but she chafes at not cooking on a larger scale. I'm hoping this bakery-café is the best of both worlds."

"I think Melody misses 'real baking.' Making someone else's recipes just doesn't suit her."

"Talking about us?" Rachel sidled up to Alex, slid an arm around him, and gave him a quick kiss.

"Talking about how brilliant you're going to be."

"Liar. You're warning him about how crazy things are about to get and how little you two are going to see us for the next few months."

Justin looked from Rachel to Alex, who didn't seem at all perturbed by the comment. He kissed the tip of his girlfriend's nose. "Which is why I said we should elope before all the work starts."

"Women don't want to elope. We want the church and the big dress. Especially ones like me, who rarely get to feel pretty."

Alex leaned down to whisper in Rachel's ear, but Justin still caught the words: "You're always pretty, love, chef whites or white dress."

Justin moved away, feeling like he was intruding on a moment. It was plain to anyone who cared to look that Rachel and Alex were mad about each other, completely comfortable and settled in the idea of their life to come. Justin had always shied away from that kind of commitment, knowing how hard it was to make it work, but as he watched Melody across the dining table, he wondered if he hadn't been too hasty.

"Need help with anything?" Justin asked.

"You can open the wine. The reds need to breathe before we serve them." Melody plunked several dark bottles on the table and handed him a corkscrew. "Ana, can you grab the wineglasses?"

Ana moved back into the kitchen's open shelving and collected glasses, bringing them to the table in several batches. Justin took the opportunity to whisper, "So how am I doing?"

Melody smiled up at him. "They're still reserving judgment, especially Ana. She's very protective."

"You mentioned that. She doesn't have any reason to be." He squeezed Melody's waist and slid his hand across her lower back, unable to resist touching her. When he moved away to open the bottle of wine, he caught a searching look from Rachel.

A knock sounded at the door, and Ana quickly placed the last few glasses on the table. "I'll get it." A moment later she returned with a very young redheaded woman in tow. "Everyone, this is my assistant, Daphne."

Rachel made her way to Daphne to shake her hand. "Glad you could make it. I'm Rachel. Care for a glass of wine?"

Daphne glanced at Ana and then gave a timid nod.

Justin leaned over to whisper to Melody. "Let me guess, Ana terrifies her assistant?"

"I get the impression that Daphne is terrified of everyone at the firm. They're pretty intense. Ana thought getting together outside the office might loosen her up a bit, build her confidence. She's brilliant, but so painfully shy."

Watching the uncertain way the girl moved through the room, Justin wondered if it would make much of a difference.

As the time edged toward seven o'clock, the doorbell rang. Alex introduced the newcomer as Bryan Shaw, his closest friend and a professional rock climber. It took only a moment to connect his full name to the real estate mogul Mitchell Shaw, even though he looked nothing like the heir to a family fortune. The climber nabbed a glass of wine and made his way to Ana's side.

"Something between those two?" Justin asked Melody in a low voice.

"Only in Bryan's head," Melody whispered back. "He's a player, and Ana's not interested."

That wasn't what it looked like from where he stood—Ana was laughing at something Bryan had said, her body language clearly flirtatious—but Justin said nothing. He was the outsider here. There was plenty of history that he didn't understand.

He made a quick count. Seven, with eight places at the table. "Are we expecting someone else?"

"My sister, Dina," Alex said, going by with a cluster of water glasses. "Ana thought she might loosen Daphne up a little."

When the doorbell rang a couple of minutes later and Rachel admitted Dina, Justin saw why. Pretty, tattooed, and pierced, she was so bubbly that the energy level seemed to go up several notches with her presence. Within minutes, she had Daphne engaged in conversation, and the girl's shoulders were making a slow descent from her ears. He doubted Ana's assistant noticed the furtive glances Dina was sending Bryan's way every time he laughed with Ana.

Justin repressed a smile, feeling more relaxed himself. Everyone had been welcoming, and so far no one had sat him down under bright lights for interrogation. So maybe he was off the hook.

Rachel put out appetizers while she began to transfer the rest of the meal to the table. Justin hastened to make himself useful, ferrying bowls of a fragrant, pale-green soup from the kitchen as fast as Rachel filled them with a ladle. Crusty bread—Melody's contribution—went out in a basket, followed by a beautifully plated meat dish and a spring-hued salad. Finally, Rachel tapped a spoon on the side of a water glass to get their attention and call them to the table. Muted conversations continued as they shuffled into place around the table.

Justin ended up next to Melody on Rachel's end of the table, across from Alex and Dina. He didn't miss the way that Bryan swiftly changed direction to nab the seat next to Ana, earning a quickly hidden frown from Dina. Unfortunately, that landed Daphne between Bryan and Justin, which obviously made her uncomfortable again. Poor girl.

Rachel waited until everyone was seated and then stood. "Welcome, everyone. Thanks for joining us for our last May meeting of the Saturday Night Supper Club. Most of you are friends, but to our newcomers, we're glad to have you. Tonight, we're starting with a zucchini gazpacho with leek and crème fraîche, followed by a warm escarole salad with roasted baby root vegetables, and finally an herb-crusted pork tenderloin with mushrooms, fava beans, and charred asparagus. Enjoy."

She sounded like a chef on one of those cooking shows, presenting food to the judges, which made Justin smile. He murmured, "You can take a chef out of the restaurant . . ."

Melody whispered back, "She pretended that she was going to quit, but we all knew the truth."

They started with the soup, which indeed was very good, cool and flavorful. Then dishes were passed family style around the table. Justin took an extra helping of bread and winked at Melody. "Bread is the best part of the meal, in my opinion."

"A man after my own heart."

He meant it, but Rachel's food was nonetheless astounding. Somehow she made simple ingredients he'd eaten dozens of times before taste new and fresh. He put down his fork and leaned over to catch her eye. "This is incredible. I'd venture to say your café is going to be a resounding success."

Alex caught on and raised his glass. "To Rachel and Melody."

The table echoed the sentiment. Then Bryan looked between the two women. "So, when is the big opening?"

Rachel responded. "Assuming all goes well, we're planning on a soft opening June 12 and our grand opening the following Saturday."

"Which means we probably won't take a breath until autumn," Melody said.

"Are you going to continue to do the supper club?" Justin asked. "It looks like this is a pretty big undertaking."

Rachel and Melody exchanged a look he didn't quite understand, but Rachel answered, "In some fashion. It's important to me—to us—to continue it."

Melody reached for Justin's hand and squeezed it under the table. "It's a reminder of why we all cook. It's pretty easy to let work be all-consuming and forget the people who are important to you."

"I can understand that," he said, turning back to his food, fully comfortable in the midst of this friendly gathering. Too comfortable. He didn't even see the danger until it was too late.

And it started with Alex, who he thought was on his side. "Tell us a bit about yourself, Justin. You're from Colorado?"

Justin put down his fork. "Born and raised. My dad's an airline pilot based out of Denver, and my mom's a teacher. Well, they were. They're both retired. I guess I followed in both of their footsteps. I was a flight instructor before I was a commercial pilot."

"What's it like?" Dina asked curiously. "Is it as glamorous as it seems?"

"About as glamorous as being a chef," he said wryly, and Rachel flashed a smile in understanding. "Strange hours, long days, working on weekends and holidays. Last year I worked on Christmas Day."

"Is that why you're moving to Florida?" Rachel asked. Her expression seemed merely curious, but suddenly Justin felt like he'd been led onto a battlefield littered with land mines, especially with expectant faces swiveling in his direction.

Justin cleared his throat, choosing his words carefully. "I wouldn't say that's the reason, but it is something of a benefit." He explained for confused members of the party, "My brother-in-law and I are in the process of buying an island air charter in Florida. He's an aircraft mechanic."

"Wow." Dina looked even more impressed than she had before, and for a fleeting moment, he thought he might escape unscathed.

But then Rachel focused in on him with laser-like precision. "So how's that going to work, exactly? If you're moving to Florida and Melody is opening a business here . . ."

Melody stiffened beside him, tension radiating from her like heat from an oven. He placed a calming hand on her knee. "We don't really know yet. I care about Melody and I want her to do whatever is best for her. We'll work it out somehow."

"With all due respect," Ana said, "that's a bit of a cop-out, don't you think?"

Melody spoke up, her voice tight. "You know as well as I do that sometimes you have to take a leap of faith. This situation comes as no surprise to God. So why should we wrestle control from His hands?"

Rachel looked mollified, but if anything, Ana's gaze only sharpened. "I don't know. Justin strikes me as a pretty practical sort of guy. What do you think about this whole leap-of-faith theory? Because from where I'm sitting, you don't look all that convinced either."

Now Justin shifted in his seat. This was

beginning to turn from a casual questioning into a full-on inquisition, and he had the uncomfortable feeling that anything he said was going to blow up in his face. He should be smart and tell them that he was fully on board with the leap-of-faith theory, that he had full confidence God was in control of their messed-up situation. He was about to do just that, but when he opened his mouth, he said, "I believe in God. But do I believe that He's up there watching and intervening in everything I do? Honestly, no. I wish I did, but I've had too much evidence to the contrary. I think this is something we've got to work out for ourselves."

Ana nodded slowly. "I see. Good to know where you stand."

Silence fell over the table, and slowly, Melody's hand slid from his. A tiny kernel of cold crept into Justin's chest.

Finally, Bryan rose. "Well, props for being honest, brother. That takes some guts in this group." He walked to the kitchen, retrieved another bottle of wine, and then expertly removed the cork. He refilled Justin's glass without being asked, gave him a nod that Justin took as a show of solidarity. Or at least respect.

"Who's ready for dessert?" Melody asked tightly. She rose so quickly that she nearly knocked over her water glass, then righted it and began to collect empty plates.

Rachel moved to help, but Melody glared her back down. "Justin, can you give me a hand?"

"Of course." He collected the dishes from the other side of the table and carried them to the kitchen behind Melody.

As soon as they put down their dishes, she moved close and whispered, "I'm sorry about that. I was hoping they'd take it easy on you."

"I'm a big boy. I can handle it." He looked into her eyes, tried to communicate that her worry was unnecessary. "I just hope I didn't make trouble for you. I should have kept my mouth shut."

"Nothing I can't manage." She didn't look him in the eye as she pulled a plastic container from the refrigerator. "Grab the cakes from the oven for me?"

It wasn't the answer he had hoped for, but he reached for a pot holder and removed a tray of small, round cakes from the oven. "What are these anyway?"

"Citrus olive oil cakes with mascarpone whipped cream." Carefully, Melody sifted a bit of powdered sugar over each of the dessert plates, then transferred the cakes to the center of each with a spatula. He watched, fascinated, while she filled a mug with hot water, dunked a tablespoon into it, and then dipped the spoon into her bowl. What came out was a perfectly smooth, football-shaped scoop of whipped cream.

"Wow, that's cool." He peered over her shoulder to see how she did it.

"Quenelles look nicer than just a dollop, but it's the same thing."

"You're like a real-deal pastry chef, aren't you?"

She rolled her eyes. "Because I can make a fancy scoop of whipped cream?"

"No, because it matters to you that it's a fancy scoop of whipped cream." He slid his arms around her waist and pressed a kiss to her jawline, aware of the other guests watching, aware he was making a statement. "I can't wait to see you in your own place."

She leaned against him for a second, softening enough that he thought maybe they were okay, even as she continued her process of dipping, scooping, and placing the quenelles on the cakes.

"Hey," Bryan called from the table. "You can smooch later. We want our dessert."

Melody laughed, but it sounded strained. "Here, help me carry these to the table."

As soon as the desserts were placed in front of the guests, all conversation quieted. Justin wanted to believe that they were all just savoring the creamy texture and surprising flavor, but he knew better. He wasn't sure which had reflected worse on him in this group, his imminent departure or his ambivalent religious beliefs. Either way, he'd let Melody down. She'd wanted one thing—for him to make a good impression on her friends—and he hadn't even had the sense to tell them what they wanted to hear. If their relationship had been a ticking bomb before, he had just sped up the timer.

Fortunately, Melody didn't seem inclined to linger. When Rachel and Alex cleared the dishes, Melody rose. "I hate to run, but Justin and I need to be going. Rachel, the food was amazing as usual."

"Thanks. Justin, thank you again for the jellies. I'm already thinking about how to use them."

The thank-you might have been sincere, but Rachel's formality betrayed her discomfort. He shook her hand, then Alex's and Ana's. Bryan stayed seated with his glass of wine, sending him a look he could only interpret as "poor sap." He probably did deserve the sympathy.

Only when the door closed behind him and he and Melody were alone in the dark did he dare to look her in the face again. "For what it's worth, I'm sorry."

She twisted and gave him a funny look as they walked down the front steps to the car. "You don't have anything to apologize for. My friends, on the other hand . . ."

"So it doesn't bother you, what I said in there? It's the truth, Melody. I respect your faith, but I'm not sure I'm ever going to trust God like you do. There's too much water under the bridge between us."

"There's never too much water under the bridge." She stopped short of the Hornet and turned to him, raising her hand to trail fingertips down his cheek. "You're a good man, Justin Keller. You might not see it, but I do. It takes courage to be honest even when it might cost you something."

With that pronouncement, she moved around the car and unlocked the driver's door, then leaned across the seat with a half smile to unlock his side.

Justin slid into the passenger seat and stared at Melody in the darkness. Of all the responses she could have given, this was the last thing he'd expected. Clearly, faith was important to her and her friends or they wouldn't have ambushed him with that not-so-subtle question. He could tell himself he had just been honest, but he'd known full well what the fallout would be when he opened his mouth. He'd been trying to force her hand, to make her drop him before he had a chance to leave and break her heart.

Instead, she had countered with understanding, her faith evidently unshaken.

He was not nearly the man she thought he was. But he suddenly wished he could be.

After the minor disaster that was the Saturday Night Supper Club, Justin wanted to stick by

Melody's side, but he had no choice. Work called, and he had no more ability to call in sick than Melody had to back off plans for Bittersweet.

The tour was a particularly heavy one: ten legs in three days, all of them short hops along the eastern seaboard. Pretty much his favorite type of schedule: very little sitting around, lots of time in the air, airports he didn't often fly into. By the time he dragged himself into the hotel at night, his body ached like he'd done physical labor. Just enough time to hear Melody's sweet voice on the phone and then collapse in a thick, dreamless sleep.

Yet a nameless dread dogged him, the source of which he knew but avoided acknowledging until he woke up on the third day of his tour in Greenwich, Connecticut, and saw the date on his phone.

Today was his five-year anniversary with AvionElite. Today was the date he was fully vested in his company stock and could access that money to fund his charter.

But instead of a leap of joy at that realization, his heart took a dive into the pit of his stomach.

He had no more excuses. As soon as he could roll over his money from his current 401(k) to their corporation, they would be able to get the loan. He would be leaving Colorado for good.

The thought dogged him throughout his morning routine, which was identical regardless of where he was staying. Drag himself out of bed, get the blood pumping with push-ups and sit-ups to remind his body that it was not in fact a sedentary lump, shower, shave, and finally shove his toiletries into his roller case. He always bypassed the fat-laden hotel breakfasts in favor of a protein bar or instant oatmeal made with water from the in-room coffeemaker.

As he waited for his F/O in the lobby—once again, someone he'd never met before this tour—his mind was spinning back toward Melody and how he was going to tell her that their relationship had to come to an end.

Instead, he found himself thinking about how he would tell Pete and Jessica that he was staying in Colorado.

His phone chimed in his pocket, and a message from Pete flashed on the lockscreen as if he knew what Justin had been thinking. Happy five-year anniversary. Ready to check out of the corporate grind?

Justin unlocked his phone and began typing a reply, which he erased and retyped three times. Everything felt like a lie. He finally settled on an excuse: Checking out of hotel. Talk later.

Fortunately, his first officer, Tarek El Shami, stepped off the elevator as soon as he pushed Send, falling into step alongside him through the sliding-glass doors of the hotel. The FBO staff at Westchester County Airport had sent the courtesy car for them, a nice service that not every city offered, and they slid into the musty fabric seats without comment.

Not so fortunately, Justin had little time to think about what this day represented. Their passengers today were nine—count them, *nine*—recent Yale grads, celebrating by heading to Florida for the week on one of their dads' fractional hours. The kids started partying from the moment they stepped on the plane, and by the time they touched down in West Palm Beach two and a half hours later, they were all pleasantly toasted.

"To be young and stupid," Justin muttered as they cleaned up the trash the kids had left behind.

"And coasting on their multimillionaire parents' money," El Shami cracked, scrubbing a smear Justin didn't really want to identify off the window.

This hadn't even been the rowdiest group he'd ever flown, that honor still going to pop stars and their entourages.

"Ever think we might have gone into the wrong line of work?"

"Frequently." Justin held open the trash bag for his F/O to deposit dirty paper towels and his latex gloves, then tied it shut. "We've got a couple hours until our next flight. Let's grab something to eat while the line crew gets started on the plane."

It had been almost a month since Justin had

been in Florida, and in that time, the weather had shifted from warm and balmy to hot and muggy. His sunglasses fogged up the minute they stepped out onto the stairs, the air condensing on his cool skin like water on a glass of sweet tea. Compared to Denver, where it stayed bone dry all summer, the air felt almost unbearably thick.

And this was where he was considering moving?

That wasn't fair, he chided himself as they walked across the apron into the FBO's lobby. The weather never bothered him when he vacationed in tropical locations. He was just reaching for any excuse to decide this move away from Melody was a bad idea.

By the time he returned to Colorado two days later, he was twisted up in the knowledge that Pete would want to move quickly now. They had already formed the C corp and completed the paperwork they needed to establish the business as a separate entity, but he'd have to put in his resignation and quickly transfer his 401(k) funds in order to get the loan and move forward with the purchase.

Yet the minute he touched down in Denver—in a snowstorm, no less—and turned his phone back on, he had a message from Pete.

Problem. The charter has another offer. And it's full price.

Justin stared at the phone, unable to believe

what he was reading. Finally he tapped out, What does that mean?

It means that unless we can come up with another $400K, it's done. Back to the drawing board.

Relief flooded Justin, followed by a wash of shame over his disloyalty. What sounded like good news to him was surely a huge blow to Pete and Jessica. How is Jess taking the news?

Disappointed. But you know Jess. She believes that God has a plan in it all.

You?

I'd like to believe it, but I'd rather God's plan didn't involve her having MS.

Justin sighed. That was the problem he always ran up against when he tried to assure himself there was a divine purpose in everything. How could he pray for a reason to stay in Denver with Melody when it meant that Pete and Jessica would have to stay as well, potentially causing her condition to deteriorate even further? Did he reassure himself with the thought that this was somewhat of a desperate chance in the first place, and there was no guarantee that she'd do better at sea level? That researchers didn't even agree on the reason for the excessive diagnosis rate of MS in Colorado? That she might well worsen in the humidity? It was just a ruse to hide his selfishness.

All he felt was relief that the decision had been taken out of his hands.

He and his F/O finished their paperwork, cleaned out the plane in record time, and then shook hands in parting, not sure if they'd ever fly together again. A shame, too, because El Shami had been good company: pleasant, competent, intelligent. It almost made Justin sad to leave AvionElite.

Or not, now that there was no reason to quit.

He checked his watch. Only 10 a.m. He'd been away for four days, which made going back to his apartment appealing. Then again, Melody had said she would be at the restaurant supervising the last phases of construction all morning. When given the choice of going home alone or being able to see her, there was no comparison.

He pushed down the handle to his case and hefted it in one hand, making his way through the snow-covered parking lot. Only when he got to the car did he allow his smile to break free.

He was staying.

He couldn't wait to tell Melody the good news.

CHAPTER THIRTY

Almost a week later, Melody still wasn't sure who she was angrier with, her friends or herself.

The situation at the supper club had been unforgivable, and she'd walked Justin straight into it. True, she'd never expected the questioning to go the direction it had. Of course she knew that Rachel and Ana would grill him about his intentions, maybe even question why he still was dating her when he was moving to Florida. But she hadn't dreamed they'd drag his faith—or in this case, lack of one—out at the dinner table for all to witness.

And maybe that was the problem. She and Justin had never really delved into what they believed, not in any significant way. She could blame it on the fact this was supposed to be short-term, but if she were honest with herself, she hadn't really wanted to know. There was no need to hear more reasons they couldn't be together when distance and future plans already seemed insurmountable.

She didn't want to hear that, once again, she'd let her heart lead her into something that could never work out in the end.

And yet, she was still utterly convinced he was a good man. Even the so-called Christian guys she'd dated got edgy after a few weeks, angling for invites to bed. Though that thought hovered between them—how could it not?—Justin seemed determined to keep things at a low simmer.

And that was one way Melody knew his ambivalent feelings about God didn't go straight to the core. What did it say that he treated her more respectfully than any of the churchgoing Christians she'd dated?

No, she was definitely more angry at Rachel and Ana for attacking someone they knew she cared about. There was no way to avoid them with the build-out on Bittersweet in full swing, and she didn't want to. But the easy, tell-all, no-topic-off-limits rapport they usually enjoyed was strained. Neither Rachel nor Ana offered an apology, and Melody didn't demand one. They didn't think they'd done anything wrong, and to push the matter would only widen the distance between them.

Justin said she was handling the matter with maturity, but the only thing she was handling well was covering up her hurt. Her sense of betrayal lingered, the suspicion that they'd tried to reveal his "faults" to get him out of her mind and shift her focus back to Bittersweet.

As if he were a distraction. Rachel was more

distracted by work and final university exams. Melody, by contrast, was on site every day, making sure the contractor was on track, making design decisions, coaxing rather than threatening the process along. So much so that it looked like they might finish ahead of schedule.

She shouldn't have thought it, though. Work ground to a halt when a late storm cruised into Denver and stayed there, shifting between rain, sleet, and heavy, wet snow while the thermometer flirted with freezing temperatures. Melody walked through the front door just as their contractor called and said he was going to be late because of road conditions. By the time the workers arrived hours later, the damp cold from the unheated space had crept into her bones.

"How's it going?" Rachel stepped inside and stamped slushy snow off her boots onto the mat their contractor had brought in, then joined Melody in the corner, where she could survey the construction.

"Good, I think. I'm liking the color we chose for the walls now that the flooring is going in. I must have second-guessed it five times even with all the swatches." She'd gone from gray to blue to green to taupe, finally settling on a gray-green that combined the things she liked most about the two colors. The old-fashioned white coin tile gave the floors a timeless feel, the black grout making it far more modern—and easier to clean—than the traditional white.

"We're still doing the tile area rug right here?" Rachel squinted, as if trying to imagine the rectangular design that was going to span the length of the counter like a permanent welcome mat.

"Yeah, but the tile we were going to use for the inset is back-ordered, so I had to come up with another idea."

All things considered, the construction was going pretty well. The paint and tile would be wrapped up by the end of the week. The cabinetry was being custom made by a craftsman in Loveland from reclaimed boxcar flooring and would take another couple of weeks, which meant that they'd have to hold the marble-look quartz countertop until it was installed.

"Did you see your ovens and the range?" Rachel asked. "That all went in yesterday while you were with the graphic designer."

"I did. It looks good. I saw they installed the outlets for my burners on my pastry bench too." Whereas a gas range was preferred for Rachel's side, Melody had ordered induction plates that would keep her candies and syrups at a steady temperature within two degrees, even as she'd choked on the price. Funny how she'd never thought twice about the cost of outfitting a restaurant kitchen until it was her turn to pay for it. "Oh, before you leave today, I need you to look at the designer's proofs for the logo and the signage."

"Let's do that now. I just dropped by to see how things were going. Alex is expecting me over at his place soon."

Melody stepped around the power tools on the floor and led Rachel back to the kitchen. Unlike the front of the house, this room was clean and spare, ready for supplies and tools to be brought in. Steel cooling racks stood along the back wall. Empty stacks of vat-sized Cambros and Rubbermaid bins waited on steel shelving to hold leavening, sugar, and flour, even though most of the time she'd pour directly from a sack to the mixer. Only the last section of her bench was incomplete, the steel frame waiting for its butcher-block top.

"Here are the logo options." Melody retrieved an envelope from her oversize tote and pulled out a stack of colored printouts.

Rachel pulled up a stool and seated herself at the worktable, spreading the papers out in front of her. "These are good."

"I know. I'm leaning toward one of these two." Melody tapped her finger on the first and last option. "The green is almost the same color as our walls. Ana is going to practically die from excitement that we listened to her about branding."

Rachel chuckled. "More likely relief that she doesn't have to lecture us anymore." She held up the papers at arm's length, one in each hand. "I like this one on the right. The Bittersweet logo is more eye-catching, and it still has 'Café and Bakery' beneath it."

"I agree. This one it is."

"That was easy."

"Compared to the paint saga, yes."

The bell on the front door jingled, and Rachel frowned. "Are you expecting anyone?"

"No." Melody rose from her stool just as a familiar head poked through the door. "Justin! What a surprise! I thought you were stuck in Oklahoma City."

"We hung out at the airport overnight. Finally got a break in the weather." He held up an overstuffed paper sack. "I figured we could both use a late lunch. Or early dinner. Whatever it is." He focused on Rachel as if noticing her for the first time. "There's plenty to share."

"No, no, I need to be going." Rachel's expression closed, and she hopped off the stool. "Call me later, Mel. I want to go over some menu changes."

Justin set the bag on the stainless-steel surface. "I hope I didn't run her off."

Melody watched Rachel's departure through the open door, resentment swelling again. "No, you didn't. She only dropped by for a few minutes."

"Good. Then I can do this." Justin took Melody's face in his hands and kissed her thoroughly.

"Wow. You know how to make an entrance. What's the occasion?"

"We're celebrating. Plus I missed you. You hungry?"

Absolutely. For another taste of him. He'd only been gone for four days this time, but even that felt way too long. She kept the thoughts to herself, plopped down, and watched as he unloaded the plastic deli containers and foil-wrapped packages. The distinctive smell of Indian food wafted to her, making her stomach rumble in response. So maybe she was hungry for lunch as well.

Justin grimaced. "I have utensils, but I didn't think about plates."

Melody pulled the lid off a container of vindaloo. "That's okay. You're not getting any of this anyway."

"Oh, really? I bet I can convince you otherwise."

She arched an eyebrow. "I don't know about that."

Justin pulled her to him again, and he was actually very convincing. Melody let out a happy sigh. Then she swiped the container from under his arm. "Nope. I'm still eating this all."

He laughed and took the stool Rachel had just

vacated. "Good thing I'm more of a tikka masala guy myself. This place has the best tikka chicken I've ever had."

Melody watched him, warmed by his mere presence. She'd done fine while he was gone. She had plenty to keep her busy. But he brought a little more color into her world. "Did you come straight from the airport?"

"I did. They're plowing the runways, but they're still pretty slick. I'm glad we made it back to Denver this morning."

"Me too. It's only supposed to get worse. Last I heard was five to seven inches, which would be a record for May."

"Oh, good. Maybe we'll get snowed in." The look he gave her could have melted the ice outside down to bare cement.

"I think we've already demonstrated that would be a very bad idea."

"Afraid you can't control yourself around me?"

"No, I'm afraid you can't control yourself around me. After all, I am irresistible."

He chuckled. "You absolutely are." He leaned over as if he were going to kiss her again . . . and grabbed the vindaloo from in front of her.

"Hey!"

He scooted out of the way and forked some of the lamb into his mouth, then held it out of reach. "Given how selfish you're being about this objectively amazing vindaloo, I think you more than made out in this situation."

"Oh yeah?" She sidled up to him and scraped a fingernail all the way down the front of his pressed white shirt. Then she threaded her hand through his hair, brought down his head toward hers, and kissed him slowly, carefully, until his attention was completely on her. Only then did she reach for the container.

"No, you don't." He shoved the container down the table and lifted her onto the stool, his mouth claiming hers completely. All thoughts of their silly game fled.

"We're just about fin—oh, sorry." A male voice intruded on the interlude, and Melody pulled away just in time to see their tile contractor's back disappear through the door.

Melody's eyes went wide. She looked back at Justin, who looked equally shocked, and then they both burst into laughter.

"Bet that's not something he's going to forget soon," he said with a crooked smile.

Melody pressed a hand to her forehead. "I'm going to have to go out there now to approve his work and pretend what he just saw never happened."

"Then fortify yourself first." He speared a piece of meat from the container that had started this whole game and fed it to her with a wicked twinkle in his eye. "I always thought this dating-a-chef fantasy involved feeding each other chocolate-covered strawberries in a dark kitchen, but I can be flexible."

Melody sighed and smoothed her hair. "That's going to have to wait. I need to go sign off on the tile work. How do I look?"

"Like you've been making out with your boyfriend in the kitchen." He smoothed his thumb over her lower lip. "I could go do it for you, but I'm really not sure what I'm supposed to be inspecting."

"No, no, I'm going." She squared her shoulders and pointed at him with the most serious expression she could muster. "You are trouble."

"I do my best."

To her relief, the contractor showed no sign of having walked in on a personal moment. He took her around the room, pointing out places he'd had to cut the tile and showing her the cement board where the inset would go. "As soon as the mosaic is finished, I can install it and we can grout the day after."

"It all looks good; thank you." She waited for him to pick up the last batch of tools and locked the door behind him. The snow had started coming down even thicker than before, blotting out the usual dusk in favor of early nightfall. She flipped off the overhead lights and went back to the kitchen, where Justin was bent over his tikka masala.

"I saved some for you," he said. "I suppose now would be the time to tell you I don't really like vindaloo."

She slid onto her stool a safe distance away, then pulled the foil-covered packet of naan toward her. "You really are trouble."

"Only around you." He grinned, but the expression quickly faded. "I have news."

"Oh? What kind of news?"

"The charter fell through."

Melody blinked at him. "What does that mean?"

"It means someone else made a better offer. It took us almost a year to find this one, so it's hard to tell how long it will take to find another suitable opportunity."

Melody studied him, afraid to let her heart grab on to the surge of joy that had surfaced as soon as he spoke the words. "You're really staying."

"For now? Yes."

Her heart squeezed with a painful intensity. She slid off the stool and threw her arms around his neck. "You have no idea how happy that makes me. I knew things were going to work out somehow. Do you believe now?"

Justin sobered. "I'm beginning to."

Melody looked into his eyes, saw the tenderness there. He was staying. He might not have said it, but she saw his devotion in their expression. For a second, a nervous flutter surfaced in her stomach, and she hid it with a quick grin. "Now about that last piece of naan . . ."

"It's yours." He grinned and surrendered the Indian flatbread willingly. When they finally finished the food, Justin began cleaning up. "How long do you have to stay?"

"I can go now. I just had to stay until the tile guy was done. I'll be back here tomorrow morning, assuming the roads are passable."

"So this is all you? Rachel's not helping?"

Melody shrugged, but her gut gave a little twist. "She's still working. And it's my design. It's easier this way."

"Things are still awkward, huh?"

"We mostly ignore it. We're partners, after all. If I think about it, I get mad all over again."

"Hey." He captured her hand and forced her to look at him. "I never wanted to put a wedge between you and your friends."

"You didn't. You just happened to reveal a side of them I've never seen before. And that is most definitely not your fault." She gathered up her tote and retrieved her parka. "Now I am going to go home and binge-watch Netflix and eat the peanut butter cookies I tested earlier this week."

"Want some company?"

Melody deposited the take-out bag in the trash and searched his face for any hidden intention. But no, he was looking at her like he always did.

"You're sure you want to go straight to my place? You haven't even been home yet."

He gestured for her to come close and pulled her back to him. This time when he kissed her, it was far more tender than heated. "As far as I'm concerned, you are home."

CHAPTER THIRTY-ONE

Over the next two weeks, Melody practically lived at Bittersweet. There were final design decisions to oversee, like the fixtures in the customer restrooms and the installation of the chalkboards they'd use for menus behind the front counter. The espresso machine had to be hooked up and the lowboy refrigerator installed under the counter. Then there was the interviewing.

"I didn't think it would be this hard," Melody said to Rachel when they'd finished talking to their tenth applicant and were no closer to finding a full-time cashier, baking assistant, or sous-chef. It didn't help that this wasn't the typical restaurant situation, so they didn't get the quality of applicants that their experience and standards demanded. Mostly they got people from the type of retail establishment she'd just left—employees who were well-meaning and hardworking, but had spent years working with premixed doughs, frozen baked goods, and mixes that were prepared in a manufacturing facility and finished on site. Not a single one of them would know how to handle a high-hydration dough like those Melody worked with or how to adjust a batch for humidity or product variations. And while Melody would love to be able to train new employees like she herself had learned, she needed to know that she could leave the bakery in good hands or she'd be working sixteen-hour days for the foreseeable future. The situation on Rachel's side was even worse.

"I don't think we're paying enough," Rachel said. "At the same time, I'm reluctant to add to our overhead."

In the end, Rachel hired the forty-year-old culinary student from her school to work as her sous-chef as well as offering an externship to another student, who jumped at the idea of working with a James Beard Award winner in a very small kitchen. Melody's solution came in a far-less-expected package.

She was stunning, a slender redhead who walked into the room with a confidence that few but Rachel could match. She held out her hand. "Talia Durand."

"Melody Johansson. Please, have a seat." Melody gestured to the chair across the café table and settled into her own, studying the woman carefully. Her long hair was pulled over her shoulder to one side, but when she reached into her bag for a portfolio, it fell away to reveal several jagged, puckered scars down the left side of her face.

Talia looked up. "Car accident. I'm fine now, but the scars are likely permanent."

"I'm sorry; I didn't mean—"

"It's okay. I find it's better to address it up front so no one feels awkward." Talia smiled, but there was something in her tone, a weariness perhaps, that made Melody think the admission was harder than she made it out to be.

"Tell me a little bit about your experience, Talia."

"I just moved from Chicago, where I worked as a pastry chef for four years, but I really consider myself a chocolatier." She withdrew a small pastry box from her bag, careful to keep it level, and pushed it across the table to Melody. "This is an example of my work."

Melody lifted the lid to the box, revealing five petite, beautifully formed chocolates. There were two hand-painted squares, each with a different fanciful design, as well as English toffee, a coconut-dusted bonbon, and a classic peanut cluster. "May I?"

"Please, I brought these for you."

Melody selected one of the hand-painted chocolates and took a tiny bite. Flavor exploded on her tongue, fruity and rich and unexpectedly layered, as complex as wine.

"Sixty-four percent Madagascar cacao with notes of red currant and blackberry and a dark chocolate ganache center."

"This is excellent." Melody took a second bite. "And I wouldn't at all mind adding some chocolate to the menu. However, we primarily do breads, French pastries, and Mediterranean desserts here."

Talia flipped open her leather portfolio. "I'm confident in my pastry work. Less so with bread at this altitude, but if you'll take the time to work with me, I'm sure I can adapt."

Her portfolio was equally impressive, divided between high-style, fine-dining pastries and simple desserts. Each was plated with an artistic eye, the technique obviously flawless. In fact, even without tasting any examples, Melody was willing to bet that Talia was at least as good as she was.

"Why do you want to work here?" Melody asked finally. "With this portfolio and what I've seen so far, you could probably get a pastry job at any restaurant in the city."

"Not all the restaurants in the city are hiring," she said with a slight smile. "And I like the idea of working at a small neighborhood bakery. I'm American, but my family is French, and growing up I spent summers in Nice. I miss the patisserie. As I understand it, you are French trained?"

"Partially." Talia had obviously done her homework prior to coming into the interview. There wasn't all that much information available on Melody online beyond her Instagram account—she would have had to do a fair bit of digging. "I tell you what. Come back tomorrow at nine for an audition. If you're half as good as your portfolio suggests, the job is yours."

They both rose, and Talia shoved her portfolio back in her bag, then stuck out her hand. "A pleasure to meet you. I'll see you tomorrow."

Melody watched the pretty woman leave the bakery, then settled back into her chair and reached for another chocolate. The bonbon she selected—hazelnut butter covered in a crisp chocolate shell—was the perfect balance of sweet, salty, and nutty, the very definition of heaven. The woman obviously had a way with confectionery, and Melody suspected her pastry would be just as good. But somehow she still didn't buy the story of wanting to work in a small bakery. Even the paltry salary of a pastry assistant in a larger restaurant would match what they were offering, with far more job security.

She pulled out her phone and typed *Talia Durand, pastry chef* in the search box of her browser. But instead of pulling up the masthead of a restaurant as she expected, Melody found herself looking at page after page of news reports.

American model suffers horrific accident.

Model Talia Durand announces permanent retirement.

Malibu car crash claims life of driver, leaves passenger disfigured.

Melody couldn't help but open news report after news report, sifting through the hyperbolic language for the truth. Talia had been in a car accident in Malibu seven years ago, right at the time she'd been at the height of her career, modeling for couture houses and designer fragrances. All that had come to a halt when the car her boyfriend was driving had slid down an embankment in Malibu Canyon, killing him and leaving her trapped for nearly eight hours before anyone noticed the vehicle. In addition to the terrible lacerations to her face, she'd broken dozens of bones, punctured a lung, and spent a good stretch in ICU recovering. That had marked the end of her modeling career and, as far as Melody could tell, the beginning of her stint as a pastry chef.

A tragedy, everyone called it. A horrible waste. Somehow the news reports rankled Melody. Sure, Talia was scarred, but she'd hardly call her disfigured. It was simply that everyone expected a woman that beautiful to be perfect. No doubt Talia had suffered under that expectation since her accident. But if what Melody tasted now was any indication, modeling wasn't even close to her greatest talent.

She pulled out her phone and texted Rachel: How do you feel about adding fine chocolate?

Rachel immediately came back: Why, are you getting bored with the four hundred items already on the menu?

Haha. Funny. I'm about to hire a pastry chef who is also a chocolatier.

420

That's your decision. Just make sure you save some samples for me.

The next morning, Melody was already hard at work when Talia arrived, dressed in a crisp white chef coat and checked trousers, her hair pulled away from her face in a tight knot. "Good morning."

Melody looked up from where she was rolling out a laminated dough on her marble table. "Morning. You can put your stuff in the staff room back there."

Talia disappeared for a moment, then returned with her knife case and pastry kit, one in each hand. "What would you like me to do?"

"While I'm making the croissants, I'd like you to make up two pounds of choux for the éclairs."

"Yes, Chef," Talia said immediately.

"Rachel gets called 'chef.' I'm just Melody or Mel."

Talia threw her a searching look as she began weighing flour for the dough, clearly comfortable with the process. "Will I get to meet her soon?"

"She should be in later this morning. Her menu is largely set. I'm still tinkering with mine and probably will be up until we open."

"Which is when?"

Melody glanced at her watch to check the date. "Five days." She stopped what she was doing. "Wow. Five days."

"You'll be ready," Talia said, moving the bowl

to the countertop mixer. "The pastry section is always ready."

It was true. Compared to the hot line, which depended on each cook performing with split-second accuracy, pastry had the advantage of advance preparation. They never knew which of their offerings were going to go over, but most of service was plating and not baking. And since only the donuts would be deep-fried to order, she'd have very little to worry about.

They'd have very little to worry about. A quick glance at the texture of the choux as Talia spooned the batter into a pastry bag told her that Talia had her recipe down to a science. Little stripes of batter went down on parchment-lined baking sheets, each perfectly uniform, a sure sign that she made these regularly. She slid them into one of the preheated ovens and then came back to the bench.

"Do you have a preference on filling? I'll make that while they're baking."

Melody pushed a binder of recipes toward Talia. "Pick two. I'd like to see how you do with my recipes."

"No problem." Talia flipped on one of the induction burners and set a small saucepan on the pad to heat. Melody barely needed to watch to know the woman knew what she was doing, scalding her cream, tempering her egg yolks. When the filling had come together, Melody dipped a spoon into the warm custard and tasted.

"That's good." She went back for a second taste. "Really good."

Talia smiled modestly, but pleasure poured off her.

A few minutes later, the pastries came out, puffed and golden, perfectly baked. Melody watched Talia fill them and sampled one of each, which was by now a formality.

Finally, Melody turned to her. "Congratulations, Talia. You're hired. You can start on Monday at seven. Beginning opening day, I'll need you here at four each morning."

"Thank you." Talia shook Melody's hand, beaming. "I'm so happy to be working here."

"And I'm happy to have you." More than happy. Melody had expected to hire a less experienced assistant and have to work alongside her. Now she was confident she could hand over her book and let Talia handle all the classic pastries while she focused on the bread and the daily specials.

For the first time, the worry that she wouldn't be ready in time fell away.

She wanted nothing more than to head to Justin's apartment and share her excitement about finally finding her pastry assistant, but he'd left on a six-day tour last night after promising that he wouldn't miss their opening night. Probably better anyway. She'd be so busy for the next several days that she'd have very little time for him . . . and the last thing she needed was to be wishing she were with him when she should be focusing on work.

She took a deep breath, happiness filling her chest. For the first time in longer than she remembered, things were falling into place. Justin. Bittersweet Café. Things were still strained with Rachel and Ana, but given time, they'd see they'd been too harsh. She had absolute confidence in that.

She'd held on through some unpleasant times, but her faith in God's blessings had proven out. Finally. She could only believe that this was all a sign she was at last headed in the right direction.

CHAPTER THIRTY-TWO

A full week off was going to feel like a luxury. Justin had purposely bid his schedule to be gone in early June and head back just in time for Bittersweet's friends-and-family night. Melody was too distracted to focus on him anyway, with the last-minute preparations taking up all her time. Their interactions had mostly consisted of him bringing dinner and coffee to the Platt Park space, then giving her a shoulder massage in the kitchen until the tension melted from her muscles. She'd plant a quick kiss on his lips and go straight back to work, his presence forgotten, leaving him with a whole lot of time alone with his thoughts.

The final days of this tour were comprised of a few long flights that pushed the limits of the Citation's range, the last being an LA-to-Atlanta leg that might or might not require a refueling stop depending on weather and winds. It was the kind of trip he enjoyed, requiring constant monitoring of speed, conditions, and fuel load, lots of planning for contingencies. Good weather and the jet stream at their back meant they made it nonstop, two hours before Tropical Storm Isobel had been expected to make landfall on the Atlantic coast.

"You staying overnight?" his F/O asked when they disembarked at Hartsfield-Jackson. By some miracle, he'd drawn Marilyn Terayasu again, who was fast becoming his favorite copilot.

"No, I need to get back to Denver by tomorrow. Flying commercial standby tonight."

Marilyn squinted at the darkening skies that indicated the leading edge of the storm. "Good luck."

"Should be chasing me home," Justin said. "On that note, I need to get going. It could be a long night." He shook Marilyn's hand and gripped his roller case as if sheer determination could get him back to Melody any faster.

But his optimism proved to be futile. As soon as he reached the terminal, he was informed that not only were there no standby slots available, they were bumping ticketed customers in order to get flight crews out of Atlanta before the storm. Already, the cascade of delays from Florida cancellations were lighting up the arrival and departure boards in a sea of blinking red.

Justin settled in to wait with a mediocre commissary salad and a Big Gulp–size cup of coffee. Time to look at alternate options. He pulled out his phone and saw that he had several text messages from Pete.

Check your e-mail! BIG news! Others followed with variations on the theme.

A flash of lightning cracked open the twilit sky,

followed by a boom of thunder. Almost instantly, a sheet of rain poured down, bringing up a roar on the airport roof and pelting the windows with a force that sounded more like pebbles than water. Justin ignored the texts and e-mails and dialed AvionElite's dispatch.

"Hey, Rebecca. Justin Keller. I'm at ATL and I need out tonight. Commercial's not going to work. What can you do for me?"

Rebecca was one of the senior dispatchers; from the noise he heard in the background of the command center, all hands were on deck. She tapped away on a keyboard. "You're in luck. I'm repositioning a Phenom from AHN to BLV. If you can get there by 8 p.m., you can ride along. But I'm not holding it for you."

"Thanks, Rebecca; I'm on my way." He grabbed his bag, tossed his coffee and the remainder of the salad, and hightailed it from the terminal to ground transportation. In good weather, Hartsfield-Jackson to Athens-Ben Epps took about ninety minutes, a drive he'd made a handful of times in his tenure at AvionElite. He had three hours until wheels up, and when Rebecca said they wouldn't wait for him, she meant it. Even then, it only got him to St. Louis, from which he'd have to find a seat back to Denver. But at least he would be out of the path of the storm. Surely twenty-four hours was enough time to make his way from Missouri to

Colorado, even if he had to rent a car and drive.

On his third try, he found a taxi willing to take him to Athens in the rain, then pulled out his phone to text Melody. He changed his mind before he could press a single button. No point worrying her unnecessarily. He'd call her when he got to St. Louis and give her an update.

Instead, he went back to the e-mails the rain had interrupted. The one on top was from Pete, a forwarded version of the e-mail immediately below it. The original was from Luis Garcia's business broker.

Justin read the message, and his whole body went cold, his stomach adding a new collection of knots. The message was phrased diplomatically, but the gist was that the other sale had fallen through and Garcia was making a counter to their initial offer.

He scrolled up to Pete's message. If he meets us halfway, I say we go for it.

Justin dropped his head back against the seat, too stunned to send a reply, looking out instead on the pelting rain. He'd been so happy a mere few hours ago, but now it felt like everything was conspiring against him and Melody. It was bad enough he might miss friends-and-family night. Even worse that he was going back to tell her the dreams they'd begun to share, the ones that involved a life together, were never going to happen. Though if he missed the biggest night of her life, it wouldn't matter. She'd never want to speak to him again.

Progress was slow, the rain coming down hard enough to make him doubt both his and his taxi driver's sanity. He gripped the handle of the door as the car plowed through standing water, sending up a spectacular rooster tail to wash his window. At this speed, he'd be lucky to make it by midnight.

And yet somehow, they pulled onto the AHN property at five minutes before eight. Justin hastily paid the driver, grabbed his suitcase, and dashed into the rain, water immediately soaking through his uniform slacks and turning the wool from navy blue to midnight black. He knew he must look like a maniac rushing through the double doors, then running to the FBO's desk, drenched to the skin, rivulets running from his hair to his face.

"AvionElite. Did I make it?"

"You must be Captain Keller." The man behind the desk looked at him sympathetically. "I'm so sorry. You just missed them. They barely made it out before they shut down the airfield."

Justin stared dumbly at the rep. Three hours in treacherous weather and significant cost to get here, only to miss his plane by mere minutes. And because Athens was a general aviation airport, that meant he'd have to go back to Atlanta or on to Greenville, South Carolina, to get on a commercial flight. Whenever that would be.

He slicked his wet hair back from his eyes and, for reasons even he couldn't explain, began to laugh. It was almost as if he were being punished for his sudden burst of optimism. Four hours ago, he'd been confident in his future with Melody, secure in his belief that he might actually be able to break the so-called pilot's curse on relationships.

He'd thought that God was distant, but until now, he'd never known He was cruel.

Chapter Thirty-Three

Melody didn't sleep the night before friends-and-family night. Which, to be honest, wasn't much of a change, because she hadn't slept much since she'd come back from Silverlark. Between the difficulty of adjusting to a daytime schedule after more than a year on the night shift and her stress over the bakery, the best she could do was grab a nap a couple times a day before she woke with a panicked flutter in her stomach.

It was not exactly what she'd expected on the day she was opening her own place.

Then again, she knew all too well from Rachel's experience that the mystique of restaurateur and proprietor was just that: mystique. The reality involved a lot of hard work and sleepless nights. The benefit was being her own boss, making her own decisions, getting to put her own stamp on the food they served. And she had a feeling the first time she saw a customer's delighted smile when they tasted her éclairs or experienced truly good bread would make up for all of it.

It had to.

The morning was still dark and cold when she left her apartment and drove south through Denver to their Platt Park location, the stars like ice chips in the night sky. A few cars illuminated the dark with the glare of their headlights, but the city mostly still slept. Unsurprisingly, Rachel's car was already parked in the alley behind the restaurant when she pulled up, light shining through the kitchen's small clerestory windows.

"Today's the day!" Rachel exclaimed the minute Melody walked through the door. She was already hard at work at her prep station, plowing through piles of vegetables with quick strokes of her knife. "I figured you might like the company. I knew you had to get the baking going early."

"Couldn't sleep either?" Melody pulled off her sweatshirt, then took her apron from where it hung outside the staff break room—really a closet that they'd appropriated for the required space. Somehow seeing Rachel in her chef's jacket and dark pants again made her feel like something in the universe had been solved, like an essential wrong had been righted. She did notice that instead of the businesslike sprayed-and-pinned low knot Rachel normally wore in the kitchen, she had her hair piled on top of her head in a messy bun, a headband holding everything back from her face.

"I haven't slept for days," Rachel admitted. "Every time I try, I remember something else I forgot."

"Tell me about it." Melody pulled out her prep list from her pocket and laid it out on the stainless-steel table, going over it one more time to make sure she had everything in the right order. First the ovens got turned on to heat. Then she'd get the autolyse started for her first batches, a simple process of mixing flour and water so it hydrated the proteins and developed gluten bonds prior to adding leavening and other ingredients. While that was sitting, she would pull the pre-ferments from the refrigerator, the yeasted starters that would give flavor and depth to her finished bread.

She was just beginning to mix the first batch of dough in the big Hobart when the back door opened. Melody looked up in surprise as Talia entered. "I didn't expect you so early! You don't need to be in until seven today."

"I know. But I thought you could use an extra set of hands." Talia dropped her coat and bag in the break room, pulled on an apron, and rolled up her sleeves. "What do you want me to do first?"

"Cream puffs, éclairs, and shortbread."

"I'm on it." Talia went to scrub her hands and then wasted no time bringing together the dough for the French pastries and the shortbread that would be the base for Melody's lemon curd bars.

Rachel sent a smile over her shoulder that clearly conveyed approval of Melody's choice.

The sous-chef showed up about an hour later, also ahead of schedule. Rachel introduced them to Samantha Caldwell, pretty and dark-skinned with wide brown eyes and a brusque attitude that seemed in total opposition to her Disney-character looks.

"An all-female kitchen," she said when she shook Melody's and Talia's hands. "I like it."

"We didn't specifically seek to hire only women," Rachel said, "but I'm not sorry that's the way it worked out."

The extra time turned out to be a blessing, because while both assistants were perfectly capable, it was going to take a while to acclimate to Rachel's and Melody's styles and expectations. They both found themselves taking time out to teach and instruct, to move supplies around the kitchen when the arrangement turned out to be inconvenient, to swap out menu items when something wasn't coming together properly. This was why they started with a friends-and-family night. Not only could they get opinions from people who loved them and would therefore be tactfully honest, it gave them the opportunity to work out the kinks before they opened for real.

Around noon, Sam cooked them lunch, a delicious pasta-and-vegetable soup to which Melody contributed half a loaf of bread. Their normal hours were such that they wouldn't have a regular family meal like in a restaurant, but today was going to be a long and tiring day.

As they sat at the long counter-height table

in the dining area, sopping up the last bit of the broth with their bread, Rachel asked, "Justin going to be here tonight?"

Melody detected no reservation in Rachel's tone. Maybe she was coming around. "He said he would. He was supposed to get home last night, but I haven't heard from him." She didn't say that she'd been checking her cell phone at every opportunity to see if he'd replied to her half-dozen texts. "How about you guys?"

Alex would be there, of course, and Sam's boyfriend and sister, but Talia just shook her head. "I grew up in Colorado, but I don't have anyone around anymore."

Melody didn't press, but there was something in the tone that told her there was more to this story. Maybe that's why Talia was so anxious to get a job. When baking was the only thing you really did well, it made a handy substitute for a real life.

At least that's what Melody had been telling herself. Now she wasn't so sure.

Then it was back to work. Rachel and Sam prepped things like stock and demi-glace that would be used in dishes later tonight, bubbling away in huge pots on the range. Melody batched bread in and out of the oven, until the baskets behind the counter out front spilled their bounty. Talia inserted tray after tray of baked goods into the case. At last, Melody and Rachel stepped back near the front door to admire their handiwork.

Bittersweet Café was at last a reality.

"It's beautiful," Rachel said with a happy sigh. "You did an incredible job on the design, Mel. I can't imagine having a prettier place."

Melody slid an arm around Rachel, and they hugged, the tension of the past weeks slipping away in the face of what they had accomplished together. It was rather impressive, hip and modern with touches that suggested old-fashioned European bakeries. When they hadn't been able to get the tile for the original "rug" in front of the counter, Melody had found an artist to instead create a mosaic that showed the Front Range skyline with its buildings and craggy mountains behind. And above it all hung Melody's funky chandelier, now transformed into a vintage showpiece, casting pools of light on the space below.

Melody glanced at her watch. "Four o'clock. Mark will be here in a few minutes to work the front, and then we'll open. Are you ready?"

"More than. We're just killing time now." Rachel took a deep breath and let it out slowly. "It's silly to be nervous, isn't it? This is a tiny menu and a tiny kitchen compared to what we're used to. We've got this."

"Of course we do. Doesn't stop me from feeling like I'm going to throw up." Melody grinned at Rachel and they hugged again. "Now let's take one more look around."

Mark, their bearded, twentysomething cashier, showed up promptly at four thirty. The irony of having a man out front and all women in the back was not lost on Melody. Mark was sharp, with barista and retail experience, and he clearly liked the idea of being in charge of the front of the house. He'd taken to the point-of-sale system immediately when Rachel trained him over the weekend, but since they weren't charging for any food tonight, the order-taking process was largely for communicating to the kitchen and making sure they didn't have any kinks in the computer system.

At 4:55, they flipped the sign on the door to Open. And three minutes later, the first guest stepped through the front door.

In the kitchen, Melody had no idea who had shown up or who hadn't; she only heard the tickets coming through on the printer on Rachel's side. Rachel and Sam worked quickly and methodically, putting together dishes from the limited hot menu.

"We need someone to run food and clean tables," Rachel called over her shoulder. "I thought Sam and I could do it ourselves, but if we get this busy during lunch rush, it's going to be a disaster."

"I'll do it." Melody gave a couple of quick instructions to Talia, then pulled her apron over her head, dusted off traces of flour from her shirt, and took the plates with the ticket.

When she stepped out into the front, she paused, her mouth dropping open.

She knew they'd invited a lot of people, but she hardly thought they'd all turn up, and definitely not at the same time. Every seat in the place was filled, and a line formed at the register and snaked out the door and down the street. She was suddenly glad they'd thought to put up a chalkboard sign on the sidewalk that said, *Closed for private party.*

Melody wrestled her surprise under control and maneuvered to the table marked with a number 3. Since there was no table-side ordering, they had opted to use table tags instead.

"Welcome!" she said brightly to Mitchell and Bryan Shaw. "Who had the pasta?"

Mitchell raised a finger and she set it down in front of him, then placed the bowl of French onion soup in front of Bryan.

"Congratulations, Melody," Bryan said. "Have you met my father, Mitchell?"

"Once in passing." She extended her hand to shake the man's. He was so unassuming and normal-seeming that one wouldn't know he was one of the wealthiest and most influential real estate developers in Denver. "I really appreciate your coming. What do you think?"

"It's perfect," Mitchell said. "Alex told me you designed the place. If you ever decide to get out of the kitchen, you could have a second career in restaurant design."

"Thank you. I can add it to my résumé, along with back waiter tonight." She smiled at both of them. "Enjoy your meals."

She hustled back into the kitchen, pausing beside Rachel. "Mitchell and Bryan are here. They seem to like the place. Complimented me on the design."

"Did you see Alex yet? He said he was going to come before seven."

"No, not yet. And no Justin either." Maybe the two men had run into each other outside and were waiting until the rush wound down. She checked her cell phone, hoping to see a text to that effect, but the screen was still blank. Where was he?

She didn't have much time to dwell on it. She took food out to the dining room as fast as Rachel and Sam made it, noting the tables that had turned over. A quick look at the bakery case showed that the croissants, lemon bars, and chocolate *dacquoise* were the most popular tonight, though there had been a pretty significant dent in the macarons as well. Only time would tell if that became a regular trend. After she had a chance to analyze the sales from the first few weeks, she'd make adjustments to their menu, dropping the slow sellers and increasing the regularly sold-out items.

On her way back to the kitchen, she felt a tug at the hem of her shirt. She whirled. "Ana!"

Ana gave Melody a tight hug. "How's it going?"

"Very well. We might not have this volume on a regular day, but at least we know we can handle it. Rachel and Sam are already a well-oiled machine."

"And you?"

"Done baking and pretending to be a server for the night. Have you seen Alex or Justin?"

"No, but Bryan is waiting outside. He said you guys had a big announcement at the end."

"We're just going to say a few words to end the night. Are you going to stick around?"

"Of course. Just waiting for my food. Hop to it, girl."

Melody stuck out her tongue and disappeared back into the kitchen. "Hey, Rach, do you have some big announcement to make?"

"Nope. You know I let my cooking talk for me."

Melody laughed. It was an automatic answer; Rachel's mind was on her food and not her words. It was good to see her back in the kitchen—and not just in the kitchen, but actually cooking. She might have loved being at the helm as executive chef, but Melody could see by the brightness in her face and the energy in her body that she found something satisfying about the hands-on process.

And that alone told Melody they'd made the right choice.

"The cream puffs and éclairs are gone," she told Talia. "I heard someone say they were the best they'd tasted. Well done."

"Your recipes," Talia said, but she beamed.

And then somehow, it was eight o'clock, the end of their event. Melody told Mark to stop taking hot orders, though he could continue to serve from the bakery cases. Rachel and Melody cleaned themselves up and moved out into the main dining room. It was slightly emptier than before, and a few stragglers waited in line at the front counter. Melody scanned the room and saw Alex seated near the front, but Justin was nowhere to be seen.

Rachel grabbed a water glass and tapped a spoon against it to get everyone's attention. "Thank you all so much for coming to the opening of Bittersweet Café and Bakery. You're all a part of getting us to where we are now, so thank you."

Applause broke out around the room, and Rachel waited until it died down. "This is a second chance for me. As most of you know, I had a rough stretch after what happened with my last restaurant. It's been almost a year since I left as chef there, and at the time I thought it was the worst thing that had ever happened to me." She met Alex's eyes and smiled. "I was wrong, of course, because it turned out to be the best thing that ever happened to me. Not least because, had

I stayed, I wouldn't have had the opportunity to co-own my dream place with one of my very best friends, Melody Johansson."

More applause, a signal that it was Melody's turn to speak. "Most of you know me mainly as a bread evangelist, pushing batards and baguettes at you with commands like 'Eat this! You've never tasted anything like this!'" Laughter rang out in response. "It really is a dream come true to be able to open a bakery like this, to make all the things that I love to eat but can rarely find on this side of the city. I make all this stuff anyway, so now I just don't have to eat it by myself. But I wouldn't have wanted to do it without Rachel, who has been a great friend and mentor to me."

They hugged amid applause. Before they could thank their guests and say good night as planned, Alex stood from the table at the corner. "I'd like to say something if I could."

Rachel's brow furrowed momentarily, but she smiled as he made his way toward her.

"As some of you know, I was the inadvertent mastermind behind Rachel's . . . ahem . . . change of direction." More scattered laughter. "I couldn't be happier for her. I know this is probably the biggest night of her life, and honestly, it's a little intimidating as her boyfriend to try to top it. So I'm not going to."

Rachel now looked completely confused, but Melody's heart picked up its beat.

Alex took Rachel's hand. "Rachel, I love you. I knew when I fell in love with you that I was not just committing to you, but also to your career and your restaurants . . . because yes, I know there will be more in the future. So it seems appropriate to ask you this tonight." He pulled a velvet box from his pocket and knelt in front of her. "Will you marry me?"

Rachel's mouth dropped open. Her hand drifted to her throat, but she remained speechless.

"Uh, Rachel? Don't leave me hanging here."

"Yes! Of course yes!" Rachel laughed as he slid a ring onto her finger and then launched herself into his arms. The room erupted in applause when they kissed, hoots and catcalls coming from their friends.

Tears pricked Melody's eyes as she waited for her turn to hug the newly engaged couple. The larger part of her was thrilled. She squeezed Rachel tight and whispered the right words in her ear, then hugged Alex as well. And when her friends got caught up in the throng of congratulations, Melody slipped back into the kitchen.

Rachel was getting married. Rachel, who had been wholly devoted to her work until she had it taken from her; Rachel, who was so skittish around men that she hadn't had a real boyfriend until Alex.

And despite the bubble of joy that welled up

within Melody from knowing that her friend had found her soul mate, there was a spike of pain that went with it. No, not pain. Envy.

She checked her cell phone, hoping that there was something from Justin, some reason for missing the biggest night of her life. Some explanation for the fact he hadn't even bothered to call or text that he wasn't going to make it.

There was nothing.

Melody shoved her phone into her pocket with an angry shake of her head and swallowed down the lump in her throat. She started the pre-ferments for tomorrow's baking and then cleaned up her station. When Rachel, Sam, and Talia bounced back through the doors, their color high and voices excited, she managed to put on a neutral expression. "So, what do you guys think? I'd say that went pretty well."

"More than well. Look!" Rachel thrust her phone in front of Melody, showing the long list of tweets that had gone out about the restaurant from their friends and associates. A quick check showed even more on Instagram, and a couple of five-star reviews had already shown up on their online listings. Their friends had clearly embraced their new venture and were doing everything they could to announce it to the world. It would be a victory for anyone, but after Rachel had been eviscerated online through no real fault of her own, it felt like redemption.

"Go home," Melody finally told Rachel. "I'll close up. I just want to finish a few things for tomorrow before I leave."

"Are you sure? I could stay . . ."

Melody gave her a stern look. "You just got engaged. Go celebrate with your new fiancé. Stop by the store and get a wedding magazine or something."

Rachel laughed, glowing with happiness from the dual successes of the night. Melody managed to keep it together until Rachel packed up her things and left, and then the first tears fell.

Alex had proposed to Rachel *and* the restaurant and her future dreams. She had someone to share her accomplishments with, and now her entire life. Up until now, Melody had held out hope that Justin could be that for her. But the fact that he hadn't shown up, hadn't even called or texted, told her that she'd been living in a fantasy world these past few months. She'd just been a way to pass time until he left. A way to stave off inevitable boredom until he got on with the next part of his life. And now that he was staying in Denver, he was rethinking the idea of her being part of it.

Melody swiped away the tears, put the labeled pre-ferments into the walk-ins, and then started to close down the bakery. Double-checked the lock on the front door, switched off all but the security lights; threw on her sweatshirt, grabbed her handbag, locked the back door behind her. When she hopped into her Jeep, she forced any thoughts of Justin out of her mind in favor of a recap of their first night. Tomorrow was the soft opening of the bakery, three days of sales before their advertised grand opening on Saturday. It would no doubt take a while for word to spread that they were open and to regain Agni's old customers, so that meant they could work out the kinks of their baking schedule without pressure.

Mark at least was worth his weight in gold. She'd noticed him chatting up the customers with a megawatt smile, pulling shots at the espresso machine like a pro, keeping the line moving without making people feel like they were being rushed through. The front of the house had been her one true concern, but now it seemed like the least of them.

It was her dream. And it was all coming true.

She drove home with surprising calm and parked on the street, where she remained, her limbs heavy, her body drained of energy. Justin would probably chide her for sitting out here in the dark in this part of the city, but then again, he—and her mother—had always had a much worse impression of her neighborhood than was actually true. Or maybe Melody really did have an unrealistically rosy perspective on things. If she'd learned anything tonight, it was that her optimism wasn't always proven out.

Chapter Thirty-Four

By the time Justin reached Denver's city limits, he was wrung out and aching, the pit in the center of his stomach filled now with rocks. To say it had been hard getting home would be an understatement. He'd thought he would be fine when by some miracle he caught a flight out of Atlanta for Seattle, a city so far removed from the East Coast weather that it should have been relatively unaffected by the delays that were stalling air travel up and down the Eastern Seaboard.

And then he'd sat at SeaTac for nearly an entire day, flight after flight to Denver filling up without any standby seats available. Finally, he'd managed to get on a flight to Colorado Springs, ninety minutes away from his house and even farther from where his car was parked at Denver International Airport. By this time of night, there were no public transportation options from the Springs, so instead he'd opted for an extremely expensive Uber ride. By the time he retrieved his car from DIA's long-term parking, it was after 11 p.m.

He'd missed Bittersweet's opening.

For the twentieth time, he pulled out his phone

and then returned it to his pocket without sending a message or making a call. It was a terrible, immature thing to do, he knew, not letting her know what had happened. But at the same time, he knew he wouldn't be able to contact Melody without spilling the news that had plagued him for the last twenty-four hours. And that was a discussion that deserved to be had in person.

He should go home to shower and change before he saw Melody. His shirt was wrinkled, and the cuffs of his wool pants were still damp from last night's downpour. He probably smelled like a wet dog. At best, he looked like the walking dead with dark circles from lack of sleep and stress and dread.

Instead, he drove straight to her apartment, hoping she would be there. Hoping she would even let him through the door.

Her Jeep was parked at the curb when he pulled up, and he parallel-parked behind her, then practically raced up the front walk. He held his breath as he pushed the buzzer and waited for her to answer. "Melody? It's me. Can I come in?"

She didn't reply, but the panel buzzed and the front door lock disengaged. At least she wasn't shutting him out completely. He slowly climbed the stairs, his anxiety now tempered.

She opened the door as soon as he knocked. The first sight of her, her beautiful brown eyes red-rimmed and swollen, punched him in the gut.

He stepped inside and reached for her. "Melody, I am *so* sorry."

She stepped out of his grasp and folded her arms over her chest. "This was the biggest night of my life, Justin. I watched for you. I thought for sure you were just running late, because you knew what this meant to me. And yet you didn't show up."

He swallowed down his misery. "You have no idea how terrible I feel. I got stuck in Georgia overnight because of the tropical storm. I finally made it to Seattle and then my flight—"

"So you're saying you were completely without phone service that entire time?" She arched an eyebrow, her tone hard.

He swallowed. "No, but—"

"No *but*s, Justin. We're not sixteen. You were having a hard time getting home. You think I wouldn't understand that? You didn't think that maybe I just wanted you to acknowledge what an accomplishment opening this bakery is? That maybe I wanted to celebrate with you, even if it had to be over the phone? What's so hard about calling me and saying, 'I'm stuck in Seattle, but I'm so proud of you'?"

"I am proud of you, Melody. What you've accomplished is worth celebrating. And yes, I should have called. Up until the last minute, I thought I could make it. It just all went wrong." He took her hand, and this time she didn't pull

449

away. Taking that as a sign she was softening toward him, he tugged her against him, enfolding her in his arms. "I never meant to hurt you. I did this completely wrong, but it wasn't because I didn't care. I just wanted so badly not to let you down."

She sighed, relaxing against him by degrees. "You did do it completely wrong. And I'm still mad at you."

"As well you have a right to be." And she would be even angrier in a moment when she found out what he was holding back.

Somehow, she must have heard that hesitation in his voice. "There's more, isn't there? What is it?"

He let her go and rubbed his hands through his hair, his momentary relief replaced immediately with the lingering dread. "Melody, sit down. I need to tell you something."

She swallowed hard and pulled up a chair at her dining room table. The very table where they'd decided to go forward with their relationship despite his imminent departure, in fact. Justin took a chair beside her, but this time he didn't take her hand.

There was no use beating around the bush. "The other offer for the charter fell through. They couldn't get their funding."

Melody stared at him, clearly not understanding what that meant.

"The owner countered our original offer. Pete wants to take it."

"And what do you think?"

He sighed. "Melody, if it were up to me, I would stay here with you. But I promised Pete and Jessica. We've already set up the corporation. I gave my notice at work today and started the process of rolling over my 401(k) for the down payment."

Melody shook her head, like she couldn't believe what she was hearing. "How long have you known this was a possibility?"

"I always knew it was a possibility, but I just found out for sure last night." He summoned the courage to say what he should have said long ago. "I've been racking my brain for another solution, but I'm not sure what else to do. This is my family. We're halfway down the road already. I can't back out. Is there any chance you'd consider . . . Do you ever think you could be happy moving to Florida with me?"

Melody stared at him, her expression stunned. "How could you ask me that? We just opened Bittersweet. It's beautiful. It's going to be a huge success. Which you would know if you'd bothered to show up."

"Mel—"

She looked away, but not fast enough. He glimpsed the tears shining in her eyes. "You know, there was a time when I absolutely would have given everything up to go with you. When the possibility of a happily ever after would have me leaving behind everything that I have here." She turned to him and drew in a shuddering breath. "But I'm tired of waiting. I'm tired of living for the future and the slim possibility that everything's going to work out."

"Melody, I never meant—"

She held up her hand. "The worst part is, I thought this time was for real. I thought for once, maybe I really could have it all." She laughed, and it transformed into a sob. "I actually believed this was my reward for hanging on, for trusting God to work it out. And if I'm being honest, I thought I could change your mind. That you'd see God really is working things for our good."

"For a little while, I started thinking the same thing." He gripped handfuls of his hair in frustration, welcoming the sting in his scalp. "Do you know what this is like for me? No matter what choice I make, I let down someone important to me. Except in my sister's case . . ."

". . . it's her health on the line. I understand. I do. I would consider me to be the less important part of that equation too." Her voice sounded dull, robotic, and that pierced him worse than her anger.

"No. No!" He grabbed her hand. "You are not less important. If I could do something . . ."

Melody pulled her hand from his. "We both knew this was only temporary. I had my eyes wide open when I walked in. Maybe our mistake was trying to make it last."

She swallowed and forced a smile. "I don't bear you any ill will. Not even for missing the opening. It makes things easier somehow. One chapter of my life ending; a new one beginning. And you're moving to Florida to begin your own chapter. You'll meet someone else, and I'll just be a memory. Hopefully a good one."

Justin cleared his throat around the lump forming there. "Is that really what you want?"

"Of course it's not what I want, but it's what has to be." She moved close enough to take his hand and then leaned over to press a brief kiss to his lips. "Good luck. I hope it all works out for you and Pete and Jessica."

He'd never believed it when people said they could feel their hearts breaking, and he was right. It wasn't broken. It was pulverized. Nothing left but a hollow spot where his last shred of hope had resided. "I'm sure Bittersweet is going to be a resounding success. Good-bye, Melody."

She walked him to the door and then closed it behind him, the bolt clicking into the frame a moment later, locking him out. Of her apartment and her life. He thought he heard sobs from the other side of the door, but that could just be his own imagination, his own wishful thinking that the decision hadn't been as easy as she'd made it seem.

He turned and slowly walked down the hall, stunned at how quickly things had changed.

It was over. His life in Denver. His relationship with Melody. All of it.

The day after he and Melody broke up, Justin woke early and began ticking off boxes on his checklist: the list of things that would dismantle his life in Denver. He gave his thirty-day notice to his landlord, even though he would be on the hook for an extra month's rent. He put in a forwarding notice for his mail to go to the business address at the Fort Lauderdale-Hollywood Airport. He ordered a storage cube to be delivered to his apartment to hold all his things until he found a permanent residence in Florida—no need to bring all his furniture with him if he was living in an extended-stay motel for a while.

And then there was his dad. Normally he would have to check Rich's schedule, but since he'd retired, he was enjoying his ability to stay in pajamas for most of the day, reading the newspaper and catching up on the five years' worth of television shows on his DVR.

"Dad?" Justin pushed the front door open and poked his head in. Silence. It was after ten, so surely he was awake. Even in retirement, he rarely slept past 6 a.m.

The smell of fresh coffee wafted from the kitchen, so he was obviously up. Justin followed the aroma deeper into the house, saw his dad's coffee cup and empty breakfast plate on the counter. And then his gaze traveled to the sliding-glass door looking out into the backyard, where his dad knelt in the dirt with a spade and a garden claw, pulling out the bindweed that had taken over the flower bed.

Justin slid the door open and stepped onto the back patio. "What are you doing?"

Rich looked up. "What does it look like I'm doing? I'm weeding."

"Yes, I can see that." Justin ambled to his side. "But why? You hate gardening."

Rich shrugged. "I'm retired. I only hated gardening because I had other things to do with my time. But now I don't, so I might as well work on the yard." He gestured with his spade. "I thought I would put a few more trees into that corner. Maybe a fire pit with some flagstone pavers. Adirondack chairs. It would be a nice place to spend some summer nights."

Justin stared at him. "Who are you and what did you do with my father?"

Rich chuckled. "Retirement makes you do strange things, Son. I enjoyed doing nothing for all of two weeks. And then I got up one morning and realized I was bored to death. There's only so much time you can spend drinking coffee and reading newspapers and watching TV. So I might as well catch up on those home improvement projects I've been talking about for the last twenty years."

"Okay, then. Whatever makes you happy and keeps you busy, I guess." Justin shook his head, repressing a laugh. Domestic tasks were normally Rich's last inclination. Justin would have thought his dad would buy a project car or a vintage plane and spend his time fixing those up. "I wanted to talk to you."

Rich pushed himself to his feet and dusted his hands off on his jeans. "Oh yeah?"

Justin told him they were about to sign the final papers for the business, that he would soon be the proud half owner of a charter with established customers and three planes. Said aloud, it did sound pretty impressive. Made him feel ungrateful for his ambivalence. "So that means I'll be gone by the end of the week."

"So soon?"

"I need to find a place to live out there, and the owner is only staying on so long for the transition. I'd feel better if I got out there as soon as possible."

Rich studied him, his expression knowing. "And the girl?"

"Melody? It's over. It was only supposed to be temporary anyway."

Justin didn't meet Rich's eyes, and his dad didn't push. "I'm sorry to hear that. It sounded like you really liked her. But . . ."

"But guys like us don't do well with long-term relationships; I know."

"I was just going to say sometimes you meet the right person at the wrong time." Rich's expression filled with sympathy. "I think you'll like Florida. I think if I were going to move away from Denver, that's where I would go. Be one of those old men driving a golf cart to the grocery store in checkered pants and a paddy hat."

"A souped-up golf cart maybe." Justin grinned, cheered by that image. "I'll leave you to your gardening."

"What's the rush? Grab a spade. As soon as I get this bed cleared, I'm going to the nursery for some annuals."

Justin shook his head, now pretty certain that his father had been snatched and replaced with a pod person. But he grabbed a spade, knelt beside his dad, and began to pull up the vines that trailed beneath the surface of the flower bed. He drew the line at selecting flowers, however, so once he'd finished his section of freshly tilled and weeded dirt, he made his excuses and escaped.

Which only put him smack into the middle of his own thoughts. It was all he could do not to drive to Melody's bakery, see it with his own eyes. Tell her that he loved her, that he missed her already, that he'd made a mistake. Tell her that he'd stay.

But he couldn't. Even if he could somehow abandon his sister and Pete that way, his entire savings was wrapped up in the business. He was on the hook for a very large bank loan, from which there was no way out.

He'd made his decision long before she said good-bye. This was his doing and he didn't have the right to be in her life, not even for a last few precious days.

He should go home and begin packing. But the thought of doing that just made him more depressed. Instead, he turned his car toward the airport, running through potential destinations in his head.

In the air, he could temporarily forget what he'd done. He could put these feelings aside in the sheer joy of flight. And forget that in keeping his promise to one woman, he'd completely betrayed another.

CHAPTER THIRTY-FIVE

Melody showed up for Bittersweet's first full day with bloodshot, swollen eyes and a pounding headache. She was already working on the first batches of cinnamon roll dough when Rachel breezed through the back door, looking deliriously happy and much too awake for the early hour.

Rachel took one look at Melody and her expression turned to alarm. "What happened?"

Melody continued to roll the dough, the exertion giving her something to focus on other than her aching heart. "Justin came by last night. It's over."

"Oh, Melody, I'm so sorry." Rachel enveloped her in a hug, but Melody just stood there stiffly, holding her sticky hands free. She couldn't let herself sink into the comfort. Couldn't tell her friend how she felt. She had twelve hours to get through here, and she was afraid that if she let the tears flow, she wouldn't be able to bottle them up again.

She cleared her throat, but her voice still came out hoarse. "I knew it was coming. I shouldn't have been surprised. I'll be okay. I'm always okay."

"Do you want to talk about it?"

"I really don't." She didn't think she could handle the attempts at comfort from her blissfully engaged friend. She didn't resent Rachel, but she knew all too well how easy it was to give advice when you were on the other side of a problem. Rachel had a man who adored her, who would give up anything for her.

Justin had proven that she wasn't worth giving up anything for.

No, that wasn't fair. He had an obligation to his sister. To her health. The plan had been in motion long before Melody had come along. She would feel terrible if he left his sister in the lurch because of her. If she got sicker because Justin wouldn't leave Melody behind.

Rachel apparently gave up on getting Melody to talk because she got set up for the day, sharpening knives and pulling out cutting boards, then started her prep. Melody went back to the cinnamon rolls, rolling out the huge lump of dough into a great sheet, then mixing together butter and her proprietary cinnamon-spice mixture to be spread as the filling. The familiar movements gave her something to focus on. A way to keep her mind off Justin and the ache that had started in her heart but wouldn't be content until it crawled through her entire body.

The worst thing was, she didn't blame him. It would be so much easier if she hated him. She could hide behind wrath until the worst of the hurt was gone. But Justin was an essentially decent guy who hadn't done anything wrong. It was just bad timing. It was no one's fault.

Except a little part of her thought it was someone's fault.

Until Justin had missed Bittersweet's opening, she'd been convinced that it was going to all work out. Her faith in that was so strong that she had refused to entertain any other possibility. God loved her. She actually thought He had brought her and Justin together. Hadn't she and Rachel and Ana talked about God dropping the perfect men in their laps since they'd had so much difficulty finding one on their own? You couldn't get any more ordained than his car breaking down in front of her work, or her grandmother leaving the Hornet to her, when Justin was the obvious choice to help her.

If He'd done all that, it was like a promise to work things out in the end, wasn't it?

"I am such a pathetic fool," she whispered. "Are You laughing at me, flitting around with this naive belief that You're going to work everything out for me?"

The worst thing was that it felt like she was being punished for wanting something permanent. For daring to believe that she could stay here and have everything she wanted. For trying to put down roots with people who loved her in a place she loved back.

Because people always left, and if you had roots, you couldn't follow.

Tears slid down her face, and she jumped back just before they could fall into her dough. She swiped a sleeve over her cheeks. If she cried now, it wasn't only over Justin. It was because everything she believed was muddled. She was lost. In the past, she would have told herself something better was around the corner, but she could no longer believe that was true.

"Mel?"

Melody opened her mouth to say she was fine, but instead the words spilled out in something that sounded like a wail. "Why doesn't anyone ever choose me?"

Rachel's face crumpled. She opened her arms again, and this time Melody went into them, her pain pouring out in great, gulping sobs. She held on tight, heedless of her sticky hands on the back of Rachel's jacket, tears pouring over both of them while her friend held her and stroked her hair.

"I love you, Melody. I picked you, remember? I couldn't do this without you. And I know it's selfish, but I'm glad you're not leaving. I need you. Bittersweet needs you."

"It's not the same," Melody mumbled.

"Well, I *hope* not." Rachel's voice sounded so wry that Melody lifted her head and let out a watery laugh.

Only then did she realize the kitchen had gone on around them, like water around an island. Both Sam and Talia had arrived, the former picking up on Rachel's prep, Talia sliding into Melody's place. She was now rolling up the cinnamon rolls and cutting them with a bench knife to be loaded into pans.

The pastry assistant flicked a look in their direction, and Melody braced herself. But all Talia said was, "Can I get started on the choux?"

Melody nodded and wiped her face with her sleeve, embarrassed. "Rachel—"

"Nope. Bittersweet needs you now. Later, we'll have cupcake therapy at my place. I'll have Ana bring the ice cream."

Melody's heart clenched, but this time it wasn't strictly from pain. She'd missed her friends. Now she wished she hadn't let her relationship with Justin drive a wedge between them. They wouldn't say anything about it, not a single "I told you so." They would let her cry and cut her off after her second bowl of ice cream so she didn't have a stomachache to contend with on top of a broken heart.

Maybe not everyone abandoned her after all.

She wiped her eyes and nose, washed her hands, and dove back into her tasks. Like the pro she was, Talia didn't even flicker an eyelash at her swollen face, handing off the baked éclair shells for Melody to fill. As the case out front began

463

to fill with all sorts of breakfast deliciousness—
cinnamon rolls, plain butter croissants, today's
special Dutch apple croissants—the sick feeling
began to ebb from her body. Seeing the raw
materials come together into beautiful, tempting,
golden-brown baked goods was an ordinary sort
of magic, but magic nonetheless.

A good thing, because it was the only magic
she still believed in.

CHAPTER THIRTY-SIX

Somewhere in the back of her mind, Melody had been concerned that their first month open would be an endless stretch of dead time and empty tables. She needn't have worried. It seemed that enough people had made Gibraltar part of their regular route that the opening of Bittersweet had seamlessly slipped into the neighborhood's morning routine. By the time they reached their grand opening on Saturday, their breakfast pastries were selling out every morning as commuters stopped by for a coffee and a croissant.

Rachel and Sam were equally busy. While Melody and Talia were turning out tray after tray of croissants and cinnamon rolls, the two cooks scrambled to meet the consistent demand for things like seafood Benedicts, fried-egg hash with chanterelles and garlic scapes, and a challah-custard French toast that was so rich and creamy it could double for bread pudding. Just because they were small didn't mean they couldn't produce food worthy of the city's finest restaurants. Rachel refused to compromise, giving every plate the same attention she had at Paisley.

Brunch in particular was a hit on Saturday and

Sunday, with lines stretching out the door and around the building. They added several benches outside the plate-glass windows to give people a place to sit and drink coffee while they waited for a free table. Melody began coming in extra early to start the bread just so she had time to circulate through the dining room, delivering plates and greeting their new regulars. In those moments, chatting with happy patrons and watching them devour her handiwork with blissful expressions, she felt something she could only describe as joy.

And yet, paradoxically, that feeling existed totally separate from the ever-present ache in her chest, the constant knowledge of the price she'd paid to have this. She couldn't stop the leap of her heart when the door opened to a man who vaguely resembled Justin, only to have it crash into her stomach when she realized it was merely a counterfeit. Of course he wasn't going to walk through the door with the rest of the brunch crowd. He was gone for good.

She knew this because she had stopped by his building in a moment of weakness and pressed the button for apartment 202, only to hear a child's voice answer. He'd moved on. Like she needed to.

She managed to convince herself that she was doing a good job of it when she was in the bakery, working from four in the morning to three or four in the afternoon every day. She smiled and laughed and said all the right things when she saw Rachel and Ana. She helped Rachel with plans for her upcoming wedding, date still undecided. And yet somehow it all took on a sense of unreality, like she was an impostor in her own life, someone who looked and sounded like Melody but didn't really belong there.

The real Melody sobbed in her bed each night when the pain she'd pushed off all day came back with unrelenting fury. The little voice in her head whispered ugly half-truths: *He left you because you weren't important. He didn't care enough. And why should he? You're unlovable. If you weren't, your relationships wouldn't keep ending.* Brandon. Sebastian. Luc. Leo. Micah. Justin. A familiar list of names, now longer by one.

Her Bible stayed firmly in the drawer where she'd left it. She couldn't summon the will or the enthusiasm to take it out and read. Her Instagram account, on the other hand, expanded exponentially as she baked her way through silent evenings, even after twelve-hour days at the café. She didn't crack the books that featured prominently in the photos, however; they were simply a painful reminder that she wasn't a fictional heroine destined for a happy ending. The girl who had collected those volumes felt like a different Melody. A hopeful Melody. One who hadn't been betrayed.

The worst thing was, it wasn't even Justin who had betrayed her. It was God.

She'd trusted Him to work things out, and He hadn't. Her faith seemed so naive, so childish now. And even that thought made her feel guilty, because she had what she'd always said she wanted—her own bakery.

She'd just thought that she could have it all, that she deserved it all. She never expected she'd have to choose, and that either choice would make her feel like part of herself was missing.

One Sunday after the kitchen closed and she and Rachel were doing their last round of cleanup, Rachel paused and looked at her. "I think it's time to talk about the Saturday Night Supper Club."

Melody stopped her scrubbing. "Oh? What are you thinking?"

"Well, as much as I love having it at my house, we've got this amazing space that's empty after six o'clock. If we move it here, we'll be able to open it to the public."

"I think that's a great idea," Melody said. "I know the supper club is getting pretty expensive to host, even though we all contribute to the cost of food. Are you thinking about rolling it into Bittersweet itself?"

"That's what I wanted to talk to you about. I don't want to make any decisions without your input. Obviously it slightly increases our overhead . . ."

Melody waved a hand. "Don't worry about that. We'll have the tickets sold out a month in advance. You've still got people begging for an invite on Instagram every time you or Alex post something. It could be a great revenue source."

"I was thinking maybe we could hold one every couple of months that was invite only. The intimacy was what appealed to me over these past nine months, but I think I'm ready to move on. If I'm putting this much time into it, which will eventually be time away from my husband, I feel like I need to be able to put a price on that." Rachel grimaced. "Does that make me a horrible, materialistic person?"

"I think that makes you a very wise person." Melody squeezed Rachel's shoulder. "What does Ana say?"

"I haven't asked her yet. I wanted to get your okay before I set her loose. You know she'll have a marketing strategy and a to-do list for us before we get off the phone."

Melody laughed. "We'd be lost without her, you know."

"I know. That's why I keep trying to pay her. She just keeps refusing." Rachel looked up. "Speaking of . . ."

Melody followed her gaze to where Ana stood outside the glass door and hurried to open it for her. "What are you doing here?"

Ana slipped inside and exchanged a glance with Rachel, who had stopped sweeping.

Dread crept into the pit of Melody's stomach. "What's going on?"

Rachel pulled three chairs off the top of a table where they'd been overturned for cleaning. "Sit down, Mel."

Melody did as they asked, as cautiously as an animal that sensed a trap. Ana and Rachel seated themselves on either side of her. "Guys, you're freaking me out here. Did someone die?"

Ana cracked a smile. "Only the Melody we know and love. We're worried about you."

Rachel reached for Melody's hand before she could pull away. "We want to know how you're really doing, Mel. Tell us the truth. Not what you think we want to hear."

Melody had told herself she wouldn't cry anymore. She had sworn that she would only be upbeat. And yet tears swelled in her eyes anyway. There was no point in keeping up the front; her friends had already seen through it. "Honestly? Not so well. I just keep wondering . . . did I make the right decision? Did I give up the love of my life to stay here? And yet I look around and I can't imagine not having Bittersweet. I feel so torn, and I feel guilty about being so torn."

There went that knowing exchange between her friends again. This time, Ana spoke. "Rachel and I owe you an apology. We feel terrible about how things went down with Justin at the supper club. We did it out of concern for you, but that probably wasn't the time or the place."

"You think?" The sarcasm and anger that spilled from Melody's lips surprised even her.

Rachel bowed her head, absorbing the jab as her due. "I want to believe that my motives were pure, but the truth is, I didn't want you to leave. I didn't want to do this by myself. But you've been so devastated since Justin left, I've realized how incredibly selfish I've been."

Melody just stared at her. "What are you saying?"

"I'm saying that if what you want is to be with Justin, you should go."

Melody's heart practically stopped before it jumped to life again. "I thought you and Ana were against Justin and me. Because of what he said about his faith."

Ana leaned forward. "You're right. We're concerned about Justin's beliefs. But then, can you honestly tell me you're not angry at God right now?"

Melody avoided Ana's eyes. Now she knew she was completely transparent.

"Have you stopped believing in Him just because you're mad?"

"No."

"So I guess we can't judge what's in Justin's heart either. You're going to have to pray about that yourself. We should never have tried to make that decision for you."

Melody turned back to Rachel. "But you need my money. And without Bittersweet, I don't have a salary."

"The real estate market in my area is hot right now. Alex and I have decided to sell my place when we get married. I'll move into his apartment. If we do that, I could buy you out." Rachel reached for her hand again. "Please understand, I'm not forcing you out. I would much rather have you as a business partner and Bittersweet's head baker and pastry chef. I'm just saying, if you want to go, you have options."

The words should have lifted a huge weight from her, but instead Melody felt like she was being crushed by the burden of decision. Up until now, she'd been telling herself that she had no choice but to stay and fulfill her obligation to Rachel. But now Rachel was giving her a free pass. What exactly was she supposed to do with it?

She looked down at her friends, who were watching her with concern and not a little bit of guilt. She sighed. No matter how misguided their actions, they loved her. They only wanted the best for her.

"Thank you, guys. Your support means a lot to me." She hugged each one in turn and reached for her handbag. "I'll think about it."

Which she did. All the way home. What was to say that Justin still even wanted her? She might have forgiven him for his absence and his silence, but it hadn't exactly been an amicable parting. Maybe in the month since they'd separated, he'd realized that he was better off without her. Wouldn't he have contacted her if he missed her? At least sent an e-mail or a text?

You haven't sent an e-mail or a text, and you miss him as much as the day he left.

She parked down the street from the apartment building and walked, lifting her face to the sky to soak up the day's last rays of sunshine. And yet the warmth didn't quite penetrate to the center of her chest.

What should she do?

She made her way up to her apartment, pushed open the door, and dropped her keys on the entryway table. She was halfway to the kitchen when movement in the living room made her whip her head around. She gasped and clutched at the dining room table for support.

"Mom! You're going to give me a heart attack! Why didn't you say something?"

Janna rose. "Last time I did, you said I scared you. I was trying not to do the same thing."

Melody exhaled her breath in a long whoosh. "You know, most normal people would call first."

"And you rarely take my calls, so I'm left with surprise visits." The words were classic Janna, but this time they lacked an edge. If anything, there was a thread of quiet regret in her voice. "I needed to see you."

Melody must have been worn out from the emotional turmoil of the last month, because she didn't have the heart to get into it with her mother today. "Do you want some tea?"

"I'd love some."

Melody wandered into the kitchen and put the kettle on, then pulled out two mismatched mugs and dropped a tea bag in each. "What brings you out here this time, Mom? I saw that you had Grandma Bev's place cleaned out already."

"That's part of it. I'm sorry I missed your restaurant opening."

Melody threw a quizzical look over her shoulder. "I didn't even know you knew about it."

"Ana called me."

"Why would she do that?"

"For some odd reason, she thought you might want me there."

Melody gave a little sardonic laugh. "But she misread the idea that *you* might want to be there; is that it?"

"Well, my flight got canceled because of the tropical storm in the southern US, and then it was so late it seemed pointless to go. It would just be another way that I failed you."

Melody waited for the jab, the twist that would

somehow make it into her fault, but it didn't come. Odd. Her mother was off her game today. She stared at the teapot, willing it to come to a boil so she had something to do, a reason not to look at Janna.

"And then when Ana called me again a couple of days ago, I thought, *Better late than never.*"

Melody twisted around. "She called you again? Why?"

"She told me what happened with Justin. I didn't even realize you were seeing someone, but she told me that it was pretty serious. That you were heartbroken. Conflicted. She thought I might be able to help."

Melody was going to have a serious talk with Ana. How on earth was her self-absorbed, self-focused mother going to help her out of this mess?

"I don't believe it. She knows you and I don't have that type of relationship." She gave the range's knob a vicious twist, took the kettle off the stove, and poured hot water into their mugs. She made up her mom's exactly how she liked it—light cream, heavy sugar—and then fixed her own.

Janna's laugh sounded uncharacteristically brittle. "You misunderstand. She called to yell at me."

"What?"

"She seems to think that you have abandonment issues because of me."

Melody stared in shock at her mother, hurt rippling through her that her friends' meddling had gone far beyond discussing her behind her back. Her mom's appearance wasn't a visit; it was an intervention.

Though if she looked at it objectively, Ana's assertion was probably true.

"I'm sure you'd love to hear every word—and she gave me an earful—but I've got something to show you." At Melody's confused expression, she waved her over to the sofa. Only then did Melody notice the cardboard box on her coffee table.

"What's in there?"

Janna reached in and pulled out an old photo album, its plastic spine cracked and the pages beginning to tear away from the rings. She sank down on an overstuffed cushion and flipped it open. "The liquidators sent me all my mother's personal effects—jewelry, photo albums—and I thought you should see these."

Melody dragged it onto her lap and flipped it open. The photos were old, pre-digital obviously, beginning to yellow with age. They were mostly of her. "What are these?"

"This right here was our trip to Disneyland." Her mother pointed to a photo of Melody wearing a pair of Mickey Mouse ears. "You couldn't have been more than three. That was a fun trip. We spent nearly a week in California. Went to the park, of course, but we spent most of the time on the beach. See, that's you in the little bikini."

Melody smiled at the image of her chubby self, blonde ringlets pulled into pigtails on the sides of her head. "I don't remember that. You'd think I'd remember."

"You were young. I'm not surprised." Janna flipped the page over. "This was us at my house in Nashville."

Melody was playing in the backyard pool, water wings on her arms, a huge smile on her face. "Who took the photo?"

"I did. Look." She pointed to another one at the bottom of the page. Janna was standing in the pool in a glamorous one-piece, big sunglasses covering her face. Melody had her arms wrapped around her neck in the water, like her mother was towing her around.

When did her mother ever play with her?

Another page flipped. "And this right here was Christmas in Denver. In Grandma Bev's house." A tinsel-studded tree. Melody sat in footie pajamas next to a big pile of presents, beaming. "This was during that time I moved back to Colorado; do you remember?"

"Right. When you lost your label."

Janna didn't respond, and Melody's eyes narrowed. "Right? It was when RCA dropped you."

Janna looked up. "RCA didn't drop me. I quit."

"What? No! You've always said your records

weren't doing well and they dropped you. You moved back home and then you got picked up by Arista and went back to Nashville."

"That's what I told you, I know. But that's not what happened. My records were doing very well. But I wasn't happy. You have to under-stand—when your father and I broke up, I was crushed. We might have gotten married because I got pregnant with you, but I loved him. I thought we could make a go of it. But he had other ideas. He wanted to go back to Sweden. After he left, I threw myself into work. I couldn't think of anything else, least of all about being a good mother. But gradually, I realized what I was giving up was your life. I couldn't do that. So I finished my last album, quit, moved back to Denver."

Melody gaped. This was a story she'd never heard, one that Grandma Bev had never told her. "I don't understand. You only stayed for a year."

"I thought I could pick up where I left off with you. I was your mother, after all. But I underestimated how long I'd been gone." Janna pressed her lips together into a semblance of a smile. "I still remember. One day you were riding your little bike out front. You crashed and scraped up your knee and started crying. I went running to pick you up, but you pushed me away and screamed, 'No, I want Gramma Bev!' "

Tears glimmered in Janna's eyes. "I didn't

blame you. You were only a little girl. But it kept happening, and I realized that I'd missed my chance with you. My mother was a better parent than I could ever be. And I thought that maybe it was best if you stayed with her." She swiped the tears away with her forefinger, somehow managing not to smear her makeup. Funny that thought should occur to Melody now. "But you were still my daughter. I thought maybe if you came on tour with me, you'd get used to me again, that I could make up for lost time. But it was like nothing I did could ever make a difference. I'd already lost you."

Melody felt sick. She flipped through the album, page after page of photos of her and her mom. Proof that Janna hadn't actually vanished from her life. Why couldn't she remember?

"No one ever thought to tell me this?"

"Would you have believed it? You would have thought I was lying to make myself look better."

"Mom, I—"

Janna shook her head. "I'm not telling you this to make you feel guilty. I'm telling you for one reason. Had I thought it was best for you, I would have chosen you over my career. Every single time. But some decisions, once they're made, they're too hard to come back from. I kept thinking I'd have another chance. And I never did."

Melody exhaled in a long, steady stream. She didn't even know what to say to this. Looking back on her history with her mother, her seeming selfishness . . . was it possible that was all born out of hurt? Out of the fear of being rejected by her daughter again and again?

She'd demonized her mother and put her grandmother on a pedestal, and yet Bev had let her believe all the horrible things she'd thought about Janna. How could she have done that to her, to both of them? Had she really known her grandmother at all?

"I've been really unfair to you, haven't I?"

"No, darlin', you haven't. I'm the one who failed you. And I've wanted to tell you, but I didn't want to guilt you into letting me back into your life. But Ana said—insisted, really—that it was time for me to step up and act like your mother. And she was right."

Melody's lips trembled as tears flooded her eyes. "I'm so sorry, Mom."

"I'm sorry too, baby." Janna put her arms around her tentatively, awkwardly. She sat there stiffly for a second and then Melody collapsed against her, sobbing, draining away decades of hurt and misunderstanding.

Janna held her as she wept, and when Melody rose, she realized that her own shoulder was damp from her mother's tears. "What do I do?"

"I'm the last one who should be giving advice," Janna said softly. "All you can do is ask yourself: Which regret can you live with? And which one would tear you apart?"

CHAPTER THIRTY-SEVEN

"Wait, when you said you would fly me to Florida, I thought you meant you were going to buy me a ticket." Melody's eyes widened when she recognized the all-too-familiar approach of Centennial Airport. She'd been too distracted by what she was about to do to realize they'd been headed south through the city rather than east to Denver International.

Janna waved a hand. "No daughter of mine is going to fly commercial if I have anything to do with it, especially when it's something this important."

Melody went straight back to obsessing, only momentarily distracted by the revelation that they'd be arriving in Fort Lauderdale on a private jet. Her small roller case was packed with a few days' worth of clothes—and a bathing suit, on her mother's insistence, though she hardly thought of this as taking a vacation. She didn't know what this was, exactly. A declaration, maybe. It was foolish to think that this would solve all her and Justin's problems.

But it was worth trying.

Rachel hadn't seemed surprised when she called her; Talia, on the other hand, was flustered at the idea of handling the weekday rush by herself. "You've got this," Melody had said, injecting confidence into her words. "You've watched me for over a month. If it makes you feel better, skip the rye until I get back. You could do the baguettes and the sourdough in your sleep."

She still felt slightly guilty about leaving the bakery, but she had no doubt Talia could manage without her. The woman had an uncanny way with pastry, and the test they'd done with some of her chocolates had gone over better than they could have imagined. So well that Melody had begun wondering if her own presence was really necessary at all.

"Melody?" Her mother nudged her, and she realized she was staring into space while the driver held the back door open for her. She stepped out and saw that while she'd zoned out yet again, they'd driven directly onto the apron where a small jet waited.

Someone else took their bags and loaded them into the cargo compartment of the aircraft while the gray-haired pilot walked down the stairs and greeted them with an outstretched hand. She missed his name, because the whole time she was imagining that it was Justin.

"So this is how you get around?" Melody whispered as they climbed the stairs into the plane. She felt slightly foolish that she hadn't known. She shouldn't be surprised, though. The lavish interior with its ivory leather seats and walnut paneling seemed just her mother's speed.

"It's lovely, isn't it? This isn't my plane—you can tell from the tail number—but we share planes among AvionElite's fleet." Janna seated herself in one of the front-facing seats and crossed her legs, smiling and waving off the pilot when he asked if they'd like something to drink. She leaned over and lowered her voice. "Usually, they're younger and better looking. You should have seen my pilot when I flew in for the funeral."

The creeping feeling of fate overtook Melody. It couldn't be. Even for her, that was too much of a coincidence. "You're an owner with AvionElite?"

"I just said I was. I'm surprised you know of them. You always seemed to feel that displays of wealth were too far beneath you to notice."

Melody pressed a cool hand to her forehead, feeling suddenly flushed. "Mom, do you remember the name of your pilot the night you came to tell me that Grandma had passed away?"

Janna shrugged. "No. I remember he was quite handsome, though. Oh, come now, don't look at me like that. I may not be as young as I used to be, but I'm not dead."

Melody was beginning to feel a little hysterical. She reached into her purse for her phone and brought up her photo gallery, then passed it to her mom. "Was that him?"

"Yes, I believe it was. Wait, you don't mean . . ."

"That's Justin." She sank back into the seat and began to laugh. Unbelievable. What were the chances? The reason Justin had gotten stuck outside her bakery was because he'd flown her mother in that night.

"Melody?" Janna leaned across the aisle, concerned.

She realized then that her laughter had turned to tears. It was all too much. The revelation that she'd been wrong about her mom. All the seemingly random coincidences that had fallen into place for her to meet Justin—a man who cared about her, who respected her. How quickly she'd turned on God because she thought He'd rewarded her faith with indifference.

And then the terrifying thought occurred to her—what if Justin hadn't been put in her life because they were meant to be together? What if the whole point of this was to reunite her with her mother? To show her the shallowness of her faith?

No, that was impossible. Wasn't it?

Melody glanced at her mom sitting there, watching her with genuine concern, and crushed the impulse to retreat into denial. If she had even once rejected Grandma Bev's insistence that she put on a happy face and make the best of things, if she had just told her mother how hurt and abandoned she'd felt, maybe they wouldn't have had to endure over two decades of distance and resentment. Maybe she would have had her mother.

Grandma Bev meant well, no doubt. She was trying to give Melody the resilience she'd needed to deal with all the changes in her young life, but it had only taught her to escape into fiction—both the kind in books and that of her own making. And instead of growing deeper in a true faith, one that was tested in tears and anguished prayers, she stuffed down her pain and retreated to superstition and magical thinking. She'd looked at God's providence like she'd looked at fairy tales—blindly and without any real belief. She'd gone from man to man, trying to buy their love at too high a price, all because she wouldn't admit how much she needed that love. How much it hurt that it always seemed to be out of reach. And because she wouldn't admit any of it, she just went on haplessly repeating her mistakes instead of turning to the One who loved her no matter what.

And now, she was about to do it again.

"Stop. Stop the jet."

Janna stared at her in disbelief. "Why? What's wrong?"

"I'm not going."

"What do you mean you're not going? I thought—"

"I can't chase him, Mom. I can't buy his love by giving up everything I care about. I've been doing this my entire life—clinging to men, begging them to choose me. If I go to him now, I'll never know if he loves me or if he simply settled for me because I made the sacrifice."

Melody's mother blinked in shock, but she rose from her seat and moved to the entrance of the jet's cockpit. "Gentlemen, I'm afraid there's been a change in plans."

Melody sat in the back of the black sedan, too stunned by her own actions to do anything but focus on her breath moving in and out of her lungs. After her mother had halted the plane, she'd changed its destination to Nashville and gotten back her car to take Melody home, but only after making her promise that she would call if she needed her. It was such an unexpectedly *motherly* thing to do that it brought tears to her eyes.

Until she followed it up with a dose of her typical passive-aggressiveness: "I sure hope you know what you're doing. A man like that doesn't wait forever."

Maybe he didn't. But that wasn't really the point. Justin had never said he loved her. He'd chosen to leave. If she ran after him now, she'd still be putting her own will above God's, acting from fear instead of faith. The nudge to her spirit had made that very clear. No, not a nudge. A kick.

She gave the driver the address of the bakery, where he took her roller case from the trunk and left it and her standing by the curb. Inside waited one of her best friends, who would no doubt have many questions. It was now or never.

"Melody!" Rachel gasped as soon as she walked through the door to the kitchen. "What are you doing here? Don't you have a plane to catch?"

"I'm not going."

Rachel set down her knife and wiped her hands on her apron. "What? Why?"

Melody told her everything that had transpired: how her mother's flight had been the reason Justin had landed on her doorstep, how she'd learned the truth about her upbringing, how she wasn't convinced the whole point hadn't been to reunite her with Janna and show her the shallowness of her own faith.

"I can't chase him and force this to work," Melody said, blinking away tears. "Not this time."

Rachel wordlessly wrapped Melody in a hug and squeezed hard. "I'm so proud of you, Mel. That can't have been an easy decision."

Melody wiped her eyes and straightened. "Yes, well, the good news is, Talia can stop hyperventilating about the bread over there."

Talia laughed from her side of the kitchen, where she'd obviously been listening but trying not to look like she was listening. "Glad to have you back, Melody."

"I'm not sure I'm glad to be back, but it's what I have to do." She dragged her suitcase into the break room, pulled down her apron, and wrapped it around herself. Her emotions felt raw, close to the surface, but deep down, she knew she'd done the right thing. She was putting her future in the hands of a God who had just been waiting for her to come around. She was taking what might be her first real step of faith in years.

Not my will but Yours be done.

Chapter Thirty-Eight

Justin had to admit, Florida was beautiful. While Denver had its wide, brilliantly clouded skies and majestic mountains, the Sunshine State was everything that its nickname suggested: beautiful light, sandy beaches, palm trees. In some ways, the weather reminded him of Denver when he was growing up, when the thunderstorms still rolled through every afternoon like clockwork, dousing them with rain and then moving out just as quickly. Of course June in Florida came with relentless humidity that was completely at odds with the arid weather to which he was accustomed.

He'd been here for almost a month, and he was still living in an extended-stay hotel while his furnishings were stored in a warehouse somewhere. He'd never actually thought to ask where they would be. He spent most of his time at the office with Luis Garcia, learning the ins and outs of the charter business, getting familiar with the various software suites, and working with the staff that had stayed on after the sale. He had the most contact with Monica Baudoin, the office manager who handled all the administrative work and probably knew just as much as or more than Luis. The pilots were equally capable: three of them were retired airline pilots; the fourth, retired Navy. All were friendly, as befitted an island charter, but it was clear they were used to operating by the book. Luis allowed nothing less, and Justin fully intended to continue that trend.

Everything he learned about the new company said they'd made a good decision.

And yet he was miserable.

He managed to keep busy between the office and the air—he was slowly familiarizing himself with their planes, though he hadn't yet taken any charters for himself. They were all small single-engine and turboprop craft, none of which required a type rating, but he was cautious enough to want to know the airplanes well before he flew passengers. He practically had to pinch himself to remember that he *owned* these planes. He should be happy. He did his best to pretend like he was.

But he couldn't lie and say distance had dampened his feelings toward Melody. If anything, it had only reinforced the fact that his interest wasn't a whim, something that could be pushed away because he lived seventeen hundred miles away. He woke up every morning wishing he could see her and went to bed every night feeling like he had made a mistake.

In short, he loved her.

He followed her social media pages, hoping for some sign that the decision hadn't been as easy as she'd made it seem, but if anything, she was taking his absence in stride. Books in the Bakery had exploded with followers as Melody ramped up her postings, displaying mouthwatering breads and desserts, all beautifully arranged and paired with her antique books, some of them staged at Bittersweet Café. It was clear she was exactly where she was meant to be; the fact he'd asked her to even consider leaving it behind left him awash with guilt.

Jessica loved Florida, though. It was too soon to know if it would have any permanent effect on her MS symptoms, but she was optimistic. Seeing the light in her eyes, the relief that was palpable in Pete's entire demeanor at the idea he might not have to watch his wife suffer through the progression of a horrible disease, made Justin swallow down his feelings and put on a happy smile. Jess felt bad enough about making him leave Denver. He didn't need her to see that every day in Florida killed a little bit more of his soul.

"So, have you found a house yet?" Jessica turned from her spot at the brand-new stove when Justin walked into her kitchen one night. That was one advantage of moving here with them: the once-a-week dinner had turned into whenever he felt like coming over. He tried not to take advantage of it. Even more importantly, he tried not to spend so much time with

Jessica that she would see through his cheery exterior.

"Not yet. I was really looking for a place on the beach, but I haven't found anything in my price range. I don't want to be house poor."

Jessica rolled her eyes. "Seriously, Justin, you're drawing a pretty big paycheck from the business. I think you can afford to raise your budget a little. You're never going to find waterfront for twelve hundred bucks a month."

Justin rolled his eyes back at her, but he was smiling. He had been scrimping and saving for so long, it was painful to shell out the cash for a nice condo here, especially when he knew his name was at the bottom of a very large bank loan. True, should they default on the loan, it would be the business assets that were seized, but since he'd put his entire retirement savings on the line, he kind of wanted to hold on to it.

"The hotel's okay for now. I don't want to commit to a lease and then realize I hate the neighborhood. I'm still getting to know the area."

Jessica didn't look convinced, but she pointed to the table with her wooden spoon. "You can set the table for me if you're going to stand there. Or you can call the kids—"

Justin was out the back door before she had a chance to finish the sentence. The small backyard was swathed in green grass, and the kids were playing some sort of game involving hopping in and out of hula hoops. "Hey, kiddos! What are you doing?"

Abby screeched, "Uncah Justin, you're burning up in the lava! Hurry!"

Ah, so the hula hoops were islands. He leapt into the center of one and swiped his arm across his forehead. "Whew. That was a close one."

"No," Andrew said gleefully. "You're all burned up now, just like Anakin Skywalker."

"Do I get a cool suit and helmet so I can become Darth Vader?"

"No, you're just burned up."

Justin chuckled. "Great. Thanks." He always forgot how bloodthirsty little kids could be.

"That's okay, because I'm a fairy and if I sprinkle pixie dust on you, your legs will grow back." Abby pulled out a saltshaker from the pocket of her princess dress. Before Justin could stop her, she shook it over his legs, covering him in a fine dusting of glitter.

"Thanks, Abby," he said wryly. "My legs are back but now they're all glittery."

She gave him an adorable grin. "You're welcome."

"I hate to break up this awesome lava-surfing party, but dinner is about to go on the table. And I think I hear your dad's car outside right now. Should we clean up this mess?"

They groaned, but they dutifully helped clean up the backyard, which really meant they picked up one hula hoop each while Justin collected the toys and lightsabers and princess accessories that littered the grass. He dropped them on the patio table and then opened the sliding-glass door for the kids.

Pete was indeed home, and he had his arms around Jessica in the corner of the kitchen.

"Hey, that's my sister you're pawing!"

Jessica made a face, but Pete let her go and she gestured to the table. "Sit down, guys. Dinner's going to get cold."

They all settled around the table, Justin getting sandwiched between the two kids as usual— something about Uncle Justin made them stick to him like Velcro. He helped portion pasta onto their little plastic plates and then carefully spooned tomato sauce over it.

"So. Justin." Jessica stabbed a piece of pasta with her fork and looked at him pointedly. "When were you going to tell us that you didn't want to move to Florida?"

Justin nearly choked on his mouthful of food. He chewed, swallowed, and wiped his mouth with a napkin before he could manage to talk. "Excuse me?"

Jessica exchanged a glance with her husband. "You're not fooling anyone. Why didn't you tell us that there was a woman?"

Justin met Pete's eye, but his friend stayed quiet.

Jessica looked at him. "Wait, you knew about this?"

Pete shrugged. "Yeah?"

"Unbelievable. Men. You know, I wouldn't even know if I hadn't talked to Dad this morning. He asked me how you were doing. Worried about you because he didn't quite believe that you were as willing to leave your girlfriend as you said you were."

"It's not important, Jess. I committed to doing this with you guys. Meeting Melody was an accident. And she knew that I was leaving the whole time we were dating, so . . ." The words came out of his mouth, but somehow they didn't make a full connection to his brain. To his heart.

"Do you love her?" Jessica asked.

"It doesn't matter."

"That's not what I asked you. Do. You. Love. Her?"

Justin set his fork down carefully. "Yes."

Jessica nodded, kept eating. And then she dropped her fork and pushed away from the table. "You two are unbelievable. I swear. Justin, I would have never asked you to give her up for me. Don't you understand that? I know this has been your plan all along, but had you said you couldn't do it, we would have understood. It's not like Pete couldn't get a job as a mechanic here . . . or in Southern California . . . or almost any other state where we could live at sea level.

And now you're committed to this business and you're hating every minute of it. Do you actually think I would want you to be miserable for my sake?"

"Jess—"

"Daddy? Why is Mommy mad?" Abby whispered.

Pete shushed her, but it didn't seem to break Jess's stride. Her eyes flashed. "If you love her, you have to go back."

"It's too late. I left her. I missed her restaurant opening. I chose this over her. How is she ever going to forgive that?"

"Trust me. If she loves you, she's going to forgive you. If she feels half as terrible as you do, she's probably crying herself to sleep every night." She seated herself and looked between the two men. "Fix it. I don't know how you're going to do it, but you are both intelligent men. You fix this."

Justin looked at Pete, who just shrugged. "I'm not dumb enough to argue with her."

No help from that quarter. He looked back at his sister. "Jess, I know what you're trying to do and I love you for it. But some things can't be fixed." He turned to his niece and nephew, who were following the conversation with confusion. "C'mon, you two. Let's go get you ready for bed."

He was playing dirty, using Abby and Andrew

to end the conversation, but no matter how much Jessica wanted to continue, she wasn't going to give up the chance for someone else to take over the bedtime routine. He lifted a kid under each arm and hustled them down the hallway, their giggles trailing behind him.

Justin got them bathed, into their pajamas, and tucked into bed with a story—all the voices included—aware that he was stalling. But when he could no longer delay, he crept out of the kids' shared bedroom and returned to the kitchen. The table had been cleared, the dishes rinsed and piled beside the sink, and a fresh pot of coffee stood waiting on the countertop. He poured himself a cup and looked out through the sliding-glass door to where Jessica sat, a mug in hand.

Reluctantly, he slid the door open and stepped outside.

She didn't look at him, just stared out onto the twilit backyard. "I know you're mad at God, Justin, but I hadn't realized you'd decided to take over for Him."

Justin frowned and pulled out the chair next to his sister. "I don't know what you mean."

She turned to face him. "Well, you've appointed yourself personally responsible for my health. And clearly you can see the future, because you're sure this Melody doesn't play any part in yours."

"Okay, okay, Jess. You've made your point."

"Have I? I don't think I have. Because if you were listening, you wouldn't be sitting here with me; you'd be booking yourself the next flight to Denver."

Justin stared out across the lawn so he didn't have to see his sister's face. "You know how hard it is to make a relationship work with what I do."

"No, what I know is that Dad has been feeding you the same line for twenty years, and somehow you still believe it. Did you ever bother to ask Mom why they broke up, or did you just take Dad's word for it?"

Justin looked at her hard now. "What do you mean?"

She gave a hard shake of her head. "I shouldn't even be telling you this."

"Then you shouldn't have brought it up. Spill."

Jessica set her mug down on the table. "It wasn't Mom's idea to get a divorce. Dad was having . . . an emotional affair, I guess you could call it . . . with another woman. He said they weren't sleeping together, and Mom believes that, but it would have almost been easier if they had been. She left, temporarily, because she needed some space. *He* needed some space to figure out what he wanted."

Justin stared, his mouth open. "Why have I never heard this?"

"Because you and Dad were so close. She

didn't want to poison you against him. She knew you needed your father."

"I needed my mother, too." He blew out his breath, understanding for the first time why Jessica had sided with her. "What happened? I never saw him with any other woman."

"I don't know. Fizzled out maybe, once it was no longer secret and forbidden. Mom wanted to move back in, but Dad was the one who pushed for a divorce. He said she deserved more than he could give her." She drilled him with a significant look. "He spent so much time playing God in the cockpit of a plane that he couldn't stop when it came to his marriage. Maybe he figured he deserved to be punished for wrecking things in the first place; I don't know. But he's been punishing himself ever since, and he brought you along for the ride."

Justin stared at his sister. She'd seemed so focused on her own life, he hadn't known she was paying that much attention to their dad's. "You think that's what I'm doing?"

"I think you're so busy being in charge of your life you can't see what God's trying to do in it, yes."

"Right. When has God done anything for us?"

Jessica reached over and placed a hand on his arm. "You can't blame God for my MS, Justin. Or for Allyson's death, or Mom and Dad's divorce. Things happen in this world—sometimes accidents, sometimes a result of our own actions—but that doesn't mean God's abandoned us. It just means that we live in a messed-up world. It's when we trust Him completely that He begins to bring good out of bad situations."

There she went again. In some ways, Jessica and Melody were absolutely alike, with their blind faith and wishful thinking. "Seems like He could have stepped in a long time ago if He had the least bit of concern for us."

"Maybe He did and you just weren't paying attention. From what Pete managed to put together, God practically dropped you on the perfect woman's doorstep. You're the one who pushed her away. You blew it, not Him." Jessica got to her feet and took her coffee mug with her. Justin barely registered the rumble of the sliding door as she went inside.

Was he making the same mistake his father had made? It sounded like Dad made the decision to divorce, regardless of what his wife wanted. Maybe it had been out of love or guilt or a mix of both, but had it really been the right thing? Or had it been an excuse?

Had Jessica's health been Justin's excuse?

He kicked his feet up on an empty chair and brought his mug to his lips, a little annoyed that his sister had his head spinning tonight. It was like eating dinner with Dr. Phil or Dr. Laura or whoever the latest celebrity shrink was. Except all those doctors urged people to take control of their lives, to accept responsibility for their actions. Which was exactly what he'd always done. He'd followed every step in his life's plan—his flight training, his jobs, and finally owning his own charter.

But you're still not happy. You're dreaming of a woman who is seventeen hundred miles away, who wasn't anywhere in your plan. How do you account for that?

Really, hadn't everything in the past three months been a disruption, a detour from his thoroughly charted future? An uncharacteristic oversight had led him to getting stuck in the snow, which led him to Melody. That was the point where his life had diverged from his plan, spun out of his control. Melody hadn't been predictable. Or temporary. She had been a fork in the road, and every step he took with her brought him further away from his carefully measured life. Even he couldn't explain the instant draw he'd felt to her—he who managed to be detached and practical, even calculated, toward women. She hadn't fit into his plans, but he'd fallen for her anyway. A bright, bubbly, impossibly optimistic baker who had shattered every assumption he'd had about how his life should look.

But when it came time to take that next step, when he was given the choice to throw away the map and see where the future took him—took *them*—he'd faltered. Wasn't that why he hadn't called Melody to let her know he wasn't going to make it back for her opening? He hadn't had the courage to admit he was scared to take a chance, so he'd orchestrated it so she'd have no choice but to dump him. To shift the blame for their breakup to her.

He was a complete and total coward.

It was an uncomfortable look at himself, an image that he didn't want to own. But he could no longer fool himself. He'd blamed his career for the fact he couldn't keep a woman. He'd blamed his sister's disease for the fact he couldn't stay with Melody. And he'd blamed God for everything else he didn't like about his life and his childhood, letting his faith be hijacked by incidents that were the result of chance or other people's choices. Instead of learning to trust Him, to let God guide him, he'd placed his confidence in his own ability to navigate his life.

It had taken making a mess of his decisions and hurting someone he loved to see the absolute ridiculousness of his thinking. Could Melody really have been put in his path to knock him off course and set him on a new direction?

"Have a little faith," she'd said. He'd need it. If he did this, he'd have no job, no money, no security. Not even any assurance that she'd take him back.

But first he had some apologies to make. To Melody, certainly. But also to God.

His prayer, even in his mind, felt rusty, hoarse, like a voice long unused. *I don't know if You really want to hear from me at this point. I've been so determined to be angry at You. But if You're trying to tell me something here . . . if You're trying to show me a way back . . . I'm sorry. I'm here. I'm ready to listen. Tell me what You want me to do.*

Justin sat there and sipped his coffee, a memory coming to mind: the night of the supper club, when he'd been so sure that he'd ruined things with Melody by being honest with her friends. Another attempt to make her call it quits so he didn't have to be responsible for the decision to leave.

"I respect your faith," he'd said, *"but I'm not sure I'm ever going to trust God like you do. There's too much water under the bridge between us."*

And in her typical, always-positive way, she'd replied, *"There's never too much water under the bridge."*

He jumped to his feet and rushed back into the kitchen. Jessica looked up from the dishwasher. "Took you long enough."

He went to her side and squeezed her into a hug. "Jess. Thank you."

"Don't thank me yet. You're still on the hook

for a half-million-dollar loan for a business that's across the country from the woman you love." She drilled him with a look. "Because you were stupid."

Justin's mouth twisted into a wry smile. "Thanks a lot, Sis."

"I call them like I see them. Now hurry up and figure out what you're going to do. This one is going to call for a lot more than roses and a pretty apology."

Jessica was right—he was going to have to make a grand gesture to show Melody how sorry he was for leaving her. And he knew exactly where to start.

CHAPTER THIRTY-NINE

Melody bent over the taut oval of dough, the edge of the razor blade in her hand flicking through the soft surface with practiced speed. Slowly, the design took shape beneath her hands: two sinuous lengthwise cuts that would form a stem, surrounded by pairs of curved slashes that would become leaves. When the bread rose, the design would take on a 3-D effect.

She pushed aside the loaf and started on the next one, number two of five of this type that she would bake today. At 3 a.m., the only sounds were the click and whoosh of the ovens preheating, the whine of the mixer kneading dough, the gentle tap of raindrops on the windows. Customers would trickle in slowly this morning because of the rain, which she'd predicted without looking at the forecast—she could feel the coming storm in the texture of her dough.

"Perfect." She straightened from the last loaves and then batched them into the oven so she could start the more ordinary boules and batards and ciabattas on the roster. Talia would be here in less than an hour, Rachel and Sam an hour after that, all bringing a sense of life and enthusiasm into the kitchen. She loved working alongside one of her best friends and two women who were fast becoming friends, but for now she would enjoy her oasis of calm.

She was just taking the decorative loaves from the oven, golden brown and beautifully bloomed, when a key rattled in the lock. Talia appeared, shaking water from the canopy of a leopard-print umbrella. "Good morning!" she sang cheerily, then gasped when she saw Melody's early work. "Mel! That's gorgeous! Are you going to Instagram it?"

"Thinking of it. I didn't bring the right book, though. I thought for sure I was going to do flowers, not leaves, so I brought *The Scarlet Pimpernel*."

Talia grinned. "I don't think it matters that much. Your houndstooth miche got four thousand likes yesterday, and I don't think it was because of *Sherlock Holmes*."

Talia was right, but her feed was called Books in the Bakery for a reason . . . and it had exploded. Hard to tell if the success of Bittersweet fueled her newfound popularity or if her Insta-success brought customers through the door, but either way, she wasn't complaining.

What had started as steady coffee-and-pastry traffic had become all-day crowds, to the point they were already talking about expanding into the space next door to accommodate the demand. Reviewers from major Denver publications had lauded Rachel's food and praised their bakery menu, going so far as to call Melody's artisan-style European bread the best in the city. Demand had spiked so much that Talia now handled all the pastry to let Melody focus exclusively on the bread menu.

They worked rapidly, side by side, on their own projects, Talia rattling off new ideas for the daily éclair flavors. Five o'clock rolled around and brought Rachel and Sam in, adding the smells of simmering stocks and the sharp bite of raw onion and garlic to the scent of wheat and sugar. Melody inhaled deeply and smiled, her heart full.

She'd never thought she could feel this contented and fulfilled at work. It was hard labor, stressful more often than not, but knowing she was building something lasting, something she wouldn't walk away from, was more satisfying than she'd dreamed.

And yet underneath it all was a vague current of sadness. She hadn't spoken of Justin since the day she returned to the café eight weeks ago, at least not aloud; her prayers were filled with him. She'd deleted his number from her phone so she wouldn't be tempted to call.

"Mel, you have the raisin bread on the menu today?" Rachel's voice snapped her out of her reverie.

"Yep, coming up at ten."

"Good. I think I'm going to do a chicken curry sandwich on raisin bread."

"Ooh," Sam said. "Save me some this time."

Melody laughed. "I did olive loaf for your *niçoise* too."

Rachel gave her a nod and a wink in thanks and turned back to her dicing.

"So, Rachel," Talia said with a knowing look, "I heard you and Alex set a date."

"June nineteenth. And then we're going to take an entire week's honeymoon in Maui. It's going to be amazing. I've always wanted to go to Hawaii."

"Even odds they never see the outside of the hotel room," Melody said sotto voce, earning a stifled laugh from Talia.

"I heard that!" Rachel said.

Melody grinned at her. "You were meant to."

"Melody and Ana have agreed to share maid of honor duties, since there's no way I can choose between them. I'm just hoping Bryan is back in time to be Alex's best man. He left for Colombia last month and hasn't contacted anyone."

Melody frowned. "That's unsettling. Are you sure he's okay?"

"He checks in every once in a while on social media, so we know he's alive." Rachel shrugged. "He went off the grid once before after a nasty breakup with his longtime girlfriend, but he hasn't been seeing anyone seriously. Alex doesn't say it, but he's worried."

Melody opened her mouth to reply, but a tapping at the front of the shop caught her attention. "You're not expecting anyone, are you, Rachel?"

"Nope. All the deliverymen come to the back door."

"Someone overeager to get Melody's bread of the day," Talia said. "Did you see this morning's masterpiece?"

Melody left the women chatting in the kitchen and pushed through to the front of the shop. A man stood half-concealed by an umbrella, the hood of his raincoat pulled up against a steady patter of raindrops.

"We don't open until six," Melody called.

The man turned, and instantly the strength left her body. Even with his face shadowed by the hood, she would recognize those blue eyes anywhere. She stood there and gaped.

"Melody? Can I come in? Or I could come back at six if you want. . . ."

The words penetrated her stunned brain, and she fumbled for her keys. The lock clicked open and Justin pushed inside, bringing with him a rush of cool, humid air. He closed his umbrella and placed it in the bucket in the corner, then shoved back his wet hood. "Hi."

Justin's gaze traveled to a point over her shoulder, and she followed it to find three women huddled in the kitchen doorway, staring with almost as much surprise as Melody felt.

"Um, guys, can we get a little privacy?"

They disappeared back into the kitchen, but no doubt they had their ears pressed against the door. That would have to do, because she wasn't stepping out in the rain to talk.

She reeled in her runaway thoughts, only now realizing that she hadn't said a word since she'd recognized Justin. Her pounding heart vibrated her whole body with every pulse, and her breath seemed to be caught somewhere between her lungs and her throat.

He was here. After all this time.

"What are you doing here?" she finally managed.

"I missed you."

"Justin—"

"No, wait. I have something to say. I owe you an apology. Yes, I know I had an obligation to my sister, but the real truth was that I was afraid. Afraid of repeating my parents' mistakes, afraid that somewhere down the line, I was going to hurt or disappoint you. So I ran away. I used my sister's health as an excuse to walk away from the woman I love."

His image swam before her eyes. "You love me?"

"I do. And I never should have asked you to give up something that means so much to you. Melody, this place is incredible! You should be so, so proud of what you've accomplished."

Her brain wasn't working fast enough to process all his words. He was here, and he was apologizing, and she needed to come up with a response, but she didn't even know what the question was. "What are you saying, then? What about your business? It was your dream."

He shook his head. "No, it wasn't. It was never my dream, not the way you feel about Bittersweet. It was just a plan . . . and once I've got a plan, it's nearly impossible to get me off course. But it turns out that my dad wasn't as keen on retirement as he thought. It didn't take too much convincing to get him to Fort Lauderdale to take the chief pilot position in my place."

Melody's hand crept to her mouth, fingertips pressed to her lips in shock. He was here. He had given up his job in Florida without knowing whether she'd take him back. "But, Justin, what are you going to do now? You gave up your captain position at AvionElite and now the charter . . ."

"I'll find another job. I'll start at the bottom if I have to. But there's no job that's going to make me happy if I don't have you to come home to." He shrugged helplessly. "I don't have the first clue how this is going to work, but if God really brought us together, He must already have a plan figured out. That's good enough for me."

Slowly, he dropped to one knee and reached into his coat.

Panic gripped her. Once upon a time, this was all she wanted, someone who would commit to her, who would promise to never leave. But his being here was already an answer to prayer in itself. For the first time in her life, she could see the value of patience. Her relationship with Justin wasn't something she wanted to rush.

And then she exhaled on a relieved laugh when the package he withdrew from his coat turned out to be not a ring box, but something flat and rectangular wrapped in flowered paper.

"I may not be as steady and reliable as Gabriel Oak, and I most certainly know nothing about sheep, but I promise you I will never be a Sergeant Troy. Will you give me another chance?"

Slowly, she pulled the paper away to reveal the last thing she'd expected: the long-desired, impossible-to-find yellowback edition of *Far from the Madding Crowd*.

Melody looked between the book and his expectant face. "I can't believe you found this. And you read it too?"

"I tried." Justin grimaced. "Melody, that's a really weird book."

"I know." She laughed and extended her hand, pulling him to his feet. "This is one of the nicest things anyone has done for me. You have a talent for grand gestures."

He squeezed her hand but kept his distance, waiting for her answer.

"You know, I think I've been obsessed with this book because I'm a lot more like Bathsheba Everdene than I'd like to admit. All this time, I've been hoping that my true love was out there, someone who would choose me in the end despite all my bad decisions. But now that I have him in front of me, you know what I've discovered?"

His smile stretched at the implications of her words. He tugged her closer. "What?"

"It's just a book." Melody tossed the volume aside and wrapped her arms around his neck, meeting his lips in a kiss that was simultaneously sweet and heated, impatient and yet filled with endless promise, familiar and wondrously new. Because for the first time, she wasn't forcing a love that wasn't hers to keep, searching for the kind of acceptance she'd never find in another person. Justin wasn't a fantasy—he was a gift.

"Melody?"

She drew back dreamily, still enveloped in a delicious haze from the kiss. "Yes?"

"That book was like a thousand dollars."

Melody gasped and jerked away, dropping to her knees to scramble for the book. "Oh my gosh! I'm so sorry! I just got caught up in the moment." She turned it over and examined the cover, the binding. "I think it's okay. I would feel terrible if I ruined it after you went to all this effort!"

Justin laughed and took the book from her hands, then set it aside on the counter. He pulled her back into his arms and looked into her eyes. "You're far more important than any book. What do you say, Melody? Should we give this a try? See if we can't find our own kind of happily ever after?"

"Yes." She stretched up and kissed him once more. "My answer is yes."

Author's Note

While I do my best to write accurate and realistic fiction, I took some dramatic liberties with the birth of Bittersweet Café. Opening any kind of eatery is an arduous process that can take nine to eighteen months or even longer. In fact, with Denver's recent rapid growth, restaurant space is at such a premium that potential restaurateurs often take *years* to select the right location. But pages of phone calls with contractors and city planners make for pretty boring fiction, so I let Melody and Rachel take advantage of their relationship with the author in order to speed things up a little (okay, a lot).

Also, a number of my favorite Denver settings were reworked for *Brunch at Bittersweet Café*. The corner storefront on Old South Pearl, where I set Gibraltar Mediterranean Bakery and later Bittersweet Café, is actually home to Duffeyroll, a Denver cinnamon-bun institution. I also borrowed the location of Bistro Barbès, an excellent European/North African restaurant, for my fictional Soyokaze. ChoLon Bistro, which inspired the interior design of Paisley in *The Saturday Night Supper Club*, makes an uncredited appearance as itself (menu and all) as the Asian restaurant where Melody brings Justin after their bookstore date. Last, Noelle Patisserie in San Francisco was inspired by the real-life Inner Sunset bakery Tartine, founded by baking superstars Chad Robertson and Elisabeth Prueitt.

ABOUT THE AUTHOR

Carla Laureano is the RITA Award–winning author of contemporary inspirational romance and Celtic fantasy (as C. E. Laureano). A graduate of Pepperdine University, she worked as a sales and marketing executive for nearly a decade before leaving corporate life behind to write fiction full-time. She currently lives in Denver with her husband and two sons, where she writes during the day and cooks things at night.

DISCUSSION QUESTIONS

1. Melody has struggled to settle down or commit to a direction for her life, always wondering if something better might be just around the corner. Are you more inclined to put down roots or keep your options open? How has that affected your life?

2. If you came into an inheritance or sudden financial windfall, with the stipulation that you use it to pursue a cherished dream, what would you do?

3. Melody finds comfort by revisiting some of her grandmother's favorite desserts and handed-down recipes. Are there specific recipes that tie you to loved ones or to cherished memories?

4. As Rachel and Melody begin to plan their bakery-café, the pieces fall into place without much effort, making Melody think it must be God's doing. Have you experienced something similar? What did it teach you about God's timing?

5. Justin attempts to control his attraction to Melody because he's sure they can't have a long-term relationship. On the surface, that seems very responsible and logical. How can our need for order and control affect our ability to see what God is doing in our lives?

6. How do Melody's past mistakes color her approach to relationships? In what ways does her caution seem wise, and where does it hold her back?

7. Both Justin and Melody bear the consequences of shaky relationships with their parents and a lack of communication. How do both come to realize they might've misinterpreted past events? How does your relationship with your parents affect how you see the world and others?

8. Ana and Rachel fear Melody is making a bad choice in dating Justin, but they voice their worries in a way that comes across as harsh and judgmental. As Melody's friends, did they have a responsibility to express their concerns? How should they have handled the situation?

9. Justin believes in God but feels he's been let down—that the tragedies and difficult circumstances he and his loved ones have endured are proof God doesn't care. Have you experienced similar doubts? What would you say to Justin in response?

10. Melody eventually comes to understand that what she saw as faith was closer to wishful thinking. How would you define faith? Is there a difference between trusting in God's blessings and trusting in God Himself?

Center Point Large Print
600 Brooks Road / PO Box 1
Thorndike, ME 04986-0001 USA

(207) 568-3717

US & Canada:
1 800 929-9108
www.centerpointlargeprint.com